"In order to

TRAN

NOVELLA COLLECTION

BOOK 2.5 IN "THE BIODOME CHRONICLES"

by
JESIKAH SUNDIN

Just Imagine...
Developmental Editing & Publishing

ISBN-13: 978-0-9913453-4-2
ISBN-10: 0991345347

Printed in the United States of America

First Edition

Just Imagine...
Developmental Editing & Publishing
Monroe, WA 98272
justimaginestory@gmail.com
jesikahsundin@gmail.com
www.jesikahsundin.com

Cover design by Amalia Chitulescu
Digital Illustration by Amalia Chitulescu
Interior design by Jesikah Sundin

DEDICATED TO

My mother-in-law, Penny Sundin

And

Jessica Jett, Hannah Miller, and Andra Perju

EMBER

"But what sort of a witch am I if I work as a milk-maid all the time and have no time for leisure? I want to live and work in peace and not suffer from back-ward people."

—*Komsomolskaya Pravda*, 1964 *

See! on yon drear and rigid bier low lies thy love, Lenore!
Come! let the burial rite be read—the funeral song be sung!—
An anthem for the queenliest dead that ever died so young—
A dirge for her the doubly dead in that she died so young.

—Edgar Allen Poe, "Lenore," *Pioneer*, February 1843 *

Take a lover who looks at you like maybe you are magic.

—Frida Kahlo, painter, 20th century *

CHAPTER ONE

New Eden Township, Salton Sea, California

Tuesday, December 1, 2054

Week Five of Project Phase Two

T he ropes beneath the mattress groaned and Ember stilled. When Leaf did not move, she untangled her leg from the blanket and resumed her shuffle toward the end of the bed. The cold floor burned her feet and sparked shivers up the length of her exposed body. Tip-toeing across the night-chilled room, she fetched her woolen chemise from the floor and shimmied into the garment. The warmth did little to ease the persistent guilt gnawing her insides.

She stole a glance over her shoulder at the rumpled covers she left behind. Fingers of moonlight touched her husband's back. Yellow and green bruises dotted his ribcage and torso. Evidence of the community's betrayal lingered still. His body was healing, his leg growing stronger with each passing day, the black eye fading from deep purples to mottled browns. His heart, however, especially where she was concerned, remained injured. Nevertheless, he loved her despite the secrets she was pressed to keep; secrets she regretted ever having at all. This choice had been made for her. Much the same as it had been for him. Time, she decided, was an ally and an enemy.

Ember glided by his side of the bed to retrieve her tunic dress, then maneuvered to the other end of the chamber with delicate steps to finish dressing. She darted her gaze back to his sleeping form, afraid the rustle of clothing in the stillness would rouse him. Yet, despite her worries, his breathing rose and fell with sleep's steady rhythm, his face pressed into the pillow that his well-muscled arms embraced. A sight that caused her pulse to falter a beat.

This night, for the first time since the Great Fire, and after the rest of the household gave way to slumber, those very arms had embraced her. Still-fresh memories of their time together— his fervent kisses, the words of love he whispered across her skin—sashayed through her mind. Pleasure burned in her stomach with each remembrance. If not for the discomforting knot tightening in her belly, she would smile. But to smile would be a disservice to the shame she rightly carried.

He loved her, and he always would. She knew. And although his vulnerability built a bridge toward healing this night, he no longer trusted her with his pain as before. For she was one of many who had deceived him. There is no turning back time. There is no undoing choices made. The course was now set and they needed to journey toward fresh beginnings. She would allow him to set the pace and guide their relationship, allow him to need and refuse her until his heart no longer ached.

For weeks they had side-stepped around each other's grief. The ash of her family home continued to shroud the biodome in bereavement. This was a public wake. Each resident carried a role in the Ceremonies of Death, each ritual another act in re-building a new future inside New Eden.

Leaf's pain, however, was private. Only a select few knew that Timothy was behind Joel's death, a decision made to protect the innocence of what remained of Skylar's family. Rather, the community believed that Timothy was banished for orchestrating the faction, the very one that harmed their King and burned down their village. Nor did the community know that Fillion was imprisoned for temporarily shutting down the biodome as a strategic move to save Leaf's life. They believed Hanley's speech, which explained the event as an unfortunate technology glitch and offered heartfelt apologies from New Eden Enterprises and the lab.

As a neighborly gesture, Hanley had personally brought in exotic fruits, a variety of cheeses, and chocolates for Sunday feast, a week after the Great Fire. The community quickly forgave their inconveniences and set aside every grievance. To sample foods not labored for was a rare treat, indeed. Leaf did not partake of the gifts, nor she, deflecting with wishes for the community to enjoy their fill.

Willow hid in a vacant apartment on the West End of the main biodome that night, too disgusted to entertain introductions with Hanley Nichols. Late the next morning, she emerged with head held high and offered no apologies or explanations to the community. The Daughter of Earth ignored the whispers and haughty stares. "New Eden is as fickle as the wind," she had declared. And she was right.

With bellies full and the wool pulled over their eyes, the village gossips turned their attentions Ember's direction. Poked and prodded for weeks now, Leaf refused to answer the gossips as to whether or not he had known of his wife's "magic" before the Great Fire. Despite his feelings of betrayal, he publicly esteemed her for negotiating his release and guiding the community in their time of distress. The words he spoke were genuine; the capacity for falsehood did not dwell inside her husband. But his eyes dulled during each exchange, a physical response he believed he hid well from her. Not so, for they were bonded. She easily discerned the most subtle of mood changes in him and knew his rhythm and nature as if they were her very own.

Regardless of his careful answers, people remained superstitious. Most especially the second generation, who viewed her as an otherworldly enigma. "Witch," they hissed in hushed tones as she passed by. Children were scooped up, some even warned to not look in her eyes. For she might bewitch them with the same magic used to subdue the men who were bent on violence to dethrone their King to raise up another.

Ember swallowed back the embarrassment and lifted her chin. Her only focus, only purpose, was to serve her husband while he poured himself out for his family and his Kingdom. To be his haven, his refuge, was an honor higher than any other—an honor she no longer held. Her betrayal of his trust was a disgrace she would rectify if it cost her everything. A sad smile pulled at her lips as the knot in her stomach intensified.

Ever so carefully, she draped her cloak along the back of her chair and studied her husband once more. He was a powerful man. More powerful than he realized. Sitting on the edge of their cot, Ember kissed her fingers then trailed them down her husband's spine in reverence. This back carried the burdens of many. Muscles moved beneath her fingertips as he awoke. Rolling to his side, Leaf squinted open his eyes. The moon's silver light threaded through the curls in his hair and caressed the smooth planes of his face, still flushed from sleep, while darkening the prominent bruising around his eye.

"Are you unwell?" he asked. The drowsy but husky quality of his deep voice filled her with warmth.

"No, My Lord. Quite well, actually." Leaf eased up to a sitting position and Ember admired his body beneath lowered lashes. He furrowed his brows and took her hand, silently noting her fully dressed state. Before he could ask, she said, "It is time for me to depart for a Guild meeting."

"I see. Why not tell me of your meeting prior to now?" She waited for him to answer his own question. A few heartbeats later, he removed his hand and looked away.

"Come with me, My Lord."

"Shall the others welcome my uninvited presence?"

"You are their beloved King, how could they not welcome you? Come, My Lord, and you shall see."

Leaf remained silent for far too long, before saying, "If it pleases you, Ember." Her name ended on a soft note, almost a hush. He rarely spoke her name. Rather, he chose to esteem her with honorary titles. Yet, she knew when he said, "My Lady," it contained layered meanings. She *was* his lady, his family, and carried his name. It was a matter of pride.

"Leaf," she whispered. He looked up. The power he so often forgot to display emanated this very moment from his posture, in the tilt of his head, to the way his eyes took her in—all of her. "You bow before no man in New Eden Township out of fear or expectation," she reassured his silhouette. "This is your Kingdom, and the Techsmith Guild yields to you. Come and receive our fealty."

"I am King, yes," he said. "But I shall be at the mercy of individuals who have led two lives within our Township. Individuals who have willingly deceived their own families. I am quite through with secrets."

Ember lowered her head with his rebuke. As The Aether, his secrets were upheld by The Code and guarded by the community. They were acceptable secrets. Unlike hers. Shame and guilt continued to form knots in her stomach and she nearly doubled over. But he deserved respect and honor, not frailty. Repositioning her stance, she pushed back her shoulders while maintaining a modest, downcast expression, holding herself with all the elegance of her station. Nor would she speak and invalidate his injuries with excuses and justifications. His offense and distrust were merited.

Leaf reached out and took her hand, whispering, "I love you," with such passion, such conviction, that a pain, sharp and bright, lanced through her chest with the grief she had caused him. He cleared his throat and blinked away his shyness before beginning again. "Others may see my uninvited presence as a move to usurp Skylar. The offices of Aether and Guild Captain were separated for reasons I know not. I shall not tread upon traditions I do not fully understand."

"Skylar is not threatened by you, My Lord. The Techsmiths follow him and he shall lead them to you."

"And yet, despite my and Skylar's many conversations, *he* has not extended an invitation." Leaf covered his face as he sighed through his nose. His broad shoulders slumped and Ember nearly reached out to comfort him. Instead, she remained steady and allowed him his privacy to internalize his thoughts as long as he needed. Finally, after a measure of time, he dropped his hands and said, "I shall go if you ask for my company this evening, My Lady. But only because *you* desire it so and not for any political reasons."

The ache in his voice gave way to understanding. Ember smiled to herself as intuition glimmered throughout her thoughts. It was a buzzing sensation that had guided her since early childhood, one that often led to hunches. Many claimed it was a magic born from being a twin. Perhaps the only magic she truly contained.

Slowly, she raised her eyes to meet his and placed her hand upon his chest. "I desire your company, My Lord. All I do, all that I am, I desire to share with you, and you alone."

She allowed her words to sink in, to reach the pulse thrumming beneath her fingertips. The longing in his eyes deepened as her message reached a sacred part inside of him, the part that feared being viewed by her as weak, cowardly, and unworthy. Her hand caressed his chest, traveling over his broad shoulder and down his arm, feeling every muscle flex under her touch, until she gingerly laced her fingers with his.

"Come, My Lord," she beckoned with a small tug. But he remained unmoving. His hand slipped from hers and she drew in a quiet breath. Unsure of what else to do, she angled away to find his clothing nearby. Gathering his tunic and breeches, she placed them into his hands without meeting his eyes and said, "Secrets are foolish creatures, I have learned. No longer do I wish to play with fools." Ember turned and did not look back. Not even when she fetched her cloak from the chair by their bed, nor when she quietly shut the door behind her.

In the living room, shadows swayed upon the walls to the tempo of her wavering nerves. Back straight and hands clasped at her waist, she waited for Leaf. Her step-mother had raised her to be genuine, compassionate, and shrewd. She oft quoted the book of Saint Matthew in the Holy Scriptures to support this lesson, saying, "Behold, I send you forth as sheep in the midst of wolves: be ye therefore wise as serpents, and harmless as doves." The juxtaposition of being prudent yet humble picked at her conscience as she waited. Had she honored Leaf this evening? Humbled herself before him? Or made matters worse?

A soft click echoed down the hallway. A breath, one she had not realized she was holding, left her lungs in a hiccup. She would not cry. Leaf moved like a whisper down the hallway, despite his limp, and paused before her, blinking as he stared at his feet.

"Shall we?" he asked, soft, wary. In a few strides, he opened their front door without waiting for her reply, and bowed. "Will you be warm enough, My Lady?"

"Yes, thank you for your kind concern."

"Ember," he began and stopped, looking away. A muscle pulsed along his jaw.

She rose on the tips of her toes and brushed a kiss across his cheek. His body stiffened. Did he regret making love to her this night? She swallowed back her shame and said, "Thank you, My Lord, for keeping me company this evening. You pay me a great honor."

"Of course," he said simply. He moved as if to return her kiss, but then stepped onto the upper deck with a shy smile. No, he did not regret their intimacies, she realized. He was comforting two separate pains, needing her for one while requiring distance to process the other. She stepped toward the stairs and his body visibly relaxed.

The night swallowed their forms as they made haste through the forest and orchard, slowing only when reaching The Rows. The jagged lines of muddy ruins and crumbled fragments of buildings glowed beneath the reflective moonlight. Both she and Leaf absorbed the scene with heavy hearts as they stood in the ashes of their loved ones in mutual mourning. Calloused fingers found hers as he lifted her hand to his lips. There truly was no love quite like that of Leaf Watson and she blushed behind the hood of her cloak. His smile was wobbly, weak, but it fortified her nonetheless. It was a promise. Their Kingdom would one day know rebirth and so would their people. But, alas, it was nearing winter—a season of rest for the heart as well as of the land.

Her hand firmly clasped with his, she followed Leaf through the rainforest until reaching Messenger Pigeon. The hatch was shut, a precaution the Guild took only when in session. Lowering her hood, she crouched by the hatch and knocked three times. She waited, but there was no answering knock. The metal hinges protested as she yanked open the metal door. If those below did not hear her knock, then surely they heard the door. Gingerly, she stepped down onto the ladder and descended into the Communications Room.

"Director," Skylar said, bowing his head and offering his assistance. "Welcome. The meeting shall commence shortly. We have received a delay from HQ. The Commander is running behind."

"Thank you, Captain. I am relieved I am not late." She released Skylar's hand as soon as her feet touched the earthen floor. "I bring a guest this eve." The Son of Wind swung his head toward the opening, his skin paling ever so slightly as he watched Leaf struggle to lower while favoring his injured leg. "His Majesty is here at my behest and only to keep me company."

The Guild members—ten aside from her and Skylar—shuffled to their feet as their King entered the Communications Room. Leaf's gaze touched on each face, eyes narrowing with his familiar expression of contemplation. The villagers stood before him with postures straight, arms behind their backs, and chins lifted high.

"Your Majesty," Skylar began with a sweeping bow. "It is an honor."

"The honor is all mine." To the villagers, Leaf said, "Carry on. I do not wish to interrupt. I shall remain a shadow." Her husband offered a kind smile as he strode to the far corner, crossing his arms over his chest as he leaned against the wall. She attempted to gain his attention, but he refused to look her way.

Hesitant, Skylar returned his attention back to the Techsmiths. "Thank you for attending on short notice. We receive new orders from our Guild Master this night." The Son of Wind angled his head toward Leaf and flinched, but continued on in a confident voice. "Stations ready."

Ember powered her Cranium and brought up a user interface. Command screens in different colors layered over one another. Brushing her finger through the air, she closed most layers save those necessary for the night's task. She logged into Messenger Pigeon. "Communications ready."

"Comm support Lead One ready."

"Comm support Lead Two ready."

"Engineering ready."

Samuel, a gardener from the village, dropped his hand from a Messenger Pigeon screen, warily peeked at Leaf, and said, "Ag ready."

Leaf turned his head as if a speck on the wall caught his interest, his chest rising and falling in a deep breath. One by one, each member declared their station's status. Peering over privacy screens, they faced the blue-lit hardwired screens in anticipation.

Ember's line opened with a pop. Then a familiar voice. "Techsmith Guild, incoming from Messenger Pigeon."

"Greetings, Guild Master," Ember said to Hanley, keeping her voice calm and steady. "Techsmith Guild on standby."

He replied, "Guardian Angels request permission for satellite connection."

"Captain, permission to connect to Guardian Angels?" she asked Skylar.

"Permission granted."

"Lead One," Ember said to the village woman by her side. "Commence connection."

Hannah tapped the blue hardwired screen and typed the password. "Connection opened."

"Thank you, Lead One." The blue of the screens gave way to a video feed of the control room at N.E.T. and Ember leveled her gaze onto Hanley. A calculating smile lifted the corners of his mouth, widening when noting Skylar's rigid form.

The Son of Wind shifted on his feet and said in a forced tone, "Welcome, Commander. A pleasure, as usual."

"Captain, it's been a few weeks. How is your family faring with the onset of Project Phase Two? Your mother still in a stupor?"

Skylar tensed even more. "Morning comes swiftly and many have chores to attend to soon. How can we serve you, Commander?"

Hanley smirked with Skylar's deflection and said, "It's time for the Comm Director to roll out the Education Plan as discussed in our previous meeting, before your father was arrested." The owner leaned back in his chair and continued as if nothing was amiss. "The Guardian Angels will send Comm Lead Two a list of residents *required* to attend technology sessions after dinner hours. The list will feature rotations to split up the community into smaller learning groups. Craniums and supplies will arrive via courier service from the lab to your engineering team within the next couple of days. Any questions?"

"Has The Aether been notified of the Education Plan?" Skylar asked.

Hanley chuckled. "This is a command from HQ to the Guild. Appoint the Comm Director to meet with him." Hanley looked at Ember and winked. "You know ways to be *persuasive*, if necessary."

Ember stilled as mortification burned across her face. She internally chanted to herself, "wise as a serpent, harmless as a dove," until her thoughts cooled. She was ready to reply, but Skylar spoke first.

"The Director and I both shall meet with His Majesty and inform him of HQ's command."

"As you see fit, Captain," Hanley said to Skylar, even though his eyes never left hers. "Any other questions?"

"Techsmiths?" Skylar asked. When no one replied, he said, "Lead One, disconnect from Messenger Pigeon."

"Sir?"

"Disconnect, Lead One."

"We are not finished. Sky—"

Hanley's voice faded into blue. Skylar drew in a breath, long and slow, then marched over to the computer towers and turned off the machines. The screens flashed to black. Their

Guild Captain leaned on the metallic table, arms stiff, head down. Silence thickened the atmosphere in the small room, hot and crackling with foreboding.

Heads shifted Ember's direction, but she stared straight ahead, unmoving. Her heart was breaking for Skylar, though. Quietly, she removed her Cranium and slipped it into her pocket. The rustle of clothing told her others followed suit. Skylar peered over his shoulder with the sound.

"You are free to return to your homes," he half whispered. "Thank you for your service." But no one dared move. "I wish to speak to our Director privately. I shall be in contact with each of you once supplies arrive and I have further instructions."

The Techsmiths reluctantly turned to leave, bowing to Leaf as they departed the underground chamber. Humiliation cloaked her husband in the shadows as his pride seemed to melt into the white-washed walls. Hanley had never made suggestive comments toward her before. Nor implied certain unladylike behavioral expectations. Normally her father—the other Guild Master—was in attendance, unlike tonight. His presence afforded her protection she had not considered necessary until this moment.

After all had departed, she lowered her head in modesty and said, "I would never manipulate you, Your Majesty. Nor have I."

Leaf flicked his gaze to Skylar and back to her. "Did I accuse you, My Queen?" His voice was soft, gentle even, but she heard the uncertainty nonetheless. "I shall wait for you above ground." The shame knotting in her stomach clenched and she grit her teeth to hold back the forming tears. He pushed off the wall and bowed before Skylar. "My Lord." Attempting to appear physically stronger than he was, Leaf climbed the stairs, holding back a grimace of pain she knew he felt.

She watched until her husband disappeared into the darkness, then said, "Worry not, I shall fare well." Slowly she pulled her gaze from the opening to Skylar. ""You need not ask."

"But I do, Your Highness." Skylar studied her, his mouth set in a thin line. "I am—"

"Please, My Lord." Ember placed her finger to his lips and Skylar's rigid posture deflated. Regret, fear, and grief stared back at her. Awareness buzzed in the forefront of her mind and she graced him with an understanding smile. "You are not to blame."

"No." He angled away and ran a finger along the screen's black surface and murmured, "But I must pay all the same, and you with me."

"You believe this is Hanley's punishment?"

"You do not?"

Ember placed her hand on his forearm. "Skylar Kane, your brother above shall defend you until his dying breath. Do not allow Hanley to divide you and Leaf."

"My father—"

"Yes, and Hanley's son loves Willow, and Leaf approves. You do your friend a discredit. Fear shall make enemies of us all." Skylar stared at her long and hard before issuing a tight nod, albeit reluctantly. She softened her voice, knowing the Son of Wind needed direction just as much as he needed a friend this moment. "All will be well, My Lord. You shall see." Her hand slipped from his arm and gripped the ladder rung. The buzzing sensations in her head grew more persistent as she stepped up toward the surface, saying, "I have a hunch."

CHAPTER TWO

Thursday, December 3, 2054

A soft head nudged her arm as she bent over to grasp the bucket's rope handles. Warm milk sloshed over the sides of the bucket and dribbled to the straw-strewn soil. Ember repositioned herself on her stool and used a rag to wipe the sweat from her forehead. "You are a naughty goat," she cooed to the Anglo-Nubian with a giggle. The sun always warmed the Mediterranean dome to uncomfortable temperatures by afternoon. Perfect for the agriculture and livestock but, alas, not for her.

"Step aside, Neesa," she said to the goat, who continued to nudge her leg as she walked to the cart. Arms and hands heavy with fatigue, she pressed a piece of waxed linen over the bucket. When finished, she scratched the goat's head and sighed. "Now, go find your friends. Shoo!" Ember pushed the goat away, then pulled the cart out of the pen, locking the gate behind her. With a soft grunt, she began walking down the service path, sweat trickling down the side of her face.

A village boy ran up and asked, "Your Highness, shall I pull the cart to the kitchen for you?"

"Yes, thank you, young sir." She smiled kindly.

"Gregory, come!" A woman called from the orange grove, just beyond the flagstone wall. The boy lowered the cart with an apologetic frown and ran to his mother. Her voice was hushed, urgent, but Ember heard every word. "Do not gaze into her eyes, have I not told you so?" The boy looked over his shoulder and the mother yanked him back to face her. "Here, this basket of oranges is needed in the kitchens. Hurry along, now."

Heat flamed Ember's cheeks and she pretended to wipe the sweat from her face once more. With a steadying breath, she began her walk to the Great Hall, dragging the cart slowly behind her. The splintered handles rubbed against her forming blisters and she winced, breathing slowly through her teeth. Gregory lifted the reed basket and wobbled by Ember in a half-run. She could have offered to carry his load, but did not wish to further upset his mother.

The air cooled considerably once she passed through the East Cave and into the main biodome. A breeze caressed her neck with a lover's touch and fingered through the strands swaying back and forth down her back. Most of her hair was contained in a head scarf, much to her relief. The crisp autumn air smelled richly of earth, a far contrast to the sweet hay and musky animal odors. Pieces of straw stuck to the edge of her skirt and milk soured on her apron. The unpleasant scent wafted upward with the breeze and she resisted the urge to wrinkle her nose.

Ember lowered the cart by the back door to the Great Hall and stretched her back before knocking. Her fingers ached from milking all day. Normally she had more assistants to ease the workload, but two milk maids had fallen ill. A few other families had mentioned similar ailments afflicting their homes as well.

She did not have long to dwell on this concerning news, however. Boisterous voices and the sounds of clanking pans tumbled through the opening doorway. A young woman, no more older than she, appeared while singing a verse to a favorite tune among the kitchen staff. Her voice ended in a laugh as she spoke to another over her shoulder, eventually turning toward Ember with a ready smile and raised eyebrows.

"Greetings, Your Highness," Killie said, stepping down to the grass. The kitchen maid peeked into the cart and grinned. "Oh, look at this bounty. Cook will be pleased. The Cheesemakers were just hounding her about the milk cart delivery."

"The goats were more than generous this day," Ember said, distracted. She watched Gregory and other village boys race toward The Orchard, their carefree laughter fairly floating on the gentle breeze.

Killie tugged Ember by the sleeve with a nod toward the door. "Your tumbler of cider is ready. Shall I fetch it?"

Ember looked down at her straw-and dirt-caked shoes. "If it is no trouble."

"No trouble at all, Your Highness." Killie dipped into a curtsy and disappeared behind the door. In a few quick heartbeats she returned and placed the vessel in Ember's hands. The cool earthen cup eased the pain in her fingers a little. "Enjoy your rest now. I shall ask a kitchen boy to return the cart." The maid hollered for assistance before closing the door.

Grabbing her wash bucket from the cart, Ember ambled over the wild grass toward the pump well. The mundane act of filling a bucket seemed never-ending as her palm and fingers throbbed with every push and pull. Air hissing through her teeth, she picked up the full bucket with one hand, holding the tumbler of cider in the other, and began her journey toward her apartment in preparations for the hour of rest. Villagers bowed and issued soft greetings as she trudged by—most villagers that is. A few still harbored suspicions and refused to look her in the eyes, heeding the escalating rumors. What could she say? After the Techsmith Guild's coming announcement, she feared the rumors would only grow more aggressive.

Back in her own apartment, she relished the quiet. The only sounds were of her footfalls, the clank of her wash bowl filling with water, and the iron handle tapping the hewn wood of her chamber door. She peeled away layer after layer of soiled garments and placed them in a pile. After scenting the water with cinnamon and clove, she washed, placing sprigs of lavender in her bindings before dressing in a freshly laundered dress. There was no time to wash her hair, so she plaited the tresses, weaving in ribbons for adornment.

Still alone, Ember enjoyed the quietude outside on the grass below, turning her back to the apartments and watchful eyes. She dumped her wash bowl into the bushes, then busied with brushing the dirt clumps and straw from her work dress and shoes. Once finished, she returned inside to rub old sprigs of sage over the inside of the bodice, hanging it on a post for the morrow.

The front door opened and she stilled, listening while Leaf's familiar footsteps grew louder as he neared their bedchamber. "My Lady," he spoke quietly as he entered. His limp seemed more pronounced than yesterday and a sharp pang seized her chest.

They had spoken little since the Guild meeting. Space and privacy were requests he made without utterance of a single word. Often she knew his needs before he did. It was a dance, generous and graceful, and her heart soared with each step spent serving her husband.

Encouraged by her thoughts, she said, "Cider, My Lord," and removed the waxed linen cover before handing him the tumbler. He eased onto the cot with a heavy sigh and enjoyed a long sip. She contemplated taking his hand in hers, a gesture of comfort and support. Instead she said, "Allow me," and knelt before him, avoiding the questions in his eyes. Wary of his injury, she unlaced his shoes until they pulled off with ease and stored them under their cot. Then she poured water from the bucket into his wash bowl, adding a few dashes of cedar and bergamot essential oils. Leaf pulled his work tunic over his head and tossed it into their laundry basket, blinking his eyes in that bashful way of his.

"The courier arrived this afternoon," he said into his tumbler, before imbibing another sip. "Jeff allowed Skylar use of The Chancery for storage until the morrow."

The knot in her stomach pulled tight and she wrapped a supportive arm around her waist. Skylar had not visited her with the news. Had he visited others from the Guild? "Thank you for sharing, My Lord," she said in quiet reply.

"Of course."

An awkward silence spanned between them and Ember clasped her hands at her waist, shoulders back, head lowered in a posture of elegance. Despite her apprehensions, she would hold herself with dignity. Leaf had worries enough and did not need to add her trepidations to the burdens he carried.

"My Lady?"

"Yes, My Lord?"

"Thank you for your kind attentions."

She gifted him a faint smile. "You are a pillar of strength in our home and in our community. There is no greater honor than serving you, My Lord." With a final curtsy, she retrieved the garment brush and his work tunic, saying, "Rest now," before gracefully slipping out of their chamber.

"Ember!" Laurel called out in a sing-song voice. "Do you like my crown of leaves?" She twirled slowly, her hands fluttering about in the air.

"Quite enchanting." Ember softly laughed as Laurel danced across the floorboards in light, whimsical steps.

Willow breezed into the apartment with a loud a huff. "I fear I shall be plucking wool fibers from my person for all of eternity." Spotting the garment brush in Ember's hands she reached out while saying, "May I? I shall brush Leaf's tunic as well."

"Oaklee, do you find my leaf crown fetching?" Laurel skipped by Willow and spun to music only she could hear.

"A beautiful autumn faerie you are, Frog." Willow leaned forward and rubbed her nose with Laurel's. "Please sprinkle your pixie dust over me and perhaps I shall no longer resemble a goat in need of shearing!" Their littlest sister covered her smile as she giggled, then wiggled her fingers. "Alas," Willow began, gliding toward the entrance. "I must away to the forest clearing over yonder for the spell to work." Willow shut the door, after sharing a playful grin with her little sister.

Laurel fell onto a chair with a melodramatic sigh. "'Tis hard work being a faerie." Fixing her dress, the youngest Watson darted a look down the shadowed hallway. "He is home?"

"Yes, sweetling."

"Rona and I were strolling through the village today," Laurel said with big eyes. "As we passed the construction station we heard the most dreadful news."

Ember placed the fire starter bowl upon the cupboard. "As women, our duty is to protect each other's hearts and reputations." The nub of a nearly finished candle plinked in the clay collection bowl for the Chandler and she placed a fresh tallow stick in the iron holder. Sparing a quick glance toward Laurel, she continued. "We should build up each other's character rather than tear down the life of another."

"I am not about to gossip, I promise."

"Very well. What is this dreadful news?"

Laurel's eyes rounded and she whispered dramatically, "There is a witch in New Eden." The hair on Ember's arms prickled and rose. A grin broke across her sister's face before she sang out, "Leaf!" and leapt from the chair. "I have ever so much to tell— whatever is in your hair?"

He scrubbed dirt-stained fingers through his dark curls and white dust poofed into the air. "I pulverized cob for reconstitution this day. Perhaps I should dunk my head in the wash bucket." Laurel's shoulders sagged a touch and her smile faltered. Leaf took note. "First, shall you tell me about your day?"

Though the exhaustion pulled on his features, his face softened when Laurel beamed, her smile brighter than the noonday sun. Her amber eyes sparkled as she resumed her position in the chair, patting the empty chair next to her. Ever a songbird with tidings for the wind, their sister's voice chirped and twittered, rising and falling with her many stories, mostly involving Rona and Blaze. Leaf listened with a kind smile, nodding his head and asking questions every so often.

Family was her husband's greatest pride. He doted upon each of them, and in unique, beautiful ways that demonstrated his devotion. Laurel needed his listening ear. Willow his patience and forgiving heart. And her? Ember blushed, smiling to herself. She relished his touch, each kiss, and losing herself to his intimate affections. Straightening her shoulders, she lit the end of a stick and focused on her tasks lest she forget entirely in her reverie.

Warm light blanketed Leaf and Laurel's conversation as Ember lit a single tallow near their chairs. The glow stretched to both hallways and chased away the dusk as she lit each candle. Shadows flickered across the walls and Ember tilted her head with wrinkled brows. Often she felt the presence of loved ones long lost. Homes contained the heartbeat of family, even those whose elements nourished the soil. Since childhood, her mother had walked among the shadows on the wall. Coal, though he believed her, did not share this sight. A sight Ember had drawn comfort from, until this night.

Witch.

The word echoed in her heart until it ached. Was she magical? Did not others possess intuition? Or see visions of their pulse dancing upon the walls? Her family was in her blood, in the very air she breathed, in the food she ate. Why was it an otherworldly phenomenon to see the very source of one's existence? She wished to hide, to turn away, to follow the shadows into the hallway. But she was a queen. Elegance and strength were her scepter, judgment and grace her crown. She would not fear superstitions, nor cower before slanderous accusations. Nor would she argue foolish notions with those enslaved by fear. They would not listen if she did, anyway. Better to remain silent and allow others the ability to walk toward understanding on their own volition—including her husband.

Leaf ignored her as she flit around the room with evening chores, though he normally tracked her every movement. Nor did he lock eyes with her in silent profession of his affection while Laurel filled the living room with her birdsong chatter. The ebb and flow of desiring her company and his desiring autonomy stilled the very air in her chest. Shrinking back would only aggravate his festering wounds. No, she would remain devoted to his needs as before. How else would he learn she was indeed a safe place? A haven for his grieving heart? Not an enemy employed by Hanley Nichols.

Not a witch.

Willow strode into the apartment with a gust of wind. Oblivious to all others, she meandered toward her room, her steps light and airy. Every thought was held captive upon her face, as if the stars and moon and the sun above sparkled and shined within her heart. Grief had transformed into longing and longing became an escape as she waited for her betrothed to return, and this just the beginning of her watch. Ember worried, however. Though she trusted the Son of Eden, his father was akin to a snake that danced to an exotic melody—beautiful, charming, hypnotic, and deadly. Wistfully, Willow's fingers trailed over the spinning wheel as she passed, humming a merry tune all her own.

Leaf's work tunic draped over a nearby chair, now freshly brushed. Ember reached for the garment before noting the carbon on her fingertips. Better to finish inspecting the lanterns in preparation for their evening travels first. With soot wiped away, the gold-toned parchment gleamed in the candlelight. A small smile of satisfaction touched her lips as she wiped her fingers on the cleaning cloth. So lost was she in her study, the eerie awareness of silence startled her. Ember peered toward the occupied chairs only to find Leaf, who inspected the dirt in his fingernails when caught staring. The door to Laurel's room shut with a quiet thud and Ember loosed a breath.

"May I help you with anything, My Lady?" Leaf asked.

"No, I am finished, but thank you, My Lord."

He studied her eyes a few heartbeats before looking away while blinking shyly. "I shall be in our bedchamber resting should you have need of me." He stood, gritting his teeth in attempt to mask the pain, then bowed, whispering, "I am entirely at your service, My Lady."

"You honor me." Ember placed her hand upon his forearm. The blisters on her hand had grown red and swollen. Shifting on his feet, he studied her hand with a frown. "Please excuse me," she said and eased toward Laurel's chamber before he could notice. "Rest well, My Lord."

The iron ring felt cool in her hand, easing the throbbing discomfort before she pushed. Her little sister grinned in greeting, plucking each leaf from her hair so Ember could brush and plait her long, gold tresses. Ember released the handle and peered at her hand. Did keeping her sores from Leaf count as a secret? Perhaps she still played with fools, after all.

ChAPTER
ThREE

Saturday, December 5, 2054

Nausea churned around the knots forming once more in her stomach. Mild but persistent, the tight, rolling sensations increased as the communal morsels of bread and wine settled. With head bowed, Ember stole glances at the villagers seated near her at Mass. Children were positioned away from her, the men seated closest. Sunlight streamed in from latticed windows nearby. The golden ribbons cast glows over a smattering of lowered heads. It was if the very fingers of God touched each hair upon their heads.

Hushed "amens" floated to the rafters above, traveling with the incense smoke. The prayers of candles and of men, the metaphor and the soul. "Amen." *So be it.* Acceptance echoed in soft murmurs off the stone walls and floors. Confessions squeezed the private chambers of her heart. The room was silent, reverent, as she bled before each person while they looked on with satisfaction, deeming her a worthy sacrifice for their fears. Did they pray for their witch's salvation or for her judgment?

The Liturgy of the Eucharist was almost at an end. Only a few families remained in line to receive communion. Quiet and meek, they returned to their seats, joining the heads bowed in prayer. Ember's eyelids slid shut and she drew in a quiet breath. The deep, peaceful tones of Brother Markus formed a backdrop for the supplications of her heart. She lifted her head when the prayer finished and pretended as though others did not look her way.

Lifting two fingers, the monk brushed the air in *signum crucis* as he said, "*In nomine Patris, et Filii, et Spiritus Sancti.* Amen."

"Amen," she whispered, the very word vibrating through her.

So be it.

Willow stood and linked her arm through hers, lips pursing in thought. "Shall I take Laurel this morn? You look peaked."

"No, she is to assist Mother and Rona this day." Ember smiled kindly. "Mother has employed her services to entertain younger children while she meets privately with their mothers."

The Daughter of Earth swept a gaze over the departing villagers. "Oh yes, I see Laurel beside Lady Brianna. Well," she said, removing her arm with a heavy sigh. "I shall see you this evening then. I must endure the agony of breaking flax this day." Willow kissed her on the cheek before melting into the throngs of villagers.

Stomach soured since waking, Ember sank onto the hard, wooden bench. Her fingers crept over each splintered groove in the wood, inching toward relief of any kind. A bird had entered the Great Hall and perched on a planked beam, cleaning its feathers. In the filtered light, the black feathers reflected tinges of blue, and she smiled. A light sensation buzzed in her head and she felt her mind drifting, wandering toward a truth bubbling to the surface.

"Daughter of Fire," Brother Markus said, pulling her from her thoughts. The tingles faded and she focused her attentions on the present rather than the abstract. Brown woolen robes swished with Brother Markus' steps, and she shifted her eyes from the coarse garment to the monk's waiting gaze.

"Peace be with you, Brother."

"And also with you, Daughter of Fire." The wrinkles on his face softened as he considered her, a pleasant smile hinting at understanding, one she knew he would not volunteer. She was to seek if she were to find. "Would you care for a walk?" he asked. "These old bones could use a jaunt to keep the rheumatism at bay. 'Tis a lovely morning, is it not?"

"Indeed. I would be honored to walk with you."

He gestured toward the large doors and she ducked her head when stepping into the morning light. Squinting her eyes, she looked toward The Rows where her husband stood in discussion with two gardeners, who pointed to the far field by the South Cave.

The village undulated with activity as the Great Hall was turned over in preparations for the first meal. A young girl dashed by, braids bouncing in merriment. "Charles, catch me!" she squealed to a little boy no more than three years of age. Face scrunched in determination, the little boy leapt from a barrel he had climbed and made chase. Little legs pumped, not stopping, not even when Brother Markus and Ember paused to allow him to pass. Gravel slipped beneath his feet and he crashed, hands and knees sliding to a halt in the dirt. Tears pooled in his bright blue eyes, his bottom lip quivering.

"There, there child," Ember said, kneeling before him. "You poor, dear." She looked around for his sister. Not finding her, Ember scooped him up and brushed earthen colored strands from his eyes. "Where is your mother, lad?" He pointed to a young woman as a contained wail emerged from his mouth. Ember kissed the side of his head and pressed him close as she walked toward the woman, who looked up, eyes widening at the sight of her son.

"Release him," the woman said, voice low, her eyes furtively taking in the villagers who had quieted to watch the exchange. "Charles, look at your mum and only me. Show me your eyes, lad." The young boy wiggled in Ember's embrace with hands stretched toward his mother. Wiping a tear from his cheek, Ember placed him on the ground and he ran into his mother's arms. "You are safe now," the young woman cooed, glaring at Ember.

"She comforted your son when he took a spill," Brother Markus said. "'Twas a kindness she showed him.'"

Ember placed a hand on the monk's arm, lowering her eyes as her face warmed. "Shall we continue our walk?"

Head downcast in what appeared to be sorrow, he took her supportive arm as they ambled toward The Orchard. Mothers with babes on hips or on backs spoke in close circles only to fall silent as she passed by. Brother Markus dipped his head while lifting prayerful hands in greeting. Moving forward was essential. Time, she reminded herself, was an ally and an enemy. Tree limbs clawed the sky in The Orchard and she lifted a small smile at the sight. Beyond the branches stood her husband and she watched his ease and familiarity within the fields.

Frowning, the old monk slowed his steps, back hunched and breath heavy. They remained quiet, time stretching onward, while enjoying the peace of barren trees and ripening fields. When villagers trickled back into the Great Hall, Brother Markus placed a weathered hand upon her forearm in comfort. She tried to smile, though her heart was not in it.

"We must labor to rest, Saint Paul tells us in the Book of Hebrews," he began. "You wear the weariness of a soul battling for peace."

"Yes, for truth."

"You are young to carry so many heavy burdens, Daughter."

Ember peered over her shoulder and studied the ruins of her family home. Lifting her eyebrow, she faced the holy man once more. "Though the community is content to forget my troubles, I cannot blame them."

"Can you not?"

"We are a community in transition from one phase to another."

"Indeed."

Ember offered a weak smile. "Transitions are seasons that force change and new growth. I have accepted that I am part of the death that shall bring new life."

Brother Markus sobered. "You have died quite enough I should think."

"Perhaps not."

"And what does His Majesty say?"

She lowered her eyes. "We do not speak of the rumors. He is not ready."

"Then speak to me, Daughter of Fire. I shall listen."

"I do not seek absolution."

"No, you seek answers. There is a question in your eyes."

Ember swallowed and tried to smile, but still she could not. In a half-whisper, she said, "I am rather confused. Why do the first generation propagate rumors that I am a witch when they, too, have known a life with technology?"

"Yes," the monk said, nodding his head. "A fine question it is." He gestured to continue walking, taking her proffered arm. "You see," he said, glancing her way, "transitions are seasons that force change and new growth." She lifted her brow once more and he smiled, warm with concern. "They are no longer from the world beyond the walls of our home. Twenty years in isolation is a long time to spend immersed in any kind of ideology and lifestyle. Wars spanning the entire globe have been waged to protect long-held beliefs and convictions."

"My father has spoken of wars from his lifetime. 'Tis truly heartbreaking."

"Since the beginning of time, men have committed unspeakable horrors against entire families, nations, races, and religions in defense of their impassioned beliefs."

"Being accused of witchcraft is hardly comparable."

The corners of his lips turned down. "'Witchcraft,' 'heresy'—these accusations are stones intended to cause injury. I do believe the emotional bruises have already formed, yes?"

She hesitated before saying, "I fare well enough."

He nodded his head, slow and thoughtful, disbelieving but placating her nonetheless. Pushing thick, white eyebrows together, he said, "In New Eden, it begs the question: What convictions are those armed with stones really protecting?"

Ember allowed the words to sink deep, to caress her thoughts. A faint tingle glimmered in the horizon of her mind and she blinked. A speech formed on the tip of her tongue, one memorized during her early years of training in the Techsmith Guild. "The idea is that children will grow up never knowing or understanding technology the same way we do," she said, each word heavy and thick in her mouth. "Instead, we hope they become fully absorbed by their environment from infancy, leaning on rocks, trees, and flowers as companions rather than electronics. We are building an Earth-like Mars colony and must know what happens should technology fail." The buzzing grew unbearable until warmth trickled through her body. She looked to Brother Markus, concealing her unraveling emotions as much as possible. "Hanley Nichols gave this speech five years before Moving Day."

Brother Markus did not ask how she knew of this speech or if she believed the statements. Nor did he encourage her to speak aloud the terror gathering within. Rather, he placed a hand, gnarled by time, onto her forearm and bowed his head. "Peace of heart is always worth fighting for, Daughter."

"Yes, indeed," she spoke softly.

Laughter from The Rows cut through the late autumn chill. Leaf's deep rumble eased as he lifted a hand in farewell and slowly ambled toward the Great Hall. Years faded from her husband's face as each feature brightened with mirth. His smiles were youthful, boyish even, though his eyes were old. Not yet twenty and already he had lived many lives.

"If you will excuse me, Daughter," the monk said, following her gaze. "It is time to bless the morning meal."

"Thank you, Brother Markus, for the pleasure of your company and for your guidance."

He studied her eyes once more, as if examining her very soul. "Do not allow the ignorance of others to destroy the beautiful truth of who you are."

The knots of shame tugged hard with his words. Ember pressed a hand to her midsection and whispered, "Who am I but a mere servant?"

Bowing his head, he said, "My Queen."

His thin, bony finger trembled as he drew a heart upon her forehead. A breeze lifted the wiry hairs upon his head, whitened with the grace and wisdom of age. Turning on his heels, he shuffled over the uneven ground, pausing only to bow to Leaf, who joined his wobbly gait to the Great Hall.

Perhaps she should join her husband and break her fast. Her stomach, however, protested the very idea. Instead, she glided past the stone building. Savory scents floated on the light breeze until she slipped into the East Cave. A voice boomed from behind, as if making an announcement. But she continued forward, lulled by her need to make herself busy, to work away the day, simply to channel her restless energy another direction.

Warmth tingled her chilled skin as she closed the large, heavy door to the Mediterranean dome. For a moment, she allowed the heat to sink to the marrow of her bones and remove winter's cloak. Waist-high flagstone walls framed the main road, rutted by heavy carts over the years. The dirt path split and she trudged toward the barns and away from the citrus and nut groves, vineyards, and grain fields. The mild honeyed scent of pollinating corn still clung to the morning dew glistening on the stones and citrus leaves.

Straightening her apron, she ambled toward the goat pens. Her hands ached, a reminder to care for them before milking began this morn. She pulled linen strips lined in salve from her apron pocket and wrapped her hands. Leaf still had not noticed her injuries, and she was glad for it. There was naught he could do, anyway. The mysterious illness had affected his workload, same as hers.

Upon reaching the gate, she looked up from bandaging her hand and her blood stilled. Against the stone wall of a barn, near the milk cart, stood Skylar. Features, usually stoic and kind, reflected the angst she carried and her stomach lurched. Gripping the gate, she fought the rising nausea. Still, the meager contents of her stomach emptied into the dry grass—the bread and the wine. Absolution had seemed counterproductive, an admission that she was in error for a choice made for her. Now, she wondered if perhaps she should have sought forgiveness for her part in what was to come.

CHAPTER FOUR

Verbal stones spat from shocked and angry faces. Their words pelted her fortitude until her confidence dimmed and flickered. She peered above the holographic screen, over the maelstrom. Each accusation drifted upward and added to the black cloud hovering above the room.

Mothers held their children tight, some silently crying over the proclamations. Ember's father pushed his way through the crowd toward the stage, much to her relief. Leaf's eyes met hers in a panic as he, too, made way from the head table to where she and Skylar stood.

Nightfall submerged the Great Hall in shadows. Candlelight did little to remove the stain of darkness in the room. It was nearly a tangible presence, thick and heady. The black cloud expanded with each acrimonious offering and she feared it would burst and consume them all. Or perhaps consume only her.

Lightheaded, she shifted on her feet when her head began to swim in the whirlpool of thoughts and sensations. The formal announcement from New Eden Biospherics & Research still wavered before her vision, the larger tile in a split screen. A list of residents selected to attend tomorrow night's first educational hour wavered in the other, smaller screen.

"Witchcraft!" A voice shouted once more above the heated murmurs.

Skylar loosed an irritated breath. "And yet when the Son of Eden employed technology no one maliciously accused him of witchcraft."

Words died on Ember's tongue as she stared past the screens. Scowls taut with paranoia and outrage swirled before her vision. The community silenced momentarily with Skylar's words. It was true and, regardless of apprehensions, they could not deny the observation. Feared at first, Fillion's magic seemed as natural to his persona as the ever-present joint hanging loosely from his mouth. People had sought his magic, desiring it to connect to loved ones beyond the walls. But from one of their own?

Betrayal.

The word simmered in the bubbling sensations overwhelming her thoughts. The intuition grew until the word fairly screamed from every corner of her mind. Her head felt heavy and she fought the blackness creeping into her vision as her heart writhed and ached. She was trained to betray. Fillion was not raised under The Code. But she was. Raised by a generation who had signed upon their honor to live a life free of modern technology.

"Technology will not bewitch your minds or homes," the Wind Element continued. "I assure you."

"She has bewitched you!"

"Your Queen and Fire Element—"

"Skylar," she said, turning off her Cranium. "Do not defend me, My Lord. All shall be well."

He turned toward her, incredulous. "How shall I call myself a gentleman?" Lowering his voice he asked, "Your Captain?" Skylar faced the crowd and sucked in a breath.

She lifted her hands in quiet protest. "Please, My Lord. Allow His Majesty to regain control."

"Her hands!"

Gasps circulated with cries of alarm and Ember raised her chin, folding her hands at her waist. Leaf sought her eyes from the crowd, near the stage, the questions and concerns burning bright. She did not look away, not even when a voice shouted, "Blisters from magic!"

"New Eden, there is a reasonable explanation!" her father boomed in response. Turning toward her, he asked, "Your Highness, how did your hands suffer such afflictions?"

Ember's gaze touched Leaf's briefly before sweeping over the crowd. "Two milk maids have fallen ill, My Lord. I have taken on their duties as well as mine."

"It was the magic!" Voices raised in protest.

"Your Majesty," her father called out.

"Please, Father," she whispered, beseeching him with her eyes. "Do not engage their fears."

Her father ignored her plea and faced Leaf. "Did you know of your wife's hands?"

Leaf looked to her, confusion written all over his face. He could not lie, incapable of it. "No." The word was soft, edged in fear. Two letters formed her judgment. Two letters released more verbal stones. The gathering roared, fury spewing from their mouths like spittle. Her husband shoved his way to the front, unwilling to meet the eyes of those he passed. Unwilling to meet her eyes as well.

"Our children will not learn magic!" a mother hollered, greeted by cheers of support.

"My Lord," Leaf said to Skylar. "Turn on your Cranium and show them your hands."

The Son of Wind obeyed. Villagers cowered, many threw their hands up to ward off an imagined attack. Ember remained steady, looking straight ahead though shame burned her skin. Skylar moved screens around, bringing up the same declaration and drafting notice from N.E.T. Gradually, he displayed his palms to the crowd.

Before the gathering could respond, Leaf said, "Let us not cast blame and false accusations to justify our trepidations. We need to work together, not slanderously tear each other apart. Shall we discuss this situation with civil tongues?"

"He is under a spell!" a man from the second generation called out, pointing to Skylar. "That is why his hands are clean!"

"Utter nonsense!" Willow spat from the head table.

Fingers pointed to Leaf. "She has bewitched you!"

"Witch!"

"Magic is on her hands!"

"Your Majesty," Ember whispered to Leaf by her side. Woozy, she placed a hand on his arm. He finally met her eyes and she nearly recoiled from the anguish he expressed. Nevertheless, she confessed, "I do not fare well."

"Shall I fetch a chair?"

"If you would be so kind."

Skylar, overhearing their exchange, dashed into the crowd to claim a chair. Tears stung Ember's eyes and she drew in a sharp breath. The community rippled in agitation, and the singular words of fury began to blend into one glaring accusation.

Betrayal.

Witch.

Hovering above the heads, black clouds stormed, the atmosphere charged with their outrage. All the while, buzzing sensations sparked through her mind, until words formed. She turned toward Leaf and they tumbled from her mouth. "Are we not fighting for project continuation?"

Leaf squinted his eyes. "Your Highness?"

"If we were to continue as a colony, what need would we have for technology?"

"Indeed," he said, cautious.

Touching her head, she closed her eyes. Where was Skylar? The chair? "It is said," she whispered, unable to stop the words, "that a house divided is easily conquered. The Techsmith Guild is an affront to the core beliefs of New Eden Township."

"Ember?"

Her husband's voice raised a notch and her eyes flew open with the sound. A metallic taste filled her mouth and she winced at the suddenness of it. Shrieks pierced the air and the community took a collective step back. Then silence. Nary a sound, not even the children. Skylar lowered a chair, his eyes darting between her father and Leaf as he paled.

Ember lifted her fingers and touched a warm, sticky substance trailing from her nose. Red coated her fingertips and dripped to the stage floor. She lifted her eyes in horror to find her emotion perfectly mirrored in Leaf's expression and that of her father's.

"Magic," a voice said. Others murmured the word, grave, fearful.

Then the black cloud burst and consumed her.

The scent of wood smoke brought her back from the black and Ember's eyes fluttered open. Pressed to her father's chest, he carried her through the forest in a harried pace. She turned her head and found Leaf beside him, his features warmed by the lantern glow and tight with worry. Trees rustled and bent with the invisible. The rushing song created flow for the anarchic current of her baffled thoughts.

Footsteps ran up from behind. "Timna is on her way, Your Majesty," Skylar said, breaths heavy. "She was already gathering her supplies when I found her."

"Thank you, My Lord," Leaf said.

Skylar matched Leaf's uneven stride. "Is she still unconscious?"

Embarrassed, she looked away when they peered her direction.

"My Lady," Leaf said, his voice hoarse with emotion. "How do you fare?"

"I am unsure." She pressed into her father's chest once more. Blood had dried on her face. Dark spots bloomed on her clothing and that of her father. His hold grew tighter, sensing her fright. Tears gathered in her eyes and rolled down her cheeks. Leaf found her wrist and provided a gentle squeeze before releasing his hold, unable to keep up with her father's speed.

He remembered her hands.

She drew in a sharp breath as more tears blurred her vision. Silence fell on their group, a sound she welcomed and that remained until they reached her and Leaf's apartment.

"Leave us," Leaf said, once she was placed upon their cot.

Her father reluctantly sought her consent and she nodded. Lowering to his knees, he kissed her on the cheek, saying, "Your mother should be here soon."

"Thank you."

"Connor," Leaf said, standing by the door. "Would you return to the Great Hall and assist Skylar and Rain as needed?"

"Yes, Your Majesty."

She held her breath lest the tears fall once more. She was confused—by what had happened and by how she felt toward her father this moment. Since age eight, he had groomed her to betray The Aether—her husband—and his people. Did he understand this truth? Or was there a greater vision she had not yet grasped?

Leaf poured water from the wash bucket into a bowl. When the door shut, he eased next to her on the cot and lifted a dampened rag to her face. Tenderness infused each touch as he wiped away the blood and tears. "Have you fallen ill?"

"It seems so," she said. The quiet that followed was tense. Leaf was brooding, though his kindness never faltered. The knot in her stomach tightened until it hurt to breathe. Holding in the tears, she half-whispered, "I am so sorry, My Lord. This night…" Ember gripped the bed linens until discomfort throbbed in each fingertip. Apologies faded from her tongue. What could she really say? How could she truly humble herself before the man who, in his heart, was still burying his murdered father? She would not insult him with paltry justifications.

"Your words in the Great Hall this eve shamed me." Leaf dipped the cloth in the bowl. Ribbons of red swirled through the clear water. Touching her face again, he said, "For weeks I have felt the same as you and pushed aside my concerns. I feared Skylar would see any move I made as retribution for the faction and Great Fire and, therefore, so would the community. Not even Dr. Nichols knew of the Techsmith Guild, my first clue that all was not well. And still, I did nothing, My Lady.

Nothing." He set the bowl on the nightstand and dabbed along her chin. "This night should not have happened. But it did and I have only myself to blame."

"Please, My Lord. Do not borrow troubles for yourself."

His hand stilled though his shoulders held a slight shake. "I have failed you." A muscle pulsed along his jaw as his face tensed.

"No, My Lord. It is I who have failed you." Ember turned her head away from his touch. "I have only wanted to serve you. Instead, I incited unrest after you battled and sacrificed for peace."

"I *love* you." His finger trailed the curve of her exposed cheek. "I would wage wars for you, Ember Lenore Watson." His finger brushed along her hairline and tucked in a stray strand. "But since the Great Fire, and especially tonight, I have failed you."

"Leaf—"

"No, allow me to speak."

He curled up next to her on the bed and continued to trace a finger down her face, her neck, and along the curves of her body. The shyness that normally claimed his affections was gone and in its place was a man made bold by humility.

"You are my family," he whispered into her neck. "I vowed to protect you all my days." He choked on the last word, his shoulders shaking again. Ever so carefully, he took her hand and kissed her palm, gently cradling her hand to his chest. "I am grieved you hid your injuries from me, but I understand why. You loved me in your pain and through your loss, and I repaid your devotion with distrust and distance. Especially this night. I should have never allowed you to stand before the community without me. I ... I fed you to the wolves. My wife..."

"I betrayed you."

"And what is the cost of this betrayal? If you had shared the truth before Fillion was poisoned, what were the consequences?"

Ember closed her eyes and forced herself to breathe. "Banishment."

"I should have asked you this question far sooner."

"You are grieving, My Lord," Ember said. "Do not add to your many sorrows. I know your heart." Leaf grazed his nose along where her neck and shoulder met as he drew in a tremored breath. She continued, "All that you had trusted proved false. You have lost so much. Are you not allowed to retreat and heal? I judge you not."

"My grief does not excuse my honor nor wipe away the tears you have shed for my selfishness." Leaf kissed her collarbone and she shivered as heat filled her body.

"Allow me to be your refuge," she whispered into his hair, "to love you."

"My Lady, I place my life into your hands." She locked eyes with her husband, left breathless by the vulnerability of his declaration. "Do with me as you will."

The air between them charged as his breath invited hers closer. Closing the gap, she claimed her honor price of a kiss, soft, hushed, a whisper of her adoration. His lips lingered on hers as his hand slipped into her hair and cupped her face, his thumb caressing her cheek. A heartbeat later his kiss deepened, though he remained gentle, only pulling away when a knock sounded on their chamber door. He blinked shyly and she could not help but smile when his bashfulness returned.

"Enter," he said, standing.

Timna strode into the room, placing her medical bag onto the end of their cot. Nerves fluttered in Ember's stomach, afraid she had the illness befalling the other milk maids. Or worse. Perhaps she was magical. Her step-mother stepped into the room and the very emotions Ember had attempted to stifle brimmed past her self-control. She could not help it. Leaf moved to the end of the bed as her step-mother bent over to hold her, swaying back and forth, caressing the hair along her temple.

"Shh," she comforted. "We shall care for you."

"Do you think I am a witch?" Ember said between quiet sobs.

"No, darling. No." Her step-mother smiled. "I think there is something brewing inside of you, but it is not the magic others speak of."

"I shall just be outside the door should you have need of me," Leaf said, with a bow.

"Please." Ember wiped the tears from her face. "Please stay, Your Majesty." He dipped his head and lowered into the chair by their cot.

Timna came around to the other side of the bed and placed the back of her hand upon her forehead. "No fever. Have you experienced any chills?"

"No, Madam."

"Nausea or vomiting?"

She dashed a worried glance to Leaf. "I have experienced mild nausea for quite some time and vomited just this morning."

"When did your courses last run?" her step-mother asked.

Ember touched her cheeks, lowering her eyes. "A week before I was married."

Timna and her step-mother shared a smile. "May I press on your abdomen, Your Highness?" Timna asked. Ember nodded, and the naturopath pressed below her stomach, her smile growing. "Lady Brianna, would you confirm?"

Ember's eyes widened. Had she misread her own body? Women her age did not speak of such things—she had so little knowledge to begin with. And everything had been tossed in confusion since the Great Fire. With so many falling ill since that time, what other explanation would she have arrived at? Elation intertwined with vindication and shimmered through the emotional mire until her limbs grew weightless. It was as if layers of grime and filth lifted from her body. She was clean. Absolved of her heresy. Lifting an eyebrow, she turned to Leaf. Did he understand? But he did not look her way, far too focused on Timna and her step-mother's ministrations.

When the examination was complete, Mother whispered in her ear, "I surmise you are eleven weeks along and due near the first of July. Nosebleeds are common in the second trimester, of which you are close. Fainting spells are unfortunate experiences in your condition as well. There is indeed something rather magical brewing inside of you, my darling." Her stepmother kissed her cheek. "I shall leave so you may share your news privately. Laurel and Oaklee are staying with us this night, so rest well."

She could not speak, not even to extend thanks. Her heart thumped wildly in her chest, more so when the door shut. Her nosebleed was not the result of magic. Nor her fainting spell. She did not carry shame. No, she carried the evidence of love. Giddy with disbelief, laughter filled her chest until it spilled out and caught fire before her very eyes.

"Is it true?" Leaf asked, his voice breathy. She patted the space next to her on their cot, laughing once more. "You are with child?" She nodded, still unable to find adequate words. The sound of his joy rushed through her and she closed her eyes, heady with bliss. Sweet and reverent, he kissed her stomach, pressing his face to her abdomen, his hands embracing her hips. "I love you, wee one," he spoke to her belly. "I am honored to be your … father."

That single word held power. By the way every muscle tightened, it was a word that swung wide the doors leading into the sacred place Leaf protected and held close. He lifted his face, a thousand emotions softening each feature. This moment, he was living numerous different beginnings and endings. The future. The past. Life and death. Family. Their family.

"Fatherhood shall be your true crown, My King."

His breath hitched. Light green eyes held hers as he brought her hand to his lips. "You have humbled me, My Queen." Slowly, carefully, he returned her hand to the bed and crawled up over her body, placing his forehead to hers. "May our child have your strength of character, unfailing compassion, wisdom—and beauty. Ember…" He said her name with a form of anguish that blazed through her soul. His gaze caressed her face, her skin burning where his eyes lingered. Then he whispered across her lips, "I am your servant."

A fiery shudder wended its way to her core with his confession. It was a powerful feeling, one she gave herself over to as her husband searched her eyes for permission.

"Yes," she whispered without hesitation.

Perhaps it was not proper, nor considerate of those awaiting news of her health or in need of reassurance from their King. But only she and Leaf existed this moment. His mouth lowered to hers and she welcomed his passion. The knots of shame in her stomach unraveled as she became his refuge, as she loved him, as he protected her against the guilt and blame. Dissension owned the world beyond the walls of their chamber. But in this room, their sanctuary, closed off from all expectations and duties, they found peace.

The candle by their bedside dripped away with each heartbeat of time. Its amber light painted the walls as her pulse walked among the shadows to dance with his.

When he later breathed deep with the rhythm of sleep's serenity, she leaned over and blew out the flame. The shame of betrayal no longer claimed her. Nor did she fear facing tomorrow. Ember placed a hand upon her stomach and smiled into the darkness.

CHAPTER FIVE

Sunday, December 6, 2054

h er elation became muted as she started out the next morn. For the village had cooled to silence. The thunderous boom of anger echoed in the Hall still, as if the stones resounded the memory. Though traces of the black cloud lingered, not one soul had hissed "witch" to her in passing. To not acknowledge her was more distressing than the verbal stones, she decided.

A low hum of tension vibrated from table to table. Dishes clanked in soft murmurs and voices remained whispers. Souls, believing themselves brave, chanced a look at her. She replied with a kind smile each time. Their ignorance was a poor excuse for her lack of compassion, especially as their Queen and Fire Element, their humble servant.

In truth, she had more pity for the villagers than anything else. The second generation were not groomed for adaptability. Nor had they much practice in the art of change. Each day had been the same. Each day until the end of September, that is. Then their world collided with another and people reacted as though Earth was a hostile enemy rather than their origin. The sudden presence of technology among their own only triggered this irrationality all the more. And strangely, it was worse among the first generation, those who should know better.

Her mind reached into the unknown for a glimmer of understanding. A sensation answered back, faint and distant. Stifling a yawn, she looked into her bowl of porridge. Bland and tasteless and growing cold, in many ways like New Eden Township. She dribbled in a spoonful of honey. Amber swirls dissolved into the oats until unseen. The sweetness, however, remained present. The enticing scent wafted upward with the waning steam.

It seemed so simple, the idea of change. On the surface, one life experience appeared to blend into the next, like honey in porridge. But this is not so, merely an illusion. Taking a bite, she appreciated the new complexity of textures and flavors not previously present. If only all experiences resulted in pleasure. With disagreements, such as now, life lacked piquancy and the sweetness turned to ash on her tongue as her heart leadened.

Ember sighed with a mild twinge of nausea and absently placed a bandaged hand upon her belly. Across the table, Skylar's gaze traveled to her hand and rested there a few heartbeats before looking away. Did he perchance hear of the coming babe? Did the community? Willow sent her a knowing smile, warm and beauteous, confirming Ember's suspicions. Of course it was announced. How else could her father and Skylar properly defend the nosebleed and fainting spell? This was why the community remained silent—they were ashamed. Embarrassed herself, Ember set her spoon on the table and lowered her eyes, the meager appetite she had entertained now gone.

"Time is both an ally and an enemy," she said under her breath.

"Your Highness?" Worry wrinkled Leaf's forehead as he angled in his chair to face her. Bending low, he asked, "Are you well?"

"Yes, quite, Your Majesty." With a smile, Ember withdrew a pinch of salt from the salt bowl and added it her porridge. She forced a small bite for Leaf's benefit.

Skylar studied her from his position on the opposite end of the table and intuition rushed through her like a mighty wind. Salt and honey, wise as serpents and gentle as doves. A revelation bloomed within the periphery of her mind and she smiled once more.

She faced Skylar. "My Lord," she began, "do you have plans following morning meal?"

"My day is yours to command." Skylar's face remained stoic, posture straight. His eyes, however, held an intensity she had not seen since the night of the Great Fire. Normally he was shuttered, private, even more so than her husband. But she knew the Son of Wind suffered, afflicted the same as Leaf. With his gaze locked onto hers, he asked, "How may I be of service, Your Highness?"

"I wish to discuss a matter of import with you and His Majesty." The room had silenced even more during their small exchange. Villagers pretended to eat with heads tilted toward the head table all the while attempting to appear inconspicuous. Ember swallowed and softened her voice. "Thank you for lending me your time, My Lord."

Skylar rose from his chair, pushed his half-eaten meal way, and splayed his hands onto the table. His fingers arched, as if clawing the wood, his chin tucked toward his chest. Normally, he shuttered away all emotion from his face. But now, the ignominy was all too clear. With a bow, he excused himself and strode from the Great Hall. All heads turned her direction, but she focused only on her porridge.

She knew where he would be when she and Leaf were ready.

The patterned sky seemed within reach, as if her hand could caress the glass surface. The biting wind buffeted against her exposed skin, her hair swirling about her face. What would it be like to fly? To soar above it all and soak in every sight? She often held this thought whilst looking over the edge of the observation deck. This morning, however, she longed to fly beyond the lined sky toward the clouds.

Back turned to her and Leaf, Skylar leaned his forearms on the railing and peered out over the main biodome. In some ways, he reminded her of Fillion. In the manner of his walk and personal carriage for sure, being both a shadow and a brilliant light. The Son of Wind was a paradox, a puzzle. He was tall and lean like the Son of Eden. He observed the world around him in the same quiet yet intense way, too.

Cousins. It was a strange thought. She was considered Fillion's cousin as well, although by marriage only. Unlike Skylar, who was Hanley's legitimate nephew. Did he know? Had Leaf shared with him? Before Leaf departed New Eden the night of the Great Fire to confront Hanley, Fillion had informed him of Mack's findings. Leaf had not been the same since. But, then again, no one had since that fated night.

Transitions, her mind whispered. They were a community in transition, rising from the ashes.

Light brown hair flew about in the wind, covering Skylar's hazel eyes as he peered over his shoulder at their approach. Lips flushed and parted, tears stained his cheeks and her heart stilled. This man had endured so much for her safety and that of Leaf. Before she could say anything, Skylar fell onto his knees before her feet.

"I beg your forgiveness." His voice shuddered in the wind, angry, broken. "Upon my honor as a man, I yield my life to you."

"There is nothing to forgive," Ember said, placing her hand on his head. "You are a man of commendable honor."

His face grimaced, teeth gritting against the storm whipping around inside of him. Lifting his eyes, he shouted, "You shall not pay for my sins! Especially... especially now..."

Ember blanched as the pain of his words gripped her. Another gust rushed by and carried off his tears. "You have committed no sins against me." She knelt before him and took his hands, forcing him to look at her, to really look at her. His hazel eyes quivered, the faint freckles on his skin surfacing as his skin deadened to an ashen color. "You are not to blame, for anything."

"My actions have called your reputation into question."

"Your father threatened you, My Lord. He used my safety as a means to motivate you." Ember squeezed his fingers, wincing with the pain in her own. "It was a strategic move to potentially marry you into position for the invisible throne." Ember looked at Leaf and said, "Though I knew not who was to become The Aether, my father did." She returned attention to Skylar. "And he allowed you to court my affections before the community, knowing full well that your father's hand was involved, that you would never willingly cause your friend harm, and that my affections were for another. You feared for me and protected me at the cost of your own honor and friendship. You knew I understood your position from the start. How can you now apologize?" Her thumb brushed over the back of his hand. She lowered her voice to barely a whisper and said, "You possess a beautiful heart, Skylar Kane."

More tears slipped past his self-control. Sacrifices of grief for the wind, sacrifices of honor. He whispered back, "The community believes you have bewitched me as well as Leaf. The villagers spoke of you controlling the hearts of men. I even heard—" He stopped, his skin reddening. Lowering his voice even more, he said, "Some women this morn even called into question whose babe you carry. My actions have dishonored you, Lady Ember."

Ember heated with mortification, grateful that Skylar kept his eyes fastened to the deck flooring. She surreptitiously glanced at Leaf, but he did not appear to have heard Skylar's hushed comment in the roaring wind. Though embarrassed, she said, "Their opinions are not a reflection of you or me, for we know the truth. They shall say anything to defend their fear and ignorance."

Skylar inhaled a sharp breath. "Hanley knew the community would punish you for his decision to roll out the Education Plan. He knew Leaf was in the room listening as well. And he knew it would break me to watch you suffer." He spat, "And still I followed through with his orders—"

"As did I. Orders I could have easily refused to obey as well." She cut him off, awareness shimmering to the forefront of her mind. "You are not the only one to have betrayed trust and good sense, or those you care about, My Lord." He hung his head, his shoulders rising and falling. "It is time you and Leaf spoke to one another. Do not grant Hanley's plan of division any morsel of victory."

"You speak with wisdom, Your Highness, as always." His gaze roamed over her face in contemplation as he whispered her words from the Communications Room: "Fear shall make enemies of us all."

Skylar helped her rise, eyebrows drawn tight and teeth clenched. His black cloak lifted in the billowing atmosphere and fluttered, his hair wild. This moment, he looked ancient and fierce, as if he contained the wind's pulse within his beating heart. Behind shifting strands, his bloodshot eyes leveled onto the Son of Earth. Skylar hesitantly reached out then grabbed Leaf's forearm as his face contorted in misery.

"I am so very sorry that my family is cause for discord yet again. Have mercy on me, on my sisters." Holding firm to Leaf's forearm, he knelt down on one leg and lowered his head. "You are my King. All that I am, all that I have is yours. The Techsmith Guild swears its fealty to you, Your Majesty."

Leaf pulled Skylar back to a stand and used the momentum to draw him close. He gripped Skylar by the shoulders, their foreheads touching. "You are my family, Sky."

The Son of Wind's body sagged as Leaf wrapped his arms around him in a tight embrace. All the grief Skylar held within his shattered life broke free and his body began to shake, his cloak snapping in the force of the air swirling and rushing by. Used and discarded, punished still, Skylar was alone. He and his sisters made reparations for sins they did not commit whilst their mother lay stricken in bed. How did one heal from such trauma? She knew not.

"We are now fatherless," Leaf began, "both of us raised up in the aristocracy to become political sons of misfortune." A shiver coursed down her spine with his words. "But it is not our identity. You stand upon your own merit, Sky. I am forever honored and deeply humbled to call you my brother."

They continued to cling to one another, Leaf's fingers digging into Skylar's back. Their unshakable bond was rich and beautiful. Another layer of filth and grime lifted off of Ember and she tilted her face to the gales galloping across the tree tops. Her generation paid for the choices of the first. But Ember was clean. They were clean.

Shyness crept in and Skylar focused on the wooden deck as he pulled away. With a need to gather himself, he wrapped his cloak tight around his body as he returned to the railing and peered out once more. Strands of her hair floated and danced in the turbulent air. The hidden turbines powering the bio-wind blasted another gust and her dress pressed hard against her body. They remained silent, lost to their own thoughts while Skylar comforted his grief.

Time slipped by, slow and steady, and she eventually sensed the need to redirect their conversation back toward a solution, the very reason she called Skylar and Leaf together. Straightening her shoulders, she angled her body toward Leaf. "Your Majesty," she began. Skylar peered over his shoulder at the sound of her voice. "How do you advise the Techsmith Guild?"

Leaf furrowed his brows at her question before covering his face with his hands. He needed to disappear within himself, to remove all distractions. Skylar moved to her side as they awaited an answer. She felt his eyes on her, though his head was downcast, and she understood his silent message of gratitude. Though she never removed her focus from Leaf, she issued a single, curt nod.

"I believe," Leaf said, dropping his hands, "New Eden needs a different form of demonstration and reassurance. How many times can the community break The Code without consequences?"

"The Techsmith Guild was created to help with transitions during Project Phase Two, Your Majesty," Skylar offered. "I had not thought of consequences, actually. Her Highness and I as well as all others within the Guild have signed an addendum to The Code, permitting us the use of technology."

Leaf squinted his eyes. "An addendum to The Code?"

"Yes," Skylar answered.

"Then have you signed the original document?"

Skylar blinked, his face relaxing into his usual stoic expression. "No, I have not. I was under the impression that we were grandfathered into it until the day you and Fillion confronted New Eden."

"Have you signed The Code?" Leaf asked her. She shook her head no, and he sighed, long and heavy. "Does it not seem like a test of honor? It feels as though Hanley is setting up the first generation to break contract. But why?" When neither she or Skylar offered an answer, Leaf whispered, "He shall never tell us."

"Shall we approach Jeff for an addendum the first generation may sign before partaking in technology education?" Skylar asked.

"No," Ember interjected, and both men turned toward her with raised brows. "Let us only offer it to the second generation who have come of age and by choice, not demand. The first generation joined New Eden to experience a life free of modern technology. The Techsmith Guild invalidates the very sacrifices they made to fully realize these convictions. We should respect their wishes."

Leaf smiled and, with such adoration, a blush crept up her neck. "Indeed, Your Highness," he said, his voice soft and full of admiration. "And what shall you teach the second generation?"

"Simple mechanics and operations," Skylar offered. "We were to introduce the idea of technology without direct application."

"Though I do believe there should be a defined purpose and use beyond introduction, do you not agree?" she asked Skylar. Ember folded her hands at her waist and shifted into a posture of regal elegance. "After all, we are fighting for project continuation. What need have we for technology?" The Son of

Wind considered her question a few heartbeats before gently nodding his head. "What do you suggest, Guild Captain?"

"I need time to ponder, if I may?" Skylar asked. Both she and Leaf dipped their heads in answer. "When do you desire an answer, Your Majesty?"

"Whenever a viable one presents itself, though I prefer soon after Yuletide, if only to not invite more trouble from Hanley."

"Very well. I also believe Lady Rain should be privy to our discussions and participate in decisions."

"Yes, indeed," Leaf said.

Skylar continued, "I shall inform her of our concerns and observations."

"Thank you, My Lord." Leaf bowed. "Let us meet at my apartment following evening meal. The education class, as it were, is hereby canceled."

The Son of Wind returned the bow, first to Leaf, then to her before departing for the village. As he passed her, he whispered for her alone, "I would gladly give my life for yours, My Queen." Their eyes locked for half a heartbeat. In that small measure of time, a bond had sealed them. Though she declared him innocent, his honor demanded a price in order to forgive himself, and he had named it. She smiled her understanding and relief softened his eyes as he strode toward the stairs.

A breeze moved through her as if she were mere vapor, leaving the chill of near winter in its wake. Leaf sidled up from behind and wrapped her in an embrace, covering her with his cloak. Together they surveyed their Kingdom in silent unity as her mind bathed in pleasurable buzzing sensations. Ember leaned the back of her head against her husband's chest, absorbing his warmth and strength. She encouraged his hands to cradle her stomach while she took hold of his cloak, pulling it tighter around them. Leaf smiled into her hair and she closed her eyes.

Their struggles were not yet over. Secrets were foolish creatures, she reminded herself. She would no longer play with fools. Time heals wounds but it also erodes memories as life weathers on. No, they would continue the fragile dance of trading one set of troubles for another all the days of their lives. Nevertheless, as she rested in deep pools of peace for the first time in weeks, she offered up a smile of her own. It was a gift for the wind to share with those who listen to its tales. Her heart whispered of hope and new beginnings for their generation and the one after. All would be well.

She had a hunch.

SKYLAR

The trees inside Biosphere 2 grew rapidly, more rapidly than they did out-side of the dome, but they also fell over before reaching maturation. After looking at the root systems and outer layers of bark, the scientists came to realize that a lack of wind in Biosphere 2 caused a deficiency of stress wood. Stress wood helps a tree position itself for optimal sun absorption and it also helps trees grow more solidly. Without stress wood, a tree can grow quickly, but it cannot support itself fully. It cannot withstand normal wear and tear, and survive. In other words, the trees needed some stress in order to thrive in the long run.

— Travis Brownley, "The Necessity of Stress," *Heads and Tales at Marin Academy*, https://travisma.wordpress.com/2013/12/12/the-necessity-of-stress/, December 12, 2013 *

The son shall not bear the iniquity of the father, neither shall the father bear the iniquity of the son: the righteousness of the righteous shall be upon him, and the wickedness of the wicked shall be upon him.

—Ezekiel 18:20, The Holy Bible, *King James Version* *

I suggested we leave, but he refused. Through his tears, he said he could not leave because the others had labeled him a bad prisoner. Even though he was feeling sick, he wanted to go back and prove he was not a bad prisoner.

At that point I said, "Listen, you are not #819. You are [his name], and my name is Dr. Zimbardo. I am a psychologist, not a prison superinten-dent, and this is not a real prison. This is just an experiment, and those are students, not prisoners, just like you. Let's go."

—"Conclusion," The Stanford Prison Experiment, www.prisonexp.org/conclusion, August 1971 *

ChAPTER ONE

New Eden Township, Salton Sea, California

Tuesday, December 8, 2054

Week Six of Project Phase Two

T he bowl of porridge heated Skylar's chilled hands. Late autumn was especially cold this morning. The trace heat delivered to the apartments courtesy of the compost digesters helped, but not enough to erase the shiver in the air. He pressed against the door with his shoulder to ensure it was shut. A draft had dropped the temperature in their home and he worried for his mother.

The hinge angled strangely and had since the day of the Great Fire. That night, men—led by the true King and Aether—had charged into his family's home in search of Skylar's father, the faction leader. The faction leader and Joel Watson's killer, a fact his father boasted of privately to him and Leaf at the lab the day following the Great Fire. Others in the community still did not know the latter bitter truth, not even his sisters. Only he and The Elements.

Skylar studied the bent hinge once more. He did not wish to bother Connor over a trivial repair. He tried to avoid the former Fire Element as much as possible, actually. But, perhaps he would discuss the need of a new hinge for his mother's sake.

The sweet scent of porridge brought him back to task and he straightened his shoulders. Dwelling on his father would have to wait. Skylar was far too busy providing for his family. His father did not deserve even a morsel of his time and energy, though he knew the mental declaration was pointless.

In a few quick strides he reached the relocated cot now placed against their living room wall. Mother stared up at the ceiling with twitching eyes and trembling limbs. Her arms seemed more rigid than earlier and he frowned. Yesterday, she had turned away from him whenever he spoke to her, refused food as well.

"Mother, 'tis time to break your fast," he said.

Behind him, Gale-Anne rushed by as the last word left his mouth, then slowed to a stop. "My Lord, I thought you had left. I heard the door."

Skylar peered at his nine-year-old sister. Brown hair spilled in waves to her waist, the ends slightly tangled. Noting his inspection, she heaved a sigh of exasperation as her lips pursed.

"Do you need assistance?" he asked.

"Windlyn left early this morn to aid the kitchen staff. Apparently a few scullery maids have fallen ill." His sister threw her hands up in the air. "However shall I braid my own hair?"

He looked to Mother and his frown deepened. Then he removed the emotion from his face lest his littlest sister believe he was displeased with her, which was often her perception. Skylar deposited the bowl of porridge upon a nearby cupboard and reached for the comb in Gale's hand.

"Do you have a ribbon?"

Her eyes rounded. "Oh!"

She dashed back to her room. Long tresses whipped behind her and disappeared into the hallway. A few heartbeats later, she skipped back into the room and, with a final jump, landed before him. Sometimes Skylar believed her energy could easily rival that of a fidgety boy. Her manners were no less inspiring at times, either. Gale-Anne never hesitated to speak what was on her mind. It was tiresome. But he could not fault her. She was willing to say anything for father's good opinion, as was their mother.

Gently, he retrieved the ribbon from her fingers. She plunked into a neighboring chair, back slouched and feet wiggling. He ran the comb through sections of wavy strands without the slightest notion of how to braid a girl's hair. Perhaps similar to braiding rope? His heart thumped heavy, afraid to disappoint her or cause further exasperation. Both he and Gale-Anne were silent, much to his relief. The only sounds were Mother's raspy breaths, shallow and perfectly rhythmic. The hair tugged his sister's head when his fingers fumbled. He drew in a shaky breath, quiet, and hopefully indiscernible to his sister's sensitivities.

"You should smile more, My Lord," she said, much to his surprise. "You are quite handsome when you do. All the girls say so. Well, at least they used to before all this." Skylar stopped his motions for a moment, unsure of how to respond. "Sometimes I miss Father," she continued when he failed to comment. "Then I see Mother and I feel angry all over again."

"We must do our best to move forward." He folded one strand over another. The braided rope formed in his mind's eye and he continued as if it were hemp slipping through his fingers.

"Though I am always much relieved for you, even if we never see him again."

"Do not worry so for me," he mumbled. "I fare well." He tried not to think of what her confession implied. Did she know? He thought his father had concealed his punishments from Gale and Windy. Skylar certainly did. Holding the end of the braid with one hand, he wrapped the ribbon until he could form a knot, then a lopsided bow. "I am finished."

Gale swung her braid over her shoulder and studied his work. The loops were rather disheveled and he postured in wait of her disappointment. Instead, she said, "Passable, I suppose, My Lord."

"Fine compliment."

"Do you trade humor now?" Gale spun to face him with a crooked grin. "Perhaps there is hope after all." She skipped toward the door. "See you in the village!"

The door slammed shut and the bowl of porridge rocked upon the cupboard. Silence settled within the apartment as he regarded Mother. She had lost a significant amount of weight. The Herbalist visited with tinctures made from valerian, stinging nettle, and St. John's wort, all beneficial for anxiety and depression, she reassured him. Still, his mother had experienced little change since the village burned and father was banished. Whispers circulated that she would die of a broken heart and mind if she did not recover soon. He was beginning to agree with the rumors for once.

He reached for spare pillows and helped her to sit upright, wary of her penchant for strange positions. The visiting psychologists referred to this as waxy flexibility, as her body could be molded as if wax and, stranger still, could hold an obscure posture for hours. Retrieving the bowl, he eased next to Mother on the cot. "Mother, it is Skylar," he said. "Killie from the kitchen has brought you porridge with cinnamon and molasses. The kitchen staff wished for me to relay that they miss the sound of your voice instructing the children, especially when you sing your lessons in French."

Dipping the spoon into the porridge, he scooped out a small amount. He wiped the spoon along the edge of the bowl until a small clump raced down the curvature back toward the cooked grains. "*Est-ce que tu aimerais prendre une bouchée?*" He lifted the spoon to her mouth and waited. Her responses were oft delayed. Eventually her lips parted and his body relaxed in relief. No aversion today. She was somewhat responsive this morn, too. Porridge mixed with drool along her chin. He caught the dribble with the spoon and promptly dumped the spittle onto a cloth. "*Une autre bouchée?*" He continued the process until half the bowl was eaten.

There were days when he could not stand the sight of his mother. It was not the weakness. He understood the obliterating pain. Rather, it was the abandonment. While she comforted her grief and trauma in a state of catatonia, he was left to face the disgrace and horror of his family alone. The community took pity on his sisters; they were young yet. They did not spare him the same courtesy.

Most forced politeness, as if charity were obligation. Nevertheless, he wondered if even those were attempts to quell any violent or aggressive tendencies he may possess—as if he might strike back or curse their home. Had he ever reacted strongly with villagers? Or anyone for that matter? Leaf often insisted that Skylar stood upon his own merit. *Lofty thoughts*, he internally argued. In one evening, his father had erased Skylar's history and inserted his own in its place. This is why the villagers had targeted the Daughter of Fire over technology even though he was the Guild Captain. They feared him. Lady Ember suffered because of him, because of his family, and in many grievous ways. It was unforgivable.

Food pushed out of Mother's mouth and he caught the rejected morsels before they fell to her chemise. "All done then," he spoke softly. He dabbed a cloth over her mouth and chin and leaned back in his chair with a heavy breath. For a brief moment, he allowed his eyes to close. Both sisters were now off to work and his mother was fed.

A knock rapped three times upon his door and he slowly opened his eyes. The door creaked open and a female voice hushed a "hello the house."

"Please, come in," Skylar said when recognizing Lady Rain's voice. She slipped in and lifted dark eyes to his as he came to a stand and bowed. A light blush colored her cheeks and he worried for a moment. "Is something amiss, My Lady?"

"No, I simply came to visit with your mother a spell." Lady Rain glided past him to Mother's bedside. "Lady Emily, this is Rain Daniels." She took Mother's hand in both of hers. "I brought soaps and lotions from the Herbalist. Shall I do your hair this day? It is ever so long and lovely. I also brought a book and thought I would read aloud to you as well."

A pang constricted Skylar's heart with her kindness.

Lady Rain peered over her shoulder at him. "Could I trouble you to fetch warmed mineral water?"

"No trouble at all," he replied. "Anything else I may do for you, My Lady? I am entirely at your service."

She released Mother's hand and tucked it beneath the covers. With graceful steps, Lady Rain reached for the iron ring on the entry door and gestured for him to follow her outside. He shut the door with a slight lift to compensate for the bent hinge. Embarrassed, he focused on the village path that separated his ground floor apartment from the forest. Two wash buckets and a basket of toiletries rested in the grass below the front window.

"I do ask one more favor, if I may?" Rain touched his forearm and he made himself meet her waiting gaze. "Would you find Canyon and ask him to deliver the mid-day meal for both your mother and me?"

"I would be honored to do so myself, My Lady. Unless, that is, you need to speak to your brother."

Her complexion warmed once more and he tried to conceal his confusion. Was she falling ill? "I simply did not wish to add to your workload this day, My Lord."

"My gesture is little, 'tis easy enough," he mumbled as his eyes shifted to a passerby. "I am deeply humbled by your care of my mother's needs, My Lady."

Long, slender fingers caressed the length of his forearm before dropping to her waist. "'Tis nothing, really. I cared for my own mother for so long, it seems strange to not do so anymore. It brings comfort to my heart. I am quite selfish, really."

Skylar smiled politely—or so he hoped he smiled—once more too moved for words. The wash buckets caught his attention from the corner of his eye. "Do you need both buckets filled?"

"Yes, please."

He opened the door for her with another bow, then strode toward The Waters. The task did not take him long and he found he rather enjoyed the solitary walk. Lady Rain was filing his mother's fingernails when he returned. Long, dark hair swished to the side when she smiled up at him and his throat tightened, unsure of what he should do next.

"If there is anything else?"

"No, My Lord. We shall fare well."

"Then I shall see you at mid-day meal."

He bowed again, flustered with shame over the state of his mother, and that neither he nor his sister Windy had thought of caring for Mother's nails until now. Had others noticed, such as Lady Brianna and Her Highness, who often cared for Mother when his family was working? Though he had two sisters, the ways and needs of women were a mystery to him. He was a man of straight lines and angles, who found tremendous comfort in rules and social customs. To provide and protect and honor, to lay down one's life for a lady, chivalry and duty, these were gentlemanly qualities he understood and upheld with utmost seriousness. But feminine nuances were almost always lost on him.

He pulled the hood of his cloak far over his head and moved in the direction of the village. His sister Gale toted a sloshing bucket and ladled water to men and women busy with rebuilding shops and apartments. They thanked her and she grinned, eager to please any who would kindly spare her a compliment. Tension stiffened the muscles in his neck and jaw as he passed by, pained by her emotional neediness. Being affectionate did not come naturally to him as it did Leaf or other men in the community, he noticed. Perhaps if he were more verbally and physically comforting rather than dutiful she might not seek constant affirmation from others. He would try harder, for his sisters and his mother.

The remains of The Forge appeared on his left. The heavy smoke accosted him and his mind raced in a panic, an unfortunate response he now endured. It was always triggered by the scent of smoke, though the intensity of reaction differed from one encounter to the next. Skylar slowed his steps and faced the wattle-constructed, open-air forge Connor employed until his shop was fully restored as before. The clank of a hammer connecting with hot metal slashed through the other work-related sounds. Skylar eased into the shadows and Connor glanced up and halted the momentum of the tool swinging in his hand.

"My Lord," Connor said with a dip of his head. "Good day to you."

"Good day to you," he parroted, also with a shallow bow of his own. The older man used tongs to pick up the iron rod he was forging and placed the object deep into the orange coals. A spray of embers flew through the air with the disruption. When finished, he removed thick work gloves and wiped his large hands across his leather apron. Skylar built up his nerves and finally said, "My apologies. I shall not take much of your time, My Lord. I came to inquire over a spare door hinge for a front entry?"

"Alas, I am out. It is a simple thing to make, though." Connor tilted his head. "Is it for your door?"

Skylar dropped his eyes, then thought better of it. Instead, he acted as if he were taking in different objects around the room before saying, "Yes, our top hinge."

"How is your mother?"

"Much the same, I am afraid."

Connor nodded his head, his movement slow and thought-ful. "You walk a difficult road at present, Son of Wind."

Skylar looked away. The words seared him and he hoped he concealed the pain he was sure had flashed across his face. Quietly, he said, "Thank you for the hinge, My Lord. Please send a shop boy when complete, though please do not rush. I know there are many needs at present. We are well."

With a quick bow, he exited and pulled the hood of his cloak even further across his face. Today he must remain as strong as possible. The dehumidifiers needed to be changed in a quarter of the occupied apartments. To face so many villagers in closed, intimate proximity liquefied his courage. But the mundane task would give his mind leave to contemplate greater problems, such as the Techsmith Guild.

Maybe it was time to lay it to rest along with his father. It was his father's project, after all. Nothing within Skylar wanted to honor anything his father had touched, save his own family. He had accepted the position of Wind Element to honor Leaf, and nothing more. For his friend, his King, he would do anything. But his father?

Skylar turned toward the East Cave to seek out the Cooper. Word had reached him that an order of activated charcoal was ready for the dehumidifiers. He straightened his shoulders, removed all thoughts from his face, and moved forward.

CHAPTER TWO

Three barrels of charcoal lined the side wall of the Cooper's shop, which was miraculously untouched by the Great Fire. At least Lady Rain's family shop had not been affected.

Skylar picked up a lump and turned it over in his hand. Sturdy but light, he scraped his fingernail over the surface and inspected the carbon. The Cooper, Lady Rain's father, shifted on his feet when Skylar blew the black dust from his finger. Next, he picked up another lump and tapped it against the first and listened for the tell-tale metallic tink. Satisfied, he threw the lumps back into the barrel and looked up. A pile of unrepairable chairs, buckets, and other hardwood pieces of furniture were mounded in the corner. So much was damaged from the Great Fire and Blood Rains.

"Does it meet your approval, My Lord?" Alex Daniels asked. He pushed a pair of spectacles up his thin nose.

"Yes, indeed. Thank you, sir." Skylar filled two buckets and tied the handles to a yoke beside several empty buckets for the waterlogged charcoal being replaced.

Alex rushed in to help. "Allow me," he said. Skylar squatted and lifted the yoke with ease. Still, Lady Rain's father fussed and ensured it was level. "All set, My Lord?"

"Yes, I believe so." He looked around and did not readily locate the evaporating bins. "Where shall I unload the damp charcoal, sir?"

"By the far corner. I shall have two aerated barrels ready upon your return."

With a dip of his head, Skylar slipped sideways out of the shop and left the village to amble through the forest toward the North apartments. He would attend his farthest locations first and save the closer apartments for when he grew tired.

The forest was rather peaceful in the early morning and he allowed his thoughts to wander where they pleased until arriving at his first location. He unslung an arm from the yoke to knock upon the door. Unsettled, as usual during home visits, his eyes trailed over the stone doorframe as he waited. Near the doorknob, a small chunk was carved from the rockery. *Strange*, he thought. It was a relief to no longer claim the only imperfect front entry, however. Skylar searched the ground for the missing piece when a middle-aged woman opened the door a crack. Her eyebrows shot up and her mouth parted.

"Forgive me, madam," he began. "May I check your dehumidifier?"

"Yes, yes, of course, My Lord." She invited him with a wave. "My eldest has fallen ill, I am afraid. Will that be a trouble?"

"No, but I am most sorry to hear of it."

The woman's eyes widened. "I did not mean to suggest that perhaps our suffering is greater than yours."

Skylar attempted a weak smile through his annoyance. "I had no such thoughts, madam. Please, be at ease. I am only here to care for your needs." He lowered the yoke and buckets to the ground. With a quick yank, he untied the collection bucket and entered her home.

The smell of sickness hit him hard. He kept his face devoid of any reaction, though he wished to gag. The woman led him first to her chamber. The dehumidifier hung from an iron candle holder upon the wall, as most were placed in private rooms. A decent pool of water had collected in the base, as he suspected. It was the same in his home. The Blood Rains had saturated the main dome beyond acceptable levels, thus the elevated humidity. The nano panels and venting systems kicked in to recalibrate the air, though not fast enough. He may need to visit all of the occupied apartments.

Carefully, he lifted the collection bucket to cover the dehumidifier, then unhooked the wooden container. It plopped to the bottom of the bucket with a loud thud. Once outside, he dumped the water plate and placed the sodden charcoal in a different bucket. With one of many rags he brought along, he dried the tarred interior until it no longer wept from the air holes, then filled it with fresh activated charcoal. He repeated this process in the apartment until all dehumidifiers were cleaned and replaced.

He was ready to leave when a thought occurred. Perhaps he should check the felted wool air filter in the natural heat return as well. The biodome had experienced far more pollutants than usual these past few months. Was this perhaps why so many were falling ill? He surely hoped not, for he could not endure one more scandal linked to his home. Skylar thought over the symptoms being reported and noted, with alarm, that some did indeed align with natural gas poisoning.

"May I check your air filter?"

Her eyes widened again. "I wash it twice a year as instructed, My Lord. I assure you."

"I have no doubts that you do. That is not my concern."

She appeared anxious, but nevertheless showed him the air return in the lower back wall. He crouched on his knees and removed the iron grate. The filter was clogged with debris, what he feared. Skylar ran a finger along the felted wool and left a noticeable streak. Over his shoulder, the woman gasped.

"Are we cursed with a Black Death?"

"No, 'tis ash from the Great Fire, fret not. Shall I send Windlyn to wash the filter for you?"

The woman sank to a chair. "You do not trust me to care for something so simple?"

"Your daughter is ill, and I did not wish to add to your burdens." Skylar resisted the urge to sigh heavily. The back and forth was growing wearisome. Did he appear upset or offended? He did not think so. Perhaps his sister was correct and he should smile more. Still, he remained bland as he awaited her reply. Emotions had always invited undesired attention in his home.

"I shall care for my filter, My Lord, never you worry."

"Then I shall take my leave." He paused at the door with a bow. "Do let me know if you are in need of anything, madam. I wish your daughter a hasty recovery."

The heavy sigh finally left his tightened chest when the door shut. Skylar picked up the yoke and carried it a few steps to the next apartment. It would be a long day, indeed.

He left the Cooper's shop and flipped up his hood, relieved of the load he had carried all day. His back ached and he rolled his shoulders and stretched. People milled about in conversation while others rushed in the direction of their apartment for the hour of rest. Pleasant savory scents infused the air from the Great Hall and his stomach grumbled. Though in need of a light repast before evening meal, he was eager to return home and decompress from this day.

Often the villagers forgot that he was in the home and spoke freely of topics and made comments he wished he had never heard or knew. His father, on the other hand, enjoyed the intrusion and would casually drop information to those who breezed by. The villagers repeated that they "heard it on the wind," as his father would oft say and, thus, the rumor mill continued to rotate at full speed.

Skylar frowned and drew his eyebrows together. His father resented him for being "too noble" and "pretentious," and for not doing his duty to ensure The Elements were informed of all goings-on within the community. A few evenings each week,

Skylar received a verbal lashing, and was struck or pinched until his skin bruised, all in attempt to gain a confession. But Skylar remained tight-lipped. His mother and sisters believed he was sequestered with Father to debrief the Wind Element on private details only The Elements and First Representatives were privy to know. Or so he thought until Gale-Anne's comment this morning.

The last of the bruises had finally faded. Never would he allow another to abuse him again—in any way. Threats and punishments no longer greeted him upon returning home as before. The initial panic still taunted him, however. Perhaps it always would, same as the panic caused by heavy wood smoke.

"My Lord."

He swiveled on his heel toward the sound of his friend's voice. "Your Majesty," Skylar said with a bow. His friend limped toward him, though his injured leg appeared to be moving with more flexibility than before.

"I searched for you earlier in the day, but you must have been making rounds," Leaf said.

"Yes. I spent most of the day on the North End, by your apartment, actually." Skylar waited for Leaf to catch up. "How may I be of service to you?"

His friend smiled at him. "I simply wished to see you."

Skylar ducked his head at the sentiments. How Leaf could seek out, let alone stand Skylar's company was beyond him. "I am glad to have crossed paths with you, Your Majesty, for a Service Announcement is needed this evening," he said. Leaf did not appear bothered by the change in subject, but narrowed his eyes as Skylar explained the situation with the filters. "My concern is that those who have fallen ill will blame the air circulation."

"Could it be poor filtration? Are the turbines and industrial air vents affected as well?"

"If the homes are affected, it stands to reason that the larger vents and filters need thorough cleansing as well. But no, I cannot imagine the illness is from poor filtration or higher levels of humidity. Not every symptom lines up with the nature of air toxicity." Skylar lifted his eyes and straightened his shoulders. "I know workloads are already strained, Your Majesty, but I shall need assistance. There is far too much for me to accomplish on my own."

"I shall assist you, My Lord."

Skylar took a step back. "No, Your Majesty. You are needed for morale in the village."

"And what of you, Sky? Your needs are also valid." Leaf placed a hand on his shoulder and squeezed. A corner of his friend's mouth tilted up as he said, "You cannot stop me. I outrank you."

Skylar's lips twitched and his friend's smile widened. "That was quite noble of you to point out."

"Yes, I am quite noble." Leaf grinned again.

The villagers looked on with curiosity, some with nervousness, and Skylar retreated to a more unreadable emotion. Did others still wish he was The Aether instead of Leaf? Or did they now berate themselves and others for the folly of their once-held political beliefs? For following a delusional, aggressive man?

"I should return home to Mother," he mumbled. "Windy is needed back in the kitchen to assist with evening meal."

Nonplussed by the attention, Leaf slipped him another smile and began walking toward the village path. Skylar relaxed his muscles a notch then fell into step next to his friend. A mild zephyr fluttered the leaves and rustled their clothing. Skylar inhaled with deep appreciation when the bio-breeze stirred up the delicious fragrance of roasted vegetables, which lessened as they traveled north. They remained in companionable silence, even as the shops gave way to apartments and the crowds thinned to an occasional villager or a child chasing another.

Before reaching his home, Skylar cut a glance Leaf's way and confessed, "I still do not have a future plan for the Techsmith Guild nor a suitable Education Plan."

"There is no hurry, My Lord. Though, Hanley hounds me almost daily for you to report back to him." Leaf flashed a sly look. "Apparently blurring the lines of our respective offices is no longer necessary. His opinions change with—"

"The wind," Skylar mumbled.

Resentment brewed within him, but he tamped it down. What were his options? Hanley—his uncle—had him cornered. The community blocked his ability to move forward, and he needed to move forward. Distance was the only hope he possessed at present. At some point, he had to admit defeat. Actually, he was ready to wipe his hands clean of the Techsmith Guild. It all seemed pointless. The dilemma of imparting technology education to firmly rooted neophytes went beyond his scope of understanding. Nor could he endure any more scandal. But, before he decided on the next course of action, he needed insight and clear direction. He stopped mid-stride and faced Leaf. An idea had surfaced with his latter thought.

"As The Aether," he began quietly, "could you request a private audience with Dr. Nichols? I am willing to travel to the lab if necessary."

"What manner of meeting do you seek?"

"I wish to discuss the psychology behind my given task." Skylar straightened his shoulders once more. "Since a lad, I was told that people learn best from their own. I am not certain if that is true anymore. And, if not, I fail to comprehend how the Techsmith Guild shall assist New Eden to transition during Project Phase Two. What are we transitioning toward, anyway? The project goal is no longer to shut down but to continue, as her High Highness kindly reminded me."

"Indeed." Leaf narrowed his eyes and nodded his head, slow and deliberate. "I shall send a message to the lab."

"Thank you, Your Majesty."

They reached Skylar's door, and Leaf thumped him amiably on the back before departing. Out of habit, he lifted the door before pushing in, but received resistance. His eyes swung up and rested on a new hinge, dark and bright against the wood and stone. The lower hinge had been replaced as well to ensure they matched. His chest tightened with Connor's gesture.

The door opened with ease and his mouth tipped up in the beginnings of a smile as he entered. Now perhaps Mother would stay warmer in the cooler months ahead. His steps faltered, however, when Lady Rain rose to a stand.

"My Lady," he said, and nearly stumbled over such simple words. He shifted his focus to the hallway and drew his eyebrows together. "Is my sister well?"

"Yes, quite." Lady Rain glided toward where he stood and folded her hands at her waist. "She has left for the kitchen. Gale-Anne assists her this eve as well."

"I see." He looked to her again and blinked back his confusion and surprise. "Thank you, once more, for coming to our family's rescue this day. I know you have tasks of your own to complete. Our family does not mean to take you from duties others are reliant upon."

"Nonsense," Lady Rain said with a dismissive wave of her hand. Then, she lowered her eyes and turned toward her shoulder saying, "It is an honor … to care for the woman responsible for my education." She cleared her throat in a dainty sound and met his eyes, though hesitant.

"I am indebted to you, My Lady." Skylar took her hand and placed it to his forehead as he bowed deeply. Warmth colored her neck and cheeks as he released her fingers and his concern from this morning grew once more. "Forgive me, but do you fare well? You seem flushed." He gestured to the chair. "Please, do not let me keep you standing."

Her eyes widened and she looked away, the color brightening. "Yes, I fare well. I do not suffer a fever. Simply … it is warm, is it not?" She touched her cheek, a delicate movement his eyes followed until her slender fingers returned back to her waist.

His forehead wrinkled, for it was not warm, though he would not press her further. "I would offer to walk you home, but we are unchaperoned."

"We are head Nobles. Surely others will think we merely speak of business."

He inspected a clump of dirt upon the floorboards. "I would not risk your reputation."

"Of course."

Lady Rain peered at his mother over her shoulder, who now sat upon a chair, prim and proper. Skylar followed her gaze and his heart jumped a beat. Mother's normally long, brown tresses were braided and crowned upon her head, dainty fern leaves tucked within the folds and loops, and a cluster of wildflowers were tucked within the latticed bodice cords of her kirtle. Her skin glowed clean and a hint of orange blossom hung in the air. For weeks her cheeks had grown sallow and her complexion waned. But this moment she appeared as though a young maiden.

"Thank you," he somehow choked out. "She looks lovely."

"Yes, she is. I told her so all day long."

The atmosphere around them shifted. It was subtle, like a light bio-breeze which stirs the air though the trees moved not. Slowly, he met Lady Rain's dark eyes and her breath fluttered. He knew he stared longer than a gentleman should. But he could not look away, far too overcome to speak or move, especially when his mind raced in tandem with his panicking pulse.

"I shall be on my way, then," she said, almost a whisper. "See you at evening meal." In a few steps, she pulled open his front entry door and disappeared into the afternoon light.

He continued to stand there like a complete dolt. Air rushed back into this lungs and his heart rate accelerated even higher. Skylar studied his mother once more. She really did look quite lovely and ... at peace. He picked up the ropes from the floor and tied one around his mother's waist and another around her thighs. Safety measure in place, he could now leave her unattended in the chair for a few moments. He gave her warm hand a gentle squeeze, then trudged to his room to freshen up. A village matriarch would arrive soon to keep Mother company while he attended evening meal with his sisters.

CHAPTER THREE

Friday, December 11, 2054

D r. Nichols breezed into The Chancery with fluid movements. Dust motes glinted and danced in a wedge of sunlight afforded by the open door. The click of her strange heeled shoes syncopated to the rhythm of Skylar's heartbeat and he steadied his bearing to ensure he appeared calm and collected. Still, he flinched when his chair scraped the floor as he came to a stand beside Leaf and Jeff.

Loosely styled raven strands swayed over slender shoulders and against a long, elegant neck with each bounce of her even steps. An embroidered silk dress—long-sleeved and high-necked—clung to every curve and ended above the knee, much to his dismay. It was her eyes that turned his mouth to sawdust, though. Haunting and gray, they were an ethereal color that appeared to see right through him. Most men in the community spoke of her allure as if Helena of Troy were merely passable in comparison. Unlike Skylar, who found her comeliness entirely unnerving and not in a pleasant way.

Since the start of Project Phase Two, Dr. Nichols had visited New Eden only once, and on the arm of her husband. People had parted for her as if she were an Earthen Queen and stared agape at her unnatural beauty. She even possessed the ability to silence the rumor mill for days following her visit, miracle of miracles. Lady Brianna, considered most fair among women in New Eden, appeared dull in her cousin's presence. And old enough to be her mother.

Hanley's wife walked into the main belly of The Chancery and his mind wandered back to their first introduction in the airlock. In front of Fillion and Leaf, she had commented on how he resembled a younger version of her husband. At the time, he had believed her observation a mere flirtation. Now he knew the truth. But did she?

He bowed, as did Leaf and Jeff. "Thank you, My Lady, for coming so swiftly and on such short notice," Skylar said as he rose.

"I had to wait until Hanley departed for New York this morning."

"Would you care for tea, My Lady?" he asked. "I can send for refreshment."

"No, but thank you." She tilted her head and arched an elegant, dark eyebrow. Lips, painted the color of wine, tipped up in a beguiling smile. "I assume you want this meeting off the record?"

"Yes, if you please." Skylar gestured to a chair and lowered into his own only when she had settled.

Leaf leaned forward and added with dry humor, "Though with all the scientists running about these days, I doubt anything is truly off the record with Hanley."

"You might be surprised." With a sly smile, her attention shifted to Jeff. Posture cool and appraising, she said, "Good to see you, Jeff."

"You look well, as always, Dr. Nichols." Jeff rose and shuffled loose leafs of paper on his desk with quaking hands. "If you will excuse me. I will leave you three to have your discussion in private." He snatched a walking stick by his chair and quickly departed The Chancery. Perhaps Skylar was not the only man who found her beauty terrifying.

"Well," Dr. Nichols began. She crossed her legs the opposite direction and leaned over her knees. Skylar focused on the floor rather than the immodest display of bare skin. "You wished to meet with me, Skylar? May I call you Skylar or do you prefer a different form of address?"

"Skylar is fine."

A cloying scent infused the air all around her and Skylar did his best to not show displeasure. Nerves rushed through him in the ensuing silence and he gripped the edge of his seat. Gray eyes roamed over him from head to toe and back up again. Was he to speak? Had she asked him a question? He could not recall, too lost was he in calming his escalating anxiety.

She brushed dark strands from her shoulder and lifted her eyebrow once more. "How is your mother? Any signs that the catatonia is waning?"

"No, not really," he murmured. "I fear she may be forever lost to us."

"Would you like her temporarily institutionalized?" Dr. Nichols reached out and placed a warm hand upon his knee. Wine-colored nails gleamed against the dark tones of his breeches, as if flecks of blood. "I promise she would have the best care until recovery. A period of rehabilitation may be necessary for atrophy, similar to that required for a stroke victim." The heat from her hand seeped through the heavy wool and he swallowed.

"Stroke?"

"Apoplexy."

Skylar stared at her fingers, lithe appendages that were far more soft and manicured than those of the women he knew. His jaw worked in agitation as he thought of Lady Rain filing his mother's nails.

"I believe she is happier with her family." He tried to sound as bored as possible to hide his turbulent thoughts. "I find she is most responsive after long visits with me or my sisters."

"Of course." Dr. Nichols smiled. "It sounds like your mother enjoys the company of her children. Whatever induces happiness and peace of mind is the best course of action in the absence of modern medicine."

"Is … my father well cared for?"

"Yes." She removed her hand and adjusted her position on the chair so that her ankles crossed to the side. Both he and Leaf focused on objects around the room and not her legs. "Formal charges are not being issued, per request," she continued, business-like. "Therefore, I signed the release papers for his permanent residence in a psychiatric home for adult patients."

"Thank you, My Lady."

"Does your mother receive regular care?"

"Several matriarchs from the village have donated their time to care for my mother whilst my sisters and I work. The Herbalist brings tinctures to reduce anxiety and depression." Skylar released his grip on the chair seat as he thought of Lady Rain. Mother appeared the happiest after her visit in particular. "She eats soft foods and can swallow water and cider," he continued. "Though she continues to lose weight." He angled away and picked up a stone figurine on the edge of Jeff's desk, similar to a chess pawn. His thumb caressed the smooth, cool surface.

"Caregiving for a dependent parent is a heavy burden to carry, especially when also raising children. I cannot imagine the stress you must be feeling at this moment. Do you find time to care for yourself?"

"My Lady, I wish to speak of other matters of import, if I may?"

She tilted her head and arched an eyebrow in that inquisitive way of hers. A sliver of light from the latticed window touched her raven tresses and violet hues glimmered in reply. Seemingly amused by his ungentlemanly staring, she asked in a light tone, "Why am I here, Skylar?"

"It concerns the Techsmith Guild." He cleared his throat and forced himself to meet her eyes to remain polite. His body stilled beneath his heavy thoughts, save his fingers, which continued to fidget with the figurine. "The community has expressed displeasure over technology education. Surprisingly, the first generation acts as though they know not of technology. At first I thought it a ruse, but…"

Dr. Nichols smiled and, in such a way, shivers raced across Skylar's skin until goosebumps appeared. "How much do you know about psychological conditioning?" she asked.

"Very little, My Lady."

"Are you familiar with mind control?"

"No," Skylar said.

"The term 'brainwashing,' perhaps?"

Leaf scooted to the edge of his seat and leaned forward. "Are you suggesting that the first generation have somehow had memories washed away?"

"Not suggesting it," she said. "From my own observations, most in New Eden no longer cling to their prior lives but adhere strictly to basic beliefs and values as a unified front, beliefs that are in strong conflict to their previous reality. The memories are still there, but they are hidden behind blind spots. Think of it as a veil, if you will."

"The first generation remembered their loved ones from the Outside when Fillion demonstrated his technology," Skylar said.

"Yes," Dr. Nichols replied. "The blind spots move and can reveal snippets of memories with certain triggers. Though, it should be noted that a trigger or token will not produce the same result with each person or situation."

"How is this possible?" Leaf asked.

The haunting smile returned. "In 1971, a renowned social psychologist by the name of Dr. Phillip Zimbardo led a breakthrough study known as the Stanford prison experiment. Groups of young men were asked to role-play as prisoners and guards. Those selected to participate in the experiment went through rigorous psychological screenings. Long story short, good, mentally healthy men were psychologically traumatized when the roles were played to realistic extremes. They had, in a sense, lost touch with their previous reality. After only six days, Dr. Zimbardo ended the experiment."

"Six days," Leaf whispered, more to himself. His face slackened as he repeated the words again.

"Surprising, I know. It was to Dr. Zimbardo as well," Dr. Nichols said. "Twenty years is a long time to behave and believe a certain way." She ironed out the wrinkles in her dress with her hands and frowned. The sudden change in her facade bothered Skylar and his pulse accelerated in response. "You were raised to believe a reality that only exists here and nowhere else," she spoke, barely above a whisper. "To impart that reality with a morally clear conscience and to discourage ICE symptoms, the first generation *had to believe* this world as well."

Skylar lifted his eyes to the wood-planked ceiling as his head fell against the back of the chair. Angry tears pricked his eyes, but he refused to give in to the strong feelings of betrayal. He knew the biodome was a social experiment. He knew they were not really on Mars. Still, to hear the intentionality of it all— —the willingness of the first generation to shed not only their pasts but their children's futures in favor of a new reality—iced the roaring blood in his veins. Skylar grit his teeth and pushed out of the chair to pace by the window. Did his father use him for revenge, to punish Hanley? To end the experiment so as to regain an original reality he could no longer live without? Did the Techsmith Guild play any part in this decision?

When the initial surge of emotions passed, he cooled his countenance to stone and asked, "Then how is it, My Lady, that The Elements remembered their prior lives with clarity when others did not?"

"Each had connection to the lab in some form that anchored them to both worlds." Dr. Nichols sought his eyes. "There are some from the village who recollect their prior lives, too."

"Since I was enlisted into the Guild as a lad," Skylar replied, "I was taught that people learn best from their own, a form of diffusion, it was called. The intent and purpose of the Techsmiths beyond providing simulation data for the lab was to aid the community in transitioning toward Outsider ways, namely technology, during Project Phase Two."

"So I have been informed, though I am still wading through years of research and data to fully confirm that statement."

Skylar rested his forearms on the back of his chair, fingers curled tight around the stone piece. "The community is vehemently opposed to the introduction of modern technology. Hanley is adamant that we educate the residents in drafted rotations. To disobey the Guild Master is insubordination and punishable with possible banishment. To disregard the community's vote dishonors my vow to represent their needs as their Wind Element." He shook his head with ill-humor. "I am not exactly the most popular man even without this test of honor, as you can imagine. The residents already fear me."

Leaf took in a shaky breath. "Sky—"

"No, do not defend my reputation," he ground out. "You and I both know it is true, which is why the Daughter of Fire was branded a witch instead of accusations being flung at me! And both you and Lady Ember allowed it." Leaf dropped his head and studied his fingers as his shoulder's fell. "My father burned the village and usurped your authority! He conspired to physically assault you, even unto death!"

The Son of Earth chanced a look at him and half whispered, "You are not to blame, Sky."

"He is not here to pay for his crimes!" Skylar slammed the stone figurine onto the desk. "Why do you protect me, Leaf? Perhaps it is best they know he murdered your father so I no longer have to carry the shame and duplicity of my heritage in secret! It shall leak out one day, I am quite sure of it. And then what?"

"Think of your sisters and your mother," Leaf said. He cast a nervous glance at Dr. Nichols, who had blanched. "I protect them as well as you."

Skylar refused to cry, to give his father the satisfaction of more tears. "You are right." He locked eyes with his King. "They deserve happiness for as long as we can falsify it. Forgive me, I have forgotten myself."

"No, My Lord." Leaf grabbed his forearm. "You have not." The Son of Earth pulled him into an embrace and whispered in his ear, "If it is forgiveness you seek, then *I forgive you*." Skylar sucked in a sharp breath and Leaf's arms tightened around him. "But punishing yourself for your father's sins shall not bring mine back, nor make yours a better man. You cannot redeem him. Stand upon your own merit, Son of Wind. Do not hide in fear and shame. Allow the community to see what an honorable, upstanding man *you* are."

Skylar's knees buckled as fury gusted through him. "And how do you advise I do such a thing, Your Majesty?" He pulled away and righted the fallen statue on Jeff's desk. "Shall I create more scandal for my family and burden the community to care for them in my banishment?" he asked. "We have canceled classes, yes. But I now fear that even offering an education opportunity to those of the second generation who have come of age will still infuriate the majority of residents and incite unrest for technology does not align with New Eden's core beliefs and values. We need to heal, not create more chaos."

A muscle pulsed in Leaf's jaw as he stood silent, eyes narrowed and limbs akimbo.

"How can we forget the visible problems with air quality as well? It is only a matter of time before fingers point to my office, accusing me of poisoning the biodome." Blood rushed in Skylar's ears as he held Leaf's steady gaze. "I am not so certain the Techsmith Guild ever had genuine purpose beyond deceit and manipulation. I cannot trust anything my father designed and managed."

"Do you believe modern technology is useful?" Dr. Nichols asked.

Both he and Leaf cut a sharp glance in her direction, having nearly forgotten her presence. She cupped knotted fingers around her bare knee and leaned forward in anticipation of his answer. The Son of Earth sank into his chair and twisted to face Skylar's direction, chin tucked toward his chest and his hands clasped tight in his lap. Strangely, the unaffected, even tone of her voice re-centered Skylar, as did the topic redirection. He blinked back the toxic emotions, ones he closeted away with eagerness, and forced his face to become even more bland.

Skylar offered Leaf an apologetic frown then acknowledged Dr. Nichols. "Yes, technology has its uses," he finally mumbled in reply.

"If you were to create a new mission statement for the Techsmith Guild, what would it be?"

He thought back over the years of simulation work and indoctrination. The problems they fixed were never real, but to test how they would respond if a real colony on Mars. Simple machines and software programs designed solely for their own education. The truth was, they mattered not. The Guardian Angels were the real engineers. Skylar slumped over to his chair and collapsed in a dispirited heap. Decorum and gentlemanly behavior required far too much energy this moment.

"I suppose," he began, "it would depend on the mission statement of New Eden Township moving forward."

"The answer will come to you and, with it, renewed purpose and vision." Dr. Nichols rose, her mouth set in a thin line. "I have a video meeting soon and need to return to the lab." She stepped toward Skylar and placed a hand upon his shoulder. "When grieving, it is normal to re-evaluate one's life. Usually there is a period of anger followed by a bargaining phase. 'If only' I had known my father's plan before he took it too far. 'If only' the Techsmith Guild had never formed. Right now, you have one foot in anger and the other in bargaining."

She removed her hand with a trembling smile as tears gathered in her eyes. The break in character disarmed Skylar and his chest tightened.

"You will never be able to accept the selfishness or aggression, nor should you. But you will find a way to appropriate grace so that you can heal and move forward." He was unsure if she spoke to him or to herself. Her eyes locked with his and he knew the intensity of pain she allowed him to see mirrored his own. "And I believe that is your desire, correct? To move forward? To begin afresh with restored honor to your family name?"

He grimaced with the enormity of heartache he contained. But, somehow, he had the presence of mind to nod his head in answer.

"Until then, give yourself permission to grieve and allow the community to grieve with you."

She opened the door at the end of the small hallway and mid-day light spilled into the office. Violet shimmers threaded through her black hair as she peered over her shoulder, and the soft light brightened her eyes a shade to silver. Even Leaf quelled all movements at the sight of the otherworldly image in the doorway. Beyond her the world appeared white, though he could hear the familiar sounds of New Eden—the clank of Connor's hammer, the cluck of whispers, and the stampede of small feet dashing toward the meadow. Her dark red lips curved in a commiserative smile before she spoke once more.

"Perhaps the fear you sense may be the community's inability to know how to behave around your stoicism rather than *your* fear of being seen as no different from your father." Dr. Nichols held his gaze a beat before bowing her head at Leaf. "A pleasure, as always." She flicked her attention back to Skylar one last time and said, "When you have a renewed vision for the future of the Techsmith Guild, contact me and we will discuss details. Leave Hanley to me."

The overly sweet scent of honey clung to the air in her wake and Skylar held his breath a few heartbeats until the perfume cleared. Leaf deflated next to him and stretched out his legs. They rolled their heads toward each other, expressions wary and relieved. Sobriety quickly gave way to laughter, however. Skylar could not help but join the lighter shift in the atmosphere.

"I think we may have bonded," Leaf said with a lopsided grin. "If we were not brothers before, surely we are now."

Skylar attempted a straight face, but laughter spurted from his compressed lips. He turned in his seat to better face his friend. "Do you believe she speaks true?"

"Yes, actually." Leaf sobered and considered Skylar. "Especially concerning you, Sky."

He released another heavy breath, long and slow, and extended a hand toward Leaf. "I am most sorry. For shouting at you today with Dr. Nichols as witness, and for all the shame I have brought your household."

Leaf shook his hand. His friend's sideways smile appeared once more. "You have not shamed my household."

"Lady Ember—"

"Is not shamed by you." Leaf diverted his focus to the floor. "If anyone is cause for shaming her reputation, it is I. We eloped, which has provided more than enough speculation for the town gossips, especially now..." Leaf blinked several times and rolled his head toward the window. "She is a strong woman, worry not."

"I ... I have given her a life debt."

Leaf looked at him again. "I know, I heard everything on the observation deck."

"This does not bother you?"

"Should I be bothered?" Leaf cast him another sidelong glance. "Is there affection between you and my wife beyond friendship?"

"No," Skylar shook his head adamantly. "Nor was there ever. I did not hold romantic affections for Lady Ember." He had never shared fully with anyone, not even Lady Ember, though she knew snippets of details. His throat tightened. Leaf deserved an explanation and Skylar's anxieties reignited. "My father," Skylar began, "would punish me." He looked away. "If I disappointed him, even over simple matters. If I did not share conversations overheard in homes I visited. If my sisters or mother embarrassed him publicly. If I did not become the next Aether."

"He would physically harm you?" Aghast, Leaf's face slackened, eyes wide and mouth agape.

"The villagers laughed at his jokes and listened with rapt attention to his many stories. Mother is patient and kind and well respected by adults and children alike. Who would believe me?" Skylar clenched his jaw. "I excused the bruises during bathing sessions as work-related injuries, nothing more."

Leaf twisted in the chair to face Skylar, his face drained of color, even his lips. It made the nearly faded black eye Leaf sported appear gruesome. "Did he touch your sisters and mother?"

"No, I ensured he took his violence out on me alone. Though I could not save them from his biting words." He squeezed his eyes shut and forced back the roiling emotions, especially the ones souring his stomach. "The only woman he had threatened to physically harm was Lady Ember. He was convinced she was the next in line to become The Aether. If … if I refused to court her and eventually marry her, then he swore he would put her life in danger and in such a way that New Eden would blame me for her death. It was a madness he possessed." He looked up at Leaf. "What choice did I have? Who would believe me? What proof could I provide beyond my word? I would be branded as mentally unstable and a disgrace, for what son dishonors his father? Not a single man or woman from the second generation has accused their parent publicly and especially over something as grievous as conspiring to murder." Skylar fidgeted with the hem of his tunic and murmured, "I am the first, though I am ashamed I waited so long to do so. Perhaps … Perhaps…"

"You are not to blame, Skylar Kane. I shall continue to repeat these very words until you believe me." Leaf shook his head. "All these years as friends and I never once suspected or thought to question the persistent bruises. You have always been methodical and careful, in all that you accomplish."

"Why would you question anything? He was the very picture of class and charm, dedicated to his family and his community." He plunked his head to the back of the chair again. "I was so angry with you, though you knew nothing of my father's threats. You were supposedly leaving and your marriage prevented me from saving her. I would have failed not only her but you. My father had diverted his attention to you by that point, but he allowed me to stew in my paranoia over Lady Ember as punishment. The rest you know."

"Thank you," Leaf whispered, voice tight, "for sacrificing your honor and our friendship to protect my family."

Skylar shoved out of his chair and strode to the window. He leaned on the sill, fingers clawing the wood, arms rigid, and placed his forehead on the cold glass to chill his roiling emotions.

Villagers passed by with baskets, balanced across their backs or atop their heads, filled to the brim with grain for animal feed and for bread, or a variety of garden produce for the kitchen and root cellars. Their heads were covered in coifs or scarves, but sweat still dripped down their foreheads. They smiled to one another and spoke in passing.

Men mixed water into powered cob from fallen buildings to rebuild walls. Mud formed gloves over their hands clear up to their elbows. A man from the second generation flicked mud from his fingers to a friend who pushed him in the shoulder in shared humor.

A mother scolded her child as another sat at her feet with tears streaking down dirt caked cheeks. She reached into her pocket and unwrapped a crust of bread from a rag and placed the remnant baguette into the distressed child's hands. Chickens pecked the soil for fallen crumbs nearby and the child laughed.

A young woman, just beyond girlhood, huddled close to another young woman and exchanged whispers while watching two young men work. Noticing their attentions, one young man intentionally hit the other in the back of the head with a plank of wood, which began a grand chase. Skylar smiled as the scene unfolded. Though they wrestled and fought, they laughed and earned humored remarks by the older men.

He had seen these very images more times than he could count. But this moment, it was as if seeing it all for the first time. "Everyone seems happy," he said aloud. His words fogged the window and he watched until it dissipated. Skylar turned toward Leaf and leaned his back against the sill. "They believe this world and have forgotten their origins, but they seem at peace."

"Yes," Leaf replied simply.

"What if," he drew out and paused. "What if we took the technology imparted to sustain our world, and used it to help disconnect New Eden from the lab entirely?" Leaf's eyes widened with interest. "Not everyone, mind you," Skylar continued. "Just those who are mechanically inclined."

"To build our own team of Guardian Angels."

"Precisely."

"And Hanley?"

Skylar lifted a shoulder in a weary shrug. "Leave him to Dr. Nichols and the Son of Eden."

"But we must convince him of this plan if we are to gain independence."

"Does he know that is what we want?"

Leaf shook his head and rested his shoes on the chair across from him. He crossed his arms across his chest as he sank lower in the chair deep in thought. "I discussed with him the possibility once and he laughed. I shall wait until Fillion returns as owner and then I shall explore buyout options with my inheritance."

"And Dr. Nichols?"

"No, she is not aware of the sincerity of our plans, nor do I wish to revisit the discussions with her until Fillion is present." Leaf leveled his gaze onto Skylar and the steel in his eyes hardened. "Her words and gestures reflect probity. I do not question her authenticity. But she is too powerful, and *knows* it." The Son of Earth lifted the corner of his mouth in a grim smile. "Sometimes I wonder if it is Hanley who is being manipulated."

Skylar flinched as goosebumps prickled the back of his neck.

He swiveled to peer through the window and reflect upon village life as Leaf's words settled. This was the most they had confided in each other since before he courted Ember. Nor did they use honorary titles to cloud their discussion. It was not necessary. He took in a deep breath and allowed the air to fill his lungs with hope.

"Leaf?" He peered over his shoulder. "When do you advise we roll out *our* Education Plan?"

"After the village is rebuilt."

"Agreed," Skylar said, relieved. "Let our community heal first."

"The community?" Leaf said with a grin. "I was thinking entirely of you and I. That was rather noble of you to think of others."

Skylar tittered, though it resembled more of a grunt. "Yes, I am quite noble."

"It must be our fine aristocratic upbringing."

"No," Skylar said. "We are far too political and scheming for that refined nonsense."

"Indeed." Leaf stood and stretched. "Well, on that note, I promised to arbitrate a disagreement between two grain growers in the Mediterranean dome."

"Happy times."

"Always." Leaf grabbed Skylar's forearm. "I shall swing by to assist you with the dehumidifiers afterward. North apartments?"

"Yes."

"Excellent. Until then, My Lord." Leaf flashed a wry grin as he bowed.

"Your Majesty," Skylar replied. He attempted a straight face to match his bored, aristocratic tone and failed. His lips twitched with a suppressed smile and Leaf quietly chuckled as they exited The Chancery.

Chickens squawked in protest as they flapped out of his and Leaf's path through the main square. Leaf slid him a blasé look in response with all the arrogance of their high-bred class. But he could not hold the expression long and erupted into sputtered mirth much to the curiosity of the villagers. Skylar hid his amusement as best he could. Then thought better of it. His friend, his brother, felt no shame in being seen with him. Why, then, should he?

Chapter Four

Monday, December 14, 2054

L eaves crunched beneath Skylar's shoes as he approached The Mill. It was mid-day and the sun was at its zenith in the reflective sky. The community currently gathered to regale their day thus far with friends and family over a meal. Skylar, on the other hand, brought a pack and planned to eat alone. A matriarch and his sisters sat with their mother.

He knew the likelihood of followers was slim. Still, as he crossed the stone bridge over the North Pond, he peeked over his shoulder. Dark fabric folded over part of his face with the movements, but in his limited sight he saw nothing save swaying trees and grass. Satisfied, he dipped two buckets into the pond and covered them with wooden lids. Then he jogged past the linden tree to the backside of The Mill where divots were dug into a corner of the cob wall. With a grunt, he hoisted himself up and scaled the wall to deposit one bucket and then quickly returned for the other. Last bucket in hand, he swung a leg over the wooden railing. He landed with a thud onto the balcony connecting to the grain bin floor. A thin layer of flour dust poofed into a small cloud and dissipated in the breeze.

At the south end of the small balcony, Skylar retrieved two long plank boards stacked against the railing. In all these years no one had questioned the need for additional planks upon a perfectly structural balcony. Perhaps the Miller knew of his family's secret. Skylar stretched the first plank toward the stone wall of the biodome. It slid across the open space to the hidden landing until it rammed a boulder. He repeated the process with the second plank. Then, he climbed onto the railing and spread his arms for balance, each hand holding a water bucket, and tiptoed to his makeshift bridge. He stepped onto the planks and bent his knees creating a slight jostle to test how they would hold. Barely a budge. He took a tentative step out into the open air, followed by another step.

The wind wrapped him in a cool embrace and his cloak fluttered and snapped behind him. Hair flew into his eyes but he continued the course, one foot in front of the other. Walking across the air was a feeling unlike any other. Even at eighteen, he could not help but pretend that he levitated and possessed the power to travel by sky. He glimpsed his shadow as it walked over bending grass several stories below while he traversed the impossible.

Not a single rumor whispered on the wind here. He was too high up for such lowly experiences, too removed from the mundane and the pain. For these few blessed moments the rushing sensations blew away his controversial existence. And he smiled. Not a mere wisp of happiness. Rather, a full-on grin, one that invaded and destroyed everything negative that he had become.

A couple steps more and a layer of birch, maple, and cypress trees lining the biodome wall came within touching distance. Skylar grabbed a limb for support and trotted the remaining way to the landing platform hidden behind several large evergreen trees.

He lowered the buckets and tossed his pack to the narrow balcony jutting from the stone wall. Carefully, he pulled one of the long planks toward him and hid it in an evergreen tree, followed by the other. The trees rustled in a gentle breeze and stirred strands of hair back over his forehead. He threw the pack across his shoulder, blew the hair out of his eyes, and spun to face the wall. A crude ladder made from hemp rope and sturdy tree limbs draped the boulders. He curled his fingers around a rung and began his long climb to the skyline. It would take multiple trips to bring up the buckets.

With a final step, both buckets now secure atop the rock wall, he crested the boulders and his hand touched the glass panels.

From all other vantage points, one could only see the Outside sky reflected back. But here, nose pressed to the glass, he could see what others could not. Beyond the glass, desert stretched on for what seemed like eternity. In the far distance, a great body of water sparkled and glimmered beneath the noonday sun. Besides Coal and now Leaf, who visited the lab at least once a week, Skylar was perhaps the only other member of the second generation to see mountains with his own eyes. They were breathtaking, especially in the evening when the sun dipped behind the jagged peaks.

He pushed himself up on the rock and pulled his knees to his chest as he surveyed Earth. Down below, scientists in white lab coats walked the grounds of N.E.T. He looked for the telltale blue trim to confirm his suspicion. These were indeed the Guardian Angels who worked within the technosphere. From his pack, he retrieved an apple and took a bite as his eyes trailed the engineers coming and going.

Skylar brushed a finger in an arc across the glass and his forehead wrinkled. A thin layer of soot still covered the dome ceiling. How on Earth could they possibly clean their sky? He bit into the apple and chewed on ideas, especially concerning the Techsmith Guild. Despite Dr. Nichols' request to leave Hanley to her, Skylar's mission was now to convince Hanley to approve their modified Education Plan without revealing their ultimate motive. His uncle was astute, though.

Skylar placed the apple core back into his pack and pulled out a small chunk of cheese and fresh bread wrapped in a linen cloth, still warmed by the ovens. The yeasty smell wafted around him and he inhaled deeply. He spread the cloth across his lap to rest his bread and cheese, and then retrieved his Cranium from the pack and positioned it against his head. Time to message Hanley, then return to work.

With a touch, his Cranium turned on. Vivid colors painted the air, though dimmer than usual in the bright light. He brought up an email screen within Messenger Pigeon and selected "Guild Master, Hanley Nichols."

> "My apologies for the delay in response, though I appreciate your efforts in reaching out. Are you perhaps available this evening for a brief session? As I am sure you have heard, the Education Plan did not roll out as designed. I do have a solution, though, one I hope you will be open to receive. I shall await your reply."

He hit "send," then enjoyed a bite of bread and cheese. The tangy goat cheese melted in his mouth and he swallowed with appreciation. A bird flew by the glass Outside and Skylar watched its wings cut through the expansive sky, seemingly unaware of the endlessness of it all. A ping echoed in his head and he returned his attention back to the message center.

> Hanley: "I am available this night. Meet me at our usual time. In the future, I expect better communication from your office."

Skylar clenched his jaw.

> "Yes, sir."

He turned off his Cranium and tossed it back into his pack. Sitting on the edge of his world inspired an idea. His insides quaked, but he was resolute. Perhaps the community would view him differently after this night. Maybe he would see himself differently, too.

Meal complete, Skylar packed up and stood. He walked the lip of the rock wall away from the ladder and toward the hidden wind machines to check the filters. Before passing an open spot in the tree border, he paused to scope out the surroundings for human movements. Several times in previous assignments he had camped on the wall ledge for hours until villagers moved far enough away that he could proceed without being seen. For this reason he always brought extra food and a skin of water.

He was able to complete most tasks at night while the residents slept. However, visiting the wind turbines required a significant amount of daylight. Candles would snuff out, and it was not safe to bring lanterns should he fall from the wall. Midday meal was a relaxed event, so it was easier to excuse his absence. Plus he enjoyed meals in solitude. Skylar checked the area surrounding the North Cave, lifted his hood, and continued to walk the sky horizon toward the roar of hidden machines.

The stone corridor appeared as the wall curved toward the North Cave. From below, it appeared as though a normal wall, as the entrance was indiscernible, an illusion. Rather clever, actually. The hallway granted access clear to the other side of the North Cave's opening before the west apartments began, to which he could walk above on the lip of the rock wall. Wind turbines were positioned discreetly throughout the domes. Though no access was granted in front, and for good reason. His father often shared a story about a worker who flew into the North Pond during a test session while the biodomes were under construction. Not even the safety ropes could save him.

Skylar yanked open an iron handle in the wall to reveal the innards to one of the many wind turbines. The whir of fans rushed in his ears and he grit his teeth at the volume and peered inside. Wires were coated in black ash which also blanketed the base. He frowned. It would have to do. There was no possible way to clean everything. Perhaps the cavity would clean itself over time. He crouched and peeked in the lower cavity and found the filter. It was buried beneath a thick layer of soot and ash.

Slow and gentle, he removed the filter and dumped it into a bucket of water to soak. He pulled out a small brush and a bar of laundry soap from his pack and scrubbed the felted wool until it no longer bled black when lathered. Given the unclean state of the wires, he surmised he would need to repeat this process once a week until the filters stopped gathering a significant collection of soot within a short duration.

Upon finishing the last filter, he studied a nearby shadow swaying by the corridor entry with a start. Mid-day meal was long over. He needed to resume replacing the dehumidifiers in the occupied apartments before his absence was noticed. Leaf had assisted him over the past two days, which had enabled Skylar to nearly finish servicing all the occupied apartments. Still, more residents grew ill.

The mumblings in homes and from passersby worried Skylar. High fevers with respiratory difficulties. Coughing spasms to the point of vomiting. He had witnessed these in two homes now. It was the latter that gave him the most concern as difficulty with breathing and vomiting were common symptoms of air toxicity. Only two facts reassured him that air quality was not to blame: The first generation was entirely unaffected by the illness, and those who fell ill suffered a fever before any other symptoms manifested. 'Twas most strange that those born after Moving Day were the only ones the illness touched. He tucked the last thought away and focused on his footing along the rock wall.

A half-hour later, both planks returned to storage along the balcony and buckets in hand, Skylar ambled along the village path toward the East Cave. He was tired. More than tired. It seemed as if he raced against the impossible. Perhaps he did. Tomorrow he would walk the circumference of the dome along the west apartments until he reached the wind turbines above the South Cave. Though with disrupted sleep promised this night, it may be best to wait an additional day to ensure his safety.

Tasks numbered in his mind until he lost sight of everything other than his myriad responsibilities. He passed villagers, but did not notice the shadowed stares or the unnatural quiet. Nor did he behold the lackluster activity within the village square. Not until a hand touched his forearm and a familiar voice said, "Son of Wind, there you are."

Skylar stopped mid-stride with a start. "Lady Rain." She wrung fingers at her waist and lifted her shoulders. He set the buckets along a shop wall and she jumped when one tipped over. Black water spilled over the earth and she took a frightened step back. Was she unwell? Concerned, he righted the result of his clumsiness and asked, "How may I assist you?"

"I have been looking for you, My Lord."

"My apologies," he said, forehead wrinkled. "I was working in the North End. Is something amiss?" Lady Rain grabbed his hand and yanked him toward the forest. "My Lady—"

"Shh!"

"This is unseemly—"

"The village is far too preoccupied to notice."

Once tucked beneath a canopy of cedar bows along the trail, she dropped his hand and lowered her hood. Her movements were frantic, though controlled. Had something happened to his mother? Sisters? Where was Leaf? Tears gathered in her eyes and crested, one drop and then another falling down her cheeks. Needing an occupation, he rummaged through his pack and pulled out the linen cloth and offered it to her.

"Forgive me," she said and dabbed her eyes.

"There is nothing to forgive, I assure you."

"Two children died this day."

The air in Skylar's lungs stilled. "From the same home?"

"No, My Lord."

Through the trees, he watched a small crowd by the entrance to the Great Hall. Hoods were raised in mourning and his heart sank. *Children*, his thoughts screamed and he winced. His mind could not form an adequate reply, hoping, praying, that air toxicity was not to blame. The mere thought that he was responsible for the deaths of two small lives was too much to process and absorb. Lady Rain glanced up at him from time to time, but he remained focused on the forest path.

Finally, he asked, "Has Timna voiced a possible diagnosis?"

"Influenza." The word repeated in his mind in a strange cadence. Lady Rain turned a sickly shade and whispered, "Under Timna's supervision, Her Highness pricked the finger of the deceased boy and used her technology to study his blood."

Skylar's pulse leapt within his chest. "Where is His Majesty?"

"Quarantined."

"What?" He knew he sounded rude and unpolished, but his panic was rising. Would the town reprise their accusations and proclaim Lady Ember a witch once more? "Is the Son of Earth ill?"

Lady Rain shook her head. "No, My Lord. It is a precaution, nothing more. For Ember's sake and for the safety of their unborn child." Color returned to her skin with her last comment and she lowered her eyes. "After interacting with the contaminated belongings and bodily fluids of the poor little boy who died, Timna asked the Watson family to remain sequestered for five days."

"Then it is not air toxicity." He loosed a slow breath.

"No, 'tis not." Compassion softened her features and Skylar blinked in confusion. "This is why I searched for you, My Lord. I worried you would hear of the deaths and feel responsible. I wished to spare you the additional grief you might suffer."

Warmth filled Skylar and he angled away from her and mumbled, "You are most kind. Thank you, My Lady." She touched his forearm and took a step closer, though she remained silent, as if gathering her thoughts. "Rain," he whispered, nearly forgetting himself, nearly forgetting everything. "We are unchaperoned."

Tears pooled in her eyes once more. "The little village boy could have easily been my youngest brother." She released a sob and pressed her fingers to her mouth in attempt to restrain her grief. "What if sickness visits my home next? Or my sister's wee babe?"

Skylar did not know what to do. Nor could he give reassurance. He knew nothing of influenza. But he felt like a complete idiot standing there as she ached with the same fears he carried over his own home. She was an unmarried woman and he a bachelor. Nevertheless, when all rules and dictates of society were stripped away, the very ones that defined the roles of males and females, both he and Rain were simply vessels comprised of the same elements. Perhaps, in moments such as these, rules mattered not.

"Leaf asked that you and I care for the community in his absence." Her body shook as she attempted to hold in her fear. Still she continued, though her voice trembled. "He wishes for us to relay our sympathies after evening meal and to reassure New Eden that he is in discussion with the lab as it appears to be an Outsider illness."

"What of the Ceremonies of Death?"

"They shall not be postponed."

He nodded his head and searched the tree limbs and dome sky. For what, he knew not. She continued to weep and he felt so utterly helpless. What could he do? It was maddening. "Rules be damned," he muttered to himself and took a small step toward the Daughter of Water. "Rain Daniels of The Seven Seas." Her eyes snapped to his with mention of her childhood nickname. Another tear trailed down her cheek. "May I have permission to comfort you?"

"Yes … yes, My Lord."

Rain leaned into him, her movements awkward and uncertain like his. Gently, he wrapped a single arm around her upper back as if the gesture came naturally. Or so he hoped. Could she hear his heartbeat thrumming wildly against his rib cage? Or feel his chest constrict as he attempted to breathe normally? They were friends, had known each other all their lives. Why should anyone judge them in this moment? Still, the many disapproving voices of society pointed fingers at him in his mind.

"Please tell me if I am too forward, My Lady." The sound of his own voice seemed strange as he spoke. "I would never wish to trespass upon your sensibilities or take advantage of your reputation."

"I am well," she whispered. Warm breath passed through his tunic and he swallowed. "You could never harm my reputation."

The forest remained unnaturally still, the village gripped in silence. The hairs on his arm rose in response. "Alas, I fear it is quite possible."

"Not with me." Her shoulders shook as another sob surfaced.

Skylar knew to what she referred. In fact, he had known for quite some time. The information never mattered to him, though. Did her mother share the truth on her deathbed? Heartsick, he whispered into her hair, "I am the son of the town murderer."

"No, you are a man of honor."

"My family's name is disgraced." He attempted to sound stoic, though his voice caught. "No father would grant their daughter's hand in marriage to me." A shudder traveled through her body and he squeezed his eyes shut for a heartbeat before stepping away from their embrace. Both looked away, embarrassed. Why did he just confess this to her? Tears continued to roll down her face as her fingers fidgeted with the strings of her cloak. "I have spoken too freely," he said quickly and grit his teeth. "I did not mean to imply ... suggest ... I am most sorry, My Lady."

"Skylar Kane of the Four Winds," she spoke softly. "I heard only your broken heart understanding mine, nothing more. I would like very much to be your friend, if I may?"

He cast her a side glance and frowned. "You already are, My Lady."

A blush touched her cheeks. His eyes rested on her lips a moment as they curved into a kind smile. Dark eyes waited for his, though she turned her head toward her shoulder. "I shall see you at evening meal, My Lord."

"Until then, My lady." Skylar bowed, his mind still berating him for his stupidity. As he rose, she closed the distance between them and kissed his cheek. Eyelashes, dampened with tears, brushed along his skin. He stilled, his heart in his throat. She was kissing him. His first kiss. Before he could speak, let alone react, she left the covering of cedar boughs and ran toward the village.

Skylar looked down to the linen cloth he clutched, one she had pressed into his hand. He fingered the soft fabric as he tried to recover from bewilderment. Were they not friends? Perhaps the fear of losing those one cared for created boldness. 'Twas compassion, nothing more. Tucking the cloth into his pocket, he stepped onto the forest path and shambled toward the village to collect his buckets, then to his apartment. For now, he was married to his family.

ChAPTER FIVE

Tuesday, December 15, 2054

F ire... fire... fire..."
Mother had entered another speech pattern phase. The house was long asleep, unlike him, and Mother, apparently. He crept down the hallway to peek in on his sisters as they slept.

Gale-Anne had refused to go to bed this eve, reduced to wild theatrics. She even threw her pillow at him. He knew she was hurting and tired. They all were. A part of him feared that if he drew a strong line, she would think him the same as Father. Instead, he picked up her pillow, put it back against the headboard, and sank onto the edge of her cot with a weary sigh. She continued to unravel about subjects he could no longer follow, but still he listened as his mind numbed.

Windlyn had cowered around the corner. Never one to raise her voice or create a fuss, she peeped through the small space between the door and door jamb.

"Windy, stop sniveling in the dark," Gale-Anne had taunted.

"Gale, that is quite enough," Skylar finally said. "Your grievances do not concern our sister."

Eyes wide, his youngest sister's bottom lip quivered. "You are mad at me?"

"I am shocked that you would use words as weapons against your sister. She has done nothing to warrant your offense." Skylar knew the game she played. Rather than acknowledge Windlyn as the victim, Gale-Anne twisted the situation around so the attention remained solely on her. It was the same game Father employed. "Please apologize."

"For what?" Gale-Anne crossed her arms and glared at him. "I did not listen in on a conversation where I was uninvited."

"The entire village has probably heard our conversation by now." Skylar stood and walked toward Windy. "Come, let us say goodnight to Mother and I shall come in to hear your prayers."

"You are mad at me!"

Skylar swiveled toward Gale and lowered until they were eye level. "I know I do not show it, but I am angry, just like you." Dr. Nichols' words about the stages of mourning floated back to his memory. "However, I do not punish you or your sister in my grief. Windy is not to blame. We are family, Gale-Anne, not your enemy."

She lowered her eyes and folded her hands at her waist. "Yes, My Lord."

"Now, offer your sister a proper apology."

Gale-Anne's jaw worked back and forth. "Windlyn, I am sorry for my hurtful words," she ground out. "Do you forgive me?"

"Yes," Windy replied, meek and quiet as a whisper. "All is forgiven."

"Now, My Lord, I suppose I must go to bed for my behavior?"

Skylar searched his sister's eyes. "No. You must go to bed for it is that proper hour and we each have work tomorrow."

Her shoulders slumped as she combed fingers through the loose ends of her braid. "You promise you are not mad at me?"

"I promise." Skylar offered a weak smile. "Now let us kiss Mother goodnight then say our prayers."

The memory faded as he opened Gale-Anne's door. Soft, rhythmic sounds greeted his ears. He leaned his head against the door jamb, relieved that she knew peace in her sleep. He did not. Mother was far too active this night. So he trudged back to the living room and collapsed into a chair. Skylar stretched out his legs and listened to Mother mumble the word "fire" in a slurred, dragged out speech over and over again. Though the room was nearly black, he could make out the white of her skin and chemise as her arm lifted up and down as if painting the air.

"The fire is over," he mumbled to the void. "The village is being rebuilt. The community is working together, Mother. You would be most proud, I think."

Silence, but for only a heartbeat. She resumed chanting, but to the word "water." He lifted his hand to his cheek, then closed his eyes. Lady Rain had abstained from looking his way most of the night, even when they stood before the community with Timna and Connor. Skylar frowned and dropped his hand back to his lap. The announcement following evening meal brought a fresh wave of grief and fear, but no one protested. No one cast blame or argued, even when several families were asked to go into quarantine. Skylar should feel relieved by the latter, but his heart remained heavy and paranoid.

Mother pronounced the word "water" with more clarity and he whipped his head her direction. Was she thirsty or did she speak of other things, such as the Blood Rains? Uncertain, he stumbled in the darkness until his hand blindly found a tumbler of water on a cupboard near her cot.

Lifting her head, he said, "*Voici de l'eau. Lentement, petites gorgées.*" Liquid dribbled from the corners of her mouth. He used the hem of his tunic to dry her face before lowering her back to the feather pillow, a gift from the feather-dresser. His hand brushed against a dangling rope and he hooked a finger around the coarse hemp. It grieved him to tie his mother to her cot, but the time to meet with Hanley was fast approaching. He found her pacing the living room earlier today. What if she left the apartment and wandered the forest? Or fell and injured herself?

"Mother, I shall return shortly." Skylar checked the last rope brace and tugged. The knot held. "I am only in my room should you have need of me." He knew she would not call out, but the pointless words brought him a modicum of comfort, nonetheless.

In his room, with the door shut, he drank in the black. Time seemed irrelevant as his mind wandered where it should not. Thoughts of his father were dangerous. Nevertheless, they came with unrelenting speed. Angry tears pricked his eyes and he grit his teeth. He would not mourn. His father was undeserving of this token of affection. Nor would he allow Hanley to destroy what remained of the life he was slowly rebuilding. Skylar swiped at the tears and rubbed his eyes with the palms of his hands. *Move forward*, he repeated in his mind.

From under his bed, he pulled out a clay bowl and fire starter. Sparks of flint flashed until the hay and dried moss caught fire. He cupped his hands over the bowl and gently blew life into the newborn flame. The fleeting embers brightened into tendrils of light and Skylar dipped a tallow candle. He lit the wrought iron sconce on his wall, followed by his lantern as the starter burned out. The scent of smoke hit his nose and he shivered into goosebumps as his heart rate accelerated a notch. Slowly, he exhaled through clenched teeth.

Straightening his shoulders, he turned on his Cranium and forced his face into an emotionless state. Screens layered before his vision and he brought Messenger Pigeon to the forefront and enlarged the viewing area. He scrolled through his contacts until his fingers settled onto Hanley's name, and then he touched the pool of light. An outgoing ping echoed in his head, much to his annoyance. The chirp-like sound always unnerved Skylar.

"Captain," Hanley said. His image appeared in the video feed, immaculately groomed as usual. "Nice to *finally* hear from you."

"My apologies, sir. Duties at home have consumed much of my time."

"Are you alone? I expected the Techsmith Guild."

"I am alone."

Hanley leaned back in a chair and sipped on a glass of wine. "Your father is making life difficult for the staff at the psychiatric home." Skylar bit his tongue and thought of the statue on Jeff's desk, carved stone, still, expressionless. "I'll need to move him to a higher security facility. He seems bent on trying to reach you. Even tried hacking a device he lifted from a nurse."

"I desire no contact."

A slow smile spread on Hanley's face. "Yes, I imagine so." He set the glass of wine on a nearby table. "My son believes all his problems stem from the media's nickname for him. Son of a Killer. Of course, that was several years ago and has nothing to do with Fillion's own choices." Hanley drummed his fingers on the arm of his chair and cocked his head to the side. "The media loves to destroy and consume. All lies, but the world doesn't care. People crave lies. It's the truth that hurts, right? Maybe you can let Fillion know how it *really* feels to have a father like yours the next time you see him. He needs a reality check."

Skylar's fingers clenched his bed linens until his arms shook. For a moment, he thought he might finally snap and release the storm that had been howling inside of him for weeks. No, years. In moments of weakness, such as with Lady Ember on the observation deck and with Leaf in The Chancery, emotions had surged and boiled over the rim of acceptability. The loss of control was too much for him. He preferred a semblance of structure in the midst of shambles—rules and order, definable expectations. Skylar focused on breathing as his fury faded into shame, and the winds, the very ones on the verge of destroying all in sight, died down to a simmer. He would not take the bait. He would not allow Hanley to rattle his self-control.

Steadying his breath once more, Skylar launched into his speech. "The community voiced concerns as the Education Plan requires all to break The Code. Unlike those in the

Techsmith Guild, the residents of New Eden are not protected with an amended contract. Villagers saw the order as a test of honor."

Hanley shook his head with humor. "The same community who had no qualms about using aggression to appoint a new leader is now too pious for technology?"

"It is too soon for change, sir." Skylar's voice trembled and he cleared his voice. "We are still rebuilding the village square. What little time and resources we possess are given to this endeavor."

"Even the children?"

"Yes, even the children, who work alongside their parents." Skylar released the bed linens.

Hanley nodded his head thoughtfully. "Of course, school is no longer in session, is it?"

The intended barb hit its mark, but Skylar remained steady. "Residents are falling ill, sir."

"So I have heard. The Aether has already debriefed me."

"Then you know that emotions are taut and there is very little energy for change." Skylar paused and maintained a level gaze. "I have a plan, one I do believe will be well received when the timing allows." Hanley sipped his wine again and said nothing, so Skylar continued. "Our world has existed without technology for twenty years. For most, the idea of integrating this Outside tool is preposterous. They are unable to conceptualize the idea of no longer living in New Eden. This is their home, their life. For their education to be real, for it to be tangible, I request a tour of the technosphere for those who show interest. Afterward, allow the Techsmith Guild to teach technology to the second generation who have come of age with real-world application. Our students need to see that their education matters. Nothing is wasted in New Eden. But, to the community, the Education Plan as it currently is drafted appears wasteful."

"Spoken like the son of a teacher. Fine speech." Hanley smirked. "What will your students do once the education session is complete?"

"Perhaps New Eden Township can create their own team of Guardian Angels." Hanley chuckled and picked at something invisible on his sleeve. "You laugh," Skylar rebutted, "but if we were truly a colony on Mars, these jobs would be necessary for our survival. This explanation is far more convincing than a required drafted rotation ordered by New Eden Biospherics & Research."

"Indeed." Hanley leaned forward in his chair with steepled fingers. "This is what the people want?"

"They do not know that this is what they want yet."

"Yes, people crave lies, don't they Captain?"

Skylar frowned. "I do not speak lies. If I train someone in technology, then they will be an engineer who works inside the technosphere."

"And if I reject your proposition?"

"Then I shall resign as Guild Captain."

Hanley's mouth curled upward. "And what makes you think I need you?"

"I know that you do not." Skylar allowed a small smile of his own. "My decision has nothing to do with your need of me, however that may be defined."

"And if your resignation demands that you leave New Eden Township?"

Skylar swallowed. "Then so be it."

"A man of principles." Hanley smiled and dipped his head in appreciation. "This is why I made you Captain of the Techsmith Guild four years ago. Once you make a decision, you stay the course." Skylar remained silent. "So you want to try your hand at being the Hero of the People instead of the Son of a Killer?" Skylar flinched. "Fine. We'll give your proposition a try."

"Those who complete training will receive occupation as an engineer within the lab's property?" Skylar asked.

"As you say, if you were a real colony on Mars, these positions within the township would be necessary for survival." Hanley leaned back against his chair again and crossed a leg over his knee. "Give the people what they want."

"Thank you, sir." Skylar dipped his eyes in substitute for a bow, per protocol when using a Cranium.

"Skylar?" A voice said from his doorway. His eyes shifted to the side and he squinted until he made out Gale-Anne's form. "Do you never sleep? What are ... oh my." His sister's mouth slackened as she stared at the holographic video feed.

"Company?" Hanley asked with a sly look.

Skylar felt his face heat with the insinuation. "My sister, sir." Gale-Anne slowly approached his cot, her eyes fixed to the bright screen. She sucked in a sharp breath upon recognizing Hanley.

"Are you finished?" Hanley shifted in his seat. "Or, do you have more to report?"

He flicked a side glance to his sister. "No, sir. I am finished."

"Check in with me in one week, Guild Captain."

"Yes, sir." Skylar happily disconnected the video feed and pulled the Cranium off his ear. Quietly, he asked, "Did I wake you?"

"No, My Lord. I had a nightmare." Gale-Anne lowered next to him. She touched the device in his hand and said, "The colors were like a dream."

"They are quite lovely, 'tis true." The shadows of flickering candles fell over his sister's face and his eyes studied the patterns. "I am sorry to hear of your nightmare. Shall I fetch you a tumbler of water?"

"Do you think Windlyn would mind if I crawled into bed with her this night?" Gale sat on her hands and kicked her feet back and forth while chewing on her bottom lip.

"I think Windy would welcome your company, actually. She cares much for you."

Her thin frame deflated as she looked away. "I know."

The dispirited posture ate at Skylar. He hesitated only a moment before placing an arm around his sister's shoulders. Affection did not come easy to him, but he made a promise to try, for her sake. Gale's face scrunched into confusion right before she launched herself into his arms and cozied up against his chest. A happy sigh escaped her lips as her body relaxed and he caressed her upper back with light motions.

Skylar stared at a candle and watched a drip descend to a pile of other waxen tears. His eyes drooped with exhaustion and he fought the urge to fall asleep. Mother was still speaking, her voice somewhat muffled by the walls. He should check on her. She was abnormally active for this hour.

"Gale?" he whispered. She did not reply.

His sister's shoulders rose and fell in a slow rhythm. A small smile touched his lips with the sight. Wisps of hair from her braid tickled his face, nevertheless he did not move away. She seemed so small and vulnerable now, despite her often big demonstrations. He was her age when she was born, a memory as vivid as if it happened yesterday. It was a night similar to this one, a gibbous moon and eerily hushed, until she took her first breath. Their house had not known quiet since.

With a grunt, he scooped up Gale's limp form and carried her to Windy's room. Their sister did not stir, not even when he pulled back the blankets. The bed linens felt rather warm to the touch and he furrowed his brows. Did Windy wear too many layers to bed, perhaps? Not wishing to intrude upon her modesty, he covered up Gale then tip-toed from the room.

He fetched a blanket off his bed and trundled to the living room where he slumped into a chair by Mother's cot. These past few weeks he had perfected the art of sleeping in a near upright position. Resigned to another night in a hard chair, he leaned back and closed his eyes. The last sound he heard was Mother's voice whispering, "water," before sleep finally claimed him.

ChAPTER
SIX

The floor creaked and groaned. A soft sound shuffled nearby and stopped. Skylar's eyes fluttered open and then squinted against the dusky light. It was morning already? Beside him lay Mother's cot. She stared at the ceiling as her head moved back and forth in slow and gentle motions. Unintelligible words exited from her chapped lips. Sometime in the night, her hands had freed themselves from their confines and now reached for the ceiling, as if she wished to be picked up. Skylar relaxed, convinced he had dreamt the other sounds.

His entire body ached, hot with pain after sleeping upright in the chair most of the night. Skylar rubbed his neck and repositioned his back and shoulders. A yawn escaped but he clamped his mouth shut to silence the sound. He did not wish to disturb Mother. The floor creaked near his side and his head whipped toward the entry door.

"Windy?" His twelve-year-old sister faced the large door barefoot and in nothing more than a thin shift, soaked with sweat. Long, light brown hair lay limp against her head and flushed skin. He repeated her name and hazel eyes, just like his, moved his direction. A gasp left her mouth and she swayed on her feet. He jumped up and rushed to her side.

With a cry, she recoiled away from him and mumbled, "Father forgive me," under her breath. "I fear I am too sick to work today. Forgive me. Please." Her body began to shake and then she shouted through her tears, "Please do not be displeased! I promise I am not weak!"

"Windlyn Mae," Skylar said, soft as a lullaby. "It is I, Skylar, your brother. Allow me to help you back to bed."

"No!" She hugged herself and ducked her head. "I am strong and shall not be an embarrassment. Please do not be displeased, Father!"

Skylar's heart shattered as his sister heaved with sobs and darted startled glances around the room. He chanced another step toward her and said, "I am not displeased with you." Her fevered eyes locked with his and her crying grew to hysterics. "I am your brother and I wish to care for you."

"Where is Father?"

"He is gone."

She gulped in a large breath that transformed with a spasm into a horrific cough. "He shall be furious with my weakness," she wheezed. "I am a disgrace to our home."

"No, Windlyn Mae, that is not true. You are brave, strong, and hard-working." Skylar took another step toward her. "I am proud of you."

"Father, I shall not disappoint you!"

Skylar halted all movement, stunned by the uncharacteristic volume of her voice. She placed a hand on the iron ring and began to push. Did she leave for work? In a panic, he grabbed the ring and shut the door. She screamed and covered her head. The sudden movements knocked her off balance and she collapsed to the floor, then she curled into herself. Unsure of what else to do, he knelt next to her and wrapped his arms around her trembling body. She was burning up. Never had he seen fever-induced delusions, though he had read about them. Maybe Skylar was still dreaming and this was all a nightmare.

Windy sobbed into his shoulder, a sound that triggered Mother, who screamed her name with startling clarity. Then again. And again. The hairs on the back of his neck stood on end. Mother continued to scream and her body thrashed against the safety ropes. Gone were the unnaturally slow movements and slurred, disconnected speech. Was she waking up? The psychologist had warned that she may go into fight-or-flight mode when coming out of a catatonic state and become dangerous, not only to those nearby, but to herself.

Gale-Anne crept into the room, eyes wide in terror. First, she studied Mother and then Windy, who leaned against Skylar, now limp, her head rolled to the side.

"Gale-Anne, please fetch help!" Skylar lifted Windy and carried her to a chair. "Grab your cloak and run!"

"Who, My Lord?"

"Timna and Joannah, if possible. If they are not home, find Lady Brianna"

Before Gale could depart, his entry door slammed open and the new hinge broke with the force. Skylar resisted the urge to swear under his breath. Five villagers ran into his house, three men and two women, who peered around the room with frantic movements, their eyes wide. Upon spotting Skylar and Gale, the oldest man in the group, Tanner Hawn, warily approached. "We heard screams and cries of distress." The man stared at their mother as color drained from his face. "Is all well, My Lord?"

"My sister suffers from a fever and slips in and out of reality." Skylar winced as his mother released another scream. Gale covered her ears. "I believe Mother was triggered by Windy's distress." A crowd began to gather outside his door and Skylar lowered his head to hide the heat suffusing his neck and face. His sister stirred in his arms and lazily blinked as she peered up into his face.

"Father, please forgive me," she wheezed. A cough wracked her body and she drew in a labored breath. "I am not weak," she pleaded. "I shall not embarrass our family."

"Shh," Skylar comforted her, and attempted to swallow back the forming tears. But he could not. His heart and mind could simply take no more. His body shuddered and he sucked in a ragged breath. "I am proud of you," he choked out. Before the last words left his mouth, her body had gone limp once more. A tear rolled down his cheek and dropped onto her face, and he wiped it away as more tears fell. He clenched his jaw and reluctantly met Tanner's concerned stare. Mother thrashed that moment and began calling out Windlyn's name in a strange, rhythmic wail.

"Let me carry your sister to her room. Care for Lady Emily, My Lord." Tanner extended his hands and Skylar eased his sister into his arms. "Suzanne?" The man called over his shoulder and a woman and her grown daughter followed him down the hallway, with Gale-Anne in the lead.

Skylar faced the crowd peering in through the windows and in from the door. "My I trouble someone to fetch Timna and Joannah?" Two young men in the front issued a curt nod and angled through the gathering.

He flinched when his mother called out for her daughter in desperation. Arms lifted, her hands clawed the air as if digging her way out of a grave. His first instinct was to back up. The grimace on her face and the snarl she released created a ripple of frightened exclamations. Spittle flew from her mouth. She had gone utterly mad. This was the agony of a broken mind. Fury gusted through his veins, a fury unlike any other. His body shook with pent-up rage. He dared not look at the community at his back who witnessed his family's pain in shocked stillness.

"Windlyn Mae! Windlyn Mae! Windlyn Mae!" she screamed.

He did not know what to do. If she saw his face, would she fear him as Windy had? Her hand clawed and grabbed in an invisible fight. He had to try before she injured herself. "I need assistance," Skylar said over his shoulder. "Two men who can help me hold her down." They pushed her cot away from the wall. Skylar eased onto the edge of the bed and dodged a flying hand. Gently, he pinned down Mother's arm while another held the right. She fought against them, but he refused to let go.

"Mother, 'tis Skylar. Look at me." She growled and more spittle sprayed the air. "Emily Kane, this is your son, Skylar. Look at me."

A tear rolled down his cheek, followed by another. His mother moaned as she opened and closed her mouth as if attempting to speak. She stopped moving, though she did not appear to have returned to a distant stupor, much to his relief. He stroked the back of her hand with his thumb. Sniffs and soft sounds came from behind him. He looked over his shoulder to find those who had gathered in various shades of grief. Through the window, he could see that the crowd had grown large. Was Dr. Nichols correct once more? Had New Eden feared his stoicism when they had longed to share in his grief? His mother was beloved, a kind and gentle soul who would do anything for another. He gulped in a breath and held back the tide of emotions.

"My Lord?" A moving voiced called from the doorway. Timna rushed to his side and leaned over Mother's bedside. "Lady Emily, you poor dear. This is Timna Lanley. You are safe and in the arms of those who love you." His mother moaned. "You are safe, My Lady."

Timna continued to speak in soft, reassuring tones. He swept an anxious gaze over the room. All eyes were riveted to the cot. Mother blinked and her pupils dilated. He gasped when she stared at him in recognition, her eyes clear and focused. Disbelieving, he whispered, "Mother?"

"Skylar." She licked her lips and blinked again. "Skylar Greysen?"

He grinned and wiped his cheeks. "Yes, Mother?" The crowd behind him murmured with excitement.

"You understand me?"

"I do," he said and laughed. "You know my name, what of yours?"

"Emily Louise Kane."

"Untie her," Skylar said to his helpers. Timna took Mother's hand with a radiant smile, one that matched the elation touching each individual inside and outside of his home. Quiet cheers and happy whispers rippled behind him and he exhaled slowly. He eased his mother to a sitting position then gathered her into an embrace. Whispering in her ear, he said, "I have missed you."

"I am so sorry." She started to cry. "I am not entirely sure what has happened."

"You were traumatized and unreachable." He pulled away. "Timna is correct, you are safe. Nothing shall happen to you. Or us, for that matter."

"I thought I heard Windlyn in distress." She touched her face in confusion, then stared at the teardrop upon her finger. For a moment, he thought the disorientation would send her back to where her mind had locked her away. But then she met his eyes. "Is she in trouble?"

"She is ill. You heard her fevered dreams, 'tis all." He looked to Timna. "If you would be so kind, I would appreciate your care of my sister."

"Of course, My Lord. A courier delivered medication from the lab early this morning. There is hope, but we must continue efforts to contain the illness." Timna turned to the crowd. "This home is hereby under quarantine. I shall provide updates during evening meals."

People bowed and curtsied, with soft words of peace and health to him and his mother in their departure. The word "miracle" and "blessed" floated on the wind they created in their exit, and he smiled. He was about to turn back to Mother, when Lady Rain caught his eye, one of the last to leave. Skylar had not realized that she was even in his home. With a shy smile that he was sure matched his own, she pressed a hand upon her heart with delicate movements, New Eden's salute in shared sorrow and joy.

"We have Outsider medicine now," he said. It was a strange thing to say, but he wished to reassure her in his, Leaf, and Lady Ember's absence.

"Yes, I heard, My Lord."

"It pains me even more for the lost little ones and their families, though I am relieved for those presently ill."

"Aye," she said simply.

"Shall you fare well on your own this week, My Lady?"

Lady Rain fidgeted with the strings of her cloak then clasped her hands at her waist. "I am not alone, My Lord." Their eyes touched one last time before she glided toward the entry door, which hung at a strange angle once more. His pulse beat wildly as he watched her depart, not sure of what else to say or do.

"Rain," his mother called out in a weak voice, and the Daughter of Water looked up. "Thank you. My memories are jumbled and rather fleeting, but I do remember your kindness. It was a special day, though I could not say so."

Lady Rain smiled, and it was one of the most beautiful images Skylar had ever beheld. "Spending the day in your company was special for me as well, Lady Emily." Then she disappeared into the dawning light as Joannah entered their home. Skylar lifted the hewn wood door to ensure it shut properly and sighed with equal parts humor and irritation.

"My apologies, I was caring for a sick family." Joannah's eyes rounded. "Emily! Oh my, what a grand pleasure." She joined them at Mother's bedside and placed her medicine basket on a nearby chair. Timna, the township's Naturopath, resumed checking Mother's vitals and neurological functions while keeping up a steady stream of conversation with both Mother and Joannah. Perhaps to keep Mother in the present?

He leaned onto the window sill, arms straight, and tracked Lady Rain's movements until she disappeared around the bend. Today was the Cremation Ceremony for Jeremy Perkins and Matilda McCauley, both wee ones under the age of seven. The illness had ravaged their community for several weeks now. Why had the lab taken so long to offer medicine?

His breath fogged the glass pane and he frowned.

Knowing that the Wind, Earth, and Fire Element homes were quarantined did not sit well with him. It made him feel paranoid, actually. Was this planned somehow? Or mere coincidence? He knew not. Later he would attempt to connect with Lady Ember via Messenger Pigeon to set up a meeting with Leaf. He still needed to brief The Aether on his conversation with the Guild Master.

Skylar pushed off from the window and said with a bow, "I shall be sitting with Windy, should you have need of me." He leaned over and kissed his mother on the cheek, then ambled down the hallway, his mind heavy. Nevertheless, it felt good to finally move forward.

And don't think the garden loses its ecstasy in winter. It's quiet, but the roots are down there riotous.

—Rumi, 13th century A.D. *

And that a young woman in love always looks— *"like Patience on a monument, Smiling at Grief."*

—Jane Austen, *Northanger Abbey*, quoting *Twelfth Night* by William Shakespeare, 1817 *

*The cold nights have been guilty
of changing the leaves on the linden trees
to take on a wintry color.
I had enjoyed high hopes for love,
and now I know that my love has ended.
I have lost the best time and place
there where I find good love
and where I can win this happiness.*

—Heinrich von Veldeke, *"Ez habent die kalte nähte getâ,"* 12th century A.D *

ChAPTER ONE

New Eden Township, Salton Sea, California

Friday, December 18, 2054

Week Seven of Project Phase Two

h ow could I know it would stop the wheel?" Rain's
youngest brother threw back in defense. Lake's face
grew red, redder than his hair. Freckles popped out on
his skin and green eyes pleaded with her to understand. "I
swear by all that is holy."

"Lake Alexander Daniels, we do not swear."

"What about handfasting vows?"

"That is wholly different."

"You can swear when you marry?"

Rain thought for a moment. "Yes, or when taking office or
when giving witness."

"I am giving witness."

She threw her hands up. How did one reason with a hot-headed seven-year-old boy? Lake stuck his hands into his pockets with a scowl. Before she could comment further, Canyon broke the water's surface and gasped for air.

"Still nothing." He blew water off his mouth and wiped wet strands from his eyes. "I shall try the other end of the waterwheel." Canyon gulped a large breath of air and dived beneath the surface once more.

"We may need to empty the millrace," Rain said in exasperation.

That would take far too much time, time that could not be wasted. The bakers needed flour for the Celebration of Life and upcoming Midwinter Feasts. She studied, with dismay, the tailrace end of the channel, which dumped into the pond. Rain gnawed at her bottom lip. The breast-shot wheel sat submerged in the North Pond. But the engineers had designed a channel lock system around it to allow drainage in the event of needed repairs. This would qualify, for sure. However, unplugging the outlet would release a slow, crawling trickle back to the pond. No, it would simply take far too much time to drain.

She faced her brother once more. "Why on Earth would you throw in Gale-Anne's rag doll?"

"She was mean to me!"

"And so, naturally, tying her doll to a rock and throwing it into the millrace will make her more amiable?"

He scuffed the ground and lifted his shoulders. "I threw it into one of the wheel slats, not the millrace. I wanted to see the horror on her face every time it came out of the water and fell back in."

Rain shook her head with a heavy sigh. Canyon emerged for the measure of time it took to fill his lungs with fresh air, then disappeared beneath the wheel. "She is in quarantine," Rain began again. "However did you find her doll?"

Lake had the decency to appear shamefaced, his head tucked toward his chest with shoulders slumped forward. He kicked the tall grass by the bank and mumbled, "I stole it from her at evening meal a few days ago."

Rain's eyes widened in disbelief. "Oh, Lake, whatever shall I do with you?"

Canyon came up for air once more with a grin. "I do believe I have rescued the doll and found the offending rock." He lifted the muddied rags that once resembled a little girl with flaxen hair. Rain's fourteen-year-old brother pushed out of the water and rolled onto the grassy bank, his chest heaving for breath.

"Shall I tell the miller the wheel is fixed?" Lake asked. His face turned hopeful and her offense melted a smidgen. He was rather adorable when his troublesome nature glowed with angelic remorse.

Rain walked past her brothers and opened the tailrace sluice gate, then moved upstream to the headrace and did the same. Water rushed through the dammed gate and splashed into the chest-deep channel. Still, the current did not move the wheel. She placed a fretful hand upon her temple, another on her hip. Why was the waterwheel not turning? Her eyes darted to the weir and the millpond. The millrace flowed at an appropriate speed.

Canyon groaned when noting the stationary wheel. Shaking the water from his titian hair, he jogged over to the penstock and studied the incoming water from the fast-moving stream that circled the biodome. He bent over at an awkward angle and inspected the headrace sluice gate. "All is clear. I do not see any debris." With another sound of annoyance, he turned the valve and raised the sluice gate. Rain, nearest to the tailrace, did the same and the current stopped.

"Shall we drain the millrace?" she asked Canyon.

"What a pain in the arse this is." He ran fingers through his hair and glared at Lake. "Is your vengeance complete?"

Their little brother stuck his tongue out at Canyon in reply. Dripping wet and shivering, Canyon growled right before dashing toward him with promises that Lake would pay for his stupidity. Rain crossed her arms over her chest as she watched her brothers chase each other in circles, Canyon spewing threats and Lake delivering flippancy as if it were the very air he breathed. Eventually Canyon caught their brother and tossed him over his shoulder. Lake kicked and pounded Canyon's back with angry fists but Canyon just laughed.

"You need to cool off, little brother," Canyon said. "Perhaps a dip in the North Pond?"

"Canyon!" Rain shouted.

But he ignored her, promptly chucking their little brother into the pond. Lake emerged from shallow waters near the bank, drenched and dripping with fury. Canyon just continued to laugh, the goading sound echoing off the water. Lake's face scrunched up in rage right as he threw a handful of mud at Canyon, which splattered across the front of his tunic.

Silence.

Then Lake laughed. Canyon jumped off the bridge with a grand splash. Lake stared wide-eyed then spun toward the bank and tried to run. But he slipped and fell in the mud. Canyon reached out and grabbed his ankle and pulled him back into the water. Rain knew it was pointless to interrupt their wrestle for power. Sometimes they were like the kids in the Mediterranean dome, jumping onto everything and butting heads.

"Rascally goats," Rain said under her breath.

"Who is winning, My Lady?" a masculine voice asked beside her.

She placed a hand to her heart. "Coal Hansen! You gave me quite a fright! For shame."

He grinned while he bowed and her heart stuttered a beat. The Outside world failed to diminish his fine looks. If anything, he had grown more handsome. Though she tried to no longer entertain romantic fancies where he was concerned, she could not help the way her heart raced at the very sight of him. Flustered, she looked away and her eyes rested on Michael, the scientist from the lab who always accompanied Coal on visits. He stared at Canyon and Lake with a faint smile.

The splashing and dunking continued and she turned back to Coal. "The waterwheel is not turning, My Lord."

"How unfortunate." He glanced at her brothers again. "I take it, My Lady, your youngest brother is somehow responsible?"

"Was there any other guess?" Rain transformed from an irritated sister to a Noblewoman and postured accordingly, shoulders back, chin lifted, and hands folded at her waist. With graceful steps she moved toward the large iron and wooden wheel submerged halfway into the water. Coal matched her stride. "Canyon dislodged the sizable rock Lake threw in and inspected the penstock and sluice gates. Still, the wheel will not turn. Perhaps one of the axles is now broken or out of alignment?"

"Unlikely," he responded. "The water can still move through the slats."

She opened her mouth to express her relief. But, much to her horror, he removed his outer garment, belt, stockings, shoes, and belongings from his pockets, and piled them into the grass until he was left wearing only a tight, short-sleeved tunic and breeches. A tattoo stretched down to his elbow and she blushed, casting her eyes to the ground. He was marked. Had Fillion's sister marked him? The very idea sent a flurry of light-headed sensations through her body. From lowered eyes, she trailed his movements until he dove into the millrace.

This moment, she wished Oaklee were here. Her friend always knew how to deflect Coal's charms with sensibility and humor, even if affected by them. Though, she would never admit it so. Rain, on the other hand, could not stop her wandering imaginations. Her helpless romantic fancies always bested her, despite all efforts to be more levelheaded and reasonable.

Her thoughts turned to the kiss she placed on Skyler's cheek in the forest. A scandalous thing to do. One that was firm grounds for marriage. Though enjoying his company unchaperoned was grounds enough. Still, she regretted nothing. She had dreamt of kissing a man for so long. And Skylar Kane was ... well, he was dashing and princely, and so utterly oblivious to her affections. And ever so kind, even a gentleman when breaking the rules for the sake of comforting her fears.

A splash grounded her thoughts and she focused on the millrace instead of her feverish musings. The water reached chest height when Coal stood to draw breath. He jerked the dampened strands from his eyes and wiped droplets from his face. "A box is lodged in the bottom slat and caught in the gravel."

"A box? What sort of box?"

"Metal from the feel of it." Coal placed his hands on the wheel and pulled until it rotated the counter direction of when in operation. At first it gave resistance but then it spun. Canyon and Lake, wet and muddied, stood beside her with clattering teeth.

"Do you need assistance, My Lord?" Canyon called out.

"No." A single word, but the tone was entirely waggish. With a puckish smile, the Son of Fire disappeared beneath the water once more.

"Showoff," Canyon muttered and rolled his eyes.

Rain could not help the unladylike snicker she smothered. Though her brother was brawny, even at fourteen, he was certainly not as physically fit as Coal Hansen.

Canyon's eyes playfully narrowed to slits. "You dare mock me, *My Lady*? Perhaps I should throw you into the North Pond next. You appear in sore need of a lesson."

"You do, and Father shall have your hide." Rain lifted her eyebrows in challenge and Canyon delivered one of his impish grins. "It is not worth it."

"To you, perhaps."

She threw her hands up again and stalked away until she stood next to Michael, as if the small, wiry man could protect her from the likes of Canyon Daniels. The scientist bestowed a sympathetic look, though the faint smile remained. Coal surfaced with a large breath, then dipped below.

Some days, such as this one, she envied Oaklee, Laurel, Corona, Windlyn, and Gale-Anne. They had older brothers who protected them, romantic heroes rather than wicked imps. With her mother now gone and her older sister busy with a newborn babe, it was left to Rain to turn her heathen brothers into civilized gentlemen. Perhaps she should allow them to remain savages and let the community mold them into proper men. Regardless, she prayed daily for their future wives. *May the good Lord bless their patient, long-suffering souls.* Rain touched her forehead, chest, then each shoulder.

"He has not drowned," Lake said with a shake of his head. "You worry too much."

"She shall pull his body from the millrace and mourn him tragically," Canyon said, throwing back the challenge by raising his eyebrows like hers. "Oh Coal," he continued in a higher voice, "If only I had not mocked my brother when he offered you assistance! You would not have died so young and so senselessly!"

"Canyon Daniels," Rain grit between clenched teeth. "I have had enough of you!" Her brother backpedaled when she stormed toward him, his lips twitching. "Go to Father now! And take Lake with you." She turned on her youngest brother and pointed a finger in his face. "I shall have Father chastise you later and provide a proper punishment."

Lake turned pleading eyes to Canyon. "You shall defend me, right?"

"Heavens, no." Canyon hit the back of his brother's head with a laugh and shocks of red hair fell into Lake's eyes. "You shall face your crimes like a man."

Bolstered by the word "man," Lake squared his shoulders and turned toward the forest. Together, her brothers trotted off, soon pushing each other and laughing, until the trees hid their shenanigans and hushed their bubbly stream of taunts.

"You have your hands full," Michael offered. "Thank goodness only two brothers, eh?"

"I once had three."

Michael's face fell. "I'm so sorry. I didn't know."

"'Twas a long time ago, sir. My brother, River, died in his sleep when he was a wee babe." Rain's lips pulled in a sad smile. "He would be ten years of age by now."

"A baby? So young."

"Indeed. Though not uncommon."

"I've heard of SIDs, but I couldn't imagine."

Sids? She tilted her head, shocked by his sentiments. "Do children not die in your world?"

"Not many, no." He stared in the direction of Coal, who pulled on the wheel once more. "Not many adults for that matter."

"How is that even possible?"

"Medicine." He looked at her now, a friendly but wary smile thinning his lips. "We have a cure for most things, and the technology to replace and repair organs, limbs—you name it."

"I see." Rain had never felt so baffled in all her life. What a strange world to live in where death did not visit and life was manufactured. Was such a reality even holy? Could one argue with God over their earthly mortality and win? She peered at the scientist in horrified wonder. Then, another thought occurred. Why were he and Coal here? It was rude to ask, and she really should not, but Coal was underwater and so she proceeded. "Have you come for the Third Ceremony following evening meal? 'Tis many hours away."

"We actually came in search of you, Ms. Daniels." Michael turned toward her. "Coal will brief you."

As if on cue, Coal stood up in the water and lifted a metal box the size of a small, personal chest. He slid the box onto the bank and then pushed out of the water. Rain's eyes widened at the definition of muscle exposed through the dark, wet tunic clinging to his body. The air caught in her chest until she grew faint. No, she would not swoon. Though, to find him leaning over her limp form as he touched her cheek, begging her to wake up, or to feel her face pressed into his neck as he carried her back to her apartment, would be a delightful way to die. Clearing her throat, she swiveled toward the forest and pretended to search for her brothers. Heat flamed her face as if she had swallowed a thousand suns. She needed to move. Head down, she focused on the tailrace sluice gate.

"Shall we test the waterwheel, My Lord?" Her fingers gripped the valve.

"On your ready," Coal hollered back.

"Ready!"

With a grunt, she turned the valve until it loosened. Round and round it went until the sluice gate lowered and water moved toward the North Pond. She locked the valve in place and faced upstream. The headrace roared as water spilled into the channel. A loud groan followed by creaks rent the air and she waited. Slowly, the waterwheel cut through the slithering current and she let out a celebratory cry.

Coal ran a hand through his strands of wet hair and slid her a victorious grin. "The miller shall be pleased."

"Yes," Rain replied, a bit breathless, trying her best to not flush like a silly girl. "I am much relieved, My Lord. Midwinter Feasts are upon us. Could you imagine Twelvetide without King Cake?"

"Heretical." His voice was muffled as he bent to retrieve his belongings piled by the bank. "Though I prefer caraway cakes soaked in cider and shall relish each bite."

"Figgy pudding 'tis one of my favorites." Rain glanced at Michael who appeared thoughtful, bemused even. Had he never tried caraway cakes or figgy pudding? "How do you celebrate Yuletide and the Twelve Days of Christmas, sir?"

"Oh, me?" Michael blinked back his surprise. "I don't celebrate anything."

"Not even Christmastide?" Rain's mouth hung open for heartbeat until she remembered her manners.

"No, not even Christmas."

She looked to Coal for an explanation, but received none. "Well, you shall accompany Coal to Midwinter Feasts, yes?"

"Yes, that's the plan, Ms. Daniels."

"Excellent," Rain said, rather pleased. "You shall be my family's personal guest, sir."

He drew his eyebrows together. "Don't go to any trouble—
—"

"Nonsense." Rain waved his concerns aside with a sweep of her hand. "We would be delighted to share our table with you." She looked to Coal. "Is this not so, My Lord?"

"This is so, Michael," he said in an overly serious tone. Rain placed her hands on hips but he continued before she could playfully chide him. "Well, My Lady, now that I have properly rescued you and good fortune hath been restored, I shall be on my merry way."

"You entered New Eden simply to rescue me?"

"Naturally."

Rain laughed as he attempted another serious expression. "How fortuitous."

He flashed her a dimpled smile as he wrung out the hem of his tunic. "Actually, once I change into dry clothes, may I speak with you?"

"Of course." Rain attempted to remain steady though her heart fluttered with his request. The bare limbs of the linden tree stretched behind Coal and her eyes wandered to the initials graved into the trunk. "Where shall we meet?"

"How about the Great Hall? I am famished."

She played with edge of her sleeve. "Do you wish for any others to join us, My Lord?"

"*Oui, Mademoiselle.* Alas, they are all in quarantine. I shall inform them later." Coal nibbled on his bottom lip and she studied his piercing. Did it hurt? "I have a message from the lab concerning the recent influenza outbreak. They seek your assistance."

Her heart fell to her stomach. "I see." She drew in a quiet breath and half-whispered, "Until then, My Lord," and lowered into a curtsy.

Coal bowed. "Until then."

She watched as he faded into the North Cave, the scientist by his side. Disappointment tinged her thoughts and, with heavy movements, she trod toward the bank, refusing to look at the linden tree. Water splashed and gurgled as it raced from one end of existence to the other. A brown-spotted leaf dodged the wheel and floated upon the surface. She trailed its journey as the current whisked it downstream. She had been foolish. Once more, her imagination and poor judgment carried her away, as if a mere leaf upon the water.

Perhaps one day she would have a home of her own and a passel of children underfoot. That is, should a man not find her sordid origins distasteful. A dispirited sigh escaped her lips at the very thought just as her foot kicked against the metal box that Coal had dislodged from the wheel. Droplets of water glistened and rolled down the sides of the box, the source of so many of her morning's troubles and yet already forgotten.

"Wherever did you come from?" she mused aloud.

Rain picked up the box and shook it. Items slid around inside and her smile widened. It was surprisingly light. She inspected the dark gray metal. Underneath, the name "Kane" was scratched into the surface. Her breath hitched. The heavier currents from the Blood Rains must have pushed it into the penstock. However did it end up in the pond? Had Timothy tossed this into the stream by the Mill? Or was this Skylar's?

Somehow the existence of the name instilled a sense of caution, and she tucked the box under her arm within her cloak. Before joining Coal at the Great Hall, she would hide the metal chest in her room. When the quarantine was lifted, she could deliver it intact to Skylar. She missed him. She missed all her friends. Though she was surrounded by people from dawn until dusk, she felt terribly lonesome.

The path split to ramble along the apartments or wend its way through the forest. Rain took a left and hummed a tune as she meandered down the village path, trying to not think of the object in her care. But it was fruitless.

Back in her apartment, she tiptoed through the house and shut her chamber door with the silence of a whispered prayer, though she was alone. It was silly, but curiosity over what could possibly be in the box amplified every sound, even her breath. Books in the lending library divulged tales of buried treasure and cursed artifacts. Her imagination was leaping at the many possibilities.

Rain placed the peculiar box upon her vanity. She traced her finger along the rounded edges and studied the shiny, metallic latch. It did not appear locked. She nibbled on her fingernail. No, she would respect the privacy due Skylar.

Resolute, she pivoted to move away just as the front entry door opened with a resounding bang and shut with a slam, one that rattled even her bedchamber door. And the metal box. She moved her attention back to her vanity. An idea emerged and she suppressed a giggle. A proper lady would honor the secrets it contained and abstain from meddlesome behavior. Rain, however, wondered that if she could steal kisses then, perhaps, she could steal secrets, too.

Across the hallway, her brother charged into his room, only to dash out just as fast. Whatever was he grabbing? She did not have long to contemplate. The front door slammed shut once more and Rain pretended to startle, gasping aloud as her fingers splayed the air in mock fright and bumped the vanity. The box rattled toward the edge but remained aloft. Rain pressed her lips together in annoyance and gave the box a hearty nudge. She held her breath. The rush of Lake's thumping scamper crescendoed by her window as the chest crashed to the floor and broke open.

With a squeal, Rain knelt on the floor and righted the toppled box. Her head was positively dizzy with excitement. A handful of small playing cards, reflecting the strangest images, spilled onto the floor in a bizarre, transparent bag. Dribbles of water pooled on her chamber floor and beaded on the material. But no water appeared to have harmed the cards.

Nimbly, she opened the bag, marveling at its flexibility, and pulled out the treasure. Her fingers rummaged through the contents one by one, until the end. Her hand stilled. Beneath the cards was a picture so lifelike, it was if she peered into a magic mirror. It was of a much younger Timothy and Lady Emily, who stared at her as if they knew her every secret. She half expected their eyes to blink or their smiles to falter. But they did not. How was this even possible?

Spooked, she shoved all the items back into the box, shut the lid, and pushed it under her cot. Rain touched her hair and smoothed out her dress, then sprinted from her apartment toward the Great Hall, her heart pounding.

Chapter Two

Rain waited for Coal to explain the reason for his visit. But whenever he opened his mouth, he filled it with food or cautiously jested with Michael. And so she waited. And sipped on her tea. And watched the goings-on of the kitchen staff with half-hearted interest while trying to push away the unsettling image in the metal box. Normally she was not so patient and would have questioned him by this point, regardless of ladylike deportment or expectations. Only his aberrant behavior stopped her.

The conversation eventually lulled and stretched from one awkward beat to another. Coal flicked his dark brown eyes her way. Rain smiled politely, trying not to think of how they were nearly black, they were so dark. How could one have hair like an angel and eyes like the devil? 'Twas divine cruelty, she decided. His gaze did not linger long, however. His attentions were fleeting, unless food was involved.

Killie flew by with a large platter of strawberries and Coal leaned back in his chair as he chewed on the last gyngerbrede candy. He tracked the freshly plucked berries until they rested upon a block table across the kitchen from the inglenook, where she, Coal, and Michael presently sat.

"Please excuse me," he said and eased from his chair.

Rain almost pitied Cook this moment. In the span of a few heartbeats, Coal had meandered across the room toward the platter. Cook stepped in front with hands on hips and clear warning in her eyes. The scene was almost comical, except Rain was still confused. Coal had been acting strangely since walking into the Great Hall. He would smile and tease, as usual. But a worried look would slip across his features when his humor ended all the while his attention darted around the room, as if he were hiding from someone or something.

"Is he in trouble?" Michael asked her. The scientist appeared to shrink under Cook's glare. He would not be the first. She was a fierce woman, though it was all bluster. She had a heart of gold beneath the gruff exterior.

"The Son of Fire is synonymous with trouble, sir," Rain replied. "I am surprised you have not learned this by now."

"Oh, I have. He's explosive at times, too."

She bit her bottom lip when Coal leaned onto the block table as if there were not a single care in the world. His odd clothing—bordering on garish—clinked with his movement.

"A dog on the hunt, you are, My Lord," Cook said. "These are for mid-day meal."

"What are, exactly?" he casually asked.

She tsked and wagged a finger in his face. "No appreciation for me work? I says no more sweets is what I say."

"You would deny a man his sweets?" Coal placed a hand over his heart as if mortally wounded.

"Listen to you talk! Deny a man his sweets? Bah!"

The kitchen maids whispered behind their aprons and hands, especially when Coal straightened to full height, followed by a gallant bow. "Madam Cook, I have never known desserts so fine as yours." For a moment, Cook pressed her lips together, skeptical. "Your sweets melt on my tongue and dissolve into happiness. Each bite allows my heart to touch Heaven and my soul sighs in pleasure. It is truly a holy experience."

The Son of Fire lifted a corner of his mouth in a lazy smile and Cook flustered, waving a hand to cool her sudden flush. Rain could not blame her, as she often had similar responses herself. Appearing pleased with himself, Coal leaned down and kissed the older woman's cheek while snaking an arm around her generous hips to the platter of strawberries. Rain gasped. The kitchen maids erupted into a flurry of stifled giggles, especially when Cook's mouth fell open.

"Coal Hansen!" She swatted him with a dish towel and he grinned, tossing a strawberry into his mouth. She grabbed a rolling pin off the block table and swung, but Coal ducked with a laugh, taking the object from her hands and placing it back onto the table. Puffing out her cheeks with hands on hips, fingers tapping in an angry rhythm, Cook loosed an irritated breath. "This is my kitchen, you … you…"

"Rascally goat!" Rain volunteered, and Coal shot her a look as if she had betrayed him.

"Thank you, My Lady!" Cook pushed Coal away with shooing sounds. "Go back to your seat, you troublesome goat. You think you can graze as you please in my kitchen?" She threw a stubby finger in his face. "Well, you are wrong you are. Rules are to be adhered to. Do you understand, young man?"

"Yes, Madam Cook."

"There will be no touching food, if you know what is good for you."

With a cherubic expression, he asked, "All food?"

"Food not offered! Gah!"

"Yes, Madam Cook."

Cook eyed Coal for several long, silent heartbeats. He raised a strawberry to his lips, blinking with innocence, a sweet smile on his face. She tried to remain firm, even attempting a scowl, but fell into laughter instead, swatting him again with her dishtowel. Cook pushed him until he stumbled back toward the nook table.

"Troublesome lad," Cook muttered under her breath. "No appreciation, says me."

Coal released his small bounty of stolen strawberries onto a trencher plate. "Really?" he asked Rain. "'Rascally goat'?"

"Are you not?"

"I do believe I am a tad more genteel than your brothers."

"Only a tad, but still a rascally goat."

Coal blinked with mock astonishment. "*Moi?* I am scandalized, *Mademoiselle.*"

Rain's heart fluttered as she wrapped her fingers around her steaming mug of tea. To be scandalized by Coal Hansen. Even better, to scandalize him! But, he belonged to Fillion's sister and the rest of the Outside world. And he was a tease. He meant nothing by the words that inspired her heated thoughts, she knew. Still, they affected her all the same.

What would Oaklee do in moments such as these? She thought of her friend and smiled. She knew exactly what Oaklee would do. Lifting her chin, Rain angled her head away, as if she were above his charms and bravado, and took a sip of her tea. There, she had properly ignored his impish behavior.

"She's coming back," Michael whispered.

Coal flicked his gaze across the kitchen with a satisfied smile. "And with a large plate."

Protestations forgotten, the sturdy, ruddy-cheeked woman, covered in flour and smelling of savory herbs, plopped a plate of hot apple tarts in the center of their table, sprinkled with candied walnuts and drizzled in honey.

"You are not eating enough, says me," Cook huffed. "Look at you, lad. Skin and bones, you are. No wonder you sneak food right under me nose." Rain hid her smile. Skin and bones he was most certainly not. "No one shall accuse Cook of not feeding you proper."

"I have missed your fare exceedingly."

"Seventeen years on St. Thomas Becket Day next week and look at you! Skin and bones." For a moment she appeared to beam with pride and said, "I shall fatten you up, never you worry."

"I am lucky, indeed, to have your exceptional care," Coal said, dimpled smile and all. "I pine for your creations."

With a loud harrumph, Cook wobbled back to her station while shouting orders at a nearby errand boy to fetch more wash water. The lad scurried from the room quicker than a blink, nearly tripping over the bucket.

Coal popped an entire apple tart into his mouth and chewed with a look akin to rapture. Rain nibbled on hers and washed down the pastry with a sip of tea. Kitchen maids and errand boys dashed to and fro, all forgiven and all forgotten.

He had insisted they dine at the kitchen nook by the cook hearth so he could charm Cook for food. But, really, it was to cover their conversation with all the riotous clamor. So far his plan had proved fruitful—on both accounts.

"Oh wow," Michael said after a bite.

"You are welcome." Coal tossed another tart into his mouth. "This is what *real* food tastes like. None of that salt-infused, unripened cardboard you Outsiders prefer." The scientist smiled. "Though, I daresay Selah prepares a fine meal for the Nichols family."

"She should, considering who she serves." Michael savored another bite with a happy grunt while nodding his head. "Is three servings of dessert before lunch normal? I always thought New Eden ate on a schedule and portioned out food."

"Yes, you speak true. I am clearly her favorite," Coal said with another look of innocence. Rain choked back a laugh and sipped on her tea to conceal her mirth. "*Ne gâchez pas l'illusion pour lui,*" he said to her, his face perfectly serious.

"*Oui, Milord,*" she replied with another laugh. "*Il semble convaincu. Ton secret est bien gardé!*"

"You know my Cranium automatically translates."

"Drat." Coal smiled in such a way that Rain gathered he already knew.

"Where's the restroom?" Michael asked.

"The public lavatory is down the corridor and on the left." With that, Michael pushed away from the small table and strode in the direction Coal indicated. A worried, distracted look shadowed Coal's features once more. The Son of Fire focused on the wooden slats of the table for several heartbeats before meeting her waiting gaze. "Is my sister well?" he asked, voice low.

"Yes, My Lord." She knew not how else to respond. Did he know of the coming babe? She wished to share the happy news, but unmarried women did not speak of such things, most especially with unattached men. "She fares well."

He chewed on his bottom lip and leaned forward. "My Lady," he whispered, "nearly a fortnight ago I sensed her distress. Did she fall ill? The lab refuses to answer my questions. My communications to the Techsmith Guild are blocked."

"Communications?" She drew her eyebrows together. He knew when Ember was troubled? "As far as I know, she has not fallen ill with influenza."

"I am much relieved." He tapped his fingers on the table and looked around the kitchen, offering a polite smile to a maid who hastened by with a bowl of various greens. He leaned over the table once more and half-whispered, "The lab is in an uproar. The media caught wind of the Perkins boy and McCauley girl who died needlessly. The Surgeon General has imposed state law on New Eden Township in response."

"Which law, My Lord?" Rain marveled at how his manner of speech had changed since leaving their community. "We are in violation of the law?"

"Yes, actually."

"Has Jeff confirmed these claims?" Rain tried her best to ignore the warmth creeping up her neck at the mention of the barrister's name. The name of her biological father. She stared into her cup of tea and hoped she hid her mortification from Coal.

"He has." Coal studied her and she pretended to focus on the cook hearth. "Worry not, My Lady. We shall not be evicted. My apologies for startling you so."

"You are kind, but I am well." She listened to the hearth crackle and watched the flames dance a spell before asking, "What law have we broken?"

"Vaccination laws. According to the state of California, all those who reside within its borders are required to be inoculated against a handful of preventable diseases, influenza being one of them."

She played with her tablet-woven belt as she thought over his words. "Are you inoculated?"

"Yes." A flash of anger crossed his face with the admission. "Which is why I am permitted to come and go within New Eden."

The sudden change in demeanor was unnerving and Rain knew not how to reply. Was inoculation dangerous? Or uncomfortable? Before she could ask, Michael returned and slid into his seat with an affable smile.

"Did I miss anything?" he asked.

"I am confused, My Lord," she said to the Son of Fire, ignoring Michael completely. "How then did influenza come to us?"

"I guess I did." Michael looked to Coal and a silent message passed between them. The Outsider turned in his chair to fully face her, his gaze darting around the kitchen. Warily, he whispered, "A scientist falsified his medical records. He no longer works for the lab."

"How shall he rectify the damages done, then?"

"My Lady," Coal said, eyes downcast. "He shall not face New Eden, though he may face a judge eventually, if Hanley presses charges."

Rain pushed away from the table and turned in her chair, folding her arms over her chest. The plate—smeared with honey and crumbs—clanked against the table. "He is not to apologize to the families who lost their precious children because of his deceit?" Her lips trembled as she tried, in vain, to contain her fury. "He is a coward."

Coal touched the plate to silence the clatter, head bowed in respect, grief etched into each of his features. The kitchen maids quieted and peered their direction. He blinked back the emotions and lifted his head with a playful smile. She drew back in confusion. "You dare attempt to take the last apple tart?"

Her pulse galloped as he stared at her unblinking, as if willing her play along. "Coal Hansen," she began hesitantly. "Have

137

you not eaten enough apple tarts already?" Rain forced a smile and her stomach sickened.

"No, I shall never eat enough, especially Cook's." He pushed the plate toward her and offered the remaining tart. "I suppose I shall share, My Lady. If I must. Cook's fine pastries shall be but a happy memory."

"You are such a rascal, My Lord."

He flashed his angelic grin, the very one that had all the matriarchs eating out of his hand. The kitchen resumed its busyness and the clank of pots and boisterous voices hid their conversation once more.

Coal's gaze grew sorrowful as he searched her eyes. "The Outside world does not demand an honor price the same way as New Eden." His voice was barely above a whisper, but cracked with the same sense of injustice she expressed.

"And so now we are found in fault before the law?"

"Yes, My Lady."

Rain lowered into her chair and gripped her mug of tea. "The whole of New Eden is to be inoc … inoc…"

"Inoculated."

"Whatever does that mean, exactly?"

"It's an easy process," Michael cut in, quick to reassure. "Painless."

"Go on."

Michael lowered his voice. "We swab the saliva in a person's inner cheek to place into a machine."

"A machine?" Rain asked, eyes rounding.

"A hand-held one that calibrates sublingual vaccine strips based on DNA."

She looked to Coal, addled by Michael's explanation. "This is your experience, My Lord?"

"No." He clenched his jaw. "My process was—not so simple."

Michael cleared his throat and adjusted his position in his seat.

Spooked, she drew in a shaky breath. "But what Michael suggests is safe? The machine will not harm the children?"

"I was advised to inform you—The Elements—that the inoculation process is perfectly harmless." Coal swallowed and blinked nervously. "I have not suffered any ill effects."

Rain set her earthen mug on the table as she stared at Coal. "Tell me you jest."

"Shoot! I need to take this call." Michael sent Coal a peculiar look, one Coal had seemed to understand explicitly. Then the scientist scurried from the kitchen toward the Great Hall.

Rain swiveled back in her seat to regard Coal and startled. Her hand flew to her chest. While distracted, he had moved next to her and leaned in close. "Coal Hansen! Once more, you have given me quite the fright."

"I need to speak quickly," he began. "Michael has been recording our conversation for Hanley." She did not understand what he meant by "record," but nodded her head anyway for him to continue. "I asked Mack to run a background check on the scientist in question and it appears as though the poor man was set up." Rain's eyes rounded, but she remained silent. Who was Mack? "The scientist was hired three weeks prior to the Great Fire and hailed from a state without stringent vaccination laws. The state of California grants three weeks to become inoculated, otherwise they will not grant you an I.D. Without an I.D., there is not much one can do."

Coal was speaking gibberish as far as she was concerned. Nevertheless she followed along enough to grasp the message. "How were his medical records falsified then?"

"They were hacked the day before the Great Fire," Coal answered. "Though he had reported symptoms of illness that very morning, he was sent in as part of the emergency team."

"Hanley wished for New Eden to fall ill?" Tears filled Rain's eyes.

"Rain," Coal whispered, narrowing his eyes. "Did any resident protest the use of Outsider medicine?" She thought over the past two days and shook her head. Actually, the first generation in particular were desperate for their children to have a cure. Coal continued. "Do you not think this odd? The Code prohibits use of modern medicine within the dome. We are to leave for Outsider medicine and intervention." Tension creased his brows. "Those who moved into the dome, including the second generation already born, were permanently inoculated against influenza."

"Dear Lord in Heaven," she breathed. "The children…"

The blood rushed from her head and an errant tear slipped down her cheek. Coal pulled a handkerchief from his pocket. Her fingers grazed his just as he abruptly straightened and flashed a distracted smile down the corridor. Rain need not peer over her shoulder to know that Michael returned. She blotted her cheeks with the linen cloth then sipped her tea to appear as if all was well.

"Is the wee Mary Norah Elizabeth faring well, My Lady?" Coal asked as he returned to his seat.

"Yes, she is precious. I dote upon her so." Rain lowered her eyes to still forming tears. "Though no one dotes upon her more so than Father. I think becoming a grandfather has eased his grief a little."

"Mist and Matthew fare well, then?"

"Yes, my sister is hearty and hale. Thank you."

"Sorry about that," Michael said, and unceremoniously flopped back into his chair. Rain never ceased to be amazed by how Outsiders moved like wet noodles, yet remained standing and sitting. "So did you tell her the plan?"

"No," Coal said, moving a crumb around on the table. "I waited for you, sir. We spoke of her family in your absence."

"OK. Good." Michael sighed with relief. "I'm surprised you haven't snatched that last apple tart from Ms. Daniels."

Coal shook his head. "I am a gentleman and would never snatch away a woman's dessert after I so generously offered it to her."

"Yes, it was quite generous of you," Rain bantered in kind, but her heart was not it. "Your sacrifice is great, though I find I no longer have an appetite." She gestured toward the plate. "Michael, would you care for the last apple tart?"

"Michael?" Coal's mouth slackened in playful offense.

"Yes, My Lord," Rain teased, biting back a smile. "He is not a rascally goat."

"She would like you," Coal said quietly. The thoughtful look on his face gave her pause. But it quickly altered to a pointed expression as he said to Michael, slowly for emphasis, "Perhaps one day Hanley shall consent for her to visit New Eden." Rain's heart fell to her stomach once more. But she forced a polite smile as he continued. Then she remembered, Hanley was somehow listening. "Michael, will you explain the plan to Lady Rain?"

"Well, we were thinking of home visits during the hour of rest. I would bring in a large team. I imagine we could inoculate every resident, even the infants, within two days."

"I see." Rain wrapped her fingers around the tea mug once more. "When shall you begin?"

"Today." She opened her mouth to protest, but Michael cut her off. "We don't want to disrupt Winter Feasts."

"Yet there is no remorse over interrupting the Ceremonies of Death? The Third Ceremony is tonight following evening meal."

"The Surgeon General has given the lab seven days to comply before imposing heavy fines and sending in health care representatives from the State." Michael lifted his hands in defeat. "Any other ideas?"

Rain's shoulders slumped a notch. "I shall make the Service Announcement during mid-day meal."

"Since The Aether and all other Elements are in quarantine," Michael continued, "we need you to go through the process publicly to demonstrate the easy, non-invasive process."

She looked to Coal in astonishment. "You would ask a lady to behave in such an undignified manner before all? I shall be humiliated, My Lord."

The Son of Fire pushed out of his chair and knelt on one knee before her and bowed his head as he took her hand in his. The tendons in his neck bulged as he clenched his jaw. The kitchen silenced, the only sounds the simmering pottage bubbling over the cook hearth. Though, she knew they could not hear her and Coal speak, not really. Their voices were barely above a hushed whisper. "I would never ask you or any other woman to accept public examination and treatment. But neither can I alter this request, though I tried."

"And if I refuse?"

Coal stiffened. "Hanley granted concession for all other individuals to endure the procedure in the privacy of their homes rather than line up publicly, though it taxes the lab to provide so many hands to visit the apartments." He met her eyes and her breath caught with the fury they contained. The consequences of her refusal were clear. "Please name your honor price for this ungentlemanly request, My Lady. I am entirely at your service."

She had dreamt of this moment more times than she could count. In her reverie, he would kiss her passionately or propose marriage. The gravity of reality changed everything. There was no romance in this gesture, only an echo of her own grievances and sense of helplessness. Tears pooled in her eyes and rolled down her cheeks. She turned her face toward her shoulder, embarrassed.

"I cannot fault you for the choices of others, My Lord."

"Rain…"

"Your kindness shall never be forgotten."

He pleaded silently with his eyes. "My Lady, I shall never forget your courage and bravery."

"I am a head Noble. 'Tis my duty to sacrifice my needs when service to my community requires it." She forced a smile through her tears. "I shall recover, never you worry."

"I shall and will continue to worry."

He pressed the handkerchief back into her hand. Kitchen maids whispered to one another and Rain noted their envious stares beneath lowered lashes. Cook barked at her staff to stop dallying and return to work, and the entire kitchen sprang into action. The gossips would be busy later and Rain closed her eyes in mortification.

"Shall I escort you to your father so I may explain the situation to him?"

"Yes, that may be wise. Thank you," she whispered. "Does Leaf know of the lab's plans to comply with state law?"

"All save the request made of you." Coal shuffled on his feet and darted a nervous glance Michael's way. "The lab agrees with quarantine methods to contain the spreading illness, most especially now that the media has agitated a few human rights activist groups." She raised her eyebrows. "Many in the world feel the community would be happiest if freed from the confines of these walls and integrated into global society."

"Oh Lord," Rain whispered. "Do they not understand that we are happy?"

Coal chuckled with ill-humor. "*They* care not what we think or how we feel, My Lady. *They* measure according to their own moral compass and definition of justice and have no qualms invalidating the true meaning of human freedom."

"How horrifying." Rain dabbed her cheeks to hide her fear, then held out the linen cloth to Coal.

"No, please. It is yours to keep."

"Thank you."

His lips thinned though he smiled, the shadowed look hardening each one of his dashing features. He lifted a hand and gestured toward the exit with a bow. Rain followed Michael out of the building, her heart in her throat. Though her feet moved beneath her, her mind remained anchored. Coal was not speaking of activists when he referred to "they." Rain understood the hidden warning and felt a shiver, one that traveled clear to her toes.

ChAPTER
ThReE

Saturday, December 19, 2054

The hood of Rain's cloak caught on the carved wooden comb in her hair. She had woven a white linen ribbon through her plaits, which she sewed into place away from her face. Lake had broken two of her bone hair pins while attempting to turn them into small sling shots for the stick knights he created. She rolled her eyes with the memory. So she resorted to sewing her hair to keep the cords and braids in place. A much easier feat when her sister visited.

Her fingers held a slight tremor from nerves. Nevertheless, they nimbly unhooked the fabric. Canyon had carved the hair fork last year as a birthday gift, depicting cresting waves, images he had seen in a book. She patted the back of her head and confirmed the complication of knots and ribbons were still in place.

"You look beautiful this evening," her father said.

She kissed him on the cheek. "Thank you, *Père*."

"Do you join the scientists once more this eve?"

"Yes," Rain said, tying the strings to her cloak. "I shall visit the Watsons and Kanes this evening during our rounds."

"Ah," her father knowingly replied. Could he hear how her heart practically sang at the very thought of seeing her friends? Rain remained steady, even when her father smiled conspiratorially. "Please give my regards to both families."

"I shall. See you at evening meal."

With a dip of his head, her father returned to his room to rest and refresh. Unable to hold back her excitement, she opened the entry door and then promptly froze. A figure jumped out at her and threw a flurry of brittle leaves in her face. Rain screamed and clutched at her heart. Her littlest brother laughed until she grabbed him by the tip of his ear and pulled him into their apartment.

"Lake Daniels!"

"Ow! Let go!" He swung an arm toward her but she maneuvered out of the way.

Canyon waltzed into the room and laughed when she swatted Lake's hand as he attempted to free her grip on his ear.

"Little brother," Canyon taunted, "you never learn, do you lad?"

"Come here, Canyon!" Lake growled, throwing another fist at Rain, who pulled on his ear again. "Ow! ... I shall trump you!"

Rain groaned with annoyance. "Will you stop moving about so?"

"Lake Daniels, hold still," their father said from the hallway. He strode over and grabbed his son by the shoulders and Rain released her hold on Lake's ear. "Whatever have you done this time?"

Her littlest brother shot Rain a glare and rubbed his ear. "I simply jumped out from the covering when Rain opened the door to leave."

"And threw leaves in my face," she added.

He scuffed the wooden floor. "And threw leaves in her face," he mumbled.

"Go ahead, daughter. I shall care for Lake, and *remind* him of how a gentleman treats a lady."

Lake deflated. "Not this speech again." He scrunched up his face and stuffed his hands into his pockets. "I am only having fun, sir."

Rain shut the door and heaved a sigh. "Troublesome sprite," she muttered under her breath. After one last check that her hair remained fastened, she trod along the village path toward the Great Hall. The scientists wished to confer with both her and Coal before knocking on doors to administer vaccinations.

Very few residents protested this medical invasion. Those who lifted their voices in outrage soon cooled their opposition to compliance. The choice given was to receive vaccinations and remain in New Eden or be forced to leave the dome and be inoculated in the lab. Re-entry would require approval from both Hanley and Leaf. Any assembled demonstrations would place project continuation at risk. The message was clear.

They had no choice.

Yesterday, during mid-day meal, was beyond humiliating. Rain believed her face would remain permanently stained red with shame. Thankfully, upon hearing the lab's request, her brother Canyon and Father insisted upon standing beside her on the stage. Canyon even went so far as to demand that he receive the inoculations first. Lake, not wishing to be out done by Canyon, announced he would be second. Never had she seen her brothers so protective of her, and she thought she might swoon with gratitude.

Following Canyon's procedure, Lake had stepped forward to receive his inoculations next, chest out, shoulders back, all the while glowering at the small scientist. Rain had trembled when it was her turn. Any and all courage had fled and she stifled the urge to whimper. Michael stuck a small stick with tufted cotton on the end into her mouth and swabbed around. She had stared at the ceiling as he invaded her sense of modesty before all. Crying would give the impression that she was in physical pain, which she was not. Only mortified. She had never been touched so intimately, let alone publicly. Let alone by a man.

Michael had sent her an apologetic frown as he inserted the strange stick into the machine and pushed a button. Words flashed across a screen of sorts as it calibrated to her DNA. How this happened was unclear to Rain.

A small measure of time passed, each heartbeat rushing water in her ears, before the machine spit out a piece of paper with a purple strip adhered to the top. The purple strip, she was told, were the vaccinations. Michael peeled the strip and asked her to open her mouth and lift her tongue.

Once more, she felt violated. To administer the vaccinations, he had held her face with one hand to steady the other hand, which deposited the strip underneath her tongue. As he pulled away, his finger brushed across her bottom lip. She wished to cry from this degradation, but held it in to demonstrate bravery and compliance for the community. The medicine had dissolved with an overly sweet flavor hinting at grapes. Not terribly unpleasant. The younger children especially appreciated this fact.

She clung to these memories with each family she visited yesterday eve. Several young women had cried, same as she. A few of the Outsiders snickered and made jokes about New Eden women being melodramatic, prudish, and ungrateful, as if she were not present to hear their insults. As if she were beneath them.

The disconcerting levels of unkindness and insensitivity tore at her heart. It was her body, not theirs. They did not have permission to decide how she should feel about anything, let alone a medical procedure forced upon her. It had nothing to do with a lack of gratitude—for she was most grateful for the protection—but, rather, a lack of human decency. The world beyond her walled garden may know how to defy mortality, but it was increasingly clear that they possessed little to no respect for life.

"Lady Rain," a voice called from behind.

She froze. Slowly, warily, she spun on her heel to face Jeff Abrams. Everything within her wanted to run while simultaneously remaining stock still. He smiled at nothing in particular, his gaze flitting from one object to another. Perhaps he was just as nervous to be in her presence as she was to be in his. Since her mother died, she had avoided the barrister completely, even at the head table. Her father, however, engaged Jeff in conversation as if nothing were amiss. Her father was ever a kind and forgiving man, though.

"May I walk with you to the Great Hall?"

She dipped her head. "If it pleases you, My Lord."

Dark hair sprinkled with silver fell over his eyes as he ambled toward her on unsteady feet. The walking stick struck the ground and the sound pounded in her head.

"Lovely evening, isn't it?" His head tilted up at the dome sky.

"Yes, quite."

When he reached where she stood, they turned in stride and moved through the village square toward the large, stone building. The breeze was light and stirred her cloak. She fidgeted with the laces and pulled the wool tighter around her person. Faint scents of tallow candles and evergreens spiced the afternoon air and she breathed deeply once more. They remained silent, and Rain focused on the thump of Jeff's walking stick and their padded footfalls shuffling across the dirt path.

"I hear Lake temporarily disabled the waterwheel yesterday morn." Jeff chuckled, disrupting their quiet. "He is a fiery one."

"Lake did not mean to disrupt mill production," she was quick to defend.

Jeff lifted his hands in amnesty. "Forgive me. I meant no offense. I simply find your brother's temperament amusing." With a side glance, Jeff said, "He reminds me of Noah."

"You knew my uncle?" Rain blinked back her surprise. She had only heard tales of Uncle Noah, her mother's younger brother, and only from her mother. It never occurred to her that others within New Eden might have known him, too, or any of her extended family for that matter.

"We were next-door neighbors," Jeff continued. "Norah's bedroom window faced mine. We spent many nights talking to each other through the tree that separated our yards."

He smiled to himself with the memory and Rain's heart panged. Within the dome, her mother had been a happily married woman. What on Earth would lead her toward the arms of another? Even one she had known for so long? They fell into silence, much to her relief. There was nothing she wished to say. But she would need to get used to conversing with him, she knew. As an Element, she would certainly face many more meetings with the village's lawyer. Perhaps so long as they focused solely on business, she could keep the haunting personal matters at bay. To encourage this, she changed the subject. "My Lord, are we in danger of violating any other state laws?"

Jeff spared her a quick glance. "No, I believe this may be the only one. I should say 'major one,' to be more specific."

"You keep abreast with current laws, then?"

"Yes. It is required to remain licensed to practice law, actually." Her eyebrows pulled together in question. Noting her look, he volunteered, "I possess a Cranium in addition to a Scroll."

He stopped and turned toward her. His hands trembled upon the walking stick and his eyes twitched. It appeared as though it took great effort to contain his body, which jerked with tremors on occasion. For a long while she had thought perhaps he was just anxious. Was he afflicted in some other capacity?

"My cousin, John, is Hanley's lawyer," he began again. "I've been in contact with him recently to ensure the wellbeing of our colony."

"I see." Rain smiled politely. "It must be nice to see family." Then she cringed, realizing her words.

"Oh, I have not visited him at the lab." Jeff shook his head. "I do not desire to enter that world ever again." Goosebumps prickled her skin with his words, words spoken as he gazed at The Rows.

She began walking once more, needing to reach the Great Hall and extricate herself from his presence. Though, she would remain polite until then. She was an Element and he the town lawyer; they would spend much time together for business purposes. She could manage a surface relationship for the sake of her community.

Her thoughts skipped around while thinking of Lake's foolhardy antics yesterday morn with the waterwheel. The metal box rested under her cot in her chamber, where it remained closed. It was most curious. The items inside disturbed her, however. The contents rightfully belonged to Skylar or his mother. Still, curiosity plagued her thoughts until, against her better judgment, she opened up conversation with Jeff once more.

"My Lord, have you ever seen a life-like image on paper of real people? One that appears as though glimpsing into a memory?"

Jeff thought for a moment. "I think you are describing a photograph."

"Is it made from magic?"

His eyes softened. "No. It's a way Outsiders hold on to memories, just as you suggested. The photograph is crafted through technology."

"Does the technology steal time in order to reflect this memory?" The very idea made her shudder.

"It gifts time by making a mere pebble of sand in one's hourglass immortal." She pondered his explanation with wonder. "Did you discover a photograph, My Lady?"

"Yesterday morn." Rain did not like to think of Timothy as sentimental. It was a rather upsetting thought. "Thank you, My Lord. I appreciate your time."

"Always," he said softly.

The warmth in his eyes stilled the air in her chest. He knew. Rain looked away, lest he see her distress. From the corner of her eye, she studied his thick, dark hair, a shade of molasses like hers. The hands on the walking stick reflected creamy beige skin tones, also similar to hers. Unlike her family, who were rosy-hued, or most others in New Eden, who seemed pale in comparison. His brown eyes possessed the same golden outer ring as hers as well, an attribute she appreciated once when given opportunity to gaze into a hand-held looking glass. How had she not noticed before her mother's deathbed confession? Had others noticed?

She was his daughter.

No, she was the daughter of Alex Daniels, the man who had raised her and treated her as though his own. The very thought was humbling. She focused on her footsteps, too afraid to meet Jeff's eyes. A few heartbeats later, they reached the Great Hall entrance and Jeff opened the door for her with a bow.

"Thank you for your company, My Lady."

Rain angled her head his direction, but averted her eyes. "You are welcome, My Lord. Good evening time." He journeyed toward the large hearth and joined a group of men. She released a tight breath and moved toward the small gathering of scientists while fortifying what remained of her nerves.

"There she is," Michael said. "Nice to see you, Ms. Daniels."

She lowered into a shallow curtsy. "You wished to speak with me, sir?" Rain looked around. "Is Coal not here?"

"He has left with a team already." Michael slung a bag over his shoulder. "We are splitting you up to cover more ground tonight. He's with the group who'll visit the Watsons."

"I am sure he shall appreciate the opportunity to visit with his sister," Rain said, hiding her disappointment. She longed to see Oaklee and Ember as well. It had been a frightful past few days without feminine company. Then a spark of hope flickered in her heart. "Am I to visit the Kanes?"

"Yes." Michael pointed to the exit and gestured for the seven scientists to follow. "Ready, Ms. Daniels?"

Rather than reply, she simply walked beside Michael. Eventually they reached the lower apartments along the village path not too far from the East Cave. The scientists split into groups of two, each team knocking upon a door. Rain remained outside and greeted each family, reassuring the young and old that the scientists would care for their needs.

CHAPTER FOUR

The hour of rest was nearly over when they stood before the Kane apartment. She convinced Michael to leave this home for last so she could visit with Lady Emily a spell before evening meal. He accommodated her further by allowing her to fetch the metal box for Skylar first.

Rain knocked upon the wooden door with bated breath. Why was she so nervous? As each heartbeat of time passed by, her anxiety leapt higher until she thought surely her pulse would fly away. To die of anticipation was not nearly as romantic as it sounded. The door creaked open and Skylar peeked through, his mouth parting slightly when recognizing her.

"My Lady?" he whispered. Worry wrinkled his forehead in that adorable way of his. "You fare well, I hope?"

"Yes, My Lord. Thank you for your kind inquiry." She offered a shaky smile. "Scientists from the lab have come to inoculate your family, if they may?"

Skylar opened the door wider and stood straighter. "Yes, of course."

She stepped into his home and moved aside to allow Michael and Sam, a fellow scientist, to enter. Skylar shut the door and spared her a passing glance as she lowered her hood, considering the box under her arm. Then his attention whipped back to her face, his gaze trailing over her hair and the curve of her cheek, before looking away. Pleased with his response, Rain bit back a smile.

In this moment, it was clear just how juvenile her flutters of excitement were around the Son of Fire. They were silly romantic fancies, nothing more. Nothing like what danced through her veins now so near the Son of Wind.

"May I take your cloak?" he offered.

She infused elegance into her movements and cast her eyes down with modesty as a woman would, rather than a blushing girl. Skylar took her cloak with a bow and hung it on the wall. She deposited the metal box below her cloak, then clasped her hands at her waist. His mouth lifted in a ghost of a smile as he met her eyes and she stared, riveted. Skylar smiled. *Smiled.* And for her! She was quite sure she was drowning this very moment, wholly submerged in every dizzying sensation.

"Rain, how delightful," Skylar's mother said from the hallway. Her voice held weakness and she seemed wobbly on her feet, yet strength emanated from her in a way that filled Rain with instant happiness. Windlyn and Gale-Anne crowded around their mother and eyed the Outsiders warily. "Lovely to see you," Lady Emily said.

Rain dropped into a curtsy and placed a hand over her heart. "My Lady, it gives me great pleasure to see you looking so well." Windy shuffled behind her mother's back. "And you as well, Windlyn."

"Thank you," Skylar's sister said in a small voice. She shrank back into the shadows of the hallway under the attention.

"Well, OK to get started?" Michael asked. Rain nearly forgot they accompanied her. "This is our last house. Skylar, willing to go first?"

"I am already inoculated, sir. The members of the Techsmith Guild were as children."

"I knew that, sorry." Michael pulled the printing machine from his bag. "Long couple of days. So, who's up next, then?"

Gale-Anne stepped forward. "I shall go first, sir." She tossed long, brown tresses over her shoulder and bounced on the balls of her toes, her nose turned upward in a glowering expression. Rain could not blame her.

Michael showed her all the tools and she relayed her understanding of the process. "Open your mouth," he said, holding up the stick with the tufted cotton end. "And hold still. It'll go faster that way." Gale narrowed her eyes, but complied. Michael stuck the swab in the machine and allowed her to push the button. That seemed to please her. The medicine printed off and he peeled it from the backing. "Open your mouth again. This time lift your tongue." He placed the medicine in her mouth and Gale bit down on his finger. Michael howled and yanked his finger back. "What the—"

"Gale-Anne Kane!" Skylar said. "That was entirely unnecessary." His face burned, but he remained cool despite the obvious embarrassment. His sister retreated to their mother with a smug smile. Lady Emily paled as she darted attention between Skylar and Michael.

"No, it's all right," Michael offered. "I get it."

Skylar frowned. "We do not resort to violence in this house to make our opinions clear." He knelt before his sister and took her hands in his. "I understand the offense. But you were never in danger. I would never allow him to harm you."

"He stuck his finger in my mouth!" Gale removed her hands and turned her back to Skylar. "It was rude! He ought to be ashamed of himself."

Lady Emily draped an arm around Gale. "There is no context for this experience, My Lord."

"I know," Skylar mumbled.

"I'm not upset." Michael gave Gale a friendly smile. "Way to defend yourself."

"Thank you, sir," she said, sticking her tongue out at Skylar. "See?"

He drew in a deep breath and peered down the hallway. "My other sister has retreated to her bedchamber. I am not so certain after this…"

"I shall administer the medicine to her, My Lord. Never you worry," Rain said, coaxing the printing machine from Michael's hands. "I have seen well over a hundred procedures."

"Wait." Michael's fingers flew across the screen. "There. It's ready."

Skylar touched her forearm. "Do you wish for my company?"

Yes, her pulse shouted. "No, My Lord," she managed in reply and daintily cleared her throat. "I think her modesty is best preserved among women."

"Of course."

"Lady Emily?" Rain asked, turning toward the hallway. In a few steps, both she and Windlyn's mother stood before her door and knocked. "Windlyn, 'tis Rain Daniels. May I come in?"

A quiet voice acknowledged her request and Rain opened the door. Tears stained Windy's cheeks as she sat upon her cot, knees drawn up to her chest and arms wrapped tight around her nightgown-draped legs.

"Will he touch me?" Windy looked past Rain and Lady Emily to the shadows. She coughed and her body spasmed.

"No, he shall not." Rain gestured to the cot. "May I?"

Windy nodded and Rain sank beside her. Out of the two sisters, Windy resembled Skylar the most. Light brown hair flowed in gentle waves to her waist. Hazel eyes fixed onto the printing machine as the color drained from her face. This made the faint smattering of freckles across her nose—what Rain's mother would call faerie kisses—more prominent. Skylar also had freckles, which made him appear boyish, though his stature was anything but.

"It does not hurt in the least, I promise. You might even enjoy the flavor of the medicine. It is like sweetened wine." Rain handed Windy the stick. "Here, hold this."

"What is this, My Lady?"

"It is a swab. Place it into your mouth and paint your inner-check until I say stop." Windlyn followed her directions, including the one to insert the swab into the designated place in the machine. A few heartbeats later they were done. "See?" Rain took Windy's hand in hers. "Painless, no?"

Windy gifted a small smile and leaned into her mother. Rain brushed a loose strand from her face and tucked it behind her ear. She was twelve, well on her way to womanhood. But her meek, timid demeanor made her appear younger than Gale-Anne at times. She was far more frail, that was for sure, and had been all her life.

"You have such beautiful eyes," Rain said with a kind smile. "They are so bright and bonny when touched by tears." She looked to Lady Emily. "Are they not?"

"Yes, indeed." Lady Emily caressed the long strands of Windy's hair and Rain's heart constricted. Oh how she missed a mother's touch. "Such lovely hair as well."

"Much like yours," Rain said. "In the sunlight it glistens as though covered in misty dew. So very romantic." Rain sighed as she looked to Windy. "May I comb your hair?"

Skylar's sister nodded bashfully. Rain practically squealed as she danced to the vanity for the wooden comb. For a measure of time, she lost herself to the task of combing and plaiting Windlyn's long strands. Lady Emily quietly sang a song in French, and Rain thought her heart would burst.

"I am so happy the earlier medicine has encouraged your recovery," Rain said, resting her head against Windy's as she embraced her from behind. "You were so very ill and I was much worried for you." A knock on the bedroom door startled her. "Oh! I forgot about Michael and Sam!"

Skylar opened the door and drew his eyebrows together. "Is all well?"

"Yes, My Lord." Rain stood and fussed with the tucks and folds of her skirt. "I was simply braiding your sister's hair. My apologies. I did not mean to take so long."

"No apology necessary." Skylar regarded his mother and sister, and his face softened. "May I return the printer to Michael? He seems eager to find Coal and return to the lab." She walked the machine to where he stood in the doorway.

Gale-Anne pushed past him and gawked at her sister. Rain had pinned part of Windlyn's hair up in an elaborate fashion. What she would give for a looking glass! Taking a step toward the youngest sister, Rain asked, "Would you care to join us, Gale?"

"Can you do that to my hair?"

"With delight!" Rain picked up a strand of Gale's hair and pretended to inspect the earthen, brown tresses. "Though, I do believe you need ribbons."

"I love ribbons," Gale-Anne said with a large grin.

Rain smiled in kind. "Yes, I thought so. Shall you fetch me your favorites?" The youngest Kane bumped past Skylar as she dashed to her room. Skylar stared at Rain, unmoving, as though a statue carved into an eternal state of bewilderment. His eyes, however, revealed everything—gratitude, admiration, and confusion. She slid him a smile as she lowered her gaze. "May I trouble you for a favor, My Lord?"

"Anything. I am entirely at your service, My Lady."

"Excuse me but a moment," Rain said to Lady Emily and Windlyn as she strode past Skylar toward the living room. "Michael, here is the printer. All is well, sir." She pointed to the machine in Skylar's hand.

"Thanks." The scientist appeared relieved, stuffing the device back into his bag. "See you on Winter Solstice."

"Remember, you shall sit beside my family."

"I look forward to it, Ms. Daniels."

She walked him to the door as if this were her own apartment. When he and Sam disappeared down the village path, she tugged on Skylar's tunic sleeve as she stepped outside.

"Rain," he whispered. "Your kindness—"

"It is nothing." She dismissed him with a wave of her hand. "It has been days since I have enjoyed the company of other women. I am quite selfish, really."

He took her hand, which had still fluttered about in the air as she spoke. "You are generous and compassionate." Slowly, he bowed over her hand in honor. "Whatever you ask of me, My Lady, I am yours to command."

Rain could not help the blush that warmed her cheeks, especially when he did not release her hand. Nor did she know how to reply. "Skylar," she began and stopped.

"You may call me Sky. I prefer it, actually."

"Sky…"

"Yes?"

Her entire body was in upheaval, from the muscles in her stomach which tightened with pleasure, to the fear stealing her breath. These were not the flutters of girlhood fancies. It was as if drops of moonlight had mixed with a warm, summer breeze and touched her pulse.

Returning to her senses, though reluctantly, she professed, "I was not seeking this manner of favor from you. I hope you do not think me forward."

"Not in the least. These are my sentiments unprovoked."

"Thank the Lord, for I would die of embarrassment."

His forehead wrinkled again and she resisted the urge to smile. "Please … please allow me to show my gratitude. Whatever you ask…"

She flushed deeper. The only request she desired to make this moment was for a kiss. Not a chaste kiss upon a cheek as before. But she could not ask for one, of any kind, not really. Though, she longed to know if his lips were soft, if he would cradle her face, or perhaps if she would lose her heart completely, never to be recovered. She touched her cheek with her free hand as the feverish musings swirled about endlessly in her head.

"Are you well?" His gaze followed the hand now resting upon her cheek. "Shall we return inside so you may sit?" He tugged gently on the hand he still held, but they did not travel far. The door whipped open. Skylar dropped her hand and she startled, jumping back a step.

"Are you leaving?" Gale-Anne asked her. The words were laced with disappointment and Rain melted a smidgen. "I have my ribbons."

"Oh, how pretty." Rain fingered the linen ribbons, some stitched with embroidered designs of flowers and leaves. "I shall be there shortly, never you worry."

Gale-Anne looked at her brother. "Do not consume all of her time for yourself, My Lord," she said, then skipped away, slamming the door behind her.

An awkward tension plucked the air in the wake of her words. The village path and forest were quiet and wrapped her and Skylar in an intimate hush. They were friends, nothing more; she had said as much just a few days prior and he had echoed her sentiments. Rain took another step backward. "Has your sister mentioned a missing doll, perchance?" The words seemed forced, but safer.

Skylar's shoulders relaxed a notch. "Have you found it?"

"Lake threw it into the millrace. I am afraid it is ruined beyond repair." She chanced a look up at him. "I am so very sorry. I shall make her another that my brother will deliver along with a proper apology."

He nodded his head, then focused on the forest. The strange tension returned. A light breeze played with the front strands of his hair. She could not look away, jealous of the wind. What she would give to know his thoughts this moment. But he was private, a quality she found both frustrating and attractive. The idea of privacy jarred her memory and she lifted her hand in exclamation.

"Goodness, I nearly forgot. I have a box of sorts that belongs to you." She pushed open his entry door, retrieved the metal chest beneath her cloak, and returned. "In your sister's room I spoke of a favor."

"Yes?"

"I simply wished for privacy as I did not know whether you permitted your sisters to see the contents. Or if they would upset your mother." Rain extended the chest to him. "Somehow, this box ended up in the millrace." Skylar's eyebrows drew together as he frowned. "Look at the base. Does that not appear to be your surname, Sky?"

"Indeed it is." He looked to her. "I have never seen this box until now."

"Please forgive me, I did not mean to pry. The box fell off my vanity and sprung open." She bit her bottom lip and lifted her shoulders. Before he could react, she spoke quickly and continued. "Inside are the strangest playing cards I have ever seen and a phot ... phot..." She could not remember the full word. "A frozen memory on shiny paper."

"Photograph?" he asked. Skylar slid the latch to the side and the lid popped open.

Rain's eyes widened. "You know of photographs?"

"Yes, I have taken a few with my Cranium." Her mouth hung open, then she remembered her manners. Though he did not see, far too focused. He rifled through the contents, his expression growing more grave. A muscle throbbed in his jaw and neck, and he shut the lid, clearing his throat, mumbling, "Thank you, My Lady."

"Of course."

Rain sobered with his switch back to formality. Skylar shifted on his feet, his body rigid, face hard but bland. Time yawned before them once more and she somehow remained quiet. Ever so many questions skipped across her mind, though.

Finally, he spared her a fleeting glance and asked, "Are you sure there is naught I can do for you?"

Skylar looked everywhere but her direction and Rain's heart sank. When agitated or troubled, her father and Canyon needed an occupation to work through their frustrations. Whatever Skylar had found in the box had clearly upset him, though he attempted to hide behind stoicism, as usual. Rain thought for a moment—wishing to help him—until an idea surfaced.

She touched his forearm and his eyes locked onto her fingers. "May I trouble you to find my father in the Great Hall and inform him that I shall arrive late? I would not wish for him to worry over my absence."

"It is no trouble at all, My Lady."

"Even though you are in quarantine?"

"My sisters are in quarantine, not I. But the community did not know I was inoculated."

"Sky—"

"My Lady, I shall deliver your message with haste as evening meal is well underway by now."

Skylar bowed and immediately turned on his heel and left, metal box tucked under his arm. Did she imagine his relief? Rain fidgeted with the hem of her sleeve and nibbled on her bottom lip. She watched him fade into the dusky light then reached for the iron ring on their front entry. But it swung open before her fingers even made contact and she stifled a startled gasp.

Gale-Anne popped her head out the door again with an exasperated sigh. "Come on, My Lady, before I expire from anticipation!"

"Oh dear. We cannot have that, now can we?"

Rain chuckled, especially when Gale grabbed her by the arm and tugged her back inside. It did her heart good to spend time with Skylar's family. But she could not shake the way grief had come over him nor the way he had dashed away. Perhaps photographs were another way for Outsiders to negotiate their mortality rather than truly live. No one, she decided, should have to bury their loved ones over and over again.

CHAPTER FIVE

Monday, December 21, 2054

B lasted reeds," Rain muttered under her breath. She pushed away the spear-like plants to traverse the edge of the outlet filter in the wetland overflow pond. The clop of her soft-soled shoes along the floating boardwalk drummed to the melodic cacophony of chirping insects.

Today, the community celebrated Yuletide. Most did no work, except for the necessities. And it was necessity that brought Rain to the wetland room to dredge organic material. The outlet had clogged with sediment. This was becoming a rather common problem since the Blood Rains. She longed to visit with her friends and join the celebration. Alas, only one more round. The water was already trickling at a steady pace.

The floating bridge wobbled as she leaned over. Rain grasped a handful of cattails to remain balanced and drug her bucket through the yellow-tinted water. She righted herself and remained still as the boardwalk undulated up and down. Feeling the rhythm beneath her feet, she set off back toward the entrance with her somewhat pungent load. The organic material released a most unpleasant odor when decomposing.

Up above, the sky was a hazy blue. In this room in particular, with only mid-height vegetation to block the view, the sky seemed infinite. Many found this room unnerving, their sense of balance and perception of depth askew. But, to Rain, it was breathtaking. Dragonflies skipped through the air. Frogs croaked in harmony, filling the constructed swamp with music she imagined the insects and other aquatic animals danced to as they went about their merry day.

The door came into sight as she rounded a corner on the curved, floating walk. Seventeen buckets of dredged material sat along the wall where she had deposited them. Canyon had left to empty two buckets in the compost and had yet to return, and that was well over an hour ago. She supposed he could finish this task tomorrow after the festivities—unlike her.

To wait another day to unclog the overflow pond invited a flood, a reality caused by the still filtering water from the Blood Rains. The domes were hermetically sealed. Their ground eventually led to a puncture-resistant liner, buried on a slope to direct water toward the wetland sump. From here, water was filtered through the natural plant and soil systems and stored in a holding tank, then allocated to the well and various streams, ponds, rainwater pipes, and more. Details swirled about in her head as she drew her eyebrows together.

The muscles in her arms shook. She set the bucket upon the walk, stretched her back and rolled her shoulders. Lifting a rag from her belt, she dabbed her forehead. Sweat dripped down the side of her cheek. A scarf held her hair back from her face but, in her rush, she had not fully tied her tresses back. Rain scrunched up her hair and enjoyed a cool breeze across the back of her neck.

Feeling rested enough, she hefted her load and continued her march back to the door. Rain nearly giggled when she lined up the final bucket next to the others along the wall. One last task: empty the slag from The Forge to the incoming gray water to help remove unhealthy levels of phosphorous. The inlet was near where she stood and, within a few heartbeats, she had emptied the slag bucket in the first of several gravel filters.

Now she was done—finally! Wiping her hands on the rag hanging from her belt, she opened the door from the wetland ancillary dome to the heat of the Mediterranean biome. It was time to ready herself for Yuletide.

Back in her chamber, Rain shimmied out of her work clothes with a wrinkled nose and tossed them toward her laundry basket. Her head scarf, too. Tomorrow was laundry day, thank goodness. She dunked her hair into a bucket of fresh water then lathered her dark, thick tresses with hair soap. Rinsing was more difficult, but accomplished without too much spillage. Once clean, she rubbed lotions, lightly scented with orange blossom, into her skin.

Dressed in a finer gown and hair decorated with a holly wreath, she twirled with arms stretched out. Nothing could dim her mood this moment. She felt positively giddy for she would see her friends, drink wassail late into the night, and dance. Rain threw open the shutters and pushed her window panes out so that she could study the shadows and determine the time. Just as the cool air touched her skin, a small head jumped up with a roar and she screamed.

"Lake Daniels!"

A chunk of red hair fell over his green eyes as he laughed. The freckles dotting his entire face were far too adorable in the dappled light, however, and her ire slowly trickled away. But, not completely. "I did not throw leaves in your face this time," he said with satisfaction, as if he had accomplished a hero's feat in restraining himself.

"Have you waited there long?"

"Yes! You take an eternity to ready." Lake shook his head. "Whatever were you doing?"

"A gentleman never asks a lady what she does in the privacy of her chamber."

Lake blew the hair out of his eyes and stuffed his hands into his pockets. "I am not a gentleman. I am only seven years old."

"A perfect age to practice. Here," Rain said, handing him Gale-Anne's new rag doll through the window. "You may begin with this peace offering and an apology."

Lake's shoulders fell. "Do I have to?"

"Yes. Now shoo!"

Rain gestured for him to run along. Lake needed no further encouragement and scampered away toward the village.

How boys transitioned from bothersome pests to men who made her pulse skip a beat and her head swim in a flood of pleasurable sensations was beyond her. Perhaps this was the true definition of magic.

With that latter thought in mind, she shut her window, grabbed her cloak, and left her apartment.

Memories of the past few days spent with Coal and Skylar swirled through her head to the pace of her strides. At sixteen, she was a woman in transition. Girlhood was a not-so-distant memory, though most of it was spent caring for her mother. Rain shook her head clear of all the nonsensical cobwebs clouding her judgment. And the grief. She was tired of feeling resentful of each initial carved into the linden tree. Love should be magic, not desperation.

This new perspective bloomed in her heart. Rather than dash her hopes upon every handsome smile tossed her way, Rain decided she would enjoy the friendly flirtations, beginning this night. Perhaps one day she would marry. Until then, her helpless romantic fancies could flutter away as they pleased.

Feeling lighter already, Rain hummed a merry tune and picked up her pace.

On the edge of the village square, a Yule tree boasted garlands made from linen scraps knotted together. Salt dough and gingerbread ornaments hung from the tips of several boughs. Rain touched a dangling star swaying in the light breeze, and smiled.

Music poured out of the Great Hall in festive beats. Anticipation crawled over her skin until she could not help but bounce on the balls of her toes. Candlelight flickered wherever she looked, glinting off window panes and spilling golden amber hues across the stone walls and wooden rafters. Every candelabra was lit, from the wrought iron wheels suspended from the ceiling, and garnished in holly garlands, to the freestanding taper holders on each table, to the lanterns resting upon each window sill.

Winter Solstice was always a grand affair in New Eden. Today, the community celebrated the Oak King's triumph over the Holly King, the Lord of Winter, a Neopagan Yuletide tradition many residents embraced prior to Moving Day. Her own mother, once belonging to a coven in the Outside world, had participated in many a mummer's play regaling the story of life, death, and rebirth during Samhain, Yule, Beltane, and Litha.

Coincidentally, this year, Samhain had fallen upon the Second Ceremony of Death held in honor of their township, the Cremation Ceremony being the Great Fire itself. The very memory painted Rain's skin in goosebumps. Following mass for All Saint's Day, the residents normally feasted to celebrate the end of Harvest and welcome the darker days of winter. This year, however, the community forwent the festivities and embraced the season of death in their unified bereavement. The ashes of the village mixed with the ashes of loved ones, and only because a founding Element had betrayed them all. The pain had been too fresh then for any form of celebration— unlike today.

Rain angled through the revelry, exchanging "blessed Yuletide" greetings with villagers. A kitchen maid placed a tumbler of wassail in her hands, kissing her cheek in greeting. The hot mulled ale warmed her fingers and she inhaled the spicy fragrance with delight.

Midwinter reflected a whole new meaning this Yule season. The Earth Element house was seen as the mighty oak and Leaf openly proclaimed the King. New Eden breathed in the allegory of hope with abandon, for the Oak King's victory ends the Lord of Winter's reign of death and darkness and secures the sun's rebirth. The spring of their lives would soon arrive. Rain closed her eyes and allowed the sweeping joy to touch every shadow in her heart. Vaccinations, deceits, ruined reputations, and sickness were pushed aside to be contemplated another day.

"There you are, you silly goose!" Rain's eyes flew open with the sound of Oaklee's voice, and she grinned. Candlelight caressed her friend's golden hair in dancing shimmers, a magical sight that elicited a wistful sigh from Rain. "Blessed Yuletide, My Lady," Oaklee said with melodramatic flair, dropping into a curtsy.

"I have missed you." Rain pulled Oaklee into a quick embrace and kissed her cheeks. "A toast, Your Highness." Rain lifted her tumbler in salute. "May dancing and merriment be ours this night!"

"Cheers!"

She slipped Oaklee a playful look. "And the smiles of handsome men."

"Rain Daniels!" Oaklee squealed. "You say such shocking things."

"Stop being so pretentious." She pushed away Oaklee's reaction with a sweep of her hand. "Feign your sensibilities all you like, Willow Oak Watson. I, for one, enjoy the attentions and shall relish each notice." Rain sighed and placed the back of her hand upon her brow. "Do catch me should I swoon."

"Dear Lord in Heaven." Oaklee groaned and rolled her eyes, though her mouth quirked with humor. "I fear my arms shall tire quickly."

"True." Rain laughed in reply. "I shall try to restrain myself."

"I am not so certain that is possible."

With a conspiratorial smile, Rain threaded her arm through Oaklee's until they formed a knot, each drinking out of her own tumbler. Both erupted into giggles as they pulled away, looping their arms together once more to promenade around the room.

Rain rose on her tip-toes, waiting for a small congestion to clear, and peered over the undulating crowd to the head table. Many seats were absent, but she noted her father and Michael engaged in conversation with Connor, Lady Brianna, and Lady Emily. Coal sat across from Leaf and Ember, laughing at his youngest brother, Blaze, who sat upon his lap. Windlyn bashfully cast surreptitious looks to Canyon, much to Rain's humor, while Lake snuck a sugar biscuit from a plate and bounded toward the great hearth where other children played.

On the other side of the room from the head table, men and women danced by the stage as the musicians plucked lively tunes. Most, however, laughed with heads bent in conversation at tables. It was as if the recent outbreak of influenza and required vaccinations were all but forgotten, a mere wisp of a memory. Rain was glad and returned her attention to the musicians.

A new song began and Rain bounced to the rhythm of the Celtic drum. With a mischievous smile, Oaklee grabbed Rain's empty tumbler and placed it on a dish return cart. They moved through the gathering, poised with the refined elegance befitting their station. Though, Rain knew, given the opportunity, they would dash to the dance floor with unfettered glee.

Eventually they arrived on the outskirts of the dance floor and Rain exhaled loudly with impatience. She clasped Oaklee's hands and waited, the anticipation roaring in her veins. When the beat returned, they stepped onto the floor and flew across the room with the other dancers.

The wind created by their movements rushed around Rain and she grinned, enjoying the feel of her hair swishing in tempo to the music. Laughter bubbled from her chest, much the same as it did from Oaklee's. Round and round they swung, their dresses fanning around their legs, the world gloriously spinning about in a haze of happiness.

The beat suddenly slowed and Rain lifted her hand and joined the forming carole dance. Fingertips touched in a star as they—the dancers—rotated together in the center. Through the tangle of limbs, a pair of hazel eyes caught hers and Rain's breath fluttered. The circle widened and the dancers took hold of each other's hands and continued to step in motion around the center of the dance floor.

Skylar held fast to Gale-Anne's hand. He did not dance often, but Rain was glad he indulged his littlest sister. Their glances touched once more and Rain smiled. He was so very handsome, especially in candlelight. Her heart refused to remain calm.

The tempo changed and the Celtic drums carried her away. She and Oaklee skipped across the floor and continued to reel until the last beat. Her chest heaved for breath when the song ended. Oaklee clapped in appreciation before threading her arm with Rain's and leading them off the dance floor.

"Shall we sample more wassail?" Oaklee asked her.

"Indeed, Your Highness." Rain smiled. "Mayhap we should stand by the kitchens and request drinks until we fall into our beds."

Oaklee's eyes darted next to Rain just as Rain felt a tug on her dress sleeve.

"Lady Rain," Gale said excitedly. "Thank you ever so much for my new doll."

"You are most welcome." Rain smiled in reply. "Did Lake apologize to you like a proper gentleman?"

"Lake? A gentleman?" Gale-Anne started giggling and turned to her brother, humor fading into a lopsided smile. "My Lord, may I join Laurel and Corona?"

"Yes, of course."

No sooner had Skylar finished when Gale-Anne gamboled to the other end of the room.

The Hall thundered with activity. But, it all felt distant, removed as Rain took in Skylar's stately presence. He wore a light-colored tunic, edged in tablet-woven trim in a darker shade. The material draped across his broad shoulders and chest, the sleeves ending just past his elbows. A dark leather belt was knotted loosely around his waist and hung down to mid-thigh. Light brown hair, somewhat rumpled from dancing, fell over his forehead and drew attention to his eyes, which appeared golden in the candlelight.

Rain's breath quickened when his gaze locked with hers. Oaklee studied her, then Skylar, then her again. It was almost comical, except Rain felt self-conscious. Flushed from the dancing, she lifted her hands to her cheeks. His forehead wrinkled with worry and Rain bit back a smile.

"Lady Rain, may I escort you and Her Highness to chairs?"

Oaklee, her face perfectly serious, replied, "Lady Rain is definitely in need of a chair, My Lord. I fear she might faint at any moment." The mischievous twinkle in her friend's eye nearly made Rain laugh aloud. Oaklee angled toward her and asked, her lips twitching, "Is this not so, My lady?"

"Yes, I do suddenly feel quite lightheaded."

Skylar blinked back the concern tightening his features as he offered his arm. Delicately, Rain placed her hand upon his forearm and allowed him to lead her toward the head table. They remained silent and her mind began to wander where it should not. She stole a glimpse over her shoulder at Oaklee, who smothered a smile behind her hand. Her friend could be such an imp.

"Please excuse me, My Lady," Oaklee said. "I shall fetch us more wassail." With a curtsy and a secretive smile, she kissed Rain's cheek then wended through the milling crowd and disappeared.

Now she and Skylar were alone. Though not considered improper in a public setting such as this. The entire community chaperoned their interaction, unlike their clandestine moment in the woods and their private conversation by his doorstep. Stalwart friend and refined gentleman, Skylar was the furthest thing from a rascally goat. Oblivious to his own charms, the Son of Wind never failed to make her feel like a woman grown in his company.

Rain's fingers tingled where they touched Skylar's arm and her heart faltered a beat. And then another. She was positively breathless.

"Thank you, Sky," she managed to say through all the heady sensations. "You are kind to concern yourself with my welfare."

"'Tis no trouble at all, I assure you," he whispered back in reply. "I am quite selfish, really."

Was that humor? She began to laugh when he smiled. Not a ghost of a smile as delivered in past exchanges. No, his entire face had transformed as his gaze lingered on her face. *Dear Lord.* He was the most dashing man her eyes had ever beheld.

Perhaps it was all the dancing, or possibly the wassail. But his smile was the last image she saw as the world happily dimmed away to the speed of her fluttering heart.

Doubt thou the stars are fire,
Doubt that the sun doth move,
Doubt truth to be a liar,
But never doubt I love.

—William Shakespeare, *Hamlet*, Act 2, Scene 2, 1603 *

I love people who make me laugh. I honestly think it's the thing I like most, to laugh. It cures a multitude of ills. It's probably the most important thing in a person.

—Audrey Hepburn, Hollywood actress, 20th century *

Rare as is true love, true friendship is rarer.

—Jean de La Fontaine, poet, 17th century *

CHAPTER ONE

Malibu, California

Saturday, April 3, 2055

Year one of Project Phase Two

Smack!

A stinging heat spread across Mack's bare ass. "Woman! Trying to sleep," he slurred into his pillow. Damn. Something had withered and died in his mouth. A nasty after-taste coated his tongue and he almost grimaced. Almost. That would take too much energy. Sleep…

"Get up," a female voice commanded nearby. One that was deeper, older, and—

Mack squinted open his eyes and finally grimaced. The light, it hurt. So did the face staring at him with expectancy. "Shit. Kris, what in the hell are you doing here?"

"It's my house."

He looked at the blurry shadow of his mom who was sporting enormously styled victory rolls in a rockabilly hairdo. That was weird. Had he died and woken up a hundred years in the past? He had to be drunk dreaming. The alcohol still swished around in his brain and filled his eyeballs.

Wait.

The girl.

Did that really happen? God he hoped so. Fuzzy brained, he turned his head to the other side of the bed. Empty.

"She's gone. Left hours ago." A pause. "Cute thing."

"Good." Mack rolled his head the other direction and closed his eyes. He hated awkward hook-up goodbyes. "Go away," he said into his pillow. "Mack no chatty. Mack sleepy."

His mom walked past him and he slid one eye open just enough to ensure she wasn't going to smack his ass again.

"Last chance. Get up."

He groaned. "It's Saturday, woman!"

"You're the minister for my wedding today. Remember?"

Mack heard the words but they dissolved into his beclouded thoughts. The alcohol, however, had no problem commandeering his tongue. "Preacher man ... I already went to church last night, desu. The altar was—" A screeching noise scratched the air in a high whine and he covered his ears. "Oh god," he cried out. Then light—bright, painful, all-consuming light—poured in from the window. He threw his hands to his eyes and hissed. Like the hiss of incinerating ashes. "What is this bright, orange orb in the sky that mocks me with its warmth?"

His mom laughed and he cracked his eyes into a glare. The sun glinted off her light purple hair and the strand of pearls around her neck. For a moment, she looked wholesome and sweet. He knew better.

"I warned you."

"No, you said 'last chance.' Not the same as 'be prepared for your retinas to burn from looking into the fires of hell.'" Mack pushed up to a sitting position and sat on the edge of the bed. "I'm up. Shit. Make it stop."

"Hey, he's finally up," a woman commented from the doorway.

Mack cupped his eyes to block the sunlight and peered in the direction of the newcomer. "Hello hot-step-mommy-number-four-to-be." At least, that's what he had thought. Wasn't sure if that's what stumbled out of his mouth.

"Yeah, and still drunk." His mom grabbed his hair and gently yanked his head up with an irritated look. But the corner of her mouth hitched up. An infinitesimal smile. Enough that he knew she was humored. "Shower. I'll make you coffee. We leave in one hour." She ruffled his hair, then patted his cheek.

He stood up and stretched. Lana, hot-step-mommy-number-four-to-be, smothered a laugh from the doorway. Yeah, he was naked. The male form was freaking hilarious. If he had more energy, he'd make a joke. But it hurt. Everything. Hurt. Still, he forced himself to strut by Lana and wink before disappearing into the bathroom.

"I'll leave your clothes out on the bed," his mom hollered to him through the bathroom door.

"I can see you now, fabric origami master, folding clothes into a swan," he said, turning toward the mirror. His eyes widened. Lipstick marks flecked his entire body—in two different shades—and he grinned. It happened. All of it. Nice. Now he knew why Lana was laughing.

Two hours, eight minutes, and forty-one seconds later, wearing khaki shorts and a vintage Hawaiian shirt plastered with floating pin-up girls in awkward positions, he stood before fifty spectators, bleary-eyed and cotton-mouthed. Coffee didn't help. Nothing helped. Not even Lynden's accusatory arched eyebrow from the second row. Damn that eyebrow. Damn this whole planet! Especially the sun. He scrunched up his face to block the ultraviolet laser beams.

That giant ball of plasma was clearly an assassin hired to kill him. Only the wind was his ally. The cool breeze comforted the pounding heat in his head. He wanted to coo with the feel of his feet sinking into the sand. He liked sandy beaches. Broad Beach was especially nice and granular this day.

Kris, his biological mother, was on marriage number six. She had married her high school sweetheart before marrying his dad. Then, after that, she filed through women as if flipping through the pages of her fashion magazine. He couldn't blame her. He had the same problem with girls.

Except, unlike her, he didn't see the purpose in marriage. It was a patriarchal throwback for breeding purposes. Required DNA recording for permanent biological stats removed the need to prove lineage through clan names and family clusters. A person could beget anyone today and the parentage was recorded while the fetus still swam around in utero. So why marry at all? The march to the altar led to divorce court anyway. Be free little birds. Go play. Have fun. No more mating for life.

His mom didn't care. She enjoyed flaunting her marriage status among the Elite. And those status-update hoarders now sat in the sand, staring at him to begin. So he did.

"Kristin McCleary Ferguson and Lana Huynh are two badass, crazy bitches."

His mom gave him the what-in-the-hell-are-you-doing look. The answer: surviving. He needed alcohol stat. Anything. His head was about to explode. She released a fake laugh to placate the spectators then cleared her throat.

"Mackenzie," she grit through a clenched smile.

"Two badass, crazy bitches *in love*," he drawled for emphasis, and her gaze softened as she focused on Lana instead of him. A photography drone hovered nearby. A hoard of human photographers moved around like ninjas in the sand. The clicks of shutters ricocheted through Mack's head. It might as well have been automatic rifles as far as he was concerned. He soldiered on. "They began as friends…"

Somehow he finished the ceremony. And only because he loved his mom. He liked seeing her happy. Lana Ferguson was officially his hot-step-mommy-number-four. He had given hugs, kissed cheeks, clapped for the new "Partners for Life." But now it was time to marinate his hangover with something hard and stiff. He smirked.

God he wished Fillion were here. He'd listen to his bad jokes and innuendos with aloof amusement. But he'd laugh on the inside. Like internally belly laugh as he analyzed every frickin' word on warp speed. That's all Mack needed to feel complete. Girls come and go, but making his best friend laugh subvocally?—Priceless.

Fillion.

Mack took a mental pause. Since November, Fillion had been sitting in the King County Youth Remand Center in Seattle awaiting trial on charges of employee sabotage. No bail hearing since he was a minor when charges were pressed. No house arrest since his parents were the prosecuting party. Lame. All of it. The worst part? The only visitors allowed were parents or legal guardians and siblings under the age of eight.

Both Mack and Lynden wrote letters and sent care packages. Despite Mack's requests, Fillion refused to collect call him and didn't write back. If that sonofabitch thought he was protecting Mack again… Mack closed the lid to that thought. His head was already pounding. Still, the rant formed.

Many times he had been tempted to follow Hanley's slime trail across the Net. Wanting to dig up something. Anything his friend could use to declare a mistrial. Or to make Hanley squirm until he dropped the charges. Trial-related info, not the dirt the collaborative hack already dug up. But Mack knew he was being watched.

The day after the zombie apocalypse attack on N.E.T.'s servers, Mack's own system was hit with a nasty spyware virus. It had drilled through all his security barriers effortlessly, which told Mack one thing—it was personal. A hack-back. He thought about hacking back the hack-back. But, in the midst of his fury, his gut screamed a loud warning. Getting him to hack back was the end goal. The temptation. That's when it hit him. Though he had cleaned up his system, his public profile was still infected. Probably his alter egos, too.

Since then, he'd been too paranoid to do anything, even incognito on the Deep Web, especially within the underground's Darknet. After all, the undercover cop who arrested Fillion was from the underground. A honeypot was out there waiting for him on the Darknet. He was sure of it. So Mack continued the illusion that he was a good boy, biding his time until the trial was over. That meant no unsanctioned visits to the underground. No hacking except what he was legally hired to do. Basically, it was the End of Days.

With a bored sigh, he faced the reception. Rainbow spotted him and moved through the crowd like a feline walking a fence line—graceful, sensual, and focused—all the while ignoring the stares and whispers. The Elite of Elites was among them, the Eco-Princess. Disinterest masked her features until she reached him.

"Well, that ceremony was all kinds of awkward," Lynden said, cozying up next to him at the bar. "Kinda like your preppy get-up. What's going on with that shirt?"

His thoughts cooled with the distraction. "It's a vintage 1950's theme. You know, nuclear family and stuff." He shrugged. "It's the up and coming trend says fashionista expert bio-mommy." He looked at her and deadpanned, "I think I look hella sexy with a pompadour. Don't ruin it for me."

She looked at his hair, dubious. "Remind me never to hire you to officiate a wedding."

Mack grunted in agreement and signaled the bartender. "Whiskey. Stout. Three shots of vodka. A pot of coffee. In that order."

"Hangover?" the bartender asked. Mack just stared, unblinking, and the bartender patted him on the shoulder.

"What happened to you after I left the club?" Her gaze floated over his outfit and hair again. He waited for her eyes to settle on his, then he bit his tongue in a silly, flirtatious grin. She pulled a look of disgust with a sound to match.

"Hairball much?"

The look of disgust morphed into irritation. "I don't want to know."

"Two words."

"Eww!" She covered her ears. "Mackenzie, stop."

He pulled a hand away from the nearest ear and leaned in close, trying not to laugh. "*Akai kuchibeni*."

"Her?!"

"Damn she was *sekushī*. Both—"

Kris hip-bumped him mid-sentence, Lana's hand in hers. His whiskey sloshed with the unexpected jerk. He quickly picked up the glass tumbler to counterbalance the movement and launched into a monologue of swear words.

Drink now safe in hand, he turned to his mom with a mock glare and received a mouthful of tulle. He playfully batted away the stiff white lace from his face, pretending to spit it out of his mouth. She pressed her cherry red lips together in annoyed amusement. Both she and Lana had dressed in retro cocktail dresses, the sides of their hair clipped back with giant, glittery flowers.

For the span of a nanosecond, Kris gawked at Lynden in surprise before kissing her on the cheek. "Look at how beautiful you've become! I should put you in my magazine. New York would love you." She turned to Lana, who was a former model of hers, now photographer. "With that tall, lanky build, I'd say black-and-white Jazz Age boudoir shot."

"Definitely. Those eyes. Magnetic." Lana took Lynden's chin in her hand and turned her head. "Nice cheekbones, too. And god, the neck of a gazelle."

Lynden emotionally retreated somewhere inside her head. But Mack didn't miss the pain she concealed. The whole world called her the ugly duckling of the Nichols family, which was insane. She was gorgeous in an otherworldly, girl-next-door kind of way. His mommies meant well, but any feature with Lynden would invite commentary and ridicule.

"I have nice cheekbones, too," Mack volunteered. "I have nice cheeks period." He waggled his eyebrows and hot-step-mommy-number-four snickered. But not bio-mommy. She looked like she was on the verge of rolling her eyes with the memory of this morning.

"My parents wanted me to convey their congratulatory wishes." Lynden flipped her hair and leaned back against the bar. "They sent a gift, too. Sorry they couldn't make it."

"How's your brother?" Kris asked.

"Peachy," Mack cut in, darting Lynden a look. The media was always listening. Everyone was always listening. Especially Hanley. "His *hikikomori* soul is finally in its element."

"I asked her! Attention whore." His mom gave him a pointed look and Mack scratched his head with his middle finger in reply. She shoved him in the arm, laughing. God he loved his mom. Turning back to Lynden, she said, "When you see him next, be sure to send my love."

"Yeah, sure. OK."

"Good to see you, darling." Kris kissed Lynden's cheek again and pulled her into a hug. "Contact me when you're ready to do a feature spread." With that, she flitted off toward the dance floor, exclaiming at a friend that it had been ages while hauling Lana over for introductions.

Mack sighed into his cup. Ages probably equated to two weeks. He pulled out a pack of cigarettes and stared at them. One second. Two seconds. Then put them back into his pocket. Pursing his lips in thought, he swirled the whiskey in his glass tumbler. Round and round, aimless motions of activity with no direction. Like him.

"You're moping."

He downed his whiskey and pushed his tumbler toward the bartender. "This isn't moping, Rainbow."

"Fine. You're pining."

"Hellz yeah." Mack looked at her now. "Still haven't grabbed that skinny ass of his or made out with him. The *bishounen* can't keep out of trouble with the law long enough." She started laughing, the kind where'd she snort. His favorite kind. He tugged on a strand of her hair and smiled.

"Maybe it's time you took another lover." She raised her eyebrow.

He nodded his head, though the throbbing pain intensified with the movement. "Yeah? Who do you suggest?" He turned around in his seat and pretended to survey the reception of Socialites and Elites.

"How about him?" Lynden pointed to a gawky dude with lime green hair, picking his nose in the corner. She started snorting again and his lips twitched with the effort to remain serious.

"I'm not into green hair," Mack said with a sly glance. "I like black."

"Hmmm… Oh, that one." She pointed to a tall, lean guy, probably around nineteen or twenty, sporting a clean-cut, athletic look and fire engine-red hair. An older woman, no doubt the man's mom, wiped something off his cheek. Lynden lowered her voice conspiratorially. "He looks like a nice boy in need of corruption."

"Hey," Mack said to the bartender. "Send that guy over there a Mac & Jack's, compliments of me."

"You got it, Mr. Ferguson."

He looked to Lynden and batted his eyes. "I hope *senpai* notices me."

Lynden shook her head and groaned. "Mac & Jack's? Really?" He smirked. "That's terrible. And wow. You move on quick. I now question whether you ever really loved Fillion at all."

"Never. Doubt. My. Love." Mack grabbed his stout and enjoyed a long sip. "Never."

"Oh my god. He got the drink. Mama's boy looks afraid." Lynden turned around to hide her snicker, eventually burying her head into her arms, her body shaking. "Maybe it's the shirt. Definitely the shirt."

Mack casually peered over his shoulder. When the athletic-looking-dude caught his eye, Mack threw him a wink and a sexy smile. The guy turned a sickly shade and shook his head no, quickly turning around. Mack almost laughed. Except, he just didn't care. It was weird, this not-caring business.

"Well, that was fantastically anticlimactic," he said to no one in particular. Lynden's body deflated in disappointment with his words and he sobered. He didn't mean it as a slam against her efforts to cheer him up. Mack hunched over his drink again, cradling the glass. "He's good-boy cute," he added, happy when she perked up again. "Not cybergoth *kawaii* enough for my taste."

"Fillion is not *kawaii*."

"Yeah, I know." Mack grinned at her. "I wasn't talking about Fillion." He shrugged his eyebrows and played with his tongue piercing suggestively. "There are plenty of fish in the underground."

"You never loved him."

"Martian monogamy isn't for all of us."

"Smart-ass."

"Gasp!" Mack covered his mouth in animated astonishment. "Lynden Norah-Leigh Nichols, the filth that comes out of your mouth." He shook his head with a tsk.

She snatched his stout and put it out of arm's reach. "You don't play nice."

"*Kusogaki*," he growled. "You touched my beer."

Mack sprang from his seat with a *kiai*, rounding his eyes into a fierce warrior look. Lynden rolled her eyes, a mocking, challenging, and bravely triumphant move. For this, she would pay. He released a slow, drawn-out "hiya," raising his arms into "praying mantis" then shoved her off her seat. She pushed back but it didn't matter. The battle was over quick and she tumbled off the stool. Victorious, he hijacked her now vacant seat and grabbed his pint, enjoying a long, theatrical sip.

Lynden plunked down in the chair he had previously occupied, arms crossed over her chest, and that damn eyebrow raised in humor, or irritation, or … whatever. Did it even need a reason? Normally he would laugh and take a victory lap, talking smack, dancing circles around the loser, or high-fiving strangers. Instead, he rubbed out a smudge on the countertop.

"You are moping!" Lynden lifted the corner of her mouth the same way Fillion did. Baiting smart-asses. Both of them. "Aw, poor Mack," she cooed. "Does someone need a romcom and ice cream?"

He ignored her. Just not in the mood to play anymore. Dubstep Elvis was making his head split. Dancers boogied away in their socks. Wait. What. He cocked his head to the side. Who in the hell came up with that stupid trend? His mom attempted to swing dance with Lana, pulling her in for a kiss, before twirling her newest wife under her raised arm.

Maybe Rainbow was right. He did feel mopey. It had been five months since he'd seen Fillion. Five. Long. Useless. Months. And even then, it was only in passing as Fillion faced a judge to plead innocent. Before that, he hadn't seen him since he'd entered New Eden, except through vid feed. But it was more than that. Fillion wasn't here. Mack's mom was getting married again, and Fillion wasn't here to celebrate with him. Like always.

"Partners for Life," he spoke into his pint. The last drop of beer left the glass and he slid the empty vessel down the countertop to join the graveyard of dirty dishes. He needed to figure something out. There had to be a loophole. A legal back door he hadn't thought of yet.

Pulling out his pack of cigarettes, he said, "It's a terrible day for rain." Lynden pretended to wipe a tear off his cheek with a wry smile. "This one's for you, mate." He lit up and savored a long draw. Lynden plucked the cigarette from his fingers and puffed. She handed it back as she exhaled, resting her head on his shoulder with a shaky sigh.

It wasn't fair. Fillion was the only family she really had. The only family that cared, at least. Visits with Coal were limited, too. Mack caught a glimpse of his mom, head back, her loud laughter filling the room as Lana hung on her, equally as humored. Lynden noticed his mommies, too.

They were two peas in a pod, he and Lynden. Loved and fought each other like siblings since preschool. Mack pulled Lynden's seat closer and wrapped his arm around her shoulders. She nuzzled in closer, settling her head in the crook of his neck.

The song changed and he almost groaned until he heard the words "great balls of fire." Mack smirked, holding in a bad joke, as he downed his shots of vodka—one, two, and finally three. The first wave of a buzz began to glimmer on the horizon. Finally. Cigarette dangling from his fingers, he enjoyed another draw.

He winked when catching Lynden's stare in the mirror over the bar. A feeble smile teased her lips in reply. The reception raged on in the background. Tiny reflected specks of gaiety over their shoulders. And then it hit him. A bullet shot to the brain. The idea that would open a back door legally.

"Oh shit," Lynden said into his neck. "I know that look. Whatever it is your half-drunk brain just schemed, Mackenzie, don't do it."

Mack laughed. He was so going to do it.

CHAPTER TWO

Seattle, Washington state

Thursday, April 8, 2055

M ack plopped into the driver seat of his car and rubbed feeling back into his limbs. Hell to the no for walking out in that garage again, even to sprint to his apartment for warmer clothes. Damn, it felt like the Arctic. After a week in Southern California, blue skies equaled warmth. He squinted up at the bright, morning sun. Well played, Mother Nature.

The dashboard lit up with facial recognition and launched the biometric stat verification process.

He twisted in his seat to peer at the spare computer and android parts littering his back seat. "Hello my pretties," Mack whispered. Metal clinked and clattered in reply as he rummaged for any signs of a forgotten hoodie.

All week, he had tried to think of a viable reason to visit Gremlin, the underground's electronics scrapper. Also the go-to black market smuggler, with extensive connections throughout the local prison systems—adult and juvenile.

The more Mack thought of Fillion, the more he knew something was wrong. It wasn't like Fillion to be *this* careful. Introvert?—Yes. Quiet?—Also true. Stubborn ass?—Ha! The most stubborn. Living with no heartbeat? Only true metaphorically. This dead-to-me business had to end. Soon. Or Mack might stage a crime simply to join his friend in detention.

The imagined screams of horror from the female population were what kept him in check. Someone had to meet their demands while Fillion was away. He was charged by The Sir to be his official fake boy, anyway. Mack was here to serve. A job he took seriously. And he promised to take care of Lynden. There was that, too.

When he had finally despaired of a believable alibi to visit Gremlin, Mack's dad came through with a save—although, he didn't know it. TalBOT industries offloaded boxes of e-waste for the underground to salvage and his dad had a shipment ready to go. So many boxes, in fact, that Mack had to dump the parts in the backseat and flatten the boxes for it all to fit in his car. The parts were young for e-waste, like maybe a year old tops. Certain circles in the underground would upcycle. Mostly, however, the vultures would pick through the scraps for gold threads and rare earth minerals. But, for Gremlin specifically, Mack selected the most valuable pieces. Bargaining chips.

The dashboard refreshed to a start-up screen. He paid it a passing glance and returned to his mission.

"Hey, Mack." Susani—the AI conversational software modded into the command center of his car—moaned his name in a silky voice. He faced the dashboard long enough to let his eyes roll back in a look of satisfaction. She purred a laugh and added, "Love it when you ride me."

Mack tossed a robotic leg the size of his forearm to the other side of the backseat. "Susani, you're my favorite girl to ride. But first I need heat."

"You want me to make you hot and sweaty?"

"Nah," he laughed. "Another time. Turn me on to room temp."

"If you want my heat, push my buttons and enter your password to start my engines."

Mack blindly pushed the start button, prompting the password screen to pop up. He had enough parts in his backseat to build an entire robot. Hell, a dozen robots. But no hoodie. Disgruntled, he turned around and swiped the code, a variation of what the girls called him. The engine roared to life.

"Mmmm... I like that." Susani's sultry voice vibrated the computer panel and he laughed again. "Where can I take you today, Mack?"

"Skyline Parking Garage."

"By the Ferry Terminal or by The Crypt?"

"The Crypt."

"At this hour?"

"Yeah. I have a work delivery." Mack rubbed his arms as his car pulled out of its slot and rolled toward the gate. "Music station. CyberBlack."

The city rolled by in flashing colors. People shuffled in and out of coffee shops and skyscrapers. Clusters of people swarmed crosswalks like vibrant hued clouds moving across the sky—one direction, straight lines, and all at the same speed. The buildings were clothed in blinking, holographic advertisements and vegetation. Green walls—required by eco-city ordinances—vertically sprawled across commercial buildings in geometric patterns. In assassin-style trench coats, with messenger bags strapped across their backs and fingers tapping privacy screens, the business class brushed by drones and androids on the sidewalk. The familiarity of it all wrapped around Mack.

Drumming his fingers on the armrest, he returned his attention to the work emails that wavered before his eyes. Sales distribution needed his assistance with an overseas order of nanotech processing chips. Again. There was always something. Nit-picky bastards. They wanted parts from TalBOT Industries, and *only* TalBOT Industries, but custom ordered *only* after shipment was received. This time, the initialization software was not to their liking and changes were demanded. He'd need to talk to dev about a patch to suit their stringent requirements.

The money was too good to blow off. So was this company's market influence.

His car stopped at a light. He closed his message center with a sulking sigh. Too much to think about. He needed to remain focused on other details. Lost in his head, Mack was absently trailing a homeless man as he limped across the street, talking to himself, when a metal object crashed into his car. Mack's head whipped toward the source.

An android's face pressed to his window and Mack jumped. The glass and computer screen eyes blinked. Mack blinked back, equally surprised. The body in casual dress still moved, walking into Mack's car with clattering bumps again and again.

Finger flying through the air, Mack turned on his Cranium and launched the scanning software he developed to breach most android security features and capture ownership details. The android shouted, "Move!" When Mack failed to comply, the android shouted his request again. Data streamed upward in Mack's vision almost immediately. The security features were that laughable.

Courier class.
Employer: Keller-Donald, Attorneys at Law.
Name: Drew 182.62.W5Y.23C
Inception date: February 3, 2051

Owner contact information uploaded into Mack's Cranium. He turned off the vid feed and closed his screens. "Gotcha, *dokyun*." He shoved his door, knocking the robot onto his metal ass. "Cheap motion sensors," he mumbled under his breath. To Drew he said, "Tell your owner to expect my bill."

"Correction. You were in my path, Mackenzie Patton Campbell Ferguson the Third." Drew lifted a hand and shook it angrily at Mack. So it had facial recognition software? But otherwise blind as a bat? Mack inclined his head and studied the courier droid. The robot twisted its head to mimic Mack's movement and said, "My owner will be in contact with you."

People stared and pointed. Some turned on Craniums to take pictures. Others shook their heads and continued walking. Horns honked behind him. Mack ignored it all and continued to analyze the courier's every movement. The android appeared to be doing the same with him.

To act casual, Mack rested his arms on the top of his car door and spit onto the road, saying, "I don't argue with computer chips. I'm your Overlord, *tesaki*." He slid back into his car and slammed the door, releasing a flood of swear words.

"Are you done playing?" Susani asked him. "The light is green."

"Yeah. Drive." Mack inhaled deeply and released a slow, shaky breath. Was Drew a warning? A signal? The car eased forward and followed traffic through the intersection. He needed to do something before his mind ate him alive. "Actually, Susani, I want manual control."

A steering wheel formed from the dashboard and moved toward him. He felt the transmission shift as he placed his foot to the accelerator pedal.

"I like it when you take control and handle my parts."

"I bet," Mack replied with a laugh. "They all do."

Five blocks later, he passed Skyline Parking Garage and pulled into an alley near The Crypt. The narrow road cut through the towering, historical brick buildings. Trash lined the walls and blew across his path. The nondescript entrance to the underground passed by on the right. Mack, however, wanted the service door at the end of the alley.

Rolling to a stop, he turned off the engine and hopped out to inspect the damage. "Shit," he said under his breath. Scratches scarred the black paint job, leaving behind a series of silver marks. "Asshole. May a rabid dog chew off your arm and piss all over your circuitry!"

The door to the drop-off opened and Gremlin poked his head out. Black hair tipped in orange spiked around his head. A tattoo of loose wires dangled down his cheek and neck, the wire ends leading to various piercings.

"Hey. Been awhile, man." Gremlin reached out and shook Mack's hand. "Whatcha got for me?"

"Mostly android parts. A few control boards." Mack opened his car's back door and grabbed a box to pop back into shape, keeping his shit together despite the chill in the air.

Dammit. He should have ran back to his apartment for warmer clothes. He was one with the sun. He was fire. He was freezing his ass off.

Gremlin whistled. "These look fresh. Still have that just-out-of-the-factory smell to 'em."

"Test parts. Honorable discharge."

"Clean? Or do the serials need scrubbed?" Gremlin briefly looked up from his inspection when Mack laughed. "Sorry, automatic question. Forgot who I was talking to."

"I have a box in my trunk *you* would appreciate." He signaled for the trunk to open and walked over. Gremlin peered inside and whistled again. "Sexy, right?" Mack asked, wiggling his eyebrows. "Go ahead. Touch. Stroke. *Nosebleed*," he added with a flirty smile. "I did."

"Let's talk."

Gremlin stuck his head inside the service door and shouted for help. Two men appeared from the shadows and propped open the door, sleep still pulling on their features. Mack understood. Ten in the morning was early after an all-nighter of subterranean activities.

"Guard the car and unload the goods," Gremlin instructed. To Mack, he said, "You can trust Ryuu and Daemon."

Mack grabbed the box from the back of his car and closed the trunk with his elbow. He stepped in front of the help and raked Ryuu and Daemon over with a critical eye. Appearing unimpressed, he asked, "Do you know who I am?" Both men nodded their heads.

Good.

He needn't say more. If they knew who he was, then they knew the consequences for being stupid. Mack felt zero remorse when the underground eliminated the criminals who betrayed the Elite who fed them.

"Lead the way," he said to Gremlin.

Mack's boots clomped across the cement and through small water puddles formed from the weeping walls. He snaked his way through dimly lit hallways cluttered with electronics, some with mortuary tags hanging off of parts. Damn, it was even colder inside.

Gremlin's office resided on the first floor. The computer underground lay several stories beneath them. But Gremlin lived on the street level for intake—human and computer. Many runaways ended up in the underground.

"Make yourself at home," the scrapper said, gesturing to his office. "Siren, guess who's here?"

A girl with ratty cotton candy-hued pink and blue hair looked up from the unmade bed pushed against the corner of the room. The sunken eyes, clammy skin, and blue tinge to her cracked lips told Mack everything he needed to know.

"Hey, Mack," she said in an airy voice. "Long time. Come for fun?"

"Not today. Business," he said with a wink. Her eyes moved to his utilikilt before she buried her face into the arms circling her knees. "Staying out of trouble?" he asked her.

"No," Gremlin answered when she didn't. "Found her huddled up in the alley early this morning, shivering to death. She's finally speaking coherent sentences."

Mack shifted his gaze back to hers as his pulse stilled. The chill left him when flaming heat fired through his veins and turned his vision red. Scrapes, drips of dried blood, and bruises lined her shins and knees like she had crawled her way to the alley. "Did that bastard hurt you?" She lifted her shoulder in a weary shrug. "God dammit."

He deposited the box he was carrying onto a desk covered in widgets and parts. Wary of any post-trauma triggers Siren may have, he eased next to her on the bed at a respectable distance, slow and steady. When she chanced a look at him from her protective position, he spoke again.

"Stay in the safe house, OK? Need me to walk you down later?"

"They don't have—"

"Yeah, that's the point. You have vasoconstriction."

"Shit, drop the harm-reduction speeches. Think I haven't heard them all by now?" She peeked at him over her arm. "The withdrawals killed me last time."

"So will dealers. Like him. Your choice." Mack never took his eyes off her. She picked at a chipped fingernail. Her knuckles were red and swollen, a few scabbed over from fresh blood. "I'd miss you," he continued. "Others would, too. We had good times, right?" Siren nodded her head and blinked back tears. "Go to the safe house. Get inhibitor shots. Find work with the hackers. You're brilliant. Don't let that go to waste." She opened her mouth and he cut her off. "I'll cover the cost."

Siren lifted her head with a dead stare, the look of drug addicts and whores. "I'll work it off, you know, if—"

"Hell no. I don't own you." Disgust wormed around in his gut. "It's a gift. Take it or leave it." He paused a beat to let his words sink in. Then, he added, "Break my heart gently," while batting his eyes.

Siren offered a shaky smile, her eyes darting away from his and then back. "I'd never break your heart."

"Good girl." He winked again. "Can you walk?" She nodded and he smiled in relief. "Give me a few minutes with Gremlin and I'll escort you to Jett. When you've cleaned up enough, Kev or Amanda will set you up." He tossed her his pack of cigarettes. "Keep a smoke or two company."

She wrapped a blanket around her thin frame and stepped out of the office. Peering out the window, Mack watched her light up before facing Gremlin. Neither of them needed to mention the obvious. She wouldn't stay in the safe house. Or get clean. It was a given.

Gremlin pointed to the box. "Whatcha want for this?"

"Still have connections inside the King County Youth Remand Center?"

He smiled so that his black-capped teeth showed. "Yeah. I smuggle in messages and small items only. No matter what you heard."

"Ah yes, the stuff of legends now lies. Going soft, old man?"

Gremlin chuckled—a menacing sound—and lit up a joint. A cloud of skunky smoke hazed around his face. "You want hits? I'll refer you. *They* owe me a favor."

"Depends. What's *their* success rate?"

"One hundred percent." The toothy grin appeared again.

Mack laughed. "Well, shit. That makes for a bad day. Remind me never to piss you off."

Gremlin lifted a shoulder in a non-committal shrug. "What's your deal?"

"I need to get a message to Fillion Nichols."

The middle-aged man considered Mack a moment. "What's the message?"

Mack peered over his shoulder to Siren, who still puffed on a cigarette near the window. Lowering his voice to a whisper, he said, "File an Inmate Marriage Request Form. Mackenzie Ferguson will appear with a minister for a counseling session when approved."

Gremlin laughed. A loud, wheezy guffaw. "Deal."

"Thanks, mate."

"Circumventing daddy surveillance?" Gremlin asked, opening his office door.

"That hurts." Mack feigned offense, placing a hand to his heart. "True. Love. Bitches. We're everybody's OTP. You've read the fan fic? O. M. G. Tell me you've read the fan fic?!"

"Yeah, yeah…" Gremlin chuckled again. "Thank your old man for the delivery."

"Will do."

"I'll send a messenger to you when the paperwork pushes through."

The grin on the man's face sent crawlers up Mack's back. He quickly shook the scrapper's hand and moved toward Siren. "Hop on. I'll carry you down."

She rubbed her cigarette out with her shoe, avoiding eye contact. He squatted low and she climbed onto his back. Blue-tipped fingers and scratched arms wrapped around his neck. Her grip was weak. She would crash soon. He was surprised she was functioning as well as she was, actually.

"Ready?" he asked. Siren nodded. "Gremlin, tell Ryuu and Daemon to guard my car longer. I'll tip them nicely on the way out."

With that, he marched to the stairway door and descended to the belly of the computer underground. Now to find a licensed minister to coax out of hiding and into the light of day. He knew just the gal. Siren's salvation would be his, too.

CHAPTER THREE

Monday, April 19, 2055

Brown eyes framed in thick, dark lashes followed Mack's movements in the strobing lights. She was the kind of beautiful that brought men to their knees. And he wanted to kneel. To pray at her altar. Beg for mercy. Anything.

But he was cooler than shit. So he did what any self-respecting man would do. In a slow scan, he appreciated every curve she presented for his viewing pleasure. Then, he delivered his best come-hither look and turned away. If she wanted him, she knew where to find him. He was desperate. But not *desperate*. Plenty of girls to choose from. Many of whom had already thrown themselves at him since he arrived. Let her feel in control. Made for better adventures.

God, he needed one.

Boredom had driven Mack to The Crypt one hour, four minutes, and fifty-two seconds ago. Pissed off with work and frustrated over no news from Fillion—After. Eleven. Nerve-wracking. Days—he had started drinking back at his apartment. It hadn't taken much to tip him over the edge once he arrived on the scene.

Now he was fluid. Moving like water as the beat vibrated through his body to hers, the one with brown eyes. God, that didn't take long. Sexy *henshin* for the win. He almost laughed. Almost. But she emptied his brain of any logical thought before he could fully react.

Fingers slid down his chest to his belt loops as her smile invited his fantasies to frolic and play. Yes ma'am. He'd hate to disappoint.

Titillating smile in place, he grabbed her hips and pulled her body tight against his. A body that seemed heavier than it should be for her size. His smile faded. The momentary confusion fled, however, when she arched her back as he moved to the song's throbbing pulse. Damn. He was officially done with all others for the evening. Sorry, ladies. And she knew it. Fisting his shirt, she crashed into him until their lips collided in mutual need.

It sounded sexier than it was.

Her movements transitioned from smooth to awkward to smooth again. Hurt a little, too. But he manned up and—oh god. Scratch that. He was melting. Intoxicated with the feel of her body owning his. Water slipping through her fingers and puddling at her feet. A moan escaped his throat as they kissed. She laughed with the pleasure of arousing him to this point. Good. Her lips were eternally soft, unnaturally so. Unlike any lips he'd ever kissed before. He wanted more. She could control the whole night for all he cared. And she did.

Strangely, she never broke a sweat while dancing. Never tired. Or complained of thirst. Damn, she was a goddess. Or maybe the buzzing sensations in his head and the lighting were playing tricks on his mind. His concentration was an elusive thing at the moment, all thoughts focused on a singular goal.

Eventually, between kisses, she said, "Let's go to your place."

"Perfect idea, *sekushī na josei*," he had meant to say. Instead, it bumbled out as, "Uh, OK."

She laughed with his unintelligent reply. Between the alcohol and hooking up, he had morphed into a Neanderthal. Mack want woman. Mack like going home. Grunt. Point to exit.

Twenty-three minutes and forty-eight seconds later—according to his Cranium—they stumbled into his apartment, shedding clothes as if they were on fire. He shuffled backwards in the dark toward his bedroom, her lips locked with his. Mack was completely unaware of anything save the way her hands trailed over his skin. Even blind to Lynden, who stared at him in frozen horror from the guest room doorway.

"Mackenzie?" She flipped on a light. "Eww ... Gross!" She finished with gagging sounds.

"Shit!" He jumped away from the brown-eyed-goddess. "What the—"

"Didn't you get my text messages?"

"Rainbow, please tell me I'm drunk and seeing things and that you're not really here."

Lynden raised that damn eyebrow of hers.

"Well, in that case, disappear." He palmed Lynden's face and pushed her back into the guest room. A cross between a growl and a scream let loose as she grabbed the hand on her face and yanked. He didn't budge. "Social cues, woman! Naked people. You're supposed to be disappearing." Lynden tried to claw his arm, but he deflected with his free hand.

Mack peered at the brown-eyed-goddess, delivering a look of long suffering and an apologetic sigh to match. "Socializing is hard for some humans. I take her to the park and let her run free, but..." He ended with a shrug. Lynden stopped moving. Steam shot out of her orifices, he was quite sure of it. The alcohol still firing through his system continued speaking, however. "We're still working on certain commands, like *go to bed*."

"Are you in a relationship?" The brown-eyed-goddess asked him.

"NO!" both he and Lynden shouted in response, followed by mutual grimaces of disgust. Their eyes locked and then Rainbow bit his hand.

"*Kusogaki!*" he growled. Lynden laughed at him. A mocking, satisfied, and overly triumphant sound. Evil. Pure evil. Her gaze then dropped below his waist. She laughed again. Oh. She. Was. Going. Down. "You wanna play, Rainbow Brite?"

"Spare me." Lynden rolled her eyes and flipped her hair. She pursed her lips to make melodramatic kissing noises and began scratching behind his ear. "You wanna play, Mack? Do ya?" she asked in a syrupy voice. "Here boy! Go fetch your male pride and shove it up your wannabe tough guy ass."

He took a step toward Lynden, indignant. But the brown-eyed-goddess slithered between them and faced Mack. "I need to speak with you."

"Speak." He continued to glare at Lynden over the goddess' shoulder.

"*Alone.*"

Mack met her eyes then, but spoke to Lynden. "What did you text me about, Rainbow?" Lynden's eyes widened a notch with the shift in his tone. Yeah, social cues. He resisted the urge to swear under his breath.

"Fillion's lawyer contacted me today about some android you hit with your car, named Drew. Says you're not returning his calls. They want to speak with you personally and not filter messages through your lawyer."

The brown-eyed-goddess lifted a corner of her mouth in an out-of-sync, humored smile. Warning bells went off in Mack's head and his brain skidded to a complete stop. Who in the hell did he take home? Trying to act casual, he studied her again while appearing to think over Lynden's words.

Flawless skin shimmered with a touch of star dust. Like she had used transparent glitter lotion or something. Not uncommon among scene girls.

Playful, dark brown eyes, the kind that were fathomless, invited him closer. They also appeared to laugh at him. Even now.

Sakura blossom pink lips curved upward in a confident smile. A color that contrasted beautifully with her ivory hair, the kind that reflected pastel hues like an opal.

Everything about her was perfection. Too perfect. Was she human? Normally he could spot a sex droid a mile away. But there was something off about her. Not really human. Not really android. But mostly human. He resisted a shudder.

"Lynden, shut the door and stay in the room."

"Why—"

"Go. Now."

Fear flickered across her face while examining the girl for the first time. The flash of emotion quickly disappeared behind a blank expression. Still, she twisted the ring on her thumb as she moved to obey his request.

When the door clicked shut, Mack brushed past the girl in question to his clothes which were tossed about the living room. Drew worked for Fillion's lawyer? The law firm name had totally eluded him. Shit. Shit. *Shit.*

"Who are you?"

"You didn't care about names before."

"Fair enough. I'll rephrase. What are you?"

"Whatever you want me to be."

He jerked strands of hair out of his eyes as he buttoned his pants. Well, this was awkward. He walked into the kitchen for a glass of water. Act natural. His mind was sobering quickly.

The girl tracked his movements. Still undressed. Creepy. Was she gathering biometric stats? Recording him? Or was she just a human with a disturbing sense of humor? It didn't matter at this point. He just needed to keep his cool. Which reminded him, where did he put his extra EMP switch?

"OK," he began again, and paused to sip on his water. "I want you to be something that makes sense to me right now. Can you perform that trick?"

She laughed. A rolling, taunting sound. "And what makes sense to you?"

He lifted his eyes. "What did you want to talk to me about?" Pretending to busy himself with the few dishes in his sink, he continued, "Speak. You have my undivided attention, *josei.*"

"I have a message for you."

"Yeah? Let me guess. You're the best kisser I've ever known? Signed—everyone."

A flirty smile teased her lips. "I'm sure you're good at lots of things."

"Pretty much. But I don't like to brag."

"Too bad it didn't get that far."

He opened up a drawer filled with odds and ends and flashed her a flirtatious look of his own. "The night's not over."

A seductive laugh filled the room as she leaned against the black granite countertop. Still naked. "You lie, Mackenzie Ferguson."

Every hair on the back of his neck stood at attention. "True," he said slowly. "Saying I'm *good* at lots of things is lowballing. 'Great' is the better word choice. Finally. Someone who gets me, and you haven't even gotten me yet." He found the EMP switch and curled it into his hand and shut the drawer with his hip. "Sad day for you."

"You're in a relationship." She slinked over to where he stood. Another amused smile flitted across her unnaturally soft lips. Dammit. He had liked those lips. A lot. He kept his gaze fixed to her eyes. "The paperwork was filed and approved," she continued in velvet tones. "He's expecting you the week of May third."

"Who sent you?"

"You know who."

Mack stilled. "I have no fucking idea what you're talking about, woman."

"Too bad it didn't work out between us."

"Yeah, my heart is breaking. You should hear it weep. It's blubbering like a baby right this very second." He angled past her into the living room. "Need a cab?"

"Your zucchini told me that you're still a virgin, despite your reputation." She swept past him to gather her clothing. Zucchini? Mack worked hard to keep his lips from twitching. "He also mentioned that you liked to cuddle and sometimes cried after messing around. Sorry to miss the show."

Mack laughed out loud. He couldn't help it. That's what Fillion told most of the girls Mack hooked up with. Old joke. It didn't prove anything. Hell, she had clearly profiled him before arriving at The Crypt tonight. Time to return the favor.

Where was his Cranium? Wait. Still on his head. Good. He touched it and launched his scanning software when she bent over to pick up her dress. The screen loaded ... and nothing. He refreshed. Two seconds. Ten seconds. Still nothing. All humans had an electronic heartbeat of some kind. A pulse of activity on the Net. Even hackers. Especially hackers. He snapped his eyes over his privacy screen to her waiting gaze.

An Untraceable.

The weirdest person he'd ever met, too. And he knew a lot of freaky people. Holy shit. Gremlin did it. Mack was so giddy this moment he could dance a jig around her bare ass. He kept his face dialed to not-giving-a-shit, though. The main channel of the Elite and badasses like him.

"See you around..." She leaned over and whispered his nickname in his ear. Goosebumps danced over his skin. That was a trade secret. What the hell? Fillion *never* shared this info.

Clothes bundled in her arms, she sauntered to the elevator. Who did that? Who willingly left someone's apartment *naked*? Nobody. She probably dressed in the elevator after the doors shut. But damn. What an exit. Gremlin was one freaky shit.

Rattled, Mack turned toward the hallway and raked shaky fingers through his hair. "You can come out now," he yelled. Pulling a pack of Marlboro's from his pocket, he lit up as Lynden tentatively stepped into the living room.

"Who ... who was that?"

"Hands down the creepiest almost hook-up *ever*." Mack hid the EMP switch in his pants pocket. "Shit. Glad you were here. Sorry about face-palming you and stuff."

She stared out the wall of windows and nibbled on her lip ring. "She looked like Pinkie."

"She wha—" He closed his mouth. Images flashed through his mind on replay. After a few seconds, he half-whispered, "It wasn't her, Lyn."

Lynden looked over her shoulder at him. City lights illuminated half of her face. The other half dissolved into the dark shadows of the room. Fear pooled in her eyes and the hair on the back of his neck rose once again.

"Sounded like her, too."

"Just coincidence." He hoped.

She shrugged a single shoulder and returned her attention back to the twinkling cityscape. "Why is the tattoo on your thigh upside down?" She glanced over her shoulder again. Mack was trying to keep it cool, face straight. Wait for it. Wait ... and there it was. She figured it out. Good job. The look of disgust on her face was priceless. "Really? That's a thing?" Gagging sounds followed. "Make the images stop!"

He laughed. "Fluffy kittens dancing on rainbows in a field of sparkling flowers."

"Ugh. Not helping. Let's change the topic. Stat." Lynden leaned her forehead on the window. "So, what happened tonight? Are you OK?"

Mack dragged on his cigarette and exhaled slowly. How to explain? An idea struck him. "One sec," he said to the dark. In the kitchen, he pulled out a spiral notebook and pen, then positioned himself next to Lynden by the window.

Scribbling in the notebook, he wrote:

Gremlin slipped note to F. Reply sent back via girl.

"Seriously?" Lynden nibbled on her lip ring again. "That's messed up." Her shoulders slumped as her head tucked toward her chest, her shoe toeing the floor. "You speak with him?"

"Hey, come here." Mack sank into the nearest leather divan and patted his lap. Lynden followed and curled up against him, resting her head on his chest. Cigarette dangling from his mouth, he used his free hand to explain his genius plan in the notebook.

Her head popped off his chest as her jaw dropped. "I need this." She plucked the cigarette from his mouth and put it into hers. Smoke escaped her lips in a thin ribbon. "So this was what lurked behind that scheming look of yours at the wedding reception."

It was a statement, not a question. Still, Mack felt compelled to answer. "Partners for life."

She laughed, a light tinkling sound as she balanced the cigarette between her fingers while covering her mouth. "I always wanted another bossy older brother." Lynden rested her head on him again and passed off the cigarette. "I guess you'll do."

Mack warmed with the underlying sentiment. One she tried to mask with humor. For a short while, he'd be the only accessible, legal relative who cared. Their loss. Wrapping his arms around her shoulder, he held her close and whispered in her ear, "'Doubt thou the stars are fire. Doubt that the sun doth move. Doubt truth to be a liar. But never doubt I love.'"

He was her family, regardless of what a silly piece of paper said. She sniffed and nuzzled closer to him, pressing her face into his neck. Her favorite spot since childhood.

His too.

CHAPTER FOUR

Tuesday, May 4, 2055

The waiting room was packed. Three hours, thirty-nine minutes, and sixteen seconds earlier, he and Jett—the woman who ran the safe house in the underground—had cleared security and checked in their personal electronics. Then waited. And waited. Paced. Stared at the wall. Tried to ignore the people crowding their space. But he couldn't get past the smell.

The public visitation hall was filled with grungy, threadbare humanity seated before wall-mounted video ports. They paid what little money they had for a twenty- to sixty-minute visitation. It was ridiculous. But jails and prisons were busting at the seams. Tax dollars only went so far. He understood both angles.

A thin woman his age, huddled in a corner, made a haunting image with pale skin, stringy hair, and pronounced dark circles under her eyes. The kind brought on by hardship. People were screaming at her to keep her child quiet. Nobody had patience for children. They were burdens. Always. The poor mite looked hungry, sounded hungry, too. Dirt stains covered the child's cheeks, his hair in matted knots.

She had most likely spent all the money she had so that her child could see his daddy. In less than two decades, the same woman would probably be here again—visiting her son. The circle of jobless, hungry, lower-class life complete.

Mack tried not to feel guilt. It wasn't his fault.

He looked at the walls again. The building was only ten years old. But the color scheme held a moldy hue. Was that butter yellow or a fading shade of white? He couldn't tell. It was gross, that's what it was.

"Mackenzie Ferguson and Jett Styles?"

Finally. Mack stood and breezed over to a petite woman with the tightest bun he'd ever seen in his life. Her eyes narrowed as she compared the real life image to the digital version on her screen.

"Follow me."

The correctional officer led Mack and Jett down the questionably colored, cement brick hallway toward the newer detention center. The one built for white-collar crimes committed by juvenile Elite who awaited trial. The holier-than-thou's received amenities the government-dependent civilians could only dream about. Unconstitutional? Maybe. Probably. Nobody fought the system. Not anymore.

Pausing at a corridor, Mack, Jett and the officer waited for a cluster of people in uniform to pass. The dirty blond hair, pulled tight into a knot, harshened the officer's features. She looked perpetually pissed. Catching her eye, he winked. Oh god. Wrong move. Now she looked pissed. Damn. He didn't think her features could harden any more. Mack held in a laugh. She'd be all kinds of fun. They started moving again, away from the entrance and the despair.

The correctional officer stopped before a door and placed a thumb onto a biometric scanner. Security cleared, the door clicked and she grabbed the knob. Mack maintained his cooler-than-shit swagger. His face remained bland, but an entire ant colony had been provoked inside of him.

"Give this to the officer at the podium to check you in."

She handed him a slip of paper. The detention and prison systems still operated in the Dark Ages compared to the rest of society. Most business and government operations would have wirelessly transmitted this data and spared a tree. To save face with the taxpaying Green Morons, if nothing else.

Mack entered an open room dotted with metal tables and chairs bolted to the floor. The light gray fixtures looked disgusting against the purulent drainage color coating the cement brick walls. It was official. This building was diseased. Rotting away from the decay of humanity who inhabited its dorms and passed through its doors daily.

The officer at the podium—an old man with silvered hair—took the slip of paper from Mack without any form of greeting. His pen scratched over Mack's paperwork.

"Show me the back of your hand," he said in a monotone voice.

Both Mack and Jett stretched out their hands, which were then stamped with invisible ink. The kind that showed up under black light. Mack almost made a joke about whether this meant they were free to roam around the amusement park. But the old man, sensing the rising sarcasm, lifted his eyes. Daring Mack to say something. Anything. Fear slithered down his spine in response. Hot damn, that man was cold. Not a drop of warmth pulsed through his veins. Alrighty, then. Silence it is.

"You're assigned to table four. Sit anywhere but the marked chair. No touching or inappropriate gesturing. Hands must remain visible at all times. No whispering or talking in a language other than English. Your visit is limited to thirty minutes because of high traffic today. Understand?"

"Yes, sir," Jett said. She elbowed Mack, who nodded his head in agreement.

"An officer will check for stamps before you can leave this room and before you can claim any checked-in belongings."

"We understand."

"You're the minister?" the officer asked her.

"Yes, sir," Jett answered.

"Ever performed a ceremony in a detention center?"

"No, sir."

"It'll happen in this room at an assigned table. Hand holding is allowed for the ceremony only. But not today."

"We understand, sir."

The officer eyed Mack with dispassion. "He'll be in shortly."

"Thank you, sir." Jett turned to Mack with humorously large eyes and gestured with her head. "Come on, Romeo. Move your ass."

Red tape identified the marked chair. Mack eased into the seat next to it, and clasped his hands together onto the table top. Looking around, he spotted several surveillance cameras. Officers roamed around the fifteen or so tables, all of which were occupied. A tense hum of conversation vibrated through the air. Two family groups sat inside a playroom, moms and dads visiting their pre-trialer sons. The younger siblings played with old, broken toys. One child snatched a toy out of another's hand. The outraged child retaliated by pushing the thief to the floor. Both families sprang into action, earning the attention of an officer.

Patience was not a virtue Mack possessed. Especially when an entire ant colony skittered through his insides. Seconds. Minutes. Hell had relocated operations to his head. Maybe he was the one imprisoned? Too deep a thought to explore right now. Then a muted buzz echoed from somewhere. A flash of dark hair reflected in the bulletproof glass of the playroom.

"Is that him?" Jett asked by his side.

Mack swung his focus to the other end of the room.

He held his breath and kept his face devoid of any reaction. A correctional officer escorted Fillion to their assigned table. Head down, his friend refused to make eye contact. Even when he sat. Even when the officer voiced his departure. It was like Mack didn't exist. Nobody did. Was he sedated with anti-anxiety meds? Or something else?

Fillion's hair had grown out since the last time Mack had seen him. Near-black hair with reddish highlights reached midcheek and fell over his eyes. It was weird seeing Fillion's natural hair tones. A long-sleeved blue, button-up shirt—same color and material as his pants—hung on him loosely. Too loosely. Had he lost weight?

Five months. What in the hell should he say?

"Hey."

Silence.

"Dad says life is boring without our larks." He paused. "Yeah, he actually used the word 'larks.' Old-timey word badassary, right?"

No movement or any indication that Fillion had even heard him.

Mack softened his voice. "Lynden sends her love."

Fillion turned his head away. Mack's pulse kicked up.

"So does my mom. She married again. Lana is my new hot-step-mommy." He smiled. "I think this one will last. You should've seen Kris. She was glowing."

Nothing.

"I filled up your commissary account. The max allowable."

A nod. Progress. Mack released a breath.

"Hey," Jett said, easing from her chair. "I need to ask the officer a question about next week. Be right back."

Mack watched her leave then said to Fillion, "I also added minutes to your calling card. I guess now that you're eighteen, you get a calling plan."

"Don't call me."

Mack's eyes widened. His voice. God how he missed it. He needed to keep him talking. "Are you breaking up with me?"

A flicker of a smile touched Fillion's lips.

Mack laughed. His friend was such a smart-ass. Nope, not on anti-anxiety meds. Fillion must be issuing Miranda rights on this conversation. And perhaps trying to appear incoherent should this ever come into question. How much of Hanley's influence penetrated these walls? Mack's eyes darted around the facility, noting each camera again. And every correctional officer.

"Well, tough shit," he said to maintain normalcy. "A queerplatonic love like ours doesn't dissolve this quickly."

Fillion lifted a single shoulder in a slight shrug, humor still on his lips, though nearly indiscernible. Like a memory of old times ghosted the corners of his mouth. To onlookers, it probably looked like he was repositioning himself in his seat.

Mack watched for gray eyes through the strands of Fillion's hair. Still nothing. He'd never seen him this cautious. Or serious. And he was the very definition of serious. Mack needed to create a code. Something Fillion could crack. Mental stimulation was his love language.

With nonchalance, Mack began tapping the table with one hand, and continued. "No," he drawled, and tapped the table in one pronounced movement. Then little taps. "Not getting rid of me. Ever. I heart my sapiosexual BFF." Mack faced Jett as she resumed her seat as before and asked, "Are you ready?"

"Yes."

When she answered, Mack gave two pronounced taps on the table. More little taps. Hopefully, it appeared as though Mack was feeling the beat to a silent tune.

"Great," he said. "Any words of wisdom you have for us before next week?"

"No, not really."

Mack issued one emphatic tap as his finger drummed away. Gray eyes finally met his. Fillion hacked the code. Good. His friend was hardwired to spot patterns. It was in his DNA. The curse of an over-thinker. Unlike Mack, who preferred to fly by the seat of his pants.

Oblivious to their silent communication, Jett asked, "Fillion, do you have a witness for next week?"

Fillion acted like he was casually taking in the scene. He ran his hand through his hair and ... there it was. He tapped his head twice before his hand returned to the table.

"Of course he does," Mack said. "My zucchini knows what he's doing." He bit down on his tongue ring and winked at Fillion. No reaction to the queerplatonic term for a partner. Damn. Tough crowd. Jett eyed Fillion, her dark purple hair falling over her face as she leaned onto the table. "Just think," Mack continued, his tone dreamy. "Next week we'll get two whole hours together. *Alone.*" Fillion touched his shirt, like he was adjusting it. Two taps on the top button. "He's happy about that, too," Mack said to Jett.

"Uh, yeah. He looks totally ecstatic about marrying you. The overwhelming joy is catching."

Mack ignored Jett's sarcasm. "Do you want to kiss me, *bishounen*?" he asked Fillion, perfectly serious. Two taps. "Wait. Really?" One tap. "I hate you." The lower part of Fillion's cheek twitched, like he had bit the inside of his mouth to keep from smiling.

"Hate is a strong word." Jett lifted her eyebrows with worry. She peered at Fillion with further concern when he appeared non-responsive, softly saying, "Let's stay positive around him."

"Pshaw. We're just frobnicating."

She inclined her head to better see Mack. "You're what?!"

"Lawyer taking care of you?" he asked Fillion, ignoring Jett again. Two subtle taps.

Hmmm ... maybe he would contact Fillion's lawyer, then. No, he'd wait until he had a chance to speak with Fillion first. Mack was paranoid about walking into a trap. Lawyers didn't request private audiences with people who already had lawyers. Especially with Elites, who were assigned lawyers at birth in many cases. It was too phishy and Mack refused to take the bait.

He lowered his voice to just above a whisper and asked, "You doing OK, mate?" Fillion's throat constricted. His friend's face remained expressionless, though. Fingers shaking, Fillion gently tapped once on his thigh while pretending to fidget with the hem of his shirt. The air leadened inside of Mack's chest.

"He's not going to talk to you," Jett said, sympathetic. She placed a hand on Mack's arm in comfort. "Looks like they sedated him. Not surprising. Maybe next week will be different."

"What do you mean, 'not surprising'?" he asked Jett, but continued to regard Fillion.

"Later."

"Fillion," Mack began softly, "Is it time to take a dump?"

Jett leaned onto the table, eyes wide and mouth slackened. "Are you high?"

"On cloud nine, woman. Never better."

Mack was happy he had selected a "Normal" to officiate the wedding, what hackers called a non-hacker in the underground. Because nobody pulled a Gabriel better than Fillion. His ability to stall and appear unaffected by chaos or details was legendary. As if reading Mack's thoughts, Fillion acted like he heard a sound and inspected the imaginary source over his shoulder. His thumb tapped the table once. No dumping info about Hanley onto the Net. Well, shit. That would have made Mack's day.

Jett studied Fillion, then examined Mack. "Nah, you're definitely off today. A braincation."

"It's the pants, isn't it?" He looked to Fillion. "Apparently, wearing my business skirt here is a matter of security. My legs are that powerful. Nobody can resist them." He faced Jett and winked. "That's *definitely* it."

"You're crazy, you know that?" She chuckled.

"Crazy in love," Mack said, wiggling his eyebrows. "He loves me, too. So much, he's speechless."

"Or he's sedated."

"Gubbish!" Mack sighed with feigned exasperation. "For a minister, your tolerance of differences is disappointing."

"Yeah, because you're so normal."

"No, you are."

"What?"

"Nothing."

Jett's eyes darted to an officer walking by. "Let's practice reciting vows then."

"Peachy."

He tracked the officer's movement, too. When he passed, Mack swiveled in his chair toward Fillion. "Do you trust me?" he asked his friend. Slivers of Fillion's gray eyes locked with Mack's through the dark strands. From the corner of his vision, Mack noted how Fillion double tapped the back of his own hand through knotted fingers.

The correctional officer walked by again. Did they suspect something? Probably not. Mack was feeling paranoid, though. Why? He had no clue. He and Fillion hadn't discussed anything dangerous or game changing. He straightened in his chair and cleared his throat. Recite vows. Act natural. Fillion met his eyes once more.

"Nothing will end between us." Mack tapped twice. "Not even our marriage." He tapped once. Shit. That was a double negative. He hoped Fillion understood, though. "Just to spend time with you—" he tapped twice "—to share my thoughts and dreams with you—" he tapped twice again "—would end my suffering." He tapped once, trying to maintain a deadpanned expression. Fillion's lower cheek twitched again.

"Wow." Jett blinked back her surprise. "Not what I was expecting. OK, Fillion?" No response. She waited. Mack waited. They remained silent and patient. After a minute, Jett patted Mack's arm.

The officer at the podium looked at Mack and tapped his wrist. Old dude, people haven't worn watches in decades. The message was clear, nonetheless. "Time is wrapping up," Mack announced. "Fillion," he continued, "next week is on, right?"

His friend tapped twice.

"Officer is coming," Jett said.

"Take care, mate." Mack tried to smile for Fillion, but fear seized him. Though they joked around, keeping anyone who was watching or listening on their toes, he now knew his gut was right. Something was wrong. Maybe not with the trial. But with Fillion. The officer gestured for Fillion to leave. "See you again, soon."

A weight crushed Mack's chest when Fillion was led away. The same helplessness that had plagued him for five months now suffocated all efforts to be cooler-than-shit. He reminded himself that this was the best he could do. Legally, his hands were tied. And Hanley was watching. Ready to pounce. Probably knew what Mack was doing. He grit his teeth. Tough shit, daddy-to-be. Hopefully, next week, he'd have a clearer picture of Fillion's needs and could take action. Something. Anything. His friend needed to regain control, and Mack would be there to ensure it happened.

"Hey," Jett nudged his shoulder. "He'll be OK. Made it this long, right?" When Fillion disappeared behind a door,

Mack acknowledged her. She smiled with understanding. "Ready?"

He tapped the table once, but got up and followed her to the door.

ϹΗΛΡΤΕΡ
ϜΙVϦ

Thursday, May 6, 2055

h is dad sipped coffee from a vintage Darth Vader mug while perusing news feeds. Mack sat on the opposite end of the table. For two years, they had met once a week for breakfast. Normally they'd shoot the breeze or discuss business needs. This morning? Silence. Mack picked at his croissant and pretended to be busy on his Cranium. But, really, he was trying not to implode.

Headlines were cropping up all over the Net this morning.

"Incarcerated Eco-Prince, Fillion Nichols, is tying the knot with long-time friend and Tech Heir, Mackenzie Ferguson, sources confirm."

"Tears of joy from stunned fangirls world-wide drown Net communities over marriage rumors."

"Net-famous bromance shocks *otaku* with secret wedding plans."

"Nichols-Ferguson nuptials a possible smoke screen for shady prison deal."

Hanley had to be shitting his pants.

Mack was surprised his own dad was so calm. Though, his dad was always calm. The calmness was on a spectrum from mellow-and-cool to eye-of-the-storm threat level. The atmosphere at the table this very moment positioned somewhere in the middle. A tension that balanced on the point of a sharp-edged blade.

Aaaand, that tension finally tipped.

The Darth Vader mug clanked loudly on the marble dining table. Dark blue eyes studied Mack over a privacy screen, the very same deep, thoughtful shade as Mack's own. But that was the only thing they shared, besides a name and similar intellect. And geeky interests. And ... OK, so they had a lot common. Still, Mack resembled his mom with a sturdy Scottish build, a playful smile advertising that he was up to no good—always—and golden brown hair. Well, his natural hair color, that is. Currently it was a solid shade of indigo-blue, like the midnight sky. His dad, by contrast, was a small man with blond hair and thin lips pressed into an eternal look of contemplation. A small man, he reminded himself, with a large presence. And right now, Mack felt it.

He resisted the urge to squirm in his seat. Dammit, he was almost nineteen. Too old for this shit. But he loved his dad. He loved his mom, too. Didn't like disappointing either of them. Or causing them problems. He was fortunate to have great parents, especially for being a corporate brat. Even more fortunate to have a healthy relationship with them in adulthood. But, in moments like this one, he understood why some had chosen to cut ties and keep family matters strictly business.

His dad continued to stare. Mack stared back. Then his dad did something unexpected. He started laughing. Not soft, jolly chuckles of the amused. Oh, no. Tears were already forming and he'd just begun. Mack opened his mouth to say something. But his dad raised a hand for Mack to stop as he lowered his head to an arm resting on the table. Still laughing. Body heaving. In-take breath growing wheezy.

Weird.

Wide-eyed, Mack focused on his uneaten croissant. What to do? He had no freaking clue. His dad had cracked. Holy shit. He broke his dad. His and Fillion's marriage was that awesome. Their upcoming union had clearly unleashed tidings of goodwill and joy to all of humankind, Net confirmed. Yin-and-yang moved into alignment. Global feng shui? Hell, maybe Earth would finally know peace.

No.

There was still the matter of Hanley. Well, dammit. Daddy-to-be ruined all the fun.

"Mack," his dad said, holding in another laugh. "This ... is ... awesome."

Yes! He knew it.

"Hanley ... oh god ... that bastard is probably experiencing an aneurysm right now."

Mack lowered his head in mock-respect and said in a solemn tone, "Our prayers have finally been answered, esteemed Father."

His dad lost it. Maybe Hanley hadn't ruined *all* the fun.

Dammit. An incoming ping echoed in Mack's head. A computer announced Hanley's name and Mack swore he saw his spirit leave his body. "Shit!" He grabbed his dad's arm. "He's calling me!"

A fresh wave of laughter seized his dad, who collapsed in his chair, tears streaming down his face. Mack let out a string of swear words as he tramped out of the dining room to the sitting area. Forget world peace. The apocalypse had begun. They were all going to die. The ephemeral thread of life, delicate as a dew drop, had finally burst. Or however that damn metaphor worked. Shit. His intelligence was fleeing, too.

"Survival of the fittest, bitches," he grit as he tapped his Cranium. "Calling to congratulate me?" he threw at Hanley. From the other room, he heard his dad laugh again.

Traitor.

"On what, exactly?" Hanley sounded like his ever charming self. "That you've finally admitted to having feelings for my son? Or for embarrassing Japan?"

Shit. He forgot about Akiko. How could *he* forget about Akiko? He'd been drooling over her for years. Damn, she was *Sekushī.* But Hanley didn't know he knew about Akiko. It was a comment meant to throw off his game. Not today, *kisama.*

"Look," Mack said, voice low. "You know this is a business arrangement, so there's nothing personal to discuss."

"You made a bad deal."

"He's eighteen." Mack sighed wistfully. "Kids grow up so fast. Transitions are hard, I know. My condolences."

Hanley chuckled, as if amused. But Mack knew it was all an illusion.

"Psychologists are concerned that Fillion is not fit to make legal decisions," daddy-to-be said. "He is still my ward in many ways."

"No, he's a ward of the state."

"Mack," Hanley continued with a silvery voice, "he is already in a contracted engagement, one he wouldn't risk breaking. Trust me. The wedding won't happen."

"Then why call me at all?"

"To give you the opportunity to do what is right. If you really love my son, you won't show up next week."

"Because he won't marry me?" Mack laughed. "Shit, Hanley. My heart is all a flutter. I didn't realize you cared about me so much. Best. Day. Ever." Hanley remained silent. The type of calm that didn't even register on his dad's spectrum. A chill wended its way up Mack's spine until the hair on the nape of his neck prickled with warning. Fillion's dad wanted him to ask about the contracted engagement, but he wouldn't. "Tell Mrs.-Fillion-Nichols-to-be that next week isn't a deal-breaker."

Hanley paused. "What assurances can you give me?"

Mack thought a moment. What had Fillion agreed to? This had to have happened after their last conversation the day of the zombie apocalypse. Either Hanley was lying or Fillion had sold his soul to the devil. The smug smile Mack heard in Hanley's voice confirmed the latter. Yet, the man was nervous. Or embarrassed. Maybe both.

He needed to give Hanley something to feel in control. He hated negotiating with the devil incarnate, but he'd made deals with lots of devils before him. Hanley would see right through lies. Then it hit him: validation. He'd stroke the narcissist's ego. Money talked. That's what this phone call was *really* about, anyway. Fillion's dad knew he couldn't stop them from marrying, regardless of their reasons for doing so. Or any prior agreements made with his son.

He clucked into the phone like he was still thinking. Bringing up a screen, he looked up the financial data on New Eden Enterprises. A slow smile crept up Mack's face. "I hear stock prices have plummeted since Fillion's incarceration. Sucks. This morning, however, prices shot up for a change and seem to be trending upward, even now. Seems public opinion favors my and Fillion's wedding. You're welcome."

"Tell me, which way will the stock move if Japan backs out of the engagement? Are you prepared to be responsible for any financial set-backs that may affect my employees? As you've so adeptly noted, Fillion has already cost me a considerable chunk of change in his choice to sabotage the experiment. He may not have any employees to manage once he comes of trust majority."

Mack rolled his eyes. "The point I'm making is that this is your moment to capitalize on regaining the public's good opinion. Make an announcement in support of your son."

"Still not good enough."

"You think Japan will want to remain in a contract with a failing company? No empire lasts forever. You know the history books. Hell, if the stock drops low enough, maybe they can buy you out." He allowed that to sink in a sec, then added, "Maybe I will."

Hanley laughed. "And what do you suggest I tell Japan, since you're so full of wisdom?"

"Sorry, that's not my problem. If you want it to be, we can discuss consulting fees."

Mack stared at the ceiling. He could feel Hanley's fury shoot through the Wi-Fi signal. Think. Think. *Think.*

"But I'm a nice guy," he continued again. "So I'll confirm that you know what to tell the betrothed family in Japan, because you already have this figured out. Am I right?"

Nothing. OK, then… Time to spell it out.

"Corporate Japan understands numbers. They speak the language of positive public opinion. It's wrapped into their culture of honor. Making an example of Fillion for the company? Sure. I get it. Sends the wrong message otherwise." Mack wanted to vomit. "But push too far and…"

"You're saying…"

"Yes." Mack smiled. "That's what I'm not saying. A temporary arrangement. Benefits everyone all the way around."

"Interesting."

"I am, it's true."

Hanley chuckled in that charming-but-slimy way of his again. "Legal back door?"

"What is this back door you speak of? I'm a good boy and abide by the laws of this land."

"If what you're not saying fails to happen," Hanley said slowly, "I'll press charges against you for taking advantage of my son while he is mentally incoherent."

Mack stilled with relief. "Yeah? Well, that's not very relational. I could think of better wedding presents. A vacation home along the Riviera. A private jet with our monograms inscribed on the side. Fine bone china for our china cabinet. Or maybe you can have a constellation named after us. Hell, all of the above."

"Oh, Mack. You know I've always thought of you like a second son."

"Nice save." He shook his head in disgust. Really? The psychopath thought he'd fall for *that*? Not in a million years, *kureejii.*

"It wasn't a save. You'd do the same if you were in my shoes. Parenting is never easy."

"I'll never be in your shoes."

"Then count yourself fortunate."

"Every day." Mack's father eased into the sitting room, traces of humor erased from his face. "All previous agreements with Fillion still standing?" Mack asked Hanley.

"I give you six months."

"Then what?"

"I revisit my agreement with Fillion."

"Deal." Mack resisted the urge to roll his eyes again. "Hey, I need to go. This chat has been ... special. I think we bonded and stuff."

"Wish I could be there next week."

"Well, you could drop charges. That'd solve so many problems."

Hanley laughed. "Always the jester, aren't you, Mack? Give your father my regards. We'll be in touch."

Silence.

Mack tapped his Cranium and let out a long breath. He felt like a balloon that had just deflated in a frenzied flight across the room.

"This chat has been special," his father mused to himself. "I'm going to use that line."

"It's all yours."

"Threats, charms, the usual baggage?"

"Pretty much."

"He let you think you won?"

"Yup, that, too."

"And, did you?"

Mack looked at his dad. "Someone will pay for my victory. I'll give you one guess as to who."

His dad sank into a chair opposite of him. "Hanley's choices are not your problem."

"Not my fault, but still my problem." He combed his fingers through his hair. "I promised Fillion I'd take care of her while he was away."

"Ever a good friend." His dad smiled, sad and reflective. "Or is there really more between you boys?"

"Nah, we joke." Mack let his head fall back on the arm of the couch as he stretched out and lit up a much needed cigarette. "Queerplatonic partners. Zero romantic attraction."

"That's what I thought."

"Hey, I have a pre-nup appointment with my lawyer in forty-five minutes." He dragged on his cigarette and blew out the smoke. "Come with me?"

"Sure. Let me move a meeting to later in the day."

"I appreciate it."

His dad squeezed Mack's shoulder and said with a wink, "Anything for my boys."

Walking away, his dad called into work to rearrange his schedule. He'd shared sentiments similar to Hanley, but Mack knew his dad spoke truth. He'd always taken care of Fillion, especially when Hanley and Della neglected to do so.

Mack would never forget the look on his dad's face when Mack brought Fillion home with a broken arm and ribs, bruised and bleeding.

School had just let out. Fillion and Mack were walking to TalBOT Industries to finish their homework before parting their separate ways, as usual. Mack's dad had given them free access to a robotics lab filled with geriatric androids and drones. Tinkering with parts and programming software to make the robots do stupid shit like fart or flip someone off was how their twelve- and thirteen-year-old minds passed most afternoons.

A block out from the school, Mack was telling Fillion of his plans to prank the seventh floor by programming the custodial Rosa to mutter, "asshat," in reply to greetings. But he never got to finish. A group of boys swarmed them, grabbing Fillion.

"Faggot!" one of the boys yelled, pushing Fillion hard.

"Pussy!"

"He even looks like a girl," another said, yanking Fillion's head back by his hair. "Gonna cry out for your dad to save you, princess?"

Fillion said nothing.

"Stop!" Mack yelled.

One of the boys spared Mack a passing glance and said, "This doesn't concern you."

"Like hell it doesn't," Mack replied, and charged him. Then charged him again. And another. He kept doing that until one of the boys shoved him to the ground. It didn't matter. They were older, stronger, and they had formed a wall around Fillion. That's when he heard four words that changed everything.

"Son of a killer!"

The next few minutes passed in a terrifying blur. Two boys held Fillion while others took turns delivering fisted blows and hard kicks. Mack cried out to passersby. Nobody would stop to help. Pedestrians looked away. Soulless humans, all of them.

Desperate, Mack stopped a Companion drone, ignoring the elementary age child it kept company. "Call the police, please."

"You have a Cranium," the hologram replied.

"It's not working. I tried." He lied. Really, he didn't want the media to trace the call back to him. All he wanted to do was protect his friend from more unwanted attention. The drone didn't seem to have facial recognition software. Or, if it did, it chose to keep the information to itself.

"Calling the police now."

"Thank you!" He sprinted across the street, back to the scene. "Hey!" he shouted. "Police drones are coming!"

"Shit!" A boy fisted another by the shirt. "Let's go." And like that, they were gone.

Mack quickly grabbed Fillion, who cried out in pain, but Mack didn't stop to consider the damage. He needed to get his friend out of there. Throwing his jacket over Fillion's head, Mack led them down an alley, which poured into another, down a side street, through a city-required permaculture garden, until reaching TalBOT Industries, only to find out that his dad had already left. The security guard alerted a chauffeur, one of two who always was on standby during business hours.

Twenty-three minutes and fifty-one seconds later, they walked into the Nichols residence. It was the first time Mack had used a timer in his Cranium. He wanted to know how long forever was inside of hell.

Fillion's body was trembling, like he was going into shock. But he kept his cool. One eye was swelling shut, blood dripped from his nose and a split lip. He cradled his left arm close to his chest, breaths shallow.

"What happened?" Hanley asked. No trace of worry. No hint of grief.

The details rushed out of Mack's mouth, slowing to a stop when Hanley circled around his son. The move was so predatory that Mack's own animal instincts stilled the blood galloping in his veins. For a few seconds, he felt suspended between the primal need to fight and the desire to pull away in self-preservation.

"Have you learned your lesson?" Hanley asked Fillion.

"Um, he didn't do anything," Mack was quick to defend. "Didn't provoke anyone."

"Some random boys appear and only want to harm Fillion?" Hanley turned to Mack. "But not you? Even when you attacked them in defense of your friend?" He shook his head with amused humor, as if Mack was so naïve. "Seems strange, don't you think?"

Mack opened his mouth to reply, but then thought better of it.

Hanley leaned down to eye level with Fillion. "Look at me." When Fillion refused to do so, he repeated the words with a threatening undertone. Gray eyes sliced over to his dad, his gaze still though his body shook with self-control and pain. "You probably deserved this," Hanley began again. "Your cocky attitude and flippancy invites trouble. Now you know the consequences. Don't pick on boys bigger than you. And, when you're older, never forget the same is true of men."

"I think his arm is broken," Mack interjected.

"I'm fine," Fillion gritted between clenched teeth.

Lynden, who had stayed home sick, appeared at the top of the stairs and gasped. "Oh my god! What happened?"

"I'm. Fine!" Fillion snapped, breath ragged.

"Since you insist that you're *fine*, I won't call for the doctor. You need to toughen up anyway. My son isn't a wimp."

"Dad!" Lynden cried out. "He's bleeding!"

"Stay out of this, Lyn," Hanley had spoken with gentleness, like he had compassion despite how it might look. "It's not for you to understand." He looked at Fillion again. "This is an important lesson, one that will prepare you for a necessary future."

That was always Hanley's justification. Like somehow he was doing Fillion a favor. Like all the suffering was "for a reason" and Hanley was God, ensuring he didn't give Fillion more than he could handle.

A core piece of Fillion had died within seconds of his dad's comment; Mack witnessed the very moment the fire turned to cold ash in his friend's eyes. Not even pain showed on his face, and he had to be in a helluva lot of pain.

Half an hour later, Hanley left for the downtown office to do "damage control" with the media. Della was out of town, as usual. Mack knew Hanley would return with a doctor, declaring "he was weak where Fillion was concerned." Bullshit. He wouldn't give the man the satisfaction of redeeming himself. Instead, he called back the chauffeur and brought Fillion and Lynden to his home.

Horror and injustice stitched into each of his dad's features upon seeing Fillion. Mack had never seen his dad cry before. He was tougher than shit. A man of logic, steady and calm. Businesses and countries cowered in his boardroom. But he knew. Somehow without being told what had happened, he knew Hanley had punished Fillion for the media fallout concerning the Watson investigation and charges. Mack even wondered sometimes if Hanley had arranged for those boys to assault his son so that he—Hanley—appeared the victim of hate crimes instead of the reverse. Perhaps to encourage Fillion to never fight back against Hanley when he was older.

"I'm sorry," Mack's dad had whispered, pulling Fillion into an embrace. "So sorry."

Fillion shattered. Broke all at once. Curled up in his dad's arms like a small child even though he was twelve. His friend had sobbed until the doctor arrived. That was the last time he'd ever seen Fillion cry. Well, until Fillion was in New Eden and his mind had slipped into a PTSD hallucination during a vid session. A psychotic episode that was triggered by memories of this day. The day that started them all.

Two weeks after the boys beat him up, Fillion began seeing things that weren't there. Talked to "the dead," especially Willow Oak Watson. Someone who needed to be saved. Just like Fillion. Both imprisoned and punished by Hanley. It was so weird. And creepy. Uber creepy. His friend knew he was mental, too, which made the delusions and self-hate worse.

Hanley spun it as evidence of Fillion's genius, which further showcased itself when Fillion graduated from high school two years early. It took everything Mack had to keep up with him academically, too. By age sixteen, the world had dropped its pitchfork and public shaming, raising *otaku* sites in worship instead. His best friend was beautiful, a *bishounen*, the kind of sensual, fine looks that made even straight men fantasize. And they did. Even now, the world continued to spin in a frenzy around their Eco-Prince.

Fillion kept it all inside, though. Showed no pain. Nothing.

But, for Mack, all he continued to see, regardless of how strong Fillion presented himself in the years that followed, was his best friend, broken, curled up, trembling, feeling protected and safe for those few, short minutes in the arms of Mack's dad. Nobody would hurt his friend again so long as Mack lived. He made sure of it, too.

"Ready?" his dad asked, walking back into the sitting room.

Mack blinked back the memory and pushed himself off the couch. Rubbing out the nub of his cigarette, he replied, "Let's roll."

"Lunch plans?"

"Nope."

"Let's make a day of it, then, to celebrate your marriage. My treat."

He smiled at his dad. "I have a few questions for you, actually."

"Yeah? Shoot."

"I think I may have met my first transhuman. An Untraceable."

His dad whipped his head toward him, eyebrows low. "That's not a question."

"So they're real?"

The car rolled out of the driveway. Once they were headed toward downtown, his dad brought up a screen and swiped: *MELISSA Project. Modulated Engineered Living Information Socio-cybernetic Systems Android. 10 humans experimented on. 3 died. Rest disappeared.*

Mack erased the message and swiped back: *When?*
21 years ago.
The one I met had to be 20, 22 tops.

His dad's faced grew darker. *Illegal augmentations. So has to be black market. Government shut down lab. Reports of nerve damage, neurological setbacks.*

How extensive were the cybernetic systems?
Not sure. But 1 was bio-hacked.

The way his dad stared at him after typing, Mack knew that was how that particular specimen had died. He erased the last line and wrote, "Almost hooked up with one. Pretty sure of it. One hell of a freaky night."

"Only you, Mack," his dad said out loud through laughter. "Robots love you."

"I'm their Overlord, *desu.*"

They pulled into the lawyer's building and Mack filed away the information. Adjusting his utilikilt, he shut the car door and marched toward the elevator. All would be set for the big day after finalizing his pre-nup. The elevator door closed and he took a deep breath.

That's right, *otaku* conspiracy theorists. Nichols-Ferguson nuptials were a smoke screen for a shady prison deal. Whatever it took to empower his friend to fight back. The conversation with Hanley had spurred an idea, too. One that would hopefully ruin daddy-to-be's future plans for control.

"I know that look," his dad said, shaking his head with warning. "That scheme you just plotted? It can't be good. Synaptic misfire."

Mack laughed. It was definitely good. Hanley would be weeping into his pillow, it was that brilliant. He grinned at his dad and winked. There was no stopping him now.

CHAPTER SIX

Tuesday, May 11, 2055

h is body moved as if someone was shaking him. Then it stopped. Good. Sleep…

Smack!

A stinging heat spread across Mack's bare ass. This was getting old. "Sleepy time," he mumbled into his pillow. "Later. Before you leave. If you're good."

"Your alarm is going off," a sexy voice cooed near his ear. "Huh?"

His head popped off his pillow. He squinted his eyes and stared at his Cranium. Sure enough, the damn thing was screaming at him. Groaning, he face-planted back into the pillow and somehow turned it off with a blind flop of his hand. Peace hath been restored. The shrieks of time, vanquished. Behold! Mackenzie Patton Campbell Ferguson the Third, Warrior-Between-the-Sheets and Robot Overlord.

Humored with himself, he rolled over to face the owner of that smooth, sexy voice and—oh god. He tried to not flinch. She was, uh … not what he was expecting. Old. She was old. Like twice his age. Maybe older. And, not attractive. Bad teeth. Dry, frizzy hair, like it had given up its will to survive. She was a little haggard looking. Damn. He never got in this much trouble when Fillion was around. How much alcohol did he have last night?

"Hey lover boy."

"Hi."

"Ready for that sendoff? I've been a good girl."

The panic, it was rising. "Sorry, can't. Just remembered I need to stop by work before my next appointment. Schedule is tight." He pulled the blankets up to his chin. Through the power of his groggy mind, he continued to send silent signals, hoping, praying, that the cougar had social cues, willing her to get out of bed.

"Feeling bashful?"

Dammit.

He nodded, slow and uncertain. Then shook his head no. Vigorously. *Act natural,* he played on repeat in his mind. "Uh, do you need a cab?"

"Nah, I live close."

"OK, then."

"Will we see each other again?"

"Nope."

"I thought we had something—"

"I'm getting married today."

Her eyes lit up. "I was your last?"

"Something like that." He cringed.

Why wouldn't she get out of bed? The rules of hooking-up, woman! No connecting beyond the physical mechanics of connecting. Still, she laid there, looking at him with expectancy. He hated awkward hook-up goodbyes. The universe was punishing him for something, he was sure of it. Fine. Be that way, Karma.

"I like this tattoo best," she drawled, tracing a finger down his arm.

Forcing a polite smile, he said mechanically, "I'm going to shower. *Alone.* Have a nice day." She leaned in for a kiss, but he jumped out of bed, covering up with pillows, and tried to walk to the bathroom like he was cooler-than-shit. It probably looked like he was stepping on Legos. Felt like it to his ego. He talked shit about liking all women, especially with older women to flirt and be silly. To make them feel good. But hell to the no. He needed to lay off the alcohol. And he needed his Fillion back.

Showered and dressed, he peeked into his room. Safe. She even made the bed. Who did that? Tip-toeing on ninja feet, he creaked open his bedroom door and peered into the hallway. Nothing. Then something. He jumped back trying to smother the horror. But failed.

"She's gone. It's safe to come out now," Lynden said. The smile on her face said it all. He narrowed his eyes and moved past her, like she hadn't caught him cowering behind his bedroom door. Or squealing in fright. "Fun night?" She asked.

"Don't want to talk about it."

"Mommy issues?"

"Ha! Ha! Very funny."

"She wanted to make you breakfast, but I told her to leave. She didn't even know who you were. Thought I was your angry, vengeful bride. Yuck!" Lynden arched that damn eyebrow. "You owe me, Mackenzie. I saved your sorry ass this morning. Literally."

He laughed. That was awful. But true. "My hero!" He batted his eyes at her, but got nothing. Not even a flicker of a smile. "All right, name your price, *Niji Doragon Ōjo.*"

She ignored his nickname for her—Rainbow Dragon Princess—and softly said, "Come home after the wedding. Don't go out." Turning her head, she nibbled on her lip ring. "Tell me all about it. We can celebrate together. I'll make us dinner."

"You can cook?"

"Yeah, Selah is giving me lessons." She shrugged. "Something to do, you know. Plus Coal is always hungry. He eats his weight in food. It's gross."

"You're so full of mumblage."

"Whatever. He doesn't stop eating. All. Day. It's not natural."

"Admit it. You think it's hella sexy to watch Farm Boy eat." He tugged on a strand of her hair, waggling his eyebrows and biting his tongue in a silly, flirtatious grin. "Kinda kinky."

Before she could verbally slap him, Mack lowered to bended knee and took Lynden's hand in his, throwing her off. Just his plan. Her eyes rounded and she darted her gaze around the room. It almost looked like she was blushing.

"Lynden Norah-Leigh Nichols," he began in the most formal voice he could conjure, "would you do me the honor of becoming my roommate? Like for reals instead of this sneaking up on me business?"

"Really?"

"For. Reals."

"Uh…"

"Yeah, you can even re-decorate the place. I don't care."

"I'm not sure I can move out yet. Need to finish school."

"I don't think Mommy and Daddy will mind. Tell Rob to come here for lessons. What's the worst that can happen?"

"I cook you dinner every night. That's what this is really about, isn't it?"

Mack tried to keep his lips from twitching. "I won't ask you to do my laundry, if that helps."

"And you clean up your own messes."

"You clean up my own messes."

"What?"

"Deal."

"Smart-ass." She flipped her hair. "Say it the right way."

"I'll clean up my own messes. Nag, nag, nag…" Mack arched his eyebrow to mock hers. "Better?"

She full-on grinned. The kind of smile that Mack had always loved. "Yes," she said with a tiny, excited jump. "I'll get some of my belongings today and meet you back here. How about steak?"

"Mack like meat."

She raised her eyebrow and he laughed again. The damn *kusogaki* beat him to the bad joke. At least she didn't groan this time. Like usual.

The rest of the morning moved on fast-forward. The next thing he knew, he was sitting in the visitation room with Jett, watching as Fillion and another inmate approached their assigned table.

"Hey," Mack said, feeling weirdly nervous all of a sudden. What the hell?

"Hey," Fillion said back, subdued. As usual. Still didn't meet his eyes, but at least he was talking.

Mack shifted his focus to a man with dark blond hair with royal blue tips and smiled with recognition. "Blue, come to witness our union, huh?" He extended his hand, which Blue shook. "Thought I heard that you were arrested. Sorry, mate."

"Good to see you, too, man."

Jett looked among them all and asked, "Are we ready?" Both Mack and Fillion nodded their heads. "OK, you may join hands."

Fillion met his eyes and Mack winked. A barely-there smile touched his friend's lips, like he was trying to hold in a laugh. But it was evident he was freaking out and playing it off as sedated, like last time. At least to Mack. Fillion's eyes darted to a camera then back to the floor, shoulders lifting a notch, no emotion to his visage. Time for fun. Face straight, Mack took Fillion's hands in his, caressing the back of Fillion's hand with his thumb. That did it. Fillion started laughing. God, it had been so long. Mack forgot how much he missed that sound.

"Still on?" He asked his friend. Fillion tapped the back of Mack's hand twice. "Go ahead," he encouraged Jett.

Rolling her eyes, Jett began. "We gather here today to witness the union of Fillion Malcolm Nichols to Mackenzie Patton Campbell Ferguson."

"The Third."

She sighed. "The Third."

"Now, say it from the beginning."

"Are you serious?"

Mack looked at her, schooling his features. "I'm always serious, *josei*."

"Yeah, no humor touches your lips. Ever."

"I'm working on it. Don't judge."

"I feel sorry for your parents." She brushed dark purple strands off her shoulder and began again. "The union of Fillion Malcolm Nichols to Mackenzie Patton Campbell Ferguson *the Third*." She waited for him to say something more, daring him almost. But he blinked flirtatiously at Fillion instead, trying to keep his friend smiling. That was his job. Make Fillion laugh. He knew it. Fillion knew it. Hell, even the *otaku* knew it. Jett leaned into Mack's field of vision. "You want my fancy speech or skip to the vows?"

"Vows," both Mack and Fillion said simultaneously.

"We're one already," Mack deadpanned. "It's a sign. Speaking of signs, I had our astrological chart done. Aries and Gemini compatibility connect on a strong physical and intellectual level." He wiggled his eyebrows. "Win-win."

Jett shook her head. "Remind me never to officiate one of your weddings again."

"Damn. That's cold." Mack feigned being scandalized and she caved in and chuckled. "I'm wooing my sapiosexual husband-to-be, *desu*. Nuptial foreplay." He returned his attention to Fillion, same playfully serious face as before. "Anyway, since our love is written in the stars, I had a constellation named after us."

"Oh god." Fillion stopped laughing long enough to ask, "Certified and registered?"

"Hellz yeah. We're now immortal." Mack grinned. "The constellation is in this shape." He lifted his middle finger.

"Nice."

"I thought so."

"Vows?"

Mack gave Jett a look of long-suffering. "Please, continue."

"Do you, Fillion Malcolm Nichols, take Mackenzie Patton Campbell Ferguson *the Third* to be your lawfully wedded husband?"

"Wait."

Jett sighed melodramatically, but finished with a kind smile for Fillion.

"Does Ha—"

"Yes." Mack lowered his voice. "Nothing has changed or will change. I made sure of it."

Fillion was still for three seconds. Fifteen seconds. Finally, he said, "I do."

Mack barely heard Jett repeat the same words as his mind started whirling around. His friend was growing more tense, even lowering his head so his hair fell over part of his face. This was the posture of fear Fillion took when tormented by his DNA donor, who inserted himself as the constant voice of reason, the way, the truth, and the light. Whatever it is was that Fillion had promised Hanley as part of the contracted engagement, it was haunting him. The world around Mack faded to red. Yet, somehow through his inner-turbulence, Mack knew to say, "I do," at the appropriate time.

"The rings?"

He reached into his pocket and pulled out matching black titanium rings, giving the one fitted for his finger to Fillion. Clearing his throat, he stood up a little taller, and in a quiet voice began. "Today I marry my best friend..." The words tumbled out awkwardly. He slid the ring onto Fillion's finger. And, as he did so, all remaining humor fled. The seriousness of the words he memorized off a wedding site hit him. This was real. Holy shit.

"OK. Fillion?"

"Today I marry my friend," he said quietly, eyes downcast. "The one I trust with my life." Fillion looked like he was ready to say more, but sobered and looked away. The same way Lynden did when battling insecurity. With a slight tremble to his hands, he slid the ring onto Mack's finger, his eyebrows knitting together, face paling.

"With the power vested in me by the state of Washington, I now pronounce you Partners for Life." Jett smiled sweetly and said, "You may kiss."

Fillion's gaze flew to Mack's. Mack smiled in response. His sexy smile. Fillion's eyes narrowed just a touch and tapped the back of Mack's hand once. In answer, Mack tapped back twice. Oh yeah. It was on.

A muscle in Fillion's lower cheek twitched. Gray eyes slipped slowly to Mack's mouth and lingered. Like he was undressing him, before raking his gaze back up to Mack's. Oozing with the controlled, seductive movements that always drove the girls and boys crazy. But Mack saw the slight smile behind his friend's invitation. Baiting smart-ass, calling his bluff. Not today, pretty boy. Mack cupped Fillion's face and lowered, hovering just above his mouth until he felt Fillion tense in an "oh shit" pose of anticipation. Mack almost laughed. Almost. Instead, he played even more.

"I hope our children have your eyes, lover," Mack whispered in his sexiest voice.

Laughter spurted from Fillion. Followed by a sound like he had held his breath, mentally escaping to his happy place until the deed was done. Mack was going to explode. Breathe in. Breathe out. Somehow he calmed himself sufficiently to move like he was going in. In the last second—at the point of no return—he diverted to kiss the tip of Fillion's nose before backing up.

"My husband is shy," Mack explained to all the spectators. The clapping and whistling grew louder. He winked at Fillion, who bent over while laughing. Unable to resist the temptation, he slapped Fillion's ass, adding, "Soon."

"No inappropriate touching," a correctional officer barked at Mack. "Next time will result in your removal."

His eyes widened. "Sorry. Got carried away in the moment, sir."

"Let's sign the docs." Jett tugged on Mack's arm and pulled him back to the table. "You sign here." She handed the stylus to Mack who flourished the air with his signature. "Now Fillion." He did the same. "And our witness." Blue signed his legal name and shot Mack a pleading look. Mack nodded his understanding. He'd keep it a secret from the underground. "We're finished," she said to the overseeing correctional officer.

"Ready?" the officer asked Fillion. Looking to Mack, the officer said, "You'll go to the private conference room first. We'll bring him in afterward."

He wiggled his eyebrows. "I'll be waiting for you, *bishounen*."

Fillion lowered his head to hide his smirk. God, he loved that smart-ass smile. Brightened his existence. Every. Damn. Time.

Mack shook Jett's hand, kissed her on the cheek, and then trailed after the correctional officer. This was it. He'd waited weeks for this moment. And all Mack felt was a sense of dread. Hanley's words spiraled through Mack's thoughts until his gut sickened with clarity. His friend had sacrificed the very thing that would have ended all of his suffering. He was pretty damn sure of it. But why? The only reason Mack could conclude created a chill so violent, it caused his entire body to shake. The world faded to red once again.

ChAPTER SEVEN

The conference room boasted the same mucus shade as the rest of the interior. Who in the hell made this decorating decision? They should be forced to wear this discharge-inspired color for all of eternity. The cement flooring with mystery stains—one in the shape of Michigan—was no more inspiring. If Fillion were in state prison, they'd get to use a trailer designed for extended family visitations. Something not as pestilent as these walls. But, as this was holding for juvenile detention, newlyweds were assigned to a non-wired room sanctioned for private legal discussions.

The correctional officer reminded Mack that sexual activities beyond kissing were prohibited and grounds for immediate removal. Though his and Fillion's time together was off-grid for prison standards, officers would interrupt every thirty minutes. Got it. Bonding through talking only. Preserve the innocence of adult incarcerated youth. When "the talk" was complete, the officer left, locking Mack inside the room.

It. Was. Maddening.

Jittery, his legs fidgeted, making the table jiggle—the one bolted down to the floor. Damn. That was talent. He knew his legs were powerful, but he didn't *how* powerful until this moment. With these findings, he supposed he could forgive the detention center for forbidding him to wear his business skirt.

Maybe.

The light above mocked Mack's eyes with its white, illuminating sneer. He squinted, sticking his tongue out at the incriminating glow. Yes. He had just taunted an inanimate object.

Sigh.

He looked down and blinked away the temporary black spots. A pen mark stained his pants above the knee. Fan-tast-ic.

What was taking so long?

He didn't like this fenced-in feeling. The way to make him spill state secrets was apparently to confine and isolate him. While Fillion's mind occupied him indefinitely, Mack needed a warm pulse to keep his beating.

Something to do.

His fingers reached up to his ear, itching to see *otaku* reactions. No Cranium.

Dammit.

Nothing. He could think of nothing.

The struggle, it was real.

He needed an occupation for his thoughts. Stat.

Pulling out his cigarettes, he lit up. It helped. Took the edge off his escalating anxiety. He enjoyed a long drag and exhaled when he heard a click. The door opened and Fillion walked in, hair still covering most of his face.

Mack stood up, feeling weirdly nervous. Like right when he had greeted his friend before the ceremony. Nothing had really changed between them. It was all a sham. The marriage was a means to an end, even though they were more than best friends. More like brothers. Hell, Mack argued their relationship went even deeper than that. But not lovers. Not husbands. Not in the truest sense, regardless of how they joked.

"Want a smoke?" Mack offered.

"Sure." Fillion collapsed into a chair. Mack reached across the table and extended a flame. Fillion leaned in until the end of his stick glowed orange. "Thanks, mate."

Fillion jerked the hair out of his eyes—finally! Mack was beginning to wonder if he'd get to see his face at all. Their gazes touched for a nanosecond before Fillion inspected the other end of the desolate room. His features looked tired and hard, broadcasting the wear and tear of battle fatigue. The fingers holding the cigarette began to quake like they had during the ceremony. Was this becoming common? Maybe Hanley was right. Maybe Fillion had cracked. Time to find out.

"No letters. No collect calls. After months of attempted connection. This kind of quiet isn't your thing, boss." Mack flicked his ashes. "My Fillion senses were tingling."

"Web slinging?" A corner of his friend's mouth lifted.

Mack shook his head. "No thrilling heroics these days. I'm being watched. Vicious spyware attack." He put the cigarette in his mouth and said, "So I decided to interrupt your ghosting efforts in person. *Bishounen*, please tell me your deliberate silence isn't some lame attempt to protect me?"

Fillion didn't answer.

"I'm a big boy so stop it. My pillow needs to dry from all the tears I've shed over your pathetic efforts to push me away." Mack paused when a shadow fell over Fillion's face. Shit. What word triggered that look? It was the look of the disturbed. One that always made the hair on the back of Mack's neck rise. Now grim faced himself, he quietly asked, "What's going on?"

"Is she still alive?"

Mack's forehead wrinkled with confusion. Had he not received his sister's letters? Or his? Maybe all contact was blocked. That would explain many things. He exhaled a stream of smoke and considered Fillion again.

"Yeah, Lyn is doing great," he answered casually. "Staying out of trouble, except when Coal's around." He paused again when Fillion flinched with his words. Fear flashed in Fillion's eyes and disappeared just as quickly. Wary, Mack continued. "She's moving in with me. Making me dinner tonight, too."

Fillion glanced at the door then at his cigarette. "Is *she* still alive?"

"They can't hear us. This is a secure room." Mack angled his head to better see Fillion's eyes. "Lynden is alive," he said, slow and punctuated. "She's even doing well with school for a change."

Gray eyes locked with his and quivered. "Willow, is she alive?" Fillion tensed as if bracing for bad news. "You ... you can tell me. Let's just get this over with."

Mack's face slackened with understanding. Oh god. Fillion thought he wanted privacy to share that Willow had died? A long breath left Mack as his shoulders slumped. He felt like an idiot. No wonder his friend seemed so jumpy and sullen.

"She's alive, mate. So are Leaf and Laur—"

He stopped. Fillion wiped away a tear and ducked his head. Dark hair fell back over his face as he drew his knees up to his chest. He dragged on the cigarette that was shaking in his fingers, trying to cover up his emotions. But there was no hiding them. Fillion swiped away another tear as he exhaled, then another.

"Shit. I should've realized you meant *her*."

"No worries, mate." Fillion offered a feeble smile. "It's all I've thought of since leaving New Eden. I'm cut off. Restraining order lifts the day before I own ..." His friend couldn't finish.

"Yeah, I heard about the restraining order."

Fillion winced again. "I can't even receive news articles about New Eden while in custody."

Mack nodded, but remained silent. He sensed there was more. And he was right.

"You seemed happy when I saw you last week," Fillion said. "You wouldn't mess with me. But I'm ... I'm..."

Too worked up, he left the words dangling in the thick atmosphere and puffed on his cigarette, eyes darting around the room. A chasm yawned before them. One Mack didn't understand how to navigate across to reach his friend. Uncertain of what else to do, he walked over to Fillion's side and sat on the tabletop next to his seat. That seemed to do it. A sob loosed from Fillion's body almost immediately. He folded up, becoming small, looking frail. Fragile. But Fillion was a warrior. Hell, he was the God of War.

For this reason, the sound of Fillion's grieving unleashed the hounds of hell inside of Mack. Everything flashed red then went dark. His thoughts. His emotions. Like a switch had been flipped. His entire body primed for combat with the rush of fury. Minutes flew by and Fillion eventually regained control of himself. Mack waited. Sensing his stare, gray eyes wandered over to Mack's fiery gaze and a light sparked. He knew. Fillion had heard Mack's silent battle cry.

It was time to "prepare for a necessary future."

Time to snip the strings held by the great puppet master.

Mack half-whispered, "I have a plan."

"I'm freaking out." Fillion sucked in a ragged breath. "I feel like if I even make a tiny mistake, Hanley will hurt her to punish me. Or Leaf. But probably her. And I won't know. I won't know it's happened until it's too late." Fillion looked at him. "Sometimes I think I'm locked up so that I can't interfere like last time."

"Wait. Hanley tried—"

"He'll blame me!" Fillion grit his teeth as he grimaced. Anguish, pain, and shame hardened his features. "He'll somehow twist it so that I'm responsible for what happens. And I'll believe him. Because I ... I couldn't save her. Can't. I can't save her."

"What are you talking about?"

"I agreed to marry Akiko."

"Agreed?" He stared at Fillion in disbelief. Mack was right about his earlier fears. And that pissed him off even more. "You have a zombie chick who has claimed your soul and your brains. For *years*. She had infected you way before she emerged from the grave. You're mental for her. Literally. But you agree to marry Akiko? What. The. Hell."

Fillion's eyebrows pushed together. "Hanley's requirement for revealing and protecting the Watsons."

Mack's mouth fell open. "Holy shit! He's extorting you?"

"If I dox him, he said he would issue a restraining order against me—"

"Done."

"Yeah." Fillion studied the cigarette balancing in his fingers. "The threat was empty."

"Then what's keeping you from pushing the red button?"

Fillion's shoulders elevated and he angled his head to the side. "I'd put the project at risk. And if he falls, then he promises to take the Watsons with him."

"He threatened you with *murder*?!"

"It wasn't said in those exact terms. But it's what he wanted me to take away from the conversation." Fillion pushed out of his seat and leaned against a nearby wall, jerking the hair out of his face. "I ... I have no proof he said it. No proof of anything. Not even what went down in New Eden." He closed his eyes. "Hanley blames everything on me and Timothy. Except his brother gets to be locked away in an insane asylum. But his own son?" Fillion chuckled with ill-humor. "Someone has to pay for what happened."

"Then press charges against Timothy. Hanley isn't above the law. Something will come up. Guaranteed. Hell, I'm a samurai for hire. The gov can pay me to hack up details."

"I promised Leaf I wouldn't. For Skylar's sake. That was also tied up in the agreement with Hanley."

A bomb of swear words exploded from Mack's mouth.

Fillion lifted a single shoulder in a weary shrug. "Justice isn't the same in New Eden as it is here. Hard to explain."

"So you're really going to marry Akiko?"

"What choice do I have?"

"Uh, I didn't think there was a choice."

Fillion turned his head away and whispered, "Exactly."

"No, I meant—"

"I know what you meant. Just drop it."

"Fillion—"

"Drop. It."

Mack blinked back his surprise. "Sorry. I can't parse that."

His friend lifted his gaze and gritted between clenched teeth, "Because I'll *own* her."

The world fell away beneath Mack's feet. For a few seconds, his heart and mind disconnected as a tsunami of thoughts hit him all at once. A crushing pain pressed the air from his lungs. Did Lynden know about Coal? He chanced a look at his friend and the suffocating pain intensified.

"That's sick," he whispered. Fillion didn't reply. Just wiped away another tear. "I had no idea, mate."

"I found out after I was removed from New Eden."

"Maybe she—"

"No." Fillion locked eyes with him. "She can't be my mistress. Her culture would punish her for immoral behavior. I won't do that to her and Leaf." He lowered his head. "Hanley said she'd never be mine before I entered New Eden ... But I never guessed..."

"The hell with Hanley. That bastard can go pound sand." Mack walked over to Fillion and leaned in close. "I have a plan—" The door opened and a correctional officer entered. "Damn your lips are smexy, lover," Mack said to Fillion, leaning in closer, before feigning surprise. He sighed dramatically, as if disappointed by the interruption. "Only kissing, nothing more. Girl Scout's honor."

The correctional officer peered at Fillion. "Everything OK?"

"Yeah. Peachy."

"Knock on the door if you're done sooner than your scheduled time." The officer considered Mack one last time before exiting.

"Well, that's awkward." Mack leaned in closer. "But your lips really are smexy." Fillion smirked and combed his fingers through his hair. "Especially when you do that."

"Do what?" He combed his fingers through his hair again. "This?"

"Not very nice of you to tease your husband."

"I'm not nice."

"True. You're the definition of naughty. Bad rap and all."

"Something like that."

"I want to grab your ass and kiss you."

"Pity. No ass grabbing."

They stared at each other. Expressions serious. Their faces tight with restrained humor. Mack winked and blew a kiss and Fillion erupted in laughter. God, how he loved that sound. He loved cheering up his best friend even more.

"Since, you're a bad, bad boy," Mack continued, "we might as well give the *otaku* the *yaoi* story they've always wanted. I'll title it 'Imprisoned by His Love: A Memoir' by Mackenzie Patton Campbell Ferguson-Nichols. Damn. I need another last name to add to my collection. Notice I dropped 'the Third' at the end? Only for you, lover." Fillion started laughing again, so hard that he had to press a hand to his stomach and lean against the wall for support. Mack added, "I've been taking my job as your official fake boy seriously, too."

"Oh god, don't tell me."

"Making the fangirls cry out in pleasure on all the forums, thinking it's you, when really it's me, is the best thing. Ever."

"You're welcome."

"Lots of action."

He cringed with the image of the cougar in his bed this morning. Really? Of all the hook-ups he could insta-remember? Then he thought of the brown-eyed-goddess and shuddered. That freaky night came flooding back to his mind. As did her words.

Wait.

Mack narrowed his eyes and said, "Still telling girls I'm a virgin, *bishounen*? Even in jail?" Fillion tried to look bored, sparing him a passing glance. Puffed on his cigarette. Exhaled smoke. The hint of a smile still touching his mouth. Mack's eyes narrowed even more. "And that I like to cuddle? And cry after messing around?"

"Stop your gritching. It makes you look more pathetic."

Mack scratched his ass with his middle finger and Fillion flashed that smart-ass smile of his. "I think you're just jealous," Mack goaded in reply.

"I think you like attention."

"True." Mack lifted his shoulder in mock-surrender, then laughed.

The decaying walls faded from Mack's peripheral vision. Instead, all he saw was faint, golden happiness. Smoking with his friend?—good times. Laughing with his BFF?—awesomeness. Talking about girls with his new husband?—nothing better. Except the girls themselves. Add a bottle of whiskey and this day would be complete. Mack wouldn't complain, though. He was soaking up every moment with Fillion, good and bad. He needed this. Fillion needed this. Hell, the whole world needed this. Yin-and-yang had slipped into alignment. Global feng shui *om*'ed with balanced harmony. Hanley hadn't ruined all the fun, after all.

The humor eventually gave way to reflection, however. Both meditating on their own thoughts for a minute. Two minutes. Mack pulled out his pack and placed a new cigarette between his lips, offering another to Fillion. He blew smoke rings in the air and tossed the lighter through one to his friend.

Fillion lifted his gaze to his for a nanosecond, then flicked the lighter. "You have a plan?"

"Yeah. I'll file for annulment within a month or two. Hanley lost his shit." Mack scooted to the edge of the tabletop once more. "But I convinced him to seize the public support to rebuild market stability. Stock prices nosedived when you were taken into custody. News of our marriage reversed the curse." With a sly smile, he said, "True. Love. Bitches. It's magic." Fillion smiled back but darted his eyes away. "I advised him to convince Japan that our marriage was a sham for business rebuilding. After all, their honor wouldn't allow their tech heiress to settle for a loser, blah, blah, blah."

"He's satisfied?"

Mack feigned offense. "Hey. When have I ever failed a business negotiation? Making deals with devils is my specialty." Fillion rolled his eyes with another nervous smile and dragged on his cigarette, peering across the room. Sensitive to Fillion's subtle shift in mood, Mack lowered his voice. "He confirmed that all agreements you held with him previously still stand as before. I wouldn't have followed through with the marriage otherwise. But, in fairness—because I'm an honest criminal mastermind—I didn't know what the agreements were until we talked."

Fillion nodded, his fingers trembling again. "What's your plan?"

"To smite thine enemies by gaining power of attorney over your financial and mental health decisions."

Fillion's eyebrows rose. "So you did talk with my lawyer?"

"Uh, no."

His face tightened with confusion. "He hasn't contacted you?"

"His courier droid rammed into my car at a stoplight and I've been trying to settle through my lawyer. He wanted to talk to me privately, but—" Mack's eyes widened. "You asshole." Fillion's mouth curved with amusement. Damn his arrogance. "Not only did you steal my idea but you asked your lawyer to harm Susani? Willingly damage, Susani? I thought you loved me. I now question everything."

"Wi-Fi is jammed in law offices. Conversations can't be tapped." He lifted a single shoulder in a taunting gesture. "Doc's can be hacked. I know this is hard for a noob. Need me to repeat this basic lesson more slowly?"

Mack flipped him off while shaking his head. "Bit dump, pretty boy."

"I asked him to draw docs for durable power of attorney, but I didn't want Hanley to find out. Court ordered a mental health evaluation at prosecution's insistence. I was put on suicide watch for a week." Fillion's face paled with what must be gruesome memories. The world faded to red once more. "Now I'm expected to take anti-anxiety meds and pass each day sedated. It doesn't take much imagination to conclude the rest."

"He won't screw with the results now. Don't worry. I'll pick up the docs on my way home and hand deliver them to my lawyer."

"Thanks, mate." Fillion smiled with relief. "I trust you with my life."

"I'd do anything for you, husband." Mack locked eyes with this friend. His words were said in jest, but they both knew their lives were already married. From the first day of preschool when they met—both wearing the same red shirt featuring a decapitated robot on the front—they were inseparable. Two hearts beating as one. For richer or for poorer. Sickness and in health. Until death. No ceremony necessary.

Fillion bit his bottom lip in a flirty smile. "Because you're my bitch."

"Damn straight."

"So, Lyn is cooking?" Fillion's expression turned dubious.

"Yeah." Mack waggled his eyebrows. "To feed Farm Boy."

"He's good to her?"

"The best." Mack sobered. "Hey, he gave me something to keep safe until you get out. A gift from Willow Oak."

"I don't—"

"It's her dad's harvest token or something like that." His friend stilled and, for a few beats of time, Mack saw an entire story unfold in Fillion's eyes. Memories. Emotions. Endings that would never be. The crushing pain in Mack's chest returned. "The only thing that survived from your room, I guess," he continued, softly. "The fire burned the rest to ash."

"Thanks." Fillion closed his eyes and drew in a deep breath. A few seconds later, he asked, "How was your mom's wedding?"

"I officiated. You should've seen the shirt bio-mommy had me wear. Lyn thinks I should frame it."

The next hour moved along to the pace of conversations that ebbed and flowed between humorous and serious. Fillion smiled and laughed more readily than when Mack first arrived on the scene. The end, however, appeared like the sneaky bastard it was. Mack wasn't ready. Five months of longing boiled down to two quick hours. Not enough. Didn't even come close for making up for lost time. But it was a start.

"Time is up," a correctional officer said from the doorway. "Say your goodbyes and come with me," he instructed Fillion. His friend pushed off the wall, an apology darkening his eyes.

"See you next week," Mack comforted.

"Yeah." Fillion rubbed out his cigarette in the ash tray. "Tell Lyn that ... that I love her. And to stay out of trouble. Especially with Farm Boy. Or I'll kick his ass."

"I'd pay money to see that."

"And sell tickets to the show."

"That, too." Mack stepped in front of Fillion's path. "Hey, come here." He opened his arms and pulled Fillion in tight before he could protest, and whispered, "Love you, friend."

"Love you, too, mate," Fillion whispered back.

"Well, shit," he said, pulling away. "Better go before you want to cuddle." Mack's eyes stung and he swallowed back the sudden emotion. "You'd cry after messing around."

Fillion smirked. That damn smart-ass. "Another time." With a wink, he passed by and followed the officer out of the room, resuming a sedated posture, hair covering his eyes.

Four hours, eighteen minutes, and eight seconds later, Mack left his lawyer's office with durable power of attorney over Fillion's financial and mental health affairs, and walked into his apartment to the smell of sizzling steaks. Lynden bustled around in the kitchen, oblivious to his return.

"Honey, I'm home."

She turned around, eyes wide. "Holy shit."

"I'm silent like a ninja."

"Too bad you don't look like one."

"Ouch. Is that anyway to treat your brother?"

Lynden smiled, a full-on grin. "I can't believe you married, Fillion. So are you a Nichols or is he a Ferguson?"

"We're modern men and hyphenated."

She rolled her eyes. "If you were truly progressive, you'd declare that you didn't need a man's name."

"I do declare, Lynden Norah-Leigh Nichols, that in the name of a man, your culinary skills smell delicious." With a harrumph, she flipped her hair, and returned to the stove.

"Dinner will be ready in five."

Under the kitchen drop-lighting, Lynden appeared to beam. It made him smile. She was happy. He could tell by her light, whimsical movements in the kitchen. Life was finally beginning to brim with purpose. He'd done his job. And he'd freed his friend from a few strings of control. Ones the puppet master could never manipulate again.

Weep, Hanley. Drown in all the tears. Consider this a lesson in preparation for a necessary future. Because it was coming. Mack would continue to liberate and empower his friend at any cost.

"Oh god," Lynden said, dropping the spatula. "I know that look. Whatever you just schemed up in your I-just-married-my-best-friend high, don't do it."

Mack laughed. He was so going to do it.

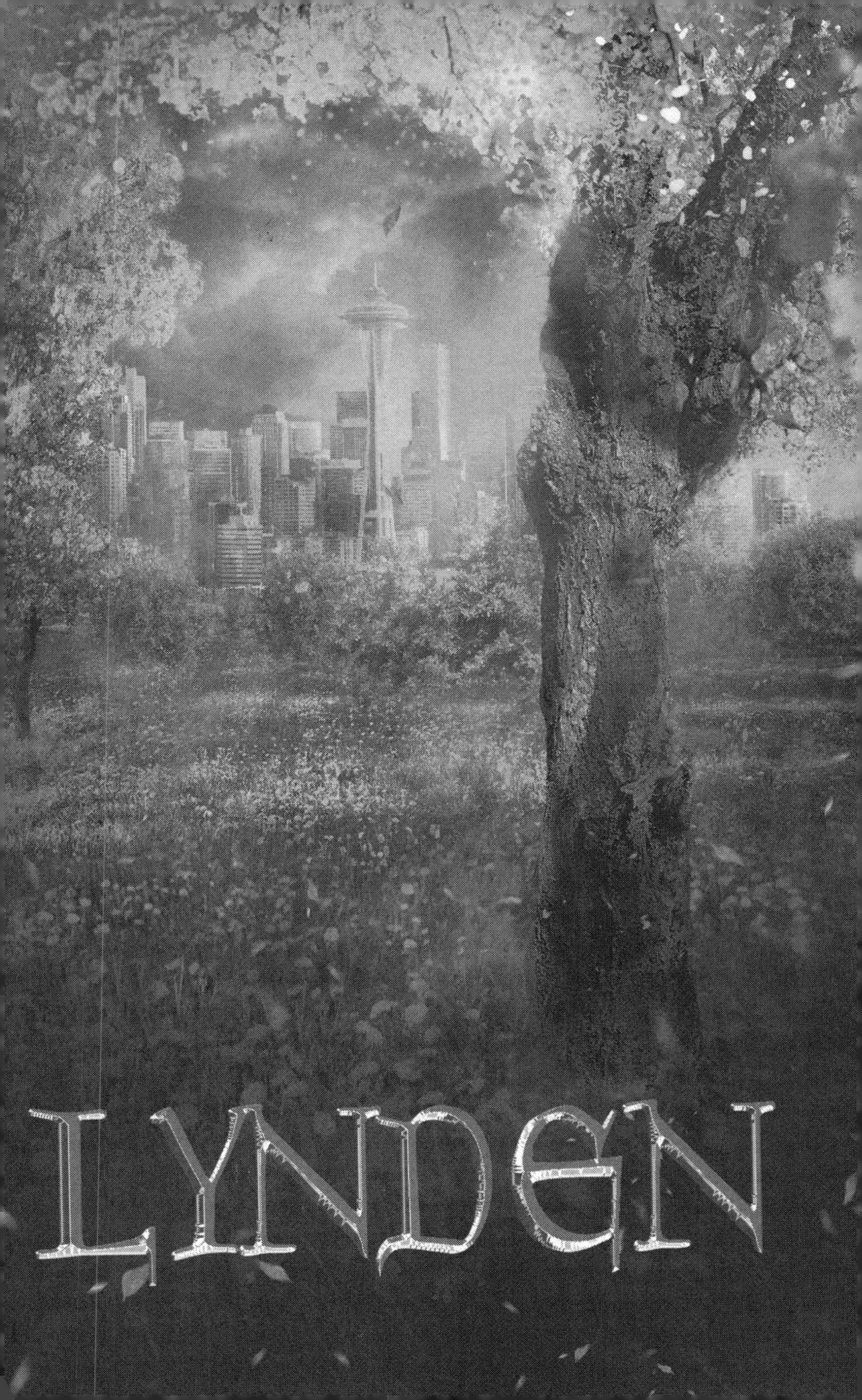
LYNDEN

Ah, dear Juliet,
Why art thou yet so fair? Shall I believe
That unsubstantial death is amorous,
And that the lean abhorrèd monster keeps
Thee here in dark to be his paramour?

—William Shakespeare, *Romeo and Juliet*, Act 5, Scene 3, 1597 *

She has secrets you know nothing of.
Her heart is unexplored territory,
her secret soul is virginal still.
She awaits an intimacy more naked than skin.

—John Mark Green, Poet, "Foolish Manboy," 21st century *

Shadows cannot see themselves in the mirror of the sun.

—Evita Peron, First Lady of Argentina, 20th century *

CHAPTER ONE

Seattle, Washington state

Wednesday, February 28, 2057

Year two of Project Phase Two

L ynden tapped the side of the coffee maker. The screen
continued to flash the happiest words on Earth—
"brewing"—while throwing digital confetti in celebration. Yet, the apparent party in a cup didn't pour into her unicorn mug. The one Fillion bought her when she was eleven.

She groaned.

"Come on," she pleaded to the machine, half desperate,
half irritated. Popping open the side compartment, she inspected the mound of freshly ground beans and shoved the tray back
into place with a threatening, "Behave."

The screen refreshed and...

Brewing.

Confetti.

The internal screams of torment.

Why wasn't this piece of high-end shit working? Lynden tilted her head in thought. Under the kitchen light, a distorted reflection in the coffee maker's screen glared back at her. Ugh. Last night, she had treated herself to an impromptu makeover—new hair, new clothes, the works. It had seemed like a good idea at the time. Now, she felt stupid. Blowing a strand of blood-red hair out of her eye, she refocused on the machine. But she had no clue what to do.

Mack's door opened and she sighed with relief—too soon. The sigh morphed into a low growl of annoyance. A girl, wearing a furry eared headband in her sea foam-colored hair, tiptoed into the hallway in nothing more than an oversized shirt and shaggy fur boots, clutching the remainder of her belongings and smothering a giggle. Then she spotted Lynden in the kitchen. The graceful doe perked her ears and froze in catatonic fright. Her perfect lips formed an "O" as her eyes blinked.

Lynden turned around.

More giggles. Different giggles.

No. Dear god.

She glanced over her shoulder to confirm. Another girl, one with pinks, lavenders, and blues through her otherwise vanilla brand of blonde hair, giggled her way on happy tip-toe dance steps to the other girl. What was with the fawn-ear headbands and shaggy fur boots? This one sported a tail, too. They whispered in each other's ears. Giggles. It couldn't be born. Lynden had yet to savor one cup—one blessed cup—of coffee. There should be rules about this.

"Oh look, his cook is here," one of the girls said. "I'll take a cappuccino in a to-go cup."

Lynden ignored her and continued to tinker around with the coffee maker.

"Maybe she doesn't speak English."

"Who cooks wearing *that*?"

"I saw her face earlier." The girl made a sound like shuddering. "She looked at me and I froze. It was like she was eating my soul."

Lynden snorted, though embarrassment wormed holes into her confidence. *Thin air thoughts.* They couldn't *really* see her. Didn't know her. Talk shit, Bambi. Go ahead. Freeze at the sight of her ugly, freckled face paired with her fine, designer clothes. Beware of the soul-eater who makes coffee.

Giggles—more irritating, bleating giggles—shot toward her.

Normally Lynden kept quiet and ignored the ignorance, trying not to cower with shame. But, this morning, all she wanted was coffee, in her own home for that matter. It should be a harassment-free event. Finding boldness, she spun on her heel, waved her hand at the wildlife, and said, "Shoo!"

In a loud, slow voice, the girl with decorated vanilla hair said, "We. Want. Coffee. Do you understand?"

"Listen Ms. Fawn-bitch," Lynden replied. "This point in a hook-up is known as the 'walk of shame.' So, tuck tail and giggle your asses out of here." She looked at the other girl. "Yes. I eat souls for breakfast. Better hurry."

Ms. Fawn-bitch narrowed her eyes and opened her mouth to reply. But nothing came out. Instead, her body writhed in a tail wag of excitement followed by high-pitched chatter with Bambi. Mack emerged from his den clothed in what appeared like a loincloth, with blue painted swirls on his skin like the savage he wished he was. Gag. Was there a convention going on or something? The girls squealed. He lifted a corner of his mouth in a sleepy smile.

Ready to projectile vomit all over the kitchen, Lynden had resumed her task when Mack caught her eye. His golden brown eyebrows furrowed slightly. Dark blue eyes darted to the girls. Thing one. Check. Thing two. Check. And back to Lynden, confusion still on his face. He blinked then looked once more to the pastel demons still haunting the living room. Red fish. Blue fish...

"Who are—" His mouth fell open and his eyes about popped out of his head. "Rainbow?"

"Is it hunting season?"

His lips twitched. "Damn. Your hair, *Niji Doragon Ōjo*. Your clothes." He wiggled his eyebrows. "Mack like. Very *sekushī*. Farm Boy is going to *nosebleed* all over the place."

"What about us?" Ms. Fawn-bitch asked with a pout, shooting a disgruntled glare at Lynden from beneath her thick lashes.

Lynden arched her eyebrow. "He's done with you." She cupped her mouth and whispered dramatically, "Walk. Of. Shame."

"Rainbow, play nice," Mack chided. His face was perfectly serious, but his eyes were laughing. "Princesses don't snarl. I might have to put you back in the closet if you don't use your manners."

"You told me we couldn't have pets. Can I keep them? Please? Pretty please?"

"She really does eat souls for breakfast," Bambi mumbled. Then it hit her. "It's... It's... " She leaned in close to her friend and whispered, both pairs of eyes riveted onto Lynden.

Ms. Fawn-bitch replied in Bambi's ear, loud enough for Lynden to hear, "*She's* telling *us* to take a 'walk of shame'?"

Lynden's stomach clenched.

"It's time to go my little doe sprites," Mack said, acting as if he heard nothing. Maybe he didn't. Sleep still creased his face. The girls wiggled while batting eyes at Mack, who strutted over and kissed both girls goodbye, before walking them to the elevator. "Alas, parting is such sweet sorrow."

The giggling wails of the pastel banshee fawns faded as the elevator sealed them away. *Damn*, Lynden thought, taking a deep breath and uncurling her fists. She had kinda hoped Ms. Fawn-bitch's tail would get caught in the door.

Mack sighed, a silly grin on his face.

Yuck.

Percolating gurgles cut through the awkward silence, and she swiveled toward the coffee maker in surprise. It was working! Unicorn mug in place, she lowered to eye level and watched as dark happiness poured into her cup. The machine chirped a song, happy with its achievement. Easing the mug away, she brought it to her nose and inhaled appreciatively.

"Thanks," Mack said, plucking the mug from her hand. To her horror, he pressed her pure, innocent unicorn mug to his filthy lips and chugged. He. Chugged. She couldn't even have the satisfaction of watching him cry out from scalding. That was too kind of a punishment, anyway. With a satisfied sigh, he plopped the mug back into her hand and headed toward the hallway, tossing a reply over his shoulder, "I needed that after last night. Those fawns put up a good chase."

Her head was about to explode. Something. She needed something to throw. Her eyes rested on the knives and she nearly laughed. Instead, she grabbed a sports bottle left in the sink and hurled it at his head.

He ducked, laughing, never breaking stride.

She released a roar of fury.

Mack scratched his ass, making sure she got a good view, then disappeared into his room.

"I hate you, Mackenzie!"

He laughed again, loud enough to ensure she heard him through the walls.

"Asshole," she mumbled.

Closing her eyes, she inhaled deep and let out a slow breath through her teeth. She went back to the coffee maker and scooped new grounds. Checked the water level. Pulled out a new mug from the cabinet. Something sanctified by the dishwasher. Then pushed the button.

Brewing.

Confetti.

The destruction of all her hopes and dreams.

"You're the soul-eater," she muttered, tapping the machine in frustration. Just as her hip fell against the counter in defeat, a ping echoed in her head. "Please be Coal," she pleaded to the universe. She brought up her message center.

        Mr. Awesome: "Happy Birthday, Lyn."

She bit back a smile and swiped a reply.

        "Thanks. Can I call you?"

257

Mr. Awesome: "In one hour? I am presently in a meeting."

"Call me when you're done."

Mr. Awesome: "Anything for the lady."

"In that case, can you destroy Mack?"

Mr. Awesome: "Easily."

Lynden suppressed a laugh.

"WILL you destroy Mack?"

Mr. Awesome: "Let us delight in his imminent doom when I call for you."

"Talk to you soon."

Mr. Awesome: "Until then, my love."

She closed her message center and studied the coffee maker once more. Forget it. Better to go downstairs to the coffee shop on the corner and order a drink. Maybe a pastry, too. Grabbing her things, she marched toward the elevator just as Mack came out of his room, fully dressed and cleaned up.

"Hey, where are you going?"

She spun on her heel and walked backwards saying, "A place where you don't exist."

"Ouch."

She walked, forward facing again, and punched the elevator button with her fist. Mack came up from behind and wrapped his arms around her, nuzzling his head on her shoulder. "I'm sorry."

"For?"

"For being me."

"Not good enough."

"Don't go yet. I'll order us food." He turned her around and rested his hands on her shoulders. "I won't touch your coffee again."

"I'll kill you next time."

Mack attempted a straight face. "You considered throwing the knives, didn't you?"

"Maybe."

"Your ninja skills are improving."

The elevator door opened. Lynden turned her head and peered out the wall of windows, twisting the thumb ring Fillion had given her on her thirteenth birthday. Rain splattered on the window and a wind gust shook the glass. The weather spoke to her loneliness and she looked away.

Today was her nineteenth birthday. Now she and Fillion were the same age for an entire month. She missed her brother. Missed his bossiness, his moods, and the way he made her feel important with his little gestures. This was the third birthday in a row where he'd been MIA. The first two he spent in juvenile detention. But, today, he was wrapping up mid-term exams at MIT. Ones that required his presence on campus. He'd been gone for two weeks now and would be gone for another two.

But, really, she longed for Coal. So much so, her heart ached. And yet, he terrified her, from the moment she found him sprawled out on her lawn to this day. He offered a world of purity and the arms of safety she yearned for, though it meant she'd have to let go. Release her grip on the ledge of self-preservation—and free fall. To what? She didn't know. She wasn't sure she wanted to know. Still, she couldn't stay away from him. The sweet addiction permeated every inch of her being.

For two years, they had sustained a long-distance relationship dotted by visits lasting anywhere from a single day to one week. Two years that her love life had entertained the world— hot alien boy and earthling girl. Her Martian romance. Boy toy from Daddy. The knight in shining armor that saved the Nichols damsel in distress. Two years that she had loved a man forged from the pages of a fairytale. But a lingering fear, one she'd never been able to shake, continued to flavor her acceptance—and her happiness.

Shortly after turning eighteen, New Eden Biospherics & Research demanded that she get an implant to monitor for pregnancy if she were to continue seeing Coal. She confronted her dad and mom, but they just brushed her accusations away with the justification that implants were standard protocol for all Earthen females who interacted with residents inside New Eden Township. No other explanation. She'd been too afraid to mention it to Coal, knowing it would send him into a rage. Same with Fillion.

But monitoring for pregnancy was not what *really* worried her. That was something of a far more personal nature.

The elevator doors closed and she let out a held in breath. Mack gently took her hand and led her to the *kotatsu* wraparound couch he had purchased a few weeks back. She collapsed onto the cushions and pulled a blanket over her legs. He eased next to her, watching her closely. She knew that look: pity, worry, and compassion. It worked on her every time, too. Damn her weak heart!

"So, you change your hair last night," he said, studying her medium-length hair shaped in edgy layers.

"Yeah. Coral's work. Something for the new grown-up me."

"I like this color on you. It's like you painted your hair with the blood of your enemies." Mack made a *kiai* sound and pretended to slice a knife across her throat.

She laughed, even though she wanted to remain mad at him. "It frightened your fawns."

"They're terrified of blood. Makes them skittish."

"Good." Lynden curled up against him and soaked up his comfort. "They'll stay away."

She didn't often criticize his hook-ups. Seeing girls tip-toe to the elevator come morning was a normal event two, sometimes three times a week. Always from Mack's room. Never from Fillion's. Her brother had turned into a monk, dedicating his life to the holy order of chain smoking and the pursuit of academics. School consumed the majority of his free time. The rest was taken up with whatever odd-end jobs their dad gave him to further train the future CEO. On those days she stayed clear of Fillion, who could be seen roaming the halls in search of a human sacrifice to appease his angry gods.

Mack adjusted the blanket covering their legs and said, "I'll pick up a new coffee maker today."

"Thanks."

"Consider it my birthday present to you."

"So you remembered."

He smiled at her, that up-to-no-good kind of grin. "Nah, my calendar just sent a notification." Lynden punched him in the arm and he laughed.

"Since you're feeling benevolent, can you bring me Coal while you're at it?"

Mack nodded his head, slow and thoughtful. "I'll see what I can do."

She rolled her eyes. "Just like that?"

"Just like that." His head fell back against the cushion. "Good thing I work today, too. One of you sounds like a dying goose when—"

"We do not!"

"Oh yeah you do. Hooooooooonk!"

He proceeded to make more pathetic, honking, dying sounds and Lynden tried to be angry, but she burst into laughter. Mack tugged a strand of her hair when she snorted, the way he always did. A handful of the loneliness melted into butterflies and fluttered away with his gesture. The sting of tears burned her eyes. She looked up, studying a hairline crack in the ceiling while spinning the ring on her thumb.

Thin air thoughts.

Bury the emotions.

She was tougher than this.

Rolling back over to his side of the cushion, his fingers drew across a canvas of air, eyes squinting in concentration. With a final tap, he closed his screen and said, "Breakfast is ordered. I added a box of hot coffee, too."

"Thanks."

"Two souls isn't enough to fill you up."

"I'm not fond of fawn souls, either."

Mack tapped his Cranium. "Jenkins? ... Yes, send him up." He looked at Lynden, a mischievous gleam in his eyes.

Damn, that was quick. What the hell did he order her for breakfast?

Pushing off the couch, he walked over to the elevator to meet the food courier. Lynden's stomach grumbled in anticipation. No, two souls wasn't enough to fill her up. She hated it when Mack was right, even about the ridiculous.

She picked at the fingernails she had painted a dark red early this morning. So dark, in fact, the color looked black except when hit with light. The blood of her enemies—ha! The linden leaf bracelet slid down her wrist and she fingered one of the copper leaves, flicking her lip ring as she tried to contain all the swirling emotions leaping through her head. She heard the elevator doors open, and her hands fell back to her lap. She peered over her shoulder with disinterest, how she greeted all strangers—

Her pulse skidded to a stop.

Coal's gaze collided with hers. At first, his eyebrows formed a crease, like she looked familiar to him but he wasn't sure. Recognition hit him a nanosecond later and his eyes flared as his mouth parted, a look of pleasure that reset her pulse. A smile stretched on his face until dimples appeared. That smile was dangerous. The kind that sent her thoughts skipping off the predictable, emotional path of safety into the wonderful, frightening unknown.

She jumped to her knees and leaned over the back of the *kotatsu*. In his hands, he carried the most beautiful roses she had ever seen, each bud afire in hues of yellow, coral, and red. She should run to him. Accept the flowers. Kiss his face silly. Instead, she blurted, "You said you were in a meeting."

"Yes, indeed. I had a press junket at New Eden Enterprises early this morning." Coal moved toward her. "I am yours until evening, however. Your father requests our presence for dinner, and then I will return to California with John."

She shrugged and looked away. From the corner of her eye, she noted how he halted all movement with her dismissive body language. What was wrong with her? She hadn't seen Coal in six weeks. Forcing herself to smile, to show emotion, she lowered the security shields walled up around her heart. He studied her face, the longing clear in his eyes. His love made her weak. Made her consider ideas that illuminated the bars to the cage she placed around her life. Thoughts and feelings that whispered, "Be free. Be fearless."

"Your smoldering gaze sucks, Son of Fire."

"Still?" he asked, moving even closer. "I shall show you in other ways, then."

His accent had softened considerably over the years. But, when confessing emotion, the lilting, British quality thickened. It was sexy and she couldn't fight its effects, even if she wanted to. Leaning down, he touched his lips to hers, tracing his thumb along the curve of her cheek.

Mack groaned a horrible sound until, much to Lynden's horror, its honking quality fully reached her ears. Oh, he was dead meat. Lynden broke away from Coal's kiss as flames radiated from her entire being. The anger burned hot with rising vengeance. To make her point further, she shifted her gaze to the knives on the kitchen counter.

"Oh shit. That's my cue to leave." Mack drew close to Coal and mock-whispered, "Beware, no coffee yet. She-demon feasting on souls."

"Mackenzie!"

"I ordered breakfast and coffee, though. Don't do *anything* until the rampage ends." Mack placed his hand on Coal's shoulder. "Be brave."

Lynden grabbed a pillow and chucked it at Mack's head. It hit with a satisfying thwump and Lynden released a wicked laugh. Mack hissed at her, lifting his fingers to form a cross and backed up slowly into the elevator. When the doors shut, a loud honking sound echoed through the walls and Lynden lost it. She couldn't hold back her laughter.

To Coal's credit, he never asked. He knew Mack well enough to know that it was usually better to leave these things alone. Jumping over the back of the *kotatsu*, he landed beside her and grinned that rascally, boyish smile that made her forget everything. Even her own name.

Gently, he rested the roses in her hands and kissed her cheek, whispering against her skin, "She is fire, forged from the sun, a brilliance that burns with each touch, each kiss, until I am nothing but ash slipping through her fingers."

She twisted the ring on her thumb and half-whispered, "That's beautiful."

"Happy birthday, my love."

His words struck an internal match and heat crept up her neck. She angled her head away, hoping Coal didn't notice. But of course he did.

"You are most becoming when you blush."

Lynden tossed the blanket and stood. "I'll go put these in water."

He tracked her escape to the kitchen, saying, "I hope the food comes soon. I am famished."

"Shocking. God, you're like a dog. Always needing to be fed, plus treats for good behavior."

"You speak as though good behavior is a rarity."

"I guess you're right. Treats are necessary."

"I am wounded, *Mademoiselle.*"

"Aww, poor Mr. Awesome," she cooed. From under the sink, she retrieved a glass vase and filled it up with water, and then began arranging the roses. "I can't believe you didn't tell me you were in Seattle."

"It is called a surprise. Pretend you like them."

A tiny smile tempted her lips. "Did Mack arrange for your visit?"

"No, your brother had, actually."

She peered over the roses. "How? It's still illegal for Fillion to have any contact with you, right?"

"True." Coal jumped over the back of the *kotatsu* and joined her in the kitchen. "As Mack would say, 'Oh ye of little faith.'"

"Oh god. You're smarter than that. Don't *ever* quote Mack."

"Ah, yes. You commissioned my services to ensure his destruction." He leaned his back against the counter, his arm touching hers, and whispered into her neck, "How else may I serve you, *Mademoiselle*?"

The breath in her lungs formed a riptide. A current that fluttered its way from her mouth in silent confession. His hand reached out until a single finger curled around one of hers. Ever respectful, ever patient. Her heart gulped loud, rapid beats to keep from drowning. But her pulse wanted him, needed him, and trembled in fear with every feeling he invoked. She could seduce him, take control and make this moment more predictable, more safe. It would be easy. In the end, however, it still wouldn't change a damn thing.

"You bewitch me," he said in a thready whisper. He planted a soft kiss beneath her earlobe. "I am completely under your spell."

"Coal..."

"Yes?"

She lifted a side glance his way. "Kiss me."

"Whatever pleases you, *mon joli petit dragon*," he whispered.

Slipping a hand up her cheek, he turned her head until his mouth captured hers. His hand traced her neck in sensual lines, whispering erotic sweet nothings across her collarbone, until his fingertips toyed with the strap of her cut-away sleeve, pulling the strings. The black silk gave way on one side, folds draping open to reveal an edge of black lace and the swell of her small breast. Satisfied, he deepened his kiss as his fingers slid along the bare skin of her shoulder, before both hands ran down the length of her back, pressing her body to his as if she were malleable, art he was crafting, a dull, uninspiring object he had the power to make beautiful with his touch alone.

Freckles faded into a creamy, velvet complexion. Her tall, boyish body transformed into a figure boasting soft, pleasing curves. Femininity continued to flame through her veins beneath his touch, incinerating each insecurity, each imperfection from her mind's eye. She was completely lost to his kiss. To him. So much so, she didn't hear the elevator doors ping open until Coal smiled against her lips. He was such a rascal.

"Leave the food on the table," he hollered over her shoulder.

"A tip," Lynden whispered.

Coal dug around in his pants pocket and pulled out a few coins. "I shall return shortly," he said with slight bow and a seductive lift to his mouth.

The heat left with Coal and Lynden dragged in a deep, ragged breath. Adjusting her clothing, she tried to appear like she didn't give a shit. Nothing affected her. Not even him. Especially him. It was too easy to forget.

But the fear clawed at her unraveled vulnerability, growing more persistent.

One day, he'd wake up from this love affair he professed for her world. And, when he did, she'd be part of the dream that faded away as reality settled. This is what terrified her the most. She wasn't the pure, spotless bride he was raised to marry, and wishful thinking or assimilation wouldn't change this fact. Despite his poetry, all the pretty promises, and his many acts of comfort and protection, he'd soon realize this truth, too.

She had never been good enough for a man like him, and never would be.

CHAPTER TWO

h alf-eaten food from a late lunch and cold cups of coffee littered the pub-style kitchen table, all but forgotten. Pressed into the folds of her bed, a supernova of heady, delirious bliss painted the night sky in her heart as Coal left stardust on her skin.

The hard planes of his body moved against her softness with sensual grace. His breath pulsed hot on her skin, flutters of passion that teased the crook of her neck. She released Coal's platinum blond hair from its tie causing silky strands to fall across her cheek in a cool, seductive caress. With a final kiss where her neck met her collarbone, he repositioned, creating momentary distance between their torsos. Her eyelids slipped shut, overwhelmed by the sweet, warm sensations exploding through her. But he was a visual feast, far better than anything her imagination could ever conjure. A mythical god. Opening her eyes, she watched the corded muscles of his chest and shoulders dance to the rhythm their bodies created. Her hands trailed down his abdomen in appreciation until she gripped his hips in an act of possession, her fingernails digging into his skin. A moan left his mouth as his lips crashed into hers.

"I love you," he whispered into their kiss.

His hands threaded into her hair, winding strand after strand over his fingers. She leaned her head back, exposing her neck once again. Wanting more of him touching more of her. Remembering the heat of his breath kissing one erogenous area after another. She arched her body with a forming sigh when his mouth connected to her offered skin, only to bite back a startled cry instead.

An image flashed violently in her mind.

Her hand reaching for a door knob. The sound of music beating on the other side. The pain shooting through her skull when *he* grabbed her hair and yanked her back to him. Toward the bed. She screamed and thrashed. He fisted a larger handful of her hair and jerked her onto blankets smelling of body odor, piss, and stale cigarette smoke. He released her hair only to slap her face. Blood spurted from her bottom lip, where his wedding ring had impacted with her face.

Lynden started clawing him. Screaming for help. Tears rolled down her face in terror. Hands, soft yet firm, gripped hers and shackled them to the bed.

"Don't touch me!" she screamed.

"Lyn, it is me," a familiar voice half-whispered. "I would never hurt you." It was a sound of safety. The fight fled her system and her body melted into the covers beneath her as she went limp. The shackles released. She opened her eyes through the tears and attempted to focus on the image sitting on the edge of the bed. "May I hold you?" the voice asked. "Only to comfort, nothing more." She loved this voice. Loved the way he embraced her in a cocoon of protection with mere words. "I shall respect your need for space, if so desired."

"Y-y-yes," she somehow got out. "Hold me." Her focus sharpened and Coal's face filled her vision. Grief tightened his features, his skin pale. "God, I'm sorry. So sorry," she said.

"Shh … there is nothing to be sorry for, my love," he spoke into her hair. Her raging thoughts swayed to the ebb and flow of his pulse. "Do not add to your sorrows."

"I ruined our only day together until who knows when."

"Not you," he said, pulling away. "Do not take blame for the actions of another." The words echoed in the hollowness she felt in hearing them. She pressed her cheek to his chest and he wrapped his arms around her shoulders. "Our day is not ruined, Lyn. I do not visit you for intimacies. I am in love with your soul, in love with *you*. I am content simply to exist in the same room as you."

She squeezed her eyes shut. Stone walls shot up to dam the terrifying emotions hurtling toward her with his words. At the same time, disgust coated her skin until the feel of his body touching hers invoked millions of invisible insect legs to skitter and crawl over every exposed surface of her skin. Panic, followed by a shudder, ripped through her and she shoved him back, pushing her way to the opposite end of the bed. Clutching the sheets, she wrapped up in the soft cotton. Shame clothed around her instead.

"Don't touch me." She swallowed back another sob. Averting her eyes, she softened her tone. "I mean, I need space. Just for a bit."

The words injured him, she knew. But he offered a tight, remorse-filled smile of understanding and said, "Of course." Coal stood with a deep breath and began to dress. "Shall I make you tea?"

"Sure." Lynden forced a flicker of emotion, a hint that she was feeling better than she was. "That'd be great."

With an apology in his eyes, he bowed to her and left her bedroom. Behind the sorrow, however, was wrath. He burned with righteous fury. Not at her. Never with her. Always at *him*. Promises of destruction flickered in Coal's dark, brown depths. But there was nothing he could do. Nothing she could do, either.

Confusion slithered through her frenzied thoughts.

Breathe, she reminded herself.

Angry tears burned in her chest and she sucked in a large breath.

The therapist, assigned by her mom, drilled into each session that the intensity behind her grief and trauma would subside with time.

But the pain would never go away.

After her assault, she felt nothing. The monster inside of her slept for months. Occasionally, she'd twinge with reminders. Faint, blurry memories that stirred when anyone demonstrated an intimidating show of anger. She'd cower and battle embarrassment, internally chanting her mantra: *Thin air thoughts. Make your feelings invisible. Toughen up. I am awesome.*

Appeased, the monster continued to slumber.

Then, with no warning, months after the incident and while enjoying the pleasure and comfort of Coal's body, the monster awakened. Then like today, she had screamed, clawed, and thrashed. Red marks had lined Coal's chest and arms where she had attacked him, blinded by her flashbacks. She had sobbed, for hours. He had held her when she needed his protection and had given her space when she needed to fight alone.

He didn't touch her intimately for several visits after that, keeping a respectful distance at all times. Ever the gentleman with care for her feelings. He had meant to be kind but, god, what an asshole move. For months she thought he had pulled away from her, too disgusted by the thought of touching someone who was damaged. Someone impure like her. Maybe if she were from his world, she would have better understood the honor behind his gesture. But she hadn't. It had felt like polite rejection, as if he didn't know how to break up with her. Nobody breaks up in New Eden. Then came another sickening thought: His honor demanded he remain bonded to her, even if she was unclean.

It wasn't true. She knew that now. But it played to her greatest fear.

Like everything.

Doubt lingered in the black spots of her mind.

"Toughen up, Rainbow," she whispered aloud. Throwing the covers aside, she lowered her feet to the floor and stood.

270

Shadows laughed from the far corner of her room. Her eyes darted to the strip of darkness and she forced her face to become like stone. "Toughen up," she whispered again. "You're not allowed to hurt me and know it," she grit between her teeth. "No pleasure from my pain."

With that, she turned her back to the shadows and dressed.

In the kitchen, Coal stared right through the electric tea kettle. A muscle twitched in his jaw and a vein pulsed in his neck. He was a coiled snake ready to strike, his anger white-hot and dangerous. Running her fingers through her hair, she visualized herself as a cat—a mighty huntress, sleek, sexy, sinew and strength combined with grace and cunning. She removed all traces of the helpless, damaged, freckle-faced girl, and moved toward him.

"Hey, Mr. Awesome."

He peered down the side of his shoulder, past her to an object just to her left. "The tea shall be ready shortly, My Lady." His accent was thick and he winced with the use of formality.

She flicked the long strands of unbound hair that fell over his eye. Still, he wouldn't look her way. The anger rolled off of him in searing waves. Feeling timid, she choked out a bleak, "Thanks."

"Lyn…"

"I'm fine. We're fine." She forced another small smile. "The episodes are becoming less common, right? That's good."

He nodded his head and returned to his vigil over the kettle. She wrapped her arms around his neck, though her body screamed in revulsion—her mind still purging the filthy memories of *his* hands on her—and planted a chaste kiss on Coal's cheek. The weather shook the wall of windows and his gaze shot over her shoulder, every muscle tight. A high-pitched whistle wound up to ear-shattering levels as steam blew from the kettle's spout. Coal started, circling his arms around her in an act of protection, and moved her away from the perceived source of danger. Realizing his hyper-alpha-male-reaction, he rolled his eyes at himself and lifted a corner of his mouth.

"My apologies," he offered.

"Nah, it was sexy." She bumped his hip with hers. "My own personal action hero."

His mouth stretched in a charming grin, but he still refused to meet her eyes.

The hot water poured into her unicorn mug in a flash of aromatic steam. Not a single drip of dried coffee tarnished the outer rim. Happy that her mug was cleansed from Mack's germs, she allowed another small smile to fully form. Coal's eyes flicked to her face for a nanosecond, before returning to his task.

"I selected 'Rainy Day' tea." He poured a cup for himself. "I thought a toast to the weather might lighten its mood."

"Flirting with rain clouds?"

"Are we jealous?"

The words were sportive. The delivery, however, was soft, uncertain, and tinged with flyaway embers of remnant anger. Still, the underlying question was unmistakable. Was she ready to play like nothing had ever happened? Like everything was normal between them?

Keeping her face bland, she sighed, "Oh please." Lynden ended by rolling her eyes as she slinked past him toward the living room, the unicorn mug snug and warm in her hands.

"Ah, the lady *is* jealous." Coal eased next to her on the *kotatsu,* ensuring ample space. Dimples appeared as he studied his own mug, and her pulse stumbled a beat. That smile was all kinds of dangerous, and he knew it. "I shall pretend otherwise as to not offend your sensibilities," he mocked in a thicker accent.

It worked. She opened her mouth to share just how much her "sensibilities" were offended by his male pride when he blinked slowly and lifted his gaze, as if overcome by the wild, snapping look he suspected existed in her eyes in the wake of his comment. And, like that, she was properly disarmed.

Damn him.

And damn every girlish sensibility.

Seizing her surprise, he pressed his forehead to hers and whispered, "*Tu es plus belle que toutes les étoiles dans le ciel nocturne. Tellement, que je fais tous les voeux de mon coeur en ton nom.*"

Now it was her turn to blink slowly, overcome. Dammit.

"What did you say?"

"I professed my love for the night sky, to make the rain clouds jealous."

Lynden snorted a laugh and his smile grew. "You're so full of shit."

"*Moi?*" Coal leaned back, creating space once more, and sipped on his tea. "No, *Mademoiselle*. I am but your devoted servant."

She dropped her gaze to her mug, nibbling on her lip ring. After a few seconds, she quietly asked, "What time is it?"

"Near time to meet your parents for dinner."

She groaned again. "Where?"

"The new restaurant along Lake Union."

"I should probably change."

She started to stand but Coal softly gripped her hand. His thumb caressed the inside of her wrist and she shivered with … pleasure. The revulsion had departed. Tears pricked her eyes and she lifted her gaze to the ceiling to hide her unexpected emotion.

"Please," he began in a half-whisper, "I am rather fond of this outfit. I shall resort to begging if necessary."

"God, you really are like a dog," she tossed out playfully in reply. "Begging? Really?"

"On hands and knees, if it pleases you."

"Barking up the wrong tree, Mr. Awesome. I'm not the swooning type."

Those damn dimples appeared again. He sent a look declaring how *she* was full of shit, and stood up. Normally he offered his hand, but the smart-ass waltzed by her with every ounce of masculine charm he possessed and swaggered into the kitchen to return their mugs. He wanted her to watch, to appreciate him, to grow faint with his show of virility.

"Shall we?" he asked, back turned.

Damn him again.

"Oh sorry. Was I supposed to faint or something?"

"Naturally."

Lynden suppressed a laugh and hit the elevator button. Lifting her eyebrow, she slipped him a mischievous look. He wanted to be playful? Good. It worked for her, too. Anything to escape the memories of this afternoon.

In her mind, the ground rumbled and split open revealing the edge into a dark abyss. The shadows were always calling to her. Laughing at her. The familiar strains of loneliness flared under their torment. Drawing in a deep breath, she screamed to the black, "You're not allowed to hurt me and know it!" Her voice echoed off the earthen walls and whispered back, "Be free. Be fearless."

Ugly. Unwanted. Whore. Dumb. Freak.

Not good enough.

"I am awesome," she murmured under her breath, twisting the ring on her thumb.

The elevator doors opened and Coal gestured for her to enter. Instead of walking ahead of him, she leapt onto his back with a triumphant laugh. The shadows shriveled into the earth with angry shrieks as the abyss closed. Layers of oppression lifted and, for a blink of time, her heart floated in zero gravity.

Coal secured her legs around his waist, flashing a grin. The rascally kind. *Oh shit.* From a squatting position, he jumped toward the elevator's glass walls now shaded in stormy hues of the indigo night. She squealed when he landed with a thunderous bang, unable to contain the laugh that followed. The doors closed and she rested her chin on his shoulder.

Coal turned his head until his cheek touched hers. "I love you, Lyn."

She nuzzled closer and buried her face into his neck, studying their reflection in the glass. The elevator began to lower and they fell through the night. His gaze collided with hers in the glass and the air in her lungs stirred, leaving in a fluttered rush of butterfly wings.

Be free.

"You set my heart on fire," he added, his voice breathy.

Be fearless.

"I love you, too."

CHAPTER THREE

Lynden nibbled on her lip ring while aimlessly pushing shrimp through rivers of citrus-infused butter sauce. Her dad held Coal's attention most of the evening, regaling them with story after story of his adventures in Antarctica, Africa, and other places around the globe. Cool and collected for someone just arriving back from Japan this morning, her mom savored dainty bites of salad and steamed vegetables. At times, her dad would ask her mom to confirm details or share a related story.

Curious eyes in the restaurant watched their table. To spectators, her family probably looked happy. Maybe even normal. Families celebrated each other's birthdays together, right? But, the hidden dysfunction churned in her soul. Lowering her fork, she stared out the window. Lake Union rippled under the magic of the night sky. Bright, flashing holographic advertisements shimmered on the surface in a pinwheel stream of colors. Rain fell in a fine mist, a gentle caress compared to the beating drops which had pounded rooftops and windows earlier in the day.

"Ms. Nichols, may I take your plate?" a waiter asked her.

The conversation halted as everyone at the table awaited her answer. "Yes, please," she said softly. The waiter nodded his head and removed her barely eaten plate. Her dad continued without missing a beat and Lynden resumed her wistful observations out the window.

"Lyn," her mom said, leaning toward her. "Are you feeling ill?"

She gave her head a faint shake, eyes fixed on the undulating water.

"If you need to talk, I'll listen."

"About what?"

Her mom's hand landed on Lynden's knee under the table. "Anything you desire."

"I have nothing to say."

The hand moved back to her mom's lap. "I understand."

Lynden forced every emotion to flee from her face.

"Life is not always—"

"Della," Hanley interjected, "I trust your visit to Japan was successful?"

Her mom issued Lynden an apologetic frown then turned a seductive gaze onto her husband. The same hand that had touched Lynden's knee, lifted and casually brushed black strands of hair from her shoulder. Her mom's nails were perfectly shaped and painted a deep burgundy. They were unlike those of Lynden, who couldn't stand salons, the catty talk of women, the demeaning stares, or the competition to be considered the most beautiful female to grace the other less fortunate women with her perfect looks. The kind that inspired men to fight wars and carve Vensuses out of marble. Gag.

Eventually, her mom's voice came back into focus and she blinked away her disgruntled thoughts.

"...wedding plans were finalized for June of next year."

"What?!"

Lynden didn't mean to blurt out her question. Horror, however, demanded a price.

Her mom softened her tone. "Fillion's studies should be complete by August if he enrolls for summer semester."

"He will." Hanley sipped on a glass of wine, tipping his head for her mom to continue.

"Your father's business schedule is demanding next year. He wishes for Fillion to join him on a world tour before trust maturity."

Lynden just got her brother back. The thought of him being carted around the world to be showcased and then married off soured what little food rolled around in her stomach. "I was wrong. I guess I don't feel too well."

Coal pushed his chair back. "May I accompany you outside for fresh air?"

"Sit down, Coal. She'll be fine," her dad said. To Lynden, he added, "You're making a scene."

She smiled with ill-humor while shaking her head in disbelief. Fine. She'd return to the meek little mouse who ate her food in silence and didn't interrupt the conversation with her childishness.

When Coal returned to his seat, Hanley continued. "You related that no expense is to be spared for Fillion and Akiko's wedding?"

"Yes, of course," Della answered. "Ms. Hirabayashi shares this opinion as well."

"I'm happy *one* of our children will have an extravagant wedding the entire world can celebrate and remember for generations to come."

Lynden whipped her head toward the window. Heat touched her cheeks until she was sure they glowed red hot. She'd give anything to feel the rain on her face this moment. If she weren't in a restaurant, she'd rest her forehead on the cool glass. Drawing in a deep breath, she slowly exhaled through clenched teeth, refusing to glance Coal's direction. The tranquil waters of Lake Union lapped against the raging torrent of her thoughts in a soothing rhythm.

Toughen up.

"Excuse me, sir," Coal said, coming to a stand. "Lyn, shall we?" He offered her his hand and helped her rise. "We will return shortly."

"She's fine," her dad said, a smile in his voice. Taking another sip of his wine, he casually added, "Lynden has a flair for the dramatic."

"Hanley," Della began with obvious caution, "She looks ill. Even I thought so earlier."

"It's called jealousy." A smug smile curved in triumph. "Green with envy. She's trying to manipulate a marriage proposal that will never come."

Lynden's mouth fell open.

Hanley smiled politely to all the onlookers, before turning sharp eyes her way. "Sit down, Lynden. Everyone is watching you."

Too shocked and hurt to think straight, she lowered into her chair. Coal remained by her side, his body rigid. Lynden avoided the whispers and studied her hands, the way each nail was filed and painted. Compared to her mom's graceful hands, she did look childish. Maybe she was overreacting. She knew Fillion was engaged. Setting a wedding date shouldn't be that surprising. And getting married had never really mattered to Lynden. New Eden's view of a bride creeped her out, anyway. Still, the ring Fillion had gifted her seemed to glare at her. She slipped it off and held it in her palm, watching how the dim light reflected off the black band.

"Sir—"

"Coal, you know I like your fire." Hanley leaned back in his chair. "I am surprised, though. She really doesn't know, does she?"

"Hanley!" her mom hissed through a forced, plastic smile. Her eyes darted around the restaurant. "She is a nineteen-year-old woman. You no longer decide whether she steps outside for fresh air or not."

Her dad gestured for Coal to resume his seat, ignoring her mom. "Impressive," her dad continued. "I knew you were a man of honor. Always valiant. But this demonstrates an entire level of trustworthiness even I never saw coming."

"Enough!" her mom challenged from across the table.

Lynden's head was ready to explode. She was tired of people talking about her as if she wasn't sitting there. Hell, this dinner was supposed to be in celebration of her birthday, not that anyone remembered. Layers of betrayal billowed the heat behind her unraveling self-control and she squeezed her hand into a fist until the black band cut into her palm.

"What is it that I *really don't know?*" she finally ground out. Every head at their table whipped her direction, mouths tight. "I asked a question. What don't I know?"

Her mom was the first to look away, unable to shield the spiral of upsetting emotions from her perfect face.

Coal dropped his gaze to a crumb on the table. A muscle twitched in his jaw and a vein pulsed in his neck.

Her dad, however, kept a steady, intense gaze, without issuing a single blink. Shadows appeared behind him, laughing at her stupidity. She had never been good enough to belong to this family. Never worth celebrating. Why was she then so surprised by her dad's exclusive statements? Or that Coal was included?

"Let me guess," she ventured. "You're going to pawn me off on someone, too, and you've contracted Coal to pretend to be madly in love with me as a publicity stunt to restore my image until my arranged marriage is to take place?"

Coal's head snapped up, his gaze white-hot with anger.

"Don't worry," Lynden directed at Coal. "I've always known we'd never last."

"You believe I am pretending?"

"Lynden," her mom pleaded. "Your offense is understandable. But, perhaps we should save this conversation for a different venue. May we come to your apartment after dinner?"

Hanley leaned over the table toward Lynden and whispered harshly, "Stop being so dramatic."

"No!" Lynden whispered back. "Does this have something to do with the implant I was required to get? So N.E.T. would know if I got knocked up?"

Coal's eyes flared before he blinked several times. "I beg your pardon?"

"Don't act like you didn't know," she shot back.

Remorse clouded his gaze and he whispered, barely above a breath, "I really did not know, Lyn. How long ..."

"Since I turned eighteen."

He sucked in an angry breath and shifted his focus back to the crumb as a flush spread over his face.

"What? Not going to ask for my hand in marriage to redeem my reputation and your honor?" Tears stung her eyes. Coal refused to meet her waiting gaze and his ensuing silence obliterated every hint of hope she had ever possessed. "Well..." she choked out, but couldn't continue.

Her dad was right about one thing.

The shadows howled in delight, reveling in her pain. In a blinding second, her heart screamed with throbbing torment right before being silenced by a fortress of stone.

Thin air thoughts.

They aren't allowed to see your pain.

Each muscle in her face relaxed, her gaze disconnecting, seeing everything and nothing all at once. Grabbing her bag, she arched out of her seat and walked with controlled, feline grace out of the restaurant and into the rain.

The weather echoed the ache knifing through her chest. Turning toward downtown, she cut through the night, swearing that the rain hissed when touching her skin. It would be a long trek, but she didn't care. It was dangerous, too. What did she have to lose? She opened her palm and stared at Fillion's ring. A part of her wanted to throw it down a dark alley. No rings. No more gifts from men. No more heartache. Her body jerked as a sob fought for release.

Her fingers, shaking with rage, slipped the black band back onto her thumb and then released the linden leaf bracelet. With a growl, she chucked it into the darkness between two buildings. The bracelet landed with a distant clatter of metal connecting to cement. The breath in her lungs stopped moving. Oh god. What had she done? It was too late. She knew this day was coming and the only option now was to leave it all behind.

Her feet, winged with fury, flew over the pavement. Her boots clomped through puddles and trampled over trash.

Drones buzzed overhead, some advertising for their employers, most racing to wherever they called home, their job complete. Couples and groups of friends passed by, not a single eye noting her existence. The shadows laughed behind every corner and in the dark patches between streetlights.

"Leave me alone," she spat at the shadows.

"Hello, Ms. Nichols." A man stepped out from the shadows. She jumped back with a stifled scream. Noting the media droid, she rolled her eyes and began walking faster, her heart still pounding with primal fear. "Is it true that you and Coal Hansen broke up?"

The words vibrated through her, but she shook them off.

The media droid continued to shoot questions at her, each one a bullet lodging deep into her body. She felt the blood run cold within her veins. Enough. She'd had enough.

"Leave me alone!" She screamed, hands fisted at her sides. People now noticed her, stopping in their tracks to gawk at "the scene" she was making. The media droid tipped his head and melted back into the shadows. Weird. They never did that. Wary, she began to turn away and resume her escape, when she caught a glimpse of Coal's figure running toward her. "Shit," she breathed. "Toughen up, Rainbow."

He stopped before her, rivulets of rain sliding down his face, his hair and clothes soaked through, breath coming in fast. The streetlight above their heads flickered, flashing glitchy light and shadows across his face.

"Lyn…"

"I don't want to talk to you." She spun on her heel toward downtown.

"You are playing into his plan."

Lynden paused mid-stride and threw her hands up into the air, shouting, "God, I'm so tired of all the lies!"

"As am I. Please…" Coal's eyes studied hers, quiet and grim. "Please let us speak somewhere private."

"I have nothing to say to you or anyone else!"

He rolled in his bottom lip. "I *love* you—"

"Don't."

"What do I have to gain in pretending this sentiment?"

She laughed, the cruel sound rumbled from the empty place in her chest. "You and I both know my dad whored me out to the son of his best friend."

The color drained from his face, his pale skin ghostly in the flickering light. "Even if that was his plan," he whispered, "every action and word I have said to you is real and honorable." Coal reached out and wove his fingers with hers. "I am in love with you, Lynden."

She yanked her hand away. "Don't touch me!"

"My sincerest apologies, My Lady." He bowed with respect. As he rose, he whispered, "I vowed to fight for your heart all the days of my life and I shall." He swallowed back emotion, and choked out, "But I am most grieved to be the cause of your pain."

"Coal … I release you from your vow."

"No." Coal stepped closer until their bodies almost touched, shaking his head in refusal. In a soft whisper he continued, "Nothing would give me greater pleasure than to call you my wife. I am yours, body and soul." He lifted his hands to cup her face, then remembered her request when she flinched. Hands dropping back to his waist, he said, "However, your father has made it impossible for us to marry."

Lynden rolled her eyes with a short laugh. "You can take your New Eden patriarchal honor and shove it up your Martian ass. I don't give a shit what my dad thinks and I don't need his *blessing* to get married. It's *my* life." Rain soaked silk clung to her skin and she shivered. "Find a pure, innocent girl who'll worship your pretty words and gestures, Coal. Don't contact me. I did my job. You've assimilated. We're done."

The fiery anger returned to his eyes and he clenched his jaw.

She angled through the crowd that had gathered without sparing another look his way. People parted for her, the dumbfounded shock written on their faces. The gaping stares distorted in her vision, the mouths growing long in silent screams. Tears of blood fell from their soulless black eyes, streaking down their cheeks alongside the rain. A cold shudder wended its way through her body and she moved faster.

Two blocks past where she left her murdered remains for the world's enjoyment, she called a cab, too frightened to keep walking. Time passed in a blur until she stormed into the apartment, dripping wet and shivering uncontrollably. She marched past Mack into the bathroom and slammed the door.

The knob turned and stuck, followed by a knock. "Let me in. Don't do anything stupid."

So Coal had called him? That thought should bring her comfort. Instead, it unsheathed a razor sharp fury that finally sliced her in half until the logical, controlled side of herself was destroyed. A raw, animalistic scream surged from somewhere deep and she swept her arm over the counter until objects flew to the other end of the bathroom.

She bared teeth at her reflection, noting each imperfection: her too wide eyes, every damn freckle, the blood-red hair now laying limp, her tall body and boyish figure. Another wave of grief slashed through her and she grabbed a metal soap dispenser and threw it at the mirror. The glass shattered. But not enough. It didn't even come close to resembling her heart.

"Lynden!" Mack shouted, banging on the door. "Open the door *now*!"

Grabbing another object, she hurled it at the cracked glass and laughed when more glittering pieces fell to the counter. They were pretty. Tiny fragments of glamour. A ruined illusion. A broken spell.

A mechanical roar came from the other side of the wall. She ignored the drill dismantling the door and grabbed another object and another, throwing them until nothing remained— like her hope. The mirror lay in shards at her feet and she danced on the broken pieces, grinding them beneath her boots.

The door was tossed to the side and Mack rushed into the room and came to an abrupt stop. "Jesus," he whispered. His eyes met hers and she cowered beneath the pity and compassion they conveyed. He gently reached out for her and she jumped back.

"Don't touch me!"

He lifted his hands in slow surrender. "You're bleeding."

"I don't care! I don't care about anything!"

"I know." His eyes filled with tears. "I know."

His open emotion battered the stone walls protecting her heart and the sob finally broke free. Her body shook as the groan heaved from her gut. A sound so haunting, so bleak, she was convinced despair uttered her pain in ways words could never describe. Her legs gave out and she fell against Mack, gasping for breath. Cradling her body to his, he picked her up and carried her out of the bathroom.

"I'm sorry—"

"Don't worry about it."

"I didn't mean…"

"It's a mirror. I can replace it. But you?" He eased into a large chair in his bedroom and wrapped a blanket around them both.

Memories of two years ago flashed in her mind. Images of waking in a hospital bed to the sound of chirping machines and Mack's face, filled with tears, like in the bathroom.

The images faded and she clutched his shirt as fresh grief rolled to the surface and spilled out of her. He never said a word. Just let her cry and scream. Let her purge and vocalize all her self-hate and fears, all the while stroking her hair or circling his arms around her. The rage eventually sputtered out, leaving her tongue thick and eyes puffy. But her grief wasn't over. Tight, clenching pain roiled in her stomach as different memories emerged.

Stop being so dramatic!

You're making a scene!

Sit down. Be quiet.

Whore.

The words mixed with her growing confusion until she blurted, "I've never once cared about getting married."

"That wasn't the point."

She shifted in Mack's arms, surprised that he had spoken. Lynden thought back over dinner and tried to find the exact moment she snapped, but her thoughts were hazy. She was so tired. Snippets of moments came rushing back—her stomach not feeling well, Coal wanting to escort her outside for fresh air, the worry in her mom's eyes. The knot in her gut intensified.

Feeling wronged suddenly felt wrong, a disturbance her mind was incapable of making right.

"If it wasn't the point, then why'd I lose my shit?"

"Hanley gaslighted you," Mack whispered into her hair. Lynden squeezed her eyes shut when he continued. "My guess? He wanted you to break up with Coal. And he wanted it to happen publicly so there was no doubt it happened."

You are playing into his plan.

She reached for her naked wrist. The hollowness in her chest gaped wider when she remembered throwing away Coal's token of affection. Bile began to rise and she pressed a hand to her gut, and set free the question trembling on the tip of her tongue.

"Why?"

"Coal loves you," Mack whispered. "And Fillion hates Akiko..." Mack opened his mouth like he was going to say more, then shut it.

Tears sprang to her eyes again and she blinked them away. Queasy sensations continued to move in nauseating circles in her stomach as his words untangled the mess in her head. "I was never good enough for him anyway."

"Yeah, because Coal is Mr. Perfect."

"That's not what I meant."

"Lynden Norah-Leigh Nichols, listen to me." Mack pulled away to look in her eyes. "A man like Coal understands what it means to play with fire."

"Mack—"

"He burns for you. *Burns.* And he likes it." Mack pulled her against him once more. "Sounds like you're plenty good enough for him."

"It's too late."

"Did you kill him?"

Lynden sighed with irritation. "Smart-ass."

"Leave my ass out of this, young lady."

"OK, mommy."

"Mack the Mother Hen says don't sass me."

A flicker of a smile touched her lips. "You'd make a good mommy."

"Yeah?" He quietly laughed. "I prefer bossy older brother. And on that note, don't ever scare me like that again. Holy shit. No boy is ever worth even a tiny scratch of self-harm, not even Mr. Perfect-Awesome-Farm-Boy. Got it?"

Tears pricked her eyes again as she nodded her head.

"But damn, that was an impressive rampage."

"I'd curtsy, but—" she stifled a yawn. Lynden sat up and said, "I should go to bed."

Mack tightened his hold. "You're not going anywhere, Rainbow."

"What?!"

"Sorry, *Niji Doragon Ōjo*. I don't trust you. The alternative is that I take you to the hospital. Your choice."

Spinning the black band on her thumb, Lynden closed her eyes with a shuddering breath. She was too tired to fight. Too tired to tell him that his male pride was gross and ridiculous. But, then again, she had destroyed a mirror and danced on the broken pieces as if they were the graves of her enemies. Dammit. She hated it when he was right.

Red eyes blinked at her from the far corner of the room.

"Fine," Lynden whispered. She buried her face into Mack's neck to hide from the shadows who were laughing at her. She hated it when they were right, too.

ChAPTER FOUR

Friday, March 16, 2057

The elevator doors opened and Lynden walked into the apartment, bags of groceries hanging off both arms. Soft, melodic minor notes filled the living room and she stilled. Sitting at the wall of windows, her brother peered out over the cityscape, Salish Sea, and Olympic Mountains while fingerpicking a tune, a cigarette dangling from his mouth. The familiar sight pulled a hint of a smile from the bleakness she'd waded through for weeks.

"You're back," she said, ambling toward the kitchen.

His fingers paused on the strings as he peered over his shoulder. "Need help?"

"Nah, just play. Keeps the monsters away." Lynden lowered the canvas bags to the ebony wood floor, happy when the song continued. "Mid-terms complete?"

"Yeah. I'll return at the end of March for my thesis presentation."

"Before or after your birthday?"

"After."

"Well, let's celebrate." She set the bag from the butcher onto the counter. "Chicken Kiev in basil-garlic sauce or steak linguine with kale salad for dinner? I can't guarantee that either will taste as good as they sound."

A corner of Fillion's mouth hitched up. "Grilled salmon, saffron jasmine rice, and tickets for two to Benaroya Hall."

"Oh." Lynden wiped every trace of emotion from her face and lifted a shoulder in a dismissive shrug. "I didn't realize Akiko was in town."

"Hell no." Fillion stopped playing and flicked the ashes from his cigarette. "I only take people I like to the symphony. I thought I'd take you out. Belated birthday present."

"Dad's idea?"

"Wow. That's low." Fillion pierced her with a haughty glare through his thick, dark hair. "Try again, Einstein."

She nibbled on her lip ring as her face relaxed into walls of granite. The arrogance behind his gaze intensified in reply. A hardness, different from the anger he carried before imprisonment, surrounded him. A new softness, too. Threads of tenderness colored most of his interactions. The unexpected gentleness behind his gestures sometimes took her breath away. The instant their dad was brought up, however, the demons howled and demanded blood.

Charged with two counts of employee sabotage, Fillion had been sentenced to twelve months of juvie. Good behavior and overcrowding had earned him an early release after only five months. Lynden had broken away from the waiting crowd and run to him, throwing her arms around his neck, not caring that she wept publicly. He had held her and whispered words of comfort in her ear, ignoring the clamor of journalists who shouted barbed questions without remorse.

Fillion was her hero, not that she'd let him know and feed that insatiable ego of his. Especially now. The man who emerged from detention was death and life incarnate. His moods flipped from one polar extreme to the other at the speed of light, usually triggered by their dad. She didn't blame him, though.

Her brother had spent more time locked up pre-trial than he had for being held guilty for the white-collar crimes he was charged with. Crimes their dad "forgave" publicly. His son, the prodigy, the hero of the people, would soon take over New Eden Biospherics & Research. According to Hanley, The Code required that he prosecute Fillion, even though his son had saved hundreds of lives and the experiment itself. But, in a closed loop system, nothing goes to waste. Prison had enabled his son to compare and contrast the journey and experience of the human experiment. To better understand nature versus nurture and its effects on isolation, confinement, and extreme environment syndrome.

The media gobbled it up. So did the shareholders.

She flitted her focus Fillion's direction. Betrayal and fury oozed from her brother's gaze. The lava drip of anger glowed bright with the promise of destruction. She understood. A similar fire simmered inside of her, too.

Lynden softened her posture and allowed a touch of emotion on her face. "Sorry," she offered. "I know you'd never sell me out to earn gold stars from the media. Dumb girl moment."

And, just like that, the anger winked out and a clearer light reflected in her brother's gaze. Fillion rubbed his cigarette out and said, "I respect your need to stay home. Whatever you want."

She didn't know what she wanted. Lately, it was an effort just to get out of bed each morning. Even breathing hurt at times. Feeling the haunting sharpness in her chest, Lynden released a slow breath through clenched teeth and busied herself with tucking away milk, eggs, and cheese in the fridge. Honeycrisp apples crowded the bottom of another canvas bag. She gathered all of the rogue pieces of fruit and deposited them into the wooden bowl on the middle shelf. It was weird, but she was usually too lazy to pull out a crisper drawer to grab a chilled apple.

Lynden righted her posture to shut the fridge door and started. Fillion stood on the other side, reached over the door, and grabbed an apple. He jerked his hair out of his eyes and took a bite, raising his eyebrow to match hers. He was such a pain in the ass sometimes. But he looked happy—for him. Was he happy to be home? Did he like school? Or maybe it was the sense of purpose he experienced in it all. She didn't have a purpose, no definable future. Not anymore.

Her gaze wandered over her brother's face, admiring his clean complexion, his full lips which often curved in a baiting, arrogant smile, and silver-gray eyes made more prominent by dark eyebrows drawn in a perpetual broody line, like he questioned and flipped off the world in a single look, all of it framed by angular features. But a slight softness in the curve of his jaw and cheekbones transformed each line that could be considered harsh into something altogether sensual. He was distinctly masculine, but beautiful in a way she'd never even come close to knowing. A gnawing pain touched her heart and she shoved it aside. Jealousy would change nothing. She slid her fingers through his chin-length hair and watched it fall back into place and then tilted her head.

"You need a makeover."

A ghost of a smile answered first, followed by, "And you need a real project." He ducked away from her hands and meandered back into the living room.

Lynden chased after him and crossed her arms over her chest. "You said 'whatever I want,' and I want you to do something with your hair. Have you even looked at yourself lately? It's scary."

"Context. Going out or staying in." He fell back into the *kotatsu* with another bite into the apple and stretched out his legs. "I'm not dyeing my hair."

"I forgot it was against your religion. I'm not sure how you can stand being around the rest of us sinners and our fake hair."

Fillion smiled. "Nice."

"That's it?"

"Pretty much."

Lynden threw her hands up in the air and marched back to the kitchen. The stomping was childish. So was slamming the groceries and cabinet doors. She wasn't entirely sure why she was overreacting. It was stupid. This entire tantrum was over the state of her brother's hair. God, she needed help. Maybe Fillion was right. Maybe she needed a real project, a purpose to plunge her into something meaningful. Embarrassment flamed up her neck and she quieted her movements.

"Lyn," Fillion called over his shoulder. "You really want to corrupt me?"

"Yes!"

"OK."

She rested carrots from the farmer's market onto the counter. "Really? God, you're so moody. What gives?"

"It would make you happy."

Lynden's shoulders deflated. "Do you think I'm petty?"

"No. I think you're bored."

"We can do something else."

Fillion smirked. "Now you're being passive aggressive."

She narrowed her eyes slightly and her brother took another bite of his apple to hide his amusement. Lynden crossed over to where he sat and said, "I get to choose everything. The hair color. The style. The piercings. *Everything.*"

His eyebrow rose again. "The piercings? That wasn't part of the original deal."

"Does Akiko like facial piercings?"

"I don't give a shit what she likes or doesn't like. Akiko will have a nuclear meltdown no matter what I do."

"Gross." Lynden couldn't hide the disgust that formed. "Then let's give Ms. Bat-shit-crazy something to cry about."

He shrugged as his lips curved in a conspiratorial smile. "Sibling tattoos while we're at it? So we can be twinsies?" He ended with a wink.

"Unicorns with heart eyes. We'll make yours a tramp stamp."

"Peachy."

"Don't tempt me. You know I'll get you drunk enough to pull it off."

A wicked gleam sparked in her brother's eyes. *Oh shit.* She knew better than to issue a challenge to Fillion. "You want to play?" he asked in a quiet voice, the dangerous kind of quiet that sent shivers of warning up her spine. "Sibling tats now out. You choose my tattoo and I choose yours."

She narrowed her eyes. "Like what?"

"Oh no," Fillion said, shaking his head slowly. "It'll be a surprise, since you like those so much."

"Think again, *Einstein*."

"Afraid?"

"Please." Lynden rolled her eyes and flipped her hair with her hand. "You tattoo something stupid on my ass and I'll kill you in your sleep, and you know it." Raising her eyebrow, she taunted, "Afraid?" He didn't answer with words. His face said it all. Fillion was delighted, giddy almost, and her pulse skidded to a stop. "Why do I have the feeling like I was just duped?"

"Tats on the forearm or wrist, so we can't escape it." His eyes slid to hers. "Steak linguine with kale salad sounds good for dinner."

Lynden's mouth fell open, before she clamped it shut with a growl of irritation. Her brother's laughter trailed after her as she marched back into the kitchen.

A few hours later, Coral and Devon arrived and began work under Lynden's instruction. Waggling his eyebrows, Mack turned up the volume on a song and scooted over to where she stood.

"Rainbow?" He offered his bottle of whiskey. She shook her head no, plucking the cigarette from Mack's mouth, who glared in reply. "Steal a man's breath, *kusogaki*? Don't you understand I need these chemicals to survive?" He tsked. "She-devil."

"Soul-eater," Lynden corrected.

Mack considered her a moment, as if taking full measure of her emotional state. "Soul-eater with the biggest heart."

Lynden rolled her eyes. "Nice try. Find new chemicals."

Mack turned desperate eyes onto Fillion. "See what I have to deal with, lover? Every. Damn. Day."

"You like feeling breathless," Fillion countered, biting his lip.

"Only when I look at you, *bishounen*."

"Don't move," Coral snapped.

The scissors slid down the front swoop of Fillion's hair, cutting away at an angle. His gaze shot daggers at Lynden. Her brother hated getting his hair cut, always had. She stuck out her tongue at him then snorted a laugh. Coral was nearly finished and Lynden appreciated Fillion's improvement from the wild, mopey appearance he was trying to pull off before. In the light, the newly dyed black hair reflected undertones of midnight blue—like a raven's feather. The left corner of his bottom lip and right side of his nose were now pierced with silver hoops, and a silver bar vertically pierced through the top of his right eyebrow. Black, angular strands fell in a swoop to a couple of inches below his left eye.

Coral fussed with the front strands of Fillion's hair, pulling the longest piece to a point, then stepped back to take in the full image. To Lynden she said, "Way better. I like the color you chose for him."

"He no longer looks weird." Lynden kept a straight face and said, "I might be able to take him out in public now."

Coral laughed as she left to join Mack and Devon.

"Thanks." Fillion's mouth compressed in a tight line. "You know how to make a man feel good about himself."

"Yeah," Lynden half-whispered, exhaling smoke. "It's the only thing I'm good at, apparently."

She didn't mean to confess her thoughts aloud. Worry creased Fillion's brows as he scrutinized her in that irritating, analytical way of his. The music's electronic beat pulsed in tandem to the echoes of life thrumming in her ears. She dragged on her cigarette, hiding any remnant of emotion from her face.

"Maybe," Fillion began, "Mack can hire you at TalBOT Industries, give you something to do."

"I don't need the money and would feel like a complete ass taking a job from someone who does."

"What about a non-profit?"

"You mean like my own?"

"Sure." Fillion patted his shirt for a lighter, pulling it from his pants pocket with an eye roll. Exhaling a thin ribbon of smoke after lighting up, he said, "Give makeovers to the lower class who secure job interviews. Make it a whole experience."

"Those already exist."

"I know." Fillion leaned forward and sought her eyes until their gazes locked. "But you have *real* assimilation skills and connections within various industries."

The reminder tightened the air in her chest. "I'll think about it."

"Who's first?" Devon asked over the music as he approached.

"Rainbow," Fillion answered in reply. He then asked Devon, "You have the picture I sent you?"

"Yep." The magenta strands of Devon's hair bobbed along with his head's movements. "Step into my shop," he said to Lynden with a wry smile and gestured toward a table propped up in the living room by the wall of windows. "Lie on your back and rest your left wrist on the edge." She eased onto the table as instructed and turned her head to the right and peered out over the twinkling city. "You know the drill. Corlan says you're not allowed to watch, upon penalty of death."

"Asshole."

The hum of a tattoo needle buzzed in her ear. Laughter floated behind her and the ghostly image of Mack—head thrown back with humor—reflected in the window as Coral animated a story. Fillion stood beside him, shoulders lifted slightly, his thumb hooked into his pants pocket, a cigarette dangling in his mouth. Lynden peered past their reflections to the few stars that had popped through the night sky in the ambient light.

Was Coal staring at the same stars? Did he make wishes for his heart's one desire, like she did? A knot of pain formed in her gut and churned, grinding against her sanity and her artificial happiness. It was unbearable and she resisted the urge to curl up into herself. She warned him years ago, begged him not to break her heart. The persistent ache was worse than anything she'd ever experienced. Worse than her assault. *He* never saw her as a real human, but Coal had intimately touched parts of her soul.

That's what hurt most. He had lied to her, intentionally. She still didn't know what her dad was talking about over dinner. But it was monumental. Coal had earned her dad's ultimate trust the moment Lynden learned she could never trust the Son of Fire again. She didn't care what Coal had to say. Didn't care if he loved her or if she still loved him. It just didn't matter anymore. The damage was already done. A tear slid down her cheek to the bed and she blinked back her emotions.

The ground of her mind rumbled until it fissured and cracked wide open. She peered over the edge into the dark abyss. Shadows hissed for her to jump, laughing at her for taking a step back.

Ugly. Unwanted. Whore. Dumb. Freak.

The vile names gusted at her on a hot wind, one that burned and blistered the fragile skin of self-respect protecting what remained of her heart.

"No, I am awesome," she whispered in her mind, then shouted, "You're not allowed to hurt me and know it!"

Loner. Cunt. Stupid. Bitch. Unlovable.

Not good enough.

"No pleasure from my pain!"

Toughen up, Rainbow.

"OK, we're done," Devin said, oblivious to her internal battle.

The tattoo pen finally silenced and her head no longer vibrated. Lynden loosed a tightened breath as the ground in her mind healed, all traces of the abyss, where the shadows hid, erased.

Devon lifted her arm and wrapped her wrist in gauze, saying "You can look now. I've blindfolded your ink until the big reveal."

Taking her other hand, he helped her to a sitting position. Fillion moved toward the bed after she quietly confirmed details with Devon. She had an idea and hoped Fillion didn't hate her for it. But the ache inside of her couldn't let go of the memorial picture in her head. Without meeting her brother's eyes, she slipped past him toward the living room in a haze and plunked down beside Mack on the *kotatsu*.

Thin air thoughts.
Bury the emotions.

"Rainbow?" Mack whispered in her ear. "Come here."

She didn't hesitate. Draping her legs in perpendicular lines across his lap, she curled up where his shoulder met his chest. Mack leaned his head on hers. She didn't have to say anything. He knew. Per their tradition, he lit up a cigarette and enjoyed the first few puffs and she stole it from his lips. Feeling bold, she also took the bottle of whiskey from his hands and drank. Mack played with the wrap around her wrist, sliding her a sympathetic look every so often. Lynden drank more and closed her eyes.

The world began to spin faster than the vortex of dark whispers in her head until the thumping music and condescending voices faded to nothing.

CHAPTER FIVE

Saturday, March 17, 2057

L yn," her brother's voice warmed her ear. "Wake up."
　　　Her eyes slit open. "What?"
　　　"Come on," Fillion said, tugging on her hand.
　　Lynden let Fillion pull her to her feet. She teetered with the weight of alcohol in her system. "I've been drinking."

"I know." Fillion's eyebrows drew together. "Let's get you to bed."

She swatted his hand away. "Stop telling me what to do. We're the same age, asshole. God, you're such a dictator."

A corner of his mouth lifted. "How does bed sound?"

"I'm so tired." She turned her head and nearly fell over when the world tipped to the side. "Where's my bedroom?"

Fillion full-on smirked. The smart-ass kind he used only when humored.

"Did Mack vanish into thin air? Like my thoughts?" She giggled and clapped a hand over her mouth with the sound.

The laughter bubbled out of her chest until she snorted, and then she giggled again. She hated giggles, especially her own. When the urge passed and sorrow took its place again, she mumbled, "Probably not good enough for him, too."

"Come on." Her brother wrapped his arm around her waist and led her forward. "Not too far."

"Why are you sad?" She walked a few steps and stopped. "Where's Mack? Did he leave you, too? That bastard."

"He's taking Coral and Devon back to the underground."

"Oh," she said through more spurts of smothered giggles. "You look hot, not that you needed help. But now you don't look like New Eden."

Fillion halted mid-stride. "What?"

"I couldn't stand it." Lynden fell into him and laughed. Fillion held her up by the waist, his posture rigid. "Aww, now you're mad at me." She patted his cheek. "Poor Fillion. Be death. Stop trying to live. It's not you. You'll never make sense of the universe. Is this why you're studying astrophysics?" Her eyes widened. "Can you read the stars? Is my name in the sky next to Coal's?" She snorted another laugh at the thought, flinging her arm toward the wall of windows. "Starlight, star bright—"

"Almost there." Gently, he turned her around and said, "The door is a few steps away."

"No!" Lynden pushed him away and staggered back. "I don't want to sleep! I'm tired of sleeping!"

"You don't have to sleep."

"I'm so tired."

"Yeah. Me, too." Fillion inched toward her. "It's hard to remain strong when it feels like any move will bring your destruction. I get it."

Lynden stared at him, tears forming despite the sputters of laughter. He took another step closer and she blinked in confusion. "Why did he choose to be more honest with Dad than me? Never mind. I know why. I tried to become a CCG. Damaged goods."

"It has nothing to do with that."

"How would you know? God, you think you know everything. Pisses me off!"

He exhaled deep and long. "I just know."

"Of course you do. Everyone knows but me." With a roar, Lynden grabbed an empty cup and threw it at Fillion. The trajectory veered far left and the cup hit a wall and shattered. Her brother's eyes grew wide. Infuriated, fists clenched at her sides, Lynden screamed, "I'm not invisible! And I'm not stupid!"

"I see you." Fillion closed the distance in quick strides and circled his arms around her. "Come on, Sis."

"You haven't called me that in ages."

He whispered in her ear. "I see you. I always see you."

"But you think I'm dumb."

"No, I think you're bored with life and want more, but very little holds meaning." Fillion pulled back and wiped away the angry tear that had escaped its prison and ran down her cheek. "I ... I want to show you something."

"What?"

"I'll show you once we're in your room. Ready?"

She nodded and he led her down the hallway and into her room. With a dispirited sigh, she sank onto her bed, covered in swirls of dark and light gray sheets and blankets, as her brother turned on a lamp. Fingers of dusky golden light undulated on the plum walls in a sickening wave and she pressed a hand to her temple. Fillion knelt next to her and unstrapped her knee length boots, pulling one off and then the other. When finished, he remained on his knees and began unwrapping the gauze that covered the tattoo on her wrist. Unraveling the last fold, he held up her arm for her to see.

Green linden leaves on winding brown twigs with dainty, ivory flower clusters circled her wrist. The delicate design was beautiful and Lynden sucked in a sharp breath, mesmerized by the intricate details. Her eyes shot to her brother's and held his gaze, tears dangerously on the edge of falling once again.

"In New Eden," he whispered, "the linden is known as the tree of love and truth." Fillion's face softened and he blinked nervously. As his face grew more bashful, he struggled to keep eye contact. "I ... I love you, Lynden. You're my world. I thought of you every day when I was in New Eden, and in prison, and while I'm at MIT. Being away from you makes me crazy."

She whispered, "I had no idea."

"Don't listen to the lies." He chanced a look her way. "If it's hard, look at the linden leaves to remember the truth."

"That I'm awesome?"

"Yeah." A corner of his mouth tipped up again. "And that I love you. No matter what. Even when I'm away."

Laughter mixed with tears and she blurted, "Did you know I threw away Coal's bracelet?"

"That's why I made it permanent."

"I'd never throw away our love," Lynden said, patting his cheek again. She snorted another laugh and leaned her forehead onto his shoulder until the rumble of giggles passed and somber emotions moved back in. Nibbling on her bottom lip ring, she eventually whispered into his neck, "I thought he was different."

Her brother's chest expanded and he held his breath for a couple of seconds. Slowly, he exhaled and whispered back, "Love has little to do with romance and everything to with honor."

"That's beautiful." She took her brother's right hand and twisted the black ring on his thumb, the one that matched hers. Next, she fondled his wedding band, worn on the opposite ring finger since the annulment, and said, "I don't understand, though."

"He honors you."

Lynden stared at his rings as her lips trembled. "No, he used me."

"Hanley used you."

"Coal hasn't tried to contact me."

"You told him not to. But he will. Trust me."

"Dad wanted us to break up so your relationship with Aki-ko could shine." Lynden sat up and mumbled, "I guess me and Coal were too bright and stole the spotlight or something."

Fillion raised an eyebrow. "*Otaku* sites say your relationship was so hot it melted the sun."

"That's the problem. The world spun around us instead of you."

Her brother smiled. "Nice."

"I'm not dumb, Mr. Astrophysics. I hated school, but I'm not dumb."

"Then do the smart thing."

"I don't want to do a thing." Lynden fell back against her pillow in a deflated heap. "And stop telling me what to do, ass-hole."

"Afraid?"

"Terrified."

"You can never lie when drunk, you know that?" Fillion eased up to the edge of her bed and bounced up and down playfully. She snorted again and gave him a push, but he remained fixed, a stubborn wall of arrogant mischief. "Let's see ... do I have a unicorn with heart eyes on my forearm?"

She snapped both hands over her mouth to hold back a loud laugh.

"Is it the word 'twinsies' in *katakana*?"

She shook her head back and forth.

"Mack's hand flipping me off?"

"Oh god, I'll do that next time. Nah, he'll be scratching his ass." Lynden shoved Fillion with her foot. "Look already!"

Fillion removed the gauze wrap around his forearm and his features transformed to glass. His eyes, however, reflected everything. Fillion was always more transparent than her, a quality she admired in him. Rolling onto her knees, Lynden rested her head on his shoulder from behind and reached around his back to trace her finger over the reddened skin. An oak tree with sprawling branches and long leaves stretched over his right forearm, the roots tangling into a Celtic knot on his wrist, to match the bicep band on the same arm.

"It's perfect," her brother whispered, breathless. The sound of his voice echoed the ache in her heart. "I was too afraid to ... to..." He didn't finish, clenching his jaw instead. After a few seconds, he turned around to see her face. Gray eyes hardened to steel and bore into her with such fierceness, she almost flinched. "You played into Hanley's plan. Don't let him win."

"Speak for yourself."

He shook his head. "Not the same."

"Seems the same—"

"Lynden," he said her name softly. "Hanley is preventing the legal act of marriage before a court of law, not a relationship. Don't confuse the two."

Her heart stilled. "But—"

"Akiko is going to hate this tattoo." A full grin transformed her brother's face and her thoughts stumbled. "Ms. Bat-shit-crazy will cry. Good job."

If he was trying to distract her, it worked. She tried to curtsy but fell over in a fit of alcohol-induced giggles. Lynden curled up on top of her bed, a hand wrapped around her stomach. The humor eased a few seconds later and she rolled to her back. The linden leaf tattoo caught her eye and the giant stone in her stomach churned around clenched knots of anxiety. Fillion lifted her blankets and covered her.

"Will you play your guitar?" she asked him. "It keeps the monsters away."

"Sure."

He mumbled a "will be right back" comment as he passed through her doorway. A minute later, he returned, his guitar in hand. The wood shimmered a vibrant, neon blue that faded to gray then black, meant to resemble the wings of a blue morpho butterfly. He told her the metaphor behind it once, but she couldn't remember the significance in the thick fog that fumed her brain.

"Any requests?" he asked as he settled into a chair.

"What you were playing when I came home this afternoon."

Head bowed, hair falling over his eyes, his fingers began plucking a minor melody. He played one song after another, each one as haunting and beautiful as the last. At some point, Mack returned home and leaned against her doorframe, smoking a cigarette. She lifted tear-stained eyes to Mack, who winked at her. She offered a feeble smile in reply.

A pocket of loneliness transformed into a rainbow of butterflies and fluttered away despite their punctured wings. A layer of oppression melted off of her with their escape and a tiny spark of hope flickered in her darkness. Lynden closed her eyes, satisfied that the shadows wouldn't visit, and allowed her brother's music to carry her away with the butterflies.

The next morning, Lynden trundled into the kitchen to make a cup of coffee. A beating pain hammered in her head and she groaned. Popping the side tray out of the coffee maker, she scooped new grounds. She then removed the water container and shuffled toward the sink and froze in horror. Beside the sink lay a handful of ceramic shards that once made up her unicorn mug.

"What the hell?" she whispered under her breath.

Peering over the counter in a panic, she scanned the living room until her eyes rested on a hole in the wall. Damn. She remembered screaming at Fillion. She remembered pain bursting from her like beams of exploding light. She didn't remember throwing anything.

Her heart sank and she sucked in a sharp breath to stifle the forming tears. A dark head popped up from the *kotatsu* with the sound, and she jumped back. Fillion looked her way, eyes half-shut with sleep.

"You slept on the couch?"

He covered a yawn and stood. "Yeah, in case you needed me or tried to leave."

The rainbow pieces and blue unicorn eyes stared at her with accusation. "I'm sorry. God, I'm such a spaz lately." She pressed a hand to her mouth and held her breath to stop the tears. "I guess Dad is right. I do have a flair for the dramatic."

"That's what he wants you to believe."

She turned away and continued her task, not in the mood to rehash events from her birthday dinner. Water container back in place, she pulled a mug from the cabinet and put it beneath the spout and pushed the button.

Brewing.

Confetti.

Dark, liquid happiness streamed into her mug.

The coffee maker chirped a song in celebration. She wrapped her hands around the mug and savored a sip. Fillion's words still lingered in her cloudy thoughts and she sighed with annoyance. No point in avoiding the obvious.

"Did I put the hole in the wall?" she asked.

Her brother reluctantly met her eyes with a single, curt nod.

"See? Dramatic. Lynden the dumb girl, famous for 'making a scene' and embarrassing the Nichols name."

"More like 'Lynden the quiet girl who is finally finding her voice.'"

"Yeah, the soul-eater is manifesting."

Fillion walked into the kitchen and grabbed a mug from the cabinet. "Good. Don't go back to sleep."

"Aww, I'm so glad you're proud of my tantrums."

"Proud? Not even close." Fillion pushed the button on the coffee maker and leaned on the counter to face her. "I'm relieved."

She looked away from him and twisted the ring on her thumb. "I feel crazy."

"That's also part of his plan." Fillion sipped his freshly brewed coffee and continued. "Image. Perception. Those illusions are the two keys to power."

"You sound like Dad."

Fillion stiffened as his own inner demons sprang to life at her careless comment. God, she could be such a bitch sometimes. Lynden sighed with remorse. Too late to take it back. When the torment passed, he dropped his voice to an intimate hush.

"You're not crazy, Lyn," he began. "It's normal for people to have feelings. It's abnormal to pretend they don't exist."

"More New Eden wisdom, Mr. Astrophysics?"

A hesitant, flicker of a smile. "Something like that."

"God, you always think you know everything."

"Because I do." The hint of a smile curved into a goading grin. "It's part of my charm."

Her face grimaced with disgust. Before she could declare how Fillion's male pride was gross, Mack trudged into the kitchen, eyes squinting with sleep, his hand running through his wild, messed up hair. He waltzed up to Fillion, patted her brother's ass with a finishing squeeze while kissing his cheek, whispering, "Good morning, lover," and reached for a mug over her brother's shoulder. "A little luck o' the Irish for you this morning." He looked at Lynden and said with a comical nod, "St. Paddy's Day."

"Not the same as getting lucky," Fillion replied with humored aloofness. "Plus, you're Scottish."

"Well, mate," Mack slurred in a half-drunk, half-sleepy haze. "It's the most action you've seen in a millennium, so I'd say it is, Irish boy." Fillion flipped him off and Mack laughed. Looking at the mug in his hand, he said, "Tell me it's Saturday. I don't want to adult today."

"It's Saturday," Fillion answered flatly.

Mack paused and blinked. "Really?"

"Really."

"Hot damn." Mack put the mug back into the cabinet. "I'm going back to bed. Hell to the no with adulting." He wiggled his eyebrows at Fillion. "Want to spoon? You can hold me if you're in the dominating mood."

"I'm busy, mate."

Mack peered at Lynden then back to Fillion. "Heartbreaker," he mumbled. "Always choosing to dominate everyone else over your never-really-happened husband."

"Jealous?"

"Hellz yeah." Mack made a kissy face at her brother and then wandered out of the kitchen, tugging on a strand of Lynden's hair before exiting.

Fillion tried to hide a laugh by sipping on his coffee. Her brother was definitely happy. School had been good for him, she concluded. In this brief period of his life, he had a purpose outside of their family—even if MIT was Hanley's idea. But, to Lynden, it seemed like an accomplishment all Fillion's own, a way to escape the shadows in his life. Her gaze touched the oak tree on his forearm then slid to the linden leaves circling her wrist.

Be free.

She wanted to know the kind of happiness Fillion had found. Desperately.

Be fearless.

"I think I'm going to look into opening a non-profit."

Fillion's gaze target-locked onto hers. "I'll help financially and set up whatever connections you need, underground and street level."

"Do you think Mack would help me run the business end of things until I'm comfortable flying solo?"

Her brother lifted his eyebrow. "You want his advice?"

"I told you," Lynden said, rolling her eyes. "Here's the official sign that I'm crazy."

"Me too, then." Fillion replied, raising his mug in a toast. With a wink he added, "Twinsies."

The sun broke through the clouds in Lynden's heart, driving away the shadows, and she allowed a genuine grin to form for the first time in weeks. Before wandering back to her room, she playfully threw out, "Kiss me, I'm Irish." Fillion smiled and kissed her cheek as she passed by. She'd need all the luck she could get.

CHAPTER SIX

Friday, March 30, 2057

The cherry trees at Jefferson Park in the Beacon Hill neighborhood branched up toward the blue sky in a profusion of pink blossoms. Lynden picnicked beneath a tree that overlooked the Seattle skyline, happy for the solitude and afternoon sun-soaked weather. Petals floated in the breeze, falling across her lap and dotting the grass around her blanket.

Hanami season had begun in Japan. Lynden honored the ancient tradition by appreciating the *sakura* trees gifted to Seattle by Japan over forty-five years ago in a gesture of century-long friendship. Most Seattleites preferred the cherry blossoms at the University of Washington. Jefferson Park, however, was her favorite. Not only was it quieter, it was breathtakingly beautiful, especially with Mount Rainier's snow-capped peak behind the Seattle cityscape.

All around Lynden, couples, friends, and mothers with their small children sprawled out on blankets beneath the blossoms. One tree over, a boy and girl kissed as if the world belonged only to them. The gentle breeze fingered their hair and Lynden watched, with longing, how the strands delicately danced in the air. Did she question his honesty? Worry that he might betray her one day? Or feel unworthy of his love, regardless of his actions?

Did he make her feel beautiful when the rest of world told her she was ugly?

Lynden tried to think of something else. Anything. But her heart ached for Coal. She saw reminders of him in everything, from the stars, to the food she made for dinner, to certain songs on her playlist. She heard his voice when afraid. Imagined his touch instead of the warm light through the wall of windows. A few times, she had felt the urge to skip, thinking of his smile whenever she was silly. God, that smile. It was dangerous. Even in her daydreams those dimples wiped her brain clean and she couldn't think. The pain throbbing in her chest wouldn't let her forget a damn thing, though.

Breathe, she reminded herself.

She had to keep moving forward and plan her life without him. It helped to lessen the heartache and fear. Investing in her own future and career had brought a form of freedom she had never experienced before. Like roll-around-in-it, throw-your-hands-in-the-air kind of happiness. She didn't ask her dad's permission. She didn't seek her mom's counsel. She plotted her own course—separate from her family, separate from empire-building for Fillion, separate from helping Coal blend in with the real world—and acted on each choice with emerging boldness.

It was terrifying, though. The persistent dread that somehow she had done something wrong or had somehow disappointed her parents gnawed at her gut. Not hearing from either her dad or mom on the subject intensified the anxiety. They had to know. But they left her alone. It was weird.

And with increased anxiety, came the internal battle.

The shadows whispered their familiar taunts and laughed at her flailing attempts to start her own business. She struggled to comprehend the logistics behind opening a non-profit organization. But she'd get it, eventually. There was no rush.

People gaped and snickered at her with disbelief at times. She ignored them. They didn't see the *real* her. Talk shit, strangers and city officials. Go ahead. Beware of the Eco-Princess, daughter of the world's Corporate King, who isn't afraid to get her hands dirty or admit that she doesn't understand laws and business requirements. If they weren't judging her over this, it would be over something else anyway.

Still, the embarrassment wormed holes in her confidence.

Lynden shifted her attention from the Seattle skyline to her new tattoo. The green linden leaves and ivory flower clusters popped out against her black and purple plaid visual *kei* dress. "I remembered," she whispered to the tattoo, as if it had the power to tell her brother, who had returned to Massachusetts yesterday. Content, she lifted the bento box on her lap close to her mouth and used chopsticks to pick up a sushi roll, when a familiar, lilting voice spoke from behind where she sat.

"'*Under the linden tree, on the heath, where we two had our bed, you might find both beautiful flattened flowers and grass. At the edge of the wood in the valley, tandaradei, the nightingale sang beautifully.*'"

The chopsticks paused mid-air. Lynden squeezed her eyes shut and fought the smile that started to form, as well as the tears.

Toughen up.

Bury your emotions.

"Allow me," he said, now before her on the blanket.

Calloused fingers coaxed the chopsticks and bento box from her hands. Searing flames shot through her veins when his skin brushed along hers. Still, she kept her eyes closed, too afraid that if she opened them, he'd disappear. Too afraid of how she'd react if he remained.

"I brought transforming strawberries," he continued, a thread of uncertainty in his thickened accent.

Her eyes flew open and landed on a face she'd yearned to see for weeks. She wanted to jump into his arms. Allow him to feed her strawberries beneath the falling petals. Kiss his face silly. Instead, she blurted, "What in the hell are you doing here?"

"Mack told me where to find you."

Her eyebrow lifted in surprise. "And how did he know?"

"Tracker."

"What?! I'll kill him."

Coal rolled in his bottom lip as a muscle pulsed in his jaw. In a choked whisper, he said, "I am so sorry, Lyn." He hesitantly met her eyes. "I had to see you. If you do not wish to see me, I shall leave your presence and cause you no further grief."

"I... It's just..." She inhaled a deep breath and exhaled slowly. "I'm freaking out."

"I am as well."

"You hurt me," she said, clenching her teeth as tears stung her eyes. "I trusted you."

"You deserved my honesty for a while now, rather than my pride. It was inevitable that you would learn of your father's ... plan. But I could not bring myself to share this detail of my life with you." Shame rolled across his features as he pulled out an envelope from his pocket. "Before you make any decision as to our future, I do ask for you to read this letter. It confesses what I am not at liberty to speak aloud. The consequences are dire." His eyes collided with hers in a thunderous storm of restrained emotion. He placed a lighter on the blanket beside the bento box. "When complete, please light each page on fire and throw it into the river."

"Does my dad know you're doing this?"

"He knows I am in Seattle, but not that I am making a full confession."

"And if he finds out?"

Coal sucked in his bottom lip again. "I am comforted in that he believed you already knew. If he did not care then, why should he now?" He rose from his kneeling position on the blanket. "I shall walk the river if you wish to find me."

"What if I don't?"

His breath hitched and he turned his face away. "Then, My Lady, please know that my greatest pleasure in life has been falling in love with you in newer, deeper ways each day since first I met you. I do not regret a single second, regardless of how our time together came to be." Bowing deeply, he whispered, "And I shall never stop fighting for your heart, Lynden Nichols."

She watched his retreating form, her pulse seeming as ephemeral as the wilted, bruised *sakura* blossoms falling into her lap. She was tougher than this, even though the hand holding his letter trembled. She could burn it right now and never know a single world. Her thoughts glitched in and out of focus until the gilded bars to her cage appeared in her vision.

What did she want?

She didn't have to please Coal. She didn't have to sell herself to promote her dad's grandiose plans for the future. She wasn't responsible for her brother's success.

Her thumb caressed the surface of the letter. She'd learn this truth one way or another. Coal declared it was inevitable.

She was a mighty huntress—sleek, sexy, sinew and strength combined with grace and cunning. Lynden removed all traces of the helpless, damaged, freckle-faced girl and slipped a fingernail beneath the seal and opened the letter.

My Dearest Lynden,

How does one even begin such a confession? I fear my heart shall bleed until the letters are no longer legible. Rather, it shall be paper smeared with remnants of fathomless emotions I never wish to see an end to and some I wish I had never known at all. I shall do my best to make sense and to honor you in the words that follow.

I love you, Lynden. I love you so completely the intensity is frightening. Every day I am humbled that I—a mere man, dust of the earth— possess the privilege of protecting the life you have bonded to mine. Before you roll your eyes and declare that my male pride is distasteful, consider this: I know your soul. For this honor you have gifted me, I would be remiss to not bare my soul in return. Yet, I did not.

For this failure in protecting you, I shall never forgive myself.

Lynden lowered the letter to her lap and wiped away her angry tears. Inhaling a deep breath, she exhaled slowly through clenched teeth and began reading again.

A few weeks following the Great Fire, I learned a terrible secret. I alone know this secret in New Eden for your father required that I sign a legal document ensuring my silence. As you know, I am not to enter New Eden without an escort and I am limited to two short visits per month, except for ceremonies and feasts. This is to ensure I remain true to the terms and agreements in that contract. The notion that I owned a choice in signing or refusal of that document is laughable. I possess little to no rights in reality.

"No," Lynden whispered. "Oh god." She knew what was coming. She re-read the last line and a shiver danced over her skin. How she had failed to recognize the signs until now, she didn't know. Maybe she hadn't wanted to see it, pretending instead that he really was forged from a fairytale. Her knight in shining armor. The dragon and the princess. Slamming the letter down, she blinked back her grief and peered out over the water. The stone in her gut scraped over her raw, blistering pain and she nearly cried out.

But I could not bring myself to share this detail of my life with you.

She understood the blinding shame. And, if Mack hadn't opened his big mouth to Coal a couple of years ago, she would've hidden the inevitable, too. She knew the degradation of being owned by another, of being seen as less than human, of being sold off for the entertainment of greedy monsters. And worst of all, her dad had known what she was doing and never interfered. Was it so she'd never feel reviled by his plan to whore her off to a man from New Eden? So she'd be easily dazzled by the romantic gestures and acts of honor, knowing they'd continue to break her spirit?

The ground in her mind split open and the shadows appeared, aroused by her festering emotions, red dripping from their exposed fangs, the blood lust blazing in their gaze. Swallowing back her fear, she picked up Coal's letter and jumped off the ledge and into the abyss, letting go of all thoughts of self-preservation. Shrieks and cackles of delight followed her descent into the black. There was no turning back now. The letter shook in her hand, and she continued to fall.

Contrary to Hanley's stated purpose, the experiment was not designed to test my generation's ability to sustain life while confined and isolated, nor to test the survival prowess of the generation before mine. It was to produce a product. Though scientists can perform miracles with human DNA, they cannot manipulate epigenetic tags the way they can design blue eyes or blonde hair and select gender. Humans have yet to permanently colonize the moon or Mars because their genetic code is programmed for Earth. They cannot separate from their mother planet for long without going mad. New Eden Biospherics & Research offered a theory to counter this problem by suggesting that colonization could be achieved through the alteration of genetic memories, by erasing remembrances of Earth through environmental conditioning.

I am the product of this science experiment. My genetic code was engineered through psychological and environmental conditioning and through transgenerational epigenetic inheritance in the lab at N.ET. Therefore, in accordance to the federal laws governing genetic engineering, I am human property of New Eden Biospherics & Research.

In my selfishness, I wished to hide my shame from you. I wanted to know that when you looked upon me, you saw a man and not a slave. Curse my male pride if you like. I shall not refuse you this satisfaction, for it is nothing compared to the grief my silence has caused you, or the physical hardship I had not known you suffered.

The implant to monitor for pregnancy was required, I have recently learned, because N.E.T. would own our child. I cannot even begin to express my sorrow with this revelation, nor the rage for how the lab has treated you. With my body, I have worshiped you, my love, and my only regret now is that I may have unwittingly caused you pain no woman should ever know. Now that we are both informed, I wish to make it explicitly clear that I would protect you with my life, even welcome death defending any child our acts of love conceive.

Lynden gulped a sharp breath. Her body began to tremble as rage settled in her bones. Like Coal, she'd die before she'd allow anyone to take a child of hers for human trafficking operations, even those glossed over as "science" for positive public opinion and support. Fury tingled in her blood, like a lit fuse.

Her dad was smart to leave her alone right now—the real reason he hadn't interfered with her business start-up plans. He knew Coal would share. And, when he did, she'd explode and make a scene unlike any to date. Hanley would appear the villain. How could he not?

Fillion was right. Their dad wanted her to believe she was crazy and melodramatic. Her hazy self-doubt would be easy for him to spin into golden threads of victimization.

She wouldn't play into his plan. Wouldn't let him win.

A strand of blood-red hair fluttered in front of her face as she returned her focus to the letter.

In my heart, Lynden Nichols, you are my wife. I shall never love another with my body and soul as I do you. However, the law forbids legal unions between human property and free humans. If we should venture to be so bold, New Eden Biospherics & Research would be required by law to permanently separate our lives upon discovery of our marriage. Lab-owned humans are allowed to breed (such a disgraceful word). But they are not to form families outside "their kind" to protect the integrity of their DNA—and, perhaps moreso, to protect that of free humans. Common law blocks our ability to live together as we would eventually be seen as domestic partners.

I have nothing to offer you save the beating heart in my chest. If it is still good enough for your love after all you know, I shall be the happiest of men. Please be warned, however, that I shall endeavor to prove myself worthy of you for as long as I draw breath. I made my vow to you as a man free to choose for whom his heart beats, a choice I would make a thousand times simply for the honor and pride of declaring that I am yours.

With all my love and affection,

Yours truly,

Coal M. Hansen

Lynden leapt to her feet and ran toward the Duwamish River, Coal's letter crumpled in her hand, the bento box, strawberries, and blanket all forgotten. Grass and pink *sakura* petals moved beneath her in a teary blur. Picnic-goers and Companion drones froze into still-frame images of shock and curiosity as she dashed past. Screaming their cruel words, the shadows chased after her. Their whips of torment lashed with each step, flaying the flesh of her self-worth until the bones and marrow of all her insecurities were revealed.

Her mind screamed, "No pleasure from my pain!"

She refused to grant them an ounce of power over her.

On the crest of the hill leading to the river, she stopped. Wind ribboned around her in cool comfort. The tight skirt of her dress pressed against her thighs, and her hair fanned away from her face. Coal stood at the bank, his back turned to her. He stood tall, a solid wall of muscle and conviction. The afternoon sun dipped low behind the bronzed buildings on the horizon, illuminating his body in a soft, golden glow. The Son of Fire was fierce, a modern mythical god, and she found that she no longer feared him.

She *burned* for him.

"Coal Hansen," she called out.

He spun toward her, eyes wide.

Their gazes collided in a clash of molten iron and swirling tide pools. The hiss of contact solidified the black abyss to obsidian and she crossed over to the other side. In the light of his presence, her shadows incinerated. Coal was wrong. She wasn't forged from the sun. He was. And she wanted him to shatter the false mirror in her heart. To destroy her in a way where she'd see her true self instead of the faulty reflections others showed her.

His breath caught as emotions openly danced and played across her face. A single finger scorched her skin where he touched, a tender caress along her cheek and lower lip, before his hands held her face with the kind of reverence she'd only seen people show for rare treasure.

"Lyn—"

She didn't let him finish that thought. They could talk later. Her mouth claimed his in a searing rush as her body flew into his, like moth to flame. She threw her arms around his neck and the letter fluttered in her fingers. He clutched her dress and pressed her closer until she melted away in pools of liquid fire. His grip relaxed and he explored the length of her back while deepening the heat of their kiss. He didn't just appreciate her body, he *cherished* her.

She was pissed that she had doubted him. Pissed that he had hidden the truth of his circumstances until now. Yet, none of that mattered anymore. It seemed so petty, so inconsequential. Her family was in the human trafficking business and she was in love with a man they had enslaved. Fury surged through her at the audacity of owning another human being. And not just the owning, but the sense of entitlement—the cruel hubris—of one human believing it was their right to physically and psychologically destroy the life of another, and the cold detachment of the humans who turned their head and looked away.

Monsters, all of them.

The kiss slowed and she eventually pulled away, untangling her breath and body from his. He opened his mouth to speak, but she touched her fingertips to his lips, whispering, "Sometimes words ruin everything."

Flicking the lighter, she lowered the first page into the tiny flame until it caught fire, then the second. She placed the pages on the bank next to the river and watched as they burned to ash. With a low, guttural scream, she kicked what remained into the water, baptizing her and Coal's shame.

She wanted to skip and dance in circles. To sing at the top of her lungs. Instead, she scooped up a handful of petals with a giggle and threw the blossom cast-offs up in the air to rain pink confetti over her and Coal.

No. Dear god.

She was giggling. *Giggling.*

Disgruntled, she blurted, "You didn't see that. It never happened."

Coal smiled until dimples appeared. "See what exactly, *Mademoiselle?*"

Dammit.

"Yeah, like I'm going to fall for that trick."

"You mean, when you *giggled?* Or when you threw flower petals?" He plucked a petal from her hair then lifted her hand to his lips and said, "Rest assured, *mon joli petit dragon*, both are normal responses after kissing me."

Lynden yanked her hand back with a groan and stalked back up the hill toward her picnic blanket to hide her smile. She knew Coal would follow. And, when he did, she spun on her heel to walk backwards and said, "Here boy!" and patted her thighs. "Do you want me pet your ego?" She asked in a syrupy coo. "Yes, you do. Oh yes you do."

Coal flashed her a grin. The rascally kind. *Oh shit.* She swiveled to face forward and broke into a run. Dumb. Pointless. So very stupid of her. In a few, quick strides, he picked her up and threw her over his shoulder.

"Put me down you asshole!" she squealed, pounding his back. "Carrying me like a caveman is not hot!" Coal just chuckled at her pathetic protests.

The picnic-goers and Companion drones froze into still-frame images once again, eyes wide and mouths parted at the scene they were making.

She didn't care. Talk shit, bystanders. Go ahead. Fill the Net with her drama.

In gentle movements, Coal lowered her to the blanket beneath him, his face inches from hers, their chests heaving for breath. The sighs of longing left her mouth in a fluttering rush of butterfly wings as *sakura* blossoms flitted and twirled on the breeze. Lynden felt magical, a princess on a bed of beautiful, flattened flowers and grass.

Coal tucked a strand of hair behind her ear. "You are so very lovely," he whispered. "I am bewitched by you."

She blushed like a silly girl, flicking her bottom lip ring, unsure of how to reply.

He repositioned himself until his hair formed an intimate curtain around their faces and she could see only him. "Lynden Nichols," he whispered, "would you do me the honor of becoming my wife?"

The blood in her veins froze.

"Not legally, right?" she whispered back.

"I spoke with Mack—"

"Oh god. Your first mistake."

Coal blinked with humor and whispered, "Rainbow Leigh, would you do me the honor of becoming Mrs. Draken Smyth?"

"I … uh … are you serious?"

"I never wish for you to doubt my love."

"What if we're discovered? I can't lose you again. The pain was torture, like I was dying."

"I shall die if you ever accuse me once more of feigning affections for you." His features hardened and the tendons in his neck flexed. "Or even suggest that I use you for intimacies."

Be free.

Lynden looked away with embarrassment. "Two people should be able to do what they want without fear of social punishment. It's nobody's damn business. God, I'm so pissed off I could set the whole world on fire and dance on the ashes." Her brother's words appeared in her mind's eye and she whispered, "Image. Perception. Those illusions are the two keys to power."

"Then let us regain power and enjoy the last laugh." Coal caressed her cheek with a petal and whispered against her lips, "Burn with me."

Her gaze crashed into his in a volcanic eruption of fury and passion. The lit fuse exploded and a pyroclastic blast rumbled from her grief, the hot, caustic current destroying the indignity others would have her feel. This was their life. *Theirs.* Nobody owned them.

Be fearless.

"Yes," she breathed. "I will burn with you."

CHAPTER SEVEN

Lake Wenatchee, Washington state

Sunday, April 1, 2057

The night wrapped around Lynden in gossamer wings of midnight blue and twinkling stars. The sight lessened her rising panic. Lifting her floor-length skirt, she maneuvered down old, rickety steps attached to her family cottage, nestled in the Cascade Mountains near Lake Wenatchee.

Inhaling a deep breath, she exhaled slowly and shook off the nerves.

The rich scent of evergreens perfumed the air as she traversed the pine needle-covered lawn toward the water edging the property. Strands of white lights illuminated a bridge to a gazebo located in the center of the small pond. It looked just like she remembered from childhood. From the gazebo's wooden ceiling hung old wrought iron lanterns lit with melted wax votive candles in various shapes and sizes, each one powered by electricity.

Her steps faltered a beat.

Beneath the faint, flickering glow, stood Coal. He faced away from her, hands clasped in front, as he gazed out over the water in a tailored suit saved for black tie charity events. Beside him, Mack waited to officiate their wedding, decked out in his family's tartan, complete with a black barathea kilt jacket.

Coal still hadn't seen her. But a soft smile warmed Mack's face as she approached. Lynden flicked her bottom lip ring in and out of her mouth. She wasn't having cold feet. Paranoia, however, formed a whirlpool of dizziness in her head. She was getting married. The muscles in her stomach clenched as the stone in her gut churned round and round.

A clandestine wedding on April Fool's Day, using their fake identities, was the crazy brain child of Mackenzie Ferguson. The layers of ridiculousness and caution ensured a perfect cover against *otaku* rumors and the law, he reassured. Mack knew the risks—from Hanley, Fillion, and the government—and shrugged them away, declaring with a closing wink that revolutionary stands always came with a price.

The word "price" vibrated through her body and she slammed shut the door to her past. This moment was about her future. About a type of owning that redeemed rather than shamed. "I am yours," she whispered across the water. "And you are mine."

Fireworks burst and glittered in her pulse as she floated across the wooden bridge in layers of charcoal colored silk and tulle. Coal's lips parted and his chest expanded. Dark and luminous, his gaze blazed with both pride and humility. Warmth crept up her neck and face as she tingled with self-awareness, forcing herself to remain steady.

Breathe, she reminded herself.

A gentle breeze skipped off the pond and enchanted her hair and dress. The same source of magic rippled the water and made the lily pads dance with bows and curtsies, as if a real princess walked past.

Lynden resisted the urge to roll her eyes at herself. God, she was such a girl. Secretly she liked it, though. All of it—the dress, makeup, starlight shimmering over the water, the intimate gathering, and the wonder on Coal's face as she approached.

Her only regret was that Fillion was not here to give her away, even though it was a stupid, demeaning patriarchal tradition. But her brother could never know she and Coal married. It was too dangerous. She fought the guilt and fear of her selfishness with each step.

Perception.

Except that it wasn't selfish.

Image.

She was tired of living in suspended animation.

Tired of feeling owned and used.

She didn't exist for the benefit and glory of others.

She wanted to live for herself.

The linden leaf tattoo caught her eye and tears pricked her eyes. She looked up and hunted for familiar constellations. Anything to distract her emotions. Her brother saw her right now. He always saw her. He would want her to be happy, consequences be damned.

Straightening her shoulders, she finished the final few steps and stopped before Coal with a bashful smile.

The charming confidence Coal normally exuded dissipated into shyness as well and he half-whispered in a shaky voice, *"Tu es plus belle que toutes les étoiles dans le ciel nocturne. Tellement, que je fais tous les voeux de mon coeur en ton nom."*

She recognized the words from her birthday and looked away. "Still professing your love for the night sky, Mr. Aw—Smyth?"

"No, I lied." He rolled his bottom lip into his mouth. Taking her hands, he released his lip and flashed her a dimpled smile that promised many things. The kinds of things where she'd forget her name and only remember his. God, that smile was dangerous. He brushed a thumb over the back of her hand and said, "I shall make a full confession later."

"You lied?"

"More like a poor translation, *Mademoiselle.*"

Lynden studied their hands and playfully replied, "Well, the honor price is probably too steep at this point."

"Nevertheless, name your price, My Lady, and I shall endeavor to earn back your good opinion of me." He dropped his voice even lower and whispered, "Whatever you require of me, I am yours to command."

Femininity roared through her veins with his words. Even when her freckle-faced and tall, boyish body was reflected back to her in Coal's eyes.

Mack cleared his throat and quietly asked, "Uh… Are we ready? Because if this continues, I might fall into a diabetic coma."

The humor moved past both her and Coal as shyness settled between them once more. The sweet atmosphere was almost too much for her, too. Though she was also reveling in it. After a few seconds, Coal nodded permission for Mack to continue. He opened his mouth to speak, then shut it, his features tensing.

"Shit," Mack mumbled. "I didn't think this would be so hard. Dammit." He rubbed his eyes and released a loud sigh. Stretching his neck and shoulders, like he was preparing to run a race, he exhaled again and began. "Rainbow Leigh and Draken Smyth are two badass, crazy bitches."

"Mackenzie!"

Coal's shoulders shook as he suppressed a laugh.

Lynden shot Coal a glare. "Don't encourage him."

Mack maintained a deadpanned expression and continued. "Two badass, crazy bitches *in love*."

She deflated with a groan of annoyance. "You forgot to remind me that I was never to hire you to officiate a wedding."

"You didn't," Mack replied, wiggling his eyebrows. "Mr. Smyth hired me."

Dammit.

"At least you're not wearing that hideous shirt." She scanned Mack from top to bottom and back up again. "Green and blue are totally your colors, by the way. Makes your legs look nice."

"Hell, I thought so, too." Mack slid Coal a sly glance and struck a pose of so-called manliness. "Behold! Mackenzie Patton Campbell Ferguson the Third."

"Indeed," Coal replied, trying hard to appear unimpressed. "A plaid skirt with a purse and ribbons on your socks. Shall I say you look pretty?"

"Don't mock the brawny highlander men of Clan Ferguson." Mack's fierce look of pride melted into a flirty smile as he batted his eyes at Coal. "But, sure, you can say that I'm pretty."

Loud laughter erupted from Coal and he turned around to contain himself.

"You're dead, Mackenzie."

"Patience, Rainbow," Mack said. "We're bonding. It's a special moment when a man calls another man pretty and means it."

She rolled her eyes and shouted, "Focus!"

"Inside voice, *Niji Doragon Ōjo*." Mack tugged on a strand of her hair and winked. "OK. Join hands ... good ... deep breath. Here we go." The soft smile returned and he began. "Do you Rainbow Leigh take Draken Smyth to be your lawfully wedded husband, for richer or for poorer, in sickness and in health, all the days of your life?"

Lynden studied her and Coal's hands, grounding her light-headed thoughts, and whispered, "I do."

Angling his body toward Coal, Mack asked, "Do you Draken Smyth take Rainbow Leigh to be your lawfully wedded wife, for richer or for poorer, in sickness and in health, all the days of your life?"

"I do."

"The rings?" Mack knew they wouldn't have rings. And the property was secure. Wi-Fi and cell reception were spotty at best in the mountains. Still, he insisted that they use their fake names and go through the motions just in case something was bugged. To Lynden he said, "Repeat after me. With this ring, I pledge my troth."

Lynden raised her eyebrow. "With this ring, I pledge my ... really?"

What in the hell was a "troth"? She shook her head at Mack and bit back a retort. Instead, she trained her thoughts onto Coal. Memories of yesterday, of Coal cradling her beneath his body and caressing her cheek with a *sakura* petal, re-set the rhythm of her heart. She allowed a smile to flutter across her lips as she fingered the old, tattered black ribbon tied around his wrist.

"With this ring," she whispered, "I vow that my life will burn for yours, always."

Coal swallowed and shifted on his feet with a deep breath. Slipping a hand into his pants pocket, he pulled out a silver bracelet featuring tiny, dangling linden leaves. Lynden pressed her fingers to her lips and grinned. For a split second, she peered at Mack in question. He bit down on his tongue ring in reply, offering zero remorse. That damn man had opened his big mouth again. She wanted to be angry with him. But other emotions competed for her attention and won.

Breathe, she reminded herself again.

"With this ring," Coal whispered intimately, clasping the bracelet around her wrist, "I vow that my life shall burn for yours, always."

Mack grinned at both her and Coal and proclaimed, "With the power vested in me by the state of Washington, I now pronounce you ... husband and wife." Softening his voice, he added, "You may kiss the bride."

What.

Her smile fell. Walls of granite turned her features to stone and shielded her heart.

A bride. She was Coal's bride.

Holy shit.

Even though she went through all the motions, she hadn't considered herself a bride until this moment. Refused to, actually.

Shame hit her with violence. All the magic she had embraced this evening vanished, too. In Coal's world, a bride was revered and celebrated as a symbol of purity and life, a goddess of Spring. Gag. She'd heard all the stories countless times until she wanted to projectile vomit all over the place with the way women were objectified and brainwashed in New Eden. And, yet, heat suffused her neck and face with her own feelings of inadequacy. As if being called a bride was an esteemed honor she had refused to acknowledge until now. Her fingers touched a silver linden leaf.

Thin air thoughts.

Toughen up, Rainbow.

A shadow fell over her face as her groom drew near. Memories of a wedding ring striking her face flashed in her mind. Terrified, she squeezed her eyes closed as hands cupped her face. Millions of insect legs skittered and crawled across her skin and she shuddered with revulsion.

Stop being so dramatic!

You're making a scene!

Sit down. Be quiet.

Whore.

His lips touched hers and she stiffened. Everything went dark. A nanosecond later, the ground in her mind winked into focus, desolate and empty. Not even shadows appeared. The sound of her emptiness echoed in the silence of her gilded cage. Far in the distance, a sliver of light moved across the barren landscape toward where she stood, followed by more tendrils of light. It was beautiful and she reached out to capture the heat.

Burn with me.

"I love you, my wife," Coal whispered against her mouth. "You set me on fire."

Bright and gentle, Coal's kiss morphed into the morning sun and warmed away the dewed veil of tears blanketing the ground. His kiss deepened—hungry, scorching, all-consuming—and the earth shook beneath her feet. She opened her mouth to scream when a vast, untamed garden broke through the hard soil and bloomed to life. Mesmerized, she pushed open the bars to the cage she had put around her life and stepped out into new territory, eyes wide at the scene that unfolded before her.

Butterflies, born from her loneliness, fluttered from flower to flower. Their wings—once punctured, now whole—shimmered in a brilliant show of colors, as soft, fragile petals continued to unfurl in her wild dark, revealing a beauty she never knew existed. Here, in this sacred place, he walked with her, neither of them ashamed of their nakedness. Lynden breathed in the intoxicating fragrance of bliss, drunk on his acceptance as his love forged new words to reconstruct the shattered mirror in her heart.

Beautiful. Intelligent. Wanted. Essential. Loved.
Free.

The morning light faded to dusk as his kiss slowed.

"Lynden Hansen," her husband whispered in her ear, "I had professed that you are lovelier than any star in the night sky. So much so, I make all the wishes of my heart in your name."

She shivered with pleasure. God, she loved this voice. It was a sound of safety and she opened her eyes. A sinful glint sparked in Coal's dark gaze as he appreciated every nuance of emotion on her face.

Desired. Playful. Treasured. Compassionate. Known.
Fearless.

"Your smoldering gaze is passable, Mr. Awesome," she whispered. "I guess."

Coal grinned. Those damn dimples. Trailing her hands over his chest, she claimed his mouth with hers, no longer afraid of the future. And, she swore, the night sky sighed with jealously as he left stardust on her lips.

Good enough.

APPENDICES

1. Author Notes

2. Hacker Terminology

3. Anime and Japanese Terminology

4. Additional Definitions

5. Translations

6. Selected Bibliography

Read THE CODE at
www.jesikahsundin.com

Reviews on Amazon, Barnes & Noble, Goodreads, iBooks, and
other retailers are *always* welcome.
Thanks in advance!

AUTHOR NOTES

TRANSITIONS is officially the byproduct of potato chips, French onion dip, way too much coffee (not really, no such thing), and inspiration from my readers. Yep, *you*!

Over the years, readers have requested stories about Ember, Skylar, Rain, Mack, and Lynden. A handful of readers also begged for a Mack and Fillion love story, even declaring that they'd sell their souls to make it happen.

Ahem. *cough, cough*

This segment in "Author Notes" is interrupted with an important message from its sponsor: *No souls were consumed or harmed in the making of TRANSITIONS*.

Phew!

However, several souls contributed to its creation.

Heart Eyes to Melissa Slager, my editor, writing partner in crime, bestie, and my manuscript Fairy Godmother who, with a flick of her wrist ... er, clickity-clack of her typing fingers ... sprinkles magic on my stories until they transform from rags to riches. *There is no sidekick'n. We are equal partners in badassary and goofyism* #SugarPacket

I am indebted to my dearest friends, fellow SVEC moms, SFF convention partners, and Girl's Movie Night peeps: Jennifer Newsom and Katie Kent, who beta read and provided invaluable feedback, and Tracy Campbell, who always reminds me of opportunities when all seems lost. *hugs you*

Penny Sundin, you are amazing. None of my books would have happened without your love and endless support. There are no adequate words to properly thank you for the time you've gifted me over the years by caring for my home while I'm off on one writing adventure after another. Love you <3

Jessica Jett, Hannah Miller, and Andra Perju, I dedicate this book to you. Thank you for your social media support, beautiful encouragement, and friendship. Never in a million years did

I think readers would one day become my personal friends. *blows kisses*

Chairelys Rojas, thank you for the fantastic quizzes and GIF-filled reviews you leave on Goodreads for my novels. They always leave a huge grin on my face. Heather Padgett, I am forever grateful for your YouTube and Twitter support. Love our bookish conversations on Goodreads, too!

Amalia Chitulescu: You. Are. Amazing. I am honored to have your artistic magic clothe one of my novels once more. THANK YOU for always caring about my world, characters, and ensuring the cover is perfect. :-*

Jennifer Cook and Claire Lalande, my heartfelt gratitude for your assistance in transforming a few fun pieces of Skylar, Rain, and Coal's dialogue into French. *Merci beaucoup.*

Myles Sundin, I make all the wishes of my heart in your name. Thank you for showing me the true meaning of romance. I love you.

To my children—Myles, Colin, and Violette—never forget the true value of your worth, for you are priceless. Your laughter sets my heart on fire.

Although I draw on the expertise of others, in various subjects, to build the near-future world of Seattle and the quasi-historical world of New Eden Township, all errors are entirely mine. In the famous words of Nennius, a ninth-century Celtic monk, "I have made a heap of all that I could find."

takes a deep breath
looks at beginning draft for GAMEMASTER
stretches fingers
And now, time to get busy finishing book three.
Tsuzuku...
(To be continued...)

HACKER TERMINOLOGY

HACKER – A hacker is an individual who breaches security in a computer system or computer network to capitalize on exposed weaknesses, for beneficial or nefarious reasons. Sometimes the term is applied to an individual with expert knowledge of computers and computer networks. A subculture now exists for hackers, formed by a real and recognized community known as the computer underground. This subculture of tech-savvy individuals has also developed a unique language and slang terms defined and collected in The Hacker's Dictionary (originally known as the Jargon File), which is searchable online.

A Lefty's Catcher Mitt – Net jargon for something people think exists, but doesn't. The term came from the anime show *Laughing Man (Ghost in the Shell)*, where a character owns a left-handed mitt inscribed with a quote by Holden Caulfield, title character in the novel *The Catcher in the Rye* by J.D. Salinger

Bagbiter – a person who always causes problems, is a whiner, and is never satisfied. Comes from the hacker term for a piece of equipment, hardware, or software that fails

Black Hat – someone who maliciously hacks into secure systems to corrupt or gain unauthorized information. The hacker subculture often refers to this person as a "cracker" rather than a "hacker"

Bletcherous (bletch) – disgusting, makes you want to vomit, usually in reference to an object, and rarely regarding people

Defragment (defrag) – an action to reduce the fragmentation of a software file by concatenating parts stored in separate locations on a disk

Faraday Cage – a grounded metal screen (usually copper) that surrounds a piece of equipment to exclude electrostatic and electromagnetic influences

Fatal Exception Error – an error that closes down and aborts a program, returning the user to the operating system

Frobnicate – to manipulate or adjust, to tweak for the fun of it, goofing off

Gabriel / "Pull a Gabriel" – [for Dick Gabriel, SAIL volleyball fanatic] An unnecessary (in the opinion of the opponent) stalling tactic, e.g., tying one's shoelaces or hair repeatedly, asking the time, etc. Also used to refer to the perpetrator of such tactics. Also, "pulling a Gabriel", "Gabriel mode"

Glitch – a sudden interruption in electric service, sanity, or program function, sometimes recoverable

Gritching (gritch) – to complain; a blend of "gripe" and "bitch"

Gubbish – nonsense; a blend of "garbage" and "rubbish"

Hack-back – Loosely defined, "hacking back" involves turning the tables on a cyberhacking assailant: thwarting or stopping the crime, or perhaps even trying to steal back what was taken

Kernel Panic – an action taken by an operating system when detecting an internal fatal error from which it cannot safely recover; also known as "the blue screen of death"

Loser – an unexpectedly bad situation, program, programmer, or person

Mumblage – The topic of one's mumbling, often used as a replacement for obscenities, "full of mumblage"

Parse – Slang for to understand or comprehend

Uncanny Valley – The hypothesis in the field of aesthetics which states that some humans feel revulsion or disturbance when robotics or 3D animation look and move almost, but not exactly, like natural beings

White Hat – someone who hacks into secure systems and instead of corrupting or taking unauthorized information, exposes the weaknesses to the system's owners so they can strengthen the breach before it can be taken advantage of by others (including **Black Hats**)

ANIME and JAPANESE TERMINOLOGY

ANIME / MANGA – Anime is a distinctly Japanese style of animation, while manga is the term for comic books that feature anime-stylized characters. Anime differs from American cartoons in that it is more often created for teens and adults with a range of topics that typically explore serious themes. It has been criticized by parents in the United States for discussing such taboo topics as teen suicide, violence, social rebellion, spiritual ideas, and sex. However, anime and manga include many genres, including romance, comedy, horror, and action, and feature several series for children, *Pokémon* being the most notable and successful in the U.S. Many video games, for general or mature audiences, feature anime-style characters and themes. In Japan, and even in the U.S., anime fans have formed a subculture with punk undertones emulating goth, emo, or cyberpunk movements.

Bishounen (bishonen, bish, bishie, bishy) – literally, "pretty boy" in Japanese, a term used to describe a young man—including those in anime, manga, and video games—who is notably beautiful and attractive

Bakayarō – dumbass, idiot, fool

Chikara – strength, power

Desu – Japanese for "it is," often said at the end of sentences to seem cute or unwitting

Dokyun – a derogatory internet slang term that spread from Japan's 2ch.net, which mostly means dumbass or idiot

Henshin – "to change or transform the body"; in anime and manga, this is usually when a character transforms into a superhero

Hikikomori – someone who purposely stays in their house all day long, isolating themselves from society, and who usually spends all their time on the Internet, playing video games, or watching anime

Jitsu – martial arts term for "technique" or "art"

Josei – woman

Kawaii – cute, Japanese culture reference.

Kiai – a Japanese term used in martial arts for the short yell or shout uttered when performing an attacking move

Kisama – No direct translation, but a good English equivalent might be "motherfucker." It is an extremely hostile and rude address, mostly toward males, that begets the air of "hate" or "detest" to whom it's directed. Historically, it was what a samurai called their enemy

Kono Yaro – translates to "that bastard"

Kotatsu – a low, wooden table frame covered by a futon, or heavy blanket, upon which a table top sits. Underneath is a heat source, often built into the table itself

Kureejii – translates to "crazy," as in a person

Kusogaki – little shit, shitty brat, damn child

Origami – The art of paper folding

Otaku – in Japan, originally a very negative term to describe a recluse who has no life, usually because their world revolves around fictional characters, such as in anime and manga; in America, the word has been applied by anime fans as a positive term for fanboy/girl

Nakoudo – translates to "matchmaker" or "go-between" and is the person who contracts a marriage between the man and woman who hope to marry

Nettomo – slang term for a friend made on the Internet

Nosebleed – used by fans about someone whom they think is hot or exciting; when an anime or manga character has become sexually excited, it is portrayed with a sudden nosebleed

Sakura – translates to "cherry blossom"

Samurai – a member of a powerful military caste in feudal Japan, especially a member of the class of military retainers of the daimyos

Sekushī – sexy

Senpai – someone who is of a higher social standing. "Notice me senpai" is usually a junior hoping he/she would get the attention of the senpai.

Tesaki – translates to "fingers," but is slang for "minion"

Yaoi – "boys love" manga and anime typically aimed at a female audience

Yuinou / Yuinou no gi – translates to "betrothal presents" and is the ceremony where the groom and bride to-be swear their engagement publicly, followed by an exchange of gifts between the two households

ADDITIONAL DEFINITIONS

Cob – a type of structural mud made from clay, sand, water, and straw that is applied wet between stones or in clumps to form walls. Cob homes, shops, and barns became the preferred building type during the Middle Ages, especially in the British Isles. The mud structures reached the height of popularity with Tudor-style architecture made famous for its external geometric timber designs, stone or brick accents, oriel window boxes, and lead multi-lit latticed windows. This is the most commonly featured style of building in fantasy storybook villages.

Cyberpunk – a literary and visual media genre that takes place in a future or near-future Earth and is most notably known for the film noir detective-like qualities of the story, high technology (computers, hackers, robotics, artificial intelligence), and a degraded society. The world or place setting is typically regulated and influenced by large corporations and wealthy elite rather than traditional governmental bodies. The protagonist is usually a rogue/misfit, a loner in society with a dark past. The cyberpunk genre is prominently featured in anime and manga in Japan.

Dungeon Master (DM) – individual in charge of organizing and planning the details and challenges of a given adventure in the table-top role-playing game "Dungeons & Dragons." He or she also is a participant in the game, but their key role is to make all the rules and control the story, telling the player characters what they hear and what they see. The only part a DM does not control are the decisions/actions of the player characters.

Emo / Emocore – an alternative rock subculture influenced by the punk music scene that emerged in the 1980s, featuring lyrics about self rather than traditional punk themes of society. The Emo scene exploded in the 1990s with the indie rock grunge scene and popularity of pop punk, and was later brought back to mainstream teen culture in the early 2000s through the Internet social media site MySpace. Individuals belonging to this subculture have a unique and notable fashion, the modern looks and trends believed to have been influenced by the anime and manga subculture. The Emo's (sometimes called Scene Kids or Ravers) are described as being "emotive" in nature, giving rise to the idea that the boys possess more feminine traits and qualities than their non-emo counterparts.

Gamemaster (GM) – an individual who officiates and referees multi-player role-playing games (table-top or live action), sometimes with other Gamemasters. They arbitrate and moderate the rules, settle disputes, create and define the game world/environment, blend and weave player character stories together, and oversee the non-player character roles and influence in the story. The Gamemaster's specific job and function is unique to each game.

Live Action Role-Playing (LARP) – a style of game that transcends traditional table-top or video game role-playing into live action where people physically become a character and act out their role in a defined fantasy setting. A LARP must contain three consistent ideas in order to be considered true live action role-playing (expanded in more depth by larping.org): collaborative (a mutual operation where everyone understands they are a character and must work together toward a common goal); pretending (a necessary element for each LARP, such as the game world/space, weapons and characterization, to name a few); and rules (agreed upon by the community of gamers and refereed by Gamemasters but usually sustained by an honor system among players).

Mundane – an object or person that does not belong to the fictional game or setting, such as a cellphone in a medieval community, or the President of the United States in ancient China. In the LARP and role-playing subculture, mundane also refers to one's "real" life versus his or her character life/world.

Visual Kei ("visual music" or "visual system") – an alternative rock music movement in Japan that features band members who typically try to emulate a unified androgynous appearance. They embody unique makeup, hair styles, and clothing that is punk in nature with mainstream success and influenced by Western concepts such as glam rock, goth, and cyberpunk. Some argue that Visual Kei is no longer about a music genre but about a subculture of individuals who reflect this fashion style and trend.

TRANSLATIONS

"*Est-ce que tu aimerais prendre une bouchée?*" He lifted the spoon to her mouth and waited.
Translation: *Shall you enjoy a bite of food?*

He caught the dribble with the spoon and promptly dumped the spittle onto a cloth. "*Une autre bouchée?*"
Translation: *Another bite?*

Lifting her head, he said, "*Voici de l'eau. Lentement, petites gorgées.*"
Translation: *Here is water. Slow, gentle sips.*

"*Ne gâchez pas l'illusion pour lui,*" he said to her, his face perfectly serious.
Translation: *Do not ruin the illusion for him.*

"*Oui, Milord,*" she replied with another laugh. "*Il semble convaincu. Ton secret est bien gardé!*"
Translation: *Yes, My Lord. / He appears convinced. Your secret is safe.*

He pulled a hand away from the nearest ear and leaned in close, trying not to laugh. "*Akai kuchibeni.*"
Translation: *Red lipstick.*

"Perfect idea, *sekushī na josei,*" he had meant to say.
Translation: *Sexy woman / sexy lady.*

"All right, name your price, *Niji Doragon Ōjo*."
Translation: *Rainbow Dragon Princess.*

Whatever pleases you, *mon joli petit dragon,*" he whispered as he lowered.
Translation: *My pretty little dragon.*

Seizing her surprise, he pressed his forehead to hers and whispered, "*Tu es plus belle que toutes les étoiles dans le ciel nocturne. Tellement, que je fais tous les voeux de mon coeur en ton nom.*"
Translation: *You are lovelier than any star in the night sky. So much so, I make all the wishes of my heart in your name.*

SELECTED BIBLIOGRAPHY

Edgar Allen Poe, "Lenore," *Pioneer* (February 1843)

Jane Austen, *Northanger Abbey* (December 1817)

John Mark Green, "Foolish Manboy," https://www.facebook.com/JohnMarkGreenPoetry (accessed February 26, 2016)

Philip G. Zimbardo, "Conclusion," *The Stanford Prison Experiment*, www.prisonexp.org/conclusion (August 1971)

Travis Brownley, "The Necessity of Stress," *Heads and Tales at Marin Academy*, https://travisma.wordpress.com/2013/12/12/the-necessity-of-stress/ (December 12, 2013)

William Shakespeare, *Twelfth Night* (February 2, 1602)

William Shakespeare, *Hamlet* (1603)

William Shakespeare, *Romeo and Juliet* (1597)

Jesikah Sundin is a sci-fi/fantasy writer mom of three nerdlets and devoted wife to a gamer geek. In addition to her family, she shares her home in Monroe, Washington with a red-footed tortoise and a collection of seatbelt purses. She is addicted to coffee, laughing, Doc Martens… Oh, and the forest is her happy place.

Discover the worlds and characters
of *The Biodome Chronicles* at:

www.jesikahsundin.com

Made in the USA
Charleston, SC
28 May 2016